Edited By
JONATHAN STRAHAN

BRIDGING INFINITY

Also Edited by Jonathan Strahan

Best Short Novels
(2004 through 2007)

Fantasy: The Very Best of 2005

Science Fiction: The Very Best
of 2005

The Best Science Fiction and
Fantasy of the Year: Volumes 1 - 10

Eclipse: New Science Fiction and
Fantasy (Vols 1-4)

The Starry Rift:
Tales of New Tomorrows

Life on Mars:
Tales of New Frontiers

Under My Hat:
Tales from the Cauldron

Godlike Machines

The Infinity Project 1:
Engineering Infinity

The Infinity Project 2:
Edge of Infinity

The Infinity Project 3:
Reach for Infinity

The Infinity Project 4:
Meeting Infinity

The Infinity Project 5:
Bridging Infinity

The Infinity Project 6:
Infinity Wars (forthcoming)

Fearsome Journeys

Fearsome Magics

Drowned Worlds, Wild Shores

With Lou Anders
Swords and Dark Magic:
The New Sword and Sorcery

With Charles N. Brown
The Locus Awards: Thirty Years
of the Best in Fantasy and Science
Fiction

With Jeremy G. Byrne
The Year's Best Australian Science
Fiction and Fantasy: Volume 1

The Year's Best Australian Science
Fiction and Fantasy: Volume 2

Eidolon 1

With Jack Dann
Legends of Australian Fantasy

With Gardner Dozois
The New Space Opera

The New Space Opera 2

With Karen Haber
Science Fiction: Best of 2003

Science Fiction: Best of 2004

Fantasy: Best of 2004

With Marianne S. Jablon
Wings of Fire

Edited By
JONATHAN STRAHAN

BRIDGING INFINITY

INCLUDING STORIES BY
ALASTAIR **REYNOLDS**
PAT **CADIGAN**
STEPHEN **BAXTER**
CHARLIE JANE **ANDERS**
TOBIAS S. **BUCKELL**
KAREN **LORD**
KARIN **LOWACHEE**
KRISTINE KATHRYN **RUSCH**
GREGORY **BENFORD**
LARRY **NIVEN**
ROBERT **REED**
PAMELA **SARGENT**
ALLEN M. **STEELE**
PAT **MURPHY**
PAUL **DOHERTY**
AN **OWOMOYELA**
THORAIYA **DYER**
KEN **LIU**

First published 2016 by Solaris
an imprint of Rebellion Publishing Ltd,
Riverside House, Osney Mead,
Oxford, OX2 0ES, UK

www.solarisbooks.com

ISBN (US): 978-1-78108-419-9
ISBN (UK): 978-1-78108-418-2

Selection and "Introduction" by Jonathan Strahan. Copyright © 2016 by Jonathan Strahan.
"Rager in Space" by Charlie Jane Anders. Copyright © 2016 Charlie Jane Anders.
"The Venus Generations" by Stephen Baxter. Copyright © 2016 Stephen Baxter.
"The Mighty Slinger" by Tobias S. Buckell & Karen Lord.
Copyright © 2016 Tobias S. Buckell & Karen Lord.
"Six Degrees of Separation Freedom" by Pat Cadigan. Copyright © 2016 Pat Cadigan.
"Induction" by Thoraiya Dyer. Copyright © 2016 Thoraiya Dyer.
"Seven Birthdays" by Ken Liu. Copyright © 2016 Ken Liu.
"Ozymandias" by Karin Lowachee. Copyright © 2016 Karin Lowachee.
"Cold Comfort" by Pat Murphy & Paul Doherty. Copyright © 2016
Pat Murphy & Paul Doherty.
"Mice Among Elephants" by Larry Niven & Gregory Benford.
Copyright © 2016 Larry Niven & Gregory Benford.
"Travelling into Nothing" by An Owomoyela. Copyright © 2016 An Owomoyela.
"Parables of Infinity" by Robert Reed. Copyright © 2016 Robert Reed.
"Sixteen Questions for Kamala Chatterjee" by Alastair Reynolds.
Copyright © 2016 Alastair Reynolds.
"The City's Edge" by Kristine Kathryn Rusch. Copyright © 2016 Kristine Kathryn Rusch.
"Monuments" by Pamela Sargent. Copyright © 2016 Pamela Sargent.
Appears by permission of the author and her agent, Richard Curtis Associates, Inc.,
200 East 72nd Street, Suite 28J, New York, NY 10021.
"Apache Charley and the Pentagons of Hex" by Allen Steele. Copyright © 2016 Allen Steele.

The right of the authors to be identified as the authors of this work has been asserted in
accordance with the Copyright, Designs and Patents Act 1988.

All rights reserved. No part of this publication may be
reproduced, stored in a retrieval system, or transmitted, in any
form or by any means, electronic, mechanical, photocopying,
recording or otherwise, without the prior permission of
the copyright owners.

10 9 8 7 6 5 4 3 2 1

A CIP catalogue record for this book is available from the
British Library.

Designed & typeset by Rebellion Publishing

REBELLION

Printed in Denmark

For Marianne,
who is far stronger than me,
and for Wendy,
who is probably stronger
than either of us.

Acknowledgements

It's always a pleasure and a privilege to work with Jonathan Oliver, Ben Smith and the team at Solaris Books. I'd like to thank them for taking the risks they have with the books we've done, and for giving me the freedom to do the books I've wanted to do. I will always be grateful to them for stepping in and for believing in the books and in me. I am also very grateful to all of the authors here, especially those who stepped in at the last moment. Special thanks to my agent Howard Morhaim who for over a decade now has had my back and helped make good things happen. Finally, most special thanks of all to Marianne, Jessica, and Sophie. I always say that every moment spent working on these books is stolen from them, but it's true, and I'm forever grateful to them for their love, support and generosity.

Contents

11 *Introduction*
Jonathan Strahan

19 *Sixteen Questions for Kamala Chatterjee*
Alastair Reynolds

39 *Six Degrees of Separation Freedom*
Pat Cadigan

63 *The Venus Generations*
Stephen Baxter

93 *Rager in Space*
Charlie Jane Anders

119 *The Mighty Slinger*
Tobias S. Buckell
& Karen Lord

159 *Ozymandias*
Karin Lowachee

189 *The City's Edge*
Kristine Kathryn Rusch

217 *Mice Among Elephants*
Gregory Benford
& Larry Niven

249 *Parables of Infinity*
Robert Reed

273 *Monuments*
Pamela Sargent

295 *Apache Charley and the Pentagons of Hex*
Allen M. Steele

323 *Cold Comfort*
Pat Murphy
& Paul Doherty

355 *Travelling into Nothing*
An Owomoyela

383 *Induction*
Thoraiya Dyer

415 *Seven Birthdays*
Ken Liu

439 *About the Authors*

JONATHAN STRAHAN
INTRODUCTION

JONATHAN STRAHAN
INTRODUCTION

SCIENCE FICTION IS about thinking big and dreaming bigger. Okay, it's not *always* about that, but it *often* is. SF can be about a lot of things, but when I started reading science fiction what grabbed me were stories that implied something greater, that opened out to a staggering, often cosmic scale. Whether it was what was implied in stories like Clarke's *Childhood's End* and "The Nine Billion Names of God", the endless grandeur of Asimov's Trantor, or the almost giddy galaxy-smashing scale of early E.E. Doc Smith, the sense of wonder was what made me want to keep reading science fiction. The sense of wonder, though, is out of fashion these days. Nonetheless, it has played an important part in the project that is science fiction, and I think it's still relevant today.

Jeff Brucher's *Brave New Words: The Oxford Dictionary of Science Fiction* defines sense of wonder as "a feeling of awakening or awe triggered by an expansion of one's awareness of what is possible or by confrontation with the vastness of space and time, as brought on by reading science fiction." It is science fiction's version of the 'sublime', which in art is defined as that "quality of greatness, whether physical, moral, intellectual, metaphysical, aesthetic, spiritual, or artistic, which especially refers to greatness beyond all possibility of calculation, measurement, or imitation. Something awe inspiring, in the truest sense." And it is often expressed in physical terms.

When I was thinking about this I began to wonder if there could be such a thing as a mechanical sublime, an engineering sublime? An instance where the tools we produce to address a problem or which we create for their own intrinsic value are of sufficient scale, sufficient scope that they evoke a sense of awe and veneration that is similar to the sublime in art? Something like the Krel machines in *Forbidden Planet*. It seemed possible. And it might connect with one of science fiction's basic tents: that problems can be solved.

Science fiction, or at least the sort of science fiction that was typical in American pulp magazines from the 1930s to the 1950s was founded on a belief that problems are *solvable*, and that those problems are solvable using technical or engineering solutions. When faced with a problem in a story in John W. Campbell's *Astounding*, our engineering hero wouldn't quail before the challenge, but would instead 'science the shit out of it' (as Andy Weir so elegantly put it) and come up with an engineering solution to the problem. And sometime it would take a big solution, a Hoover Dam or maybe moving a planet or two. It was what had worked for the American dream throughout the first half of the 20th century, but as the Atomic Age came and went we began to doubt it, and some of that doubt carries on today.

Why? By the 1960s the world seemed more complex, darker, more difficult, and the sort of human problems we faced seemed to require something other than a better screwdriver, a smarter mousetrap, or a backyard build rocket ship. With the New Wave science fiction turned inwards and, to some extent, began to set 'sense of wonder' to one side. Not that it ever went away, but it seemed like a hoarier, more clichéd, less complex way to solve a problem in a story. And yet, we keep coming back to it, as you can see in any number of hard SF adventures published over the past thirty years.

The book you're now holding, *Bridging Infinity*, is at least in part a new way of asking some old questions. Is solving problems still integral to science fiction? Do we still *believe* problems are solvable? Can we engineer our way out of the kind of problems we face today and will face in the future? And if we do, if science fiction is still at least partly about solving problems, what scale will we have to face them on? With my mind full of images of Dyson spheres and rings, of star-engulfing AI sub-strates, and of distinctly terrestrial projects that redirected rivers or reshaped continents, I turned to some of the most interesting science fiction writers working today and asked them to send me stories that looked at super-engineering projects. Anything from mad abandoned Soviet plans to re-route rivers to Australian plans to build 3,000 kilometer long canals to Dyson Spheres that enclose stars; stories about sometimes-goofy sounding projects that capture our sense of wonder while providing a chance to look at everything from the greatest of humanity's successes to our darkest motivations. These also evoke a sense of awe, a sense of the sublime. The stories could be set here on Earth, in our Solar System, or anywhere in the deepest reaches of space. The only criteria was that they be hard SF and relate to a super engineering project or projects.

In the end fifteen writers responded, and while they responded in very different ways, there were some similarities that were striking. One group of writers took to the cosmic stage, spinning classic tales of hard SF. Gregory Benford & Larry Niven, Allen M. Steele, Robert Reed, Charlie Jane Anders, and An Owomoyela all describe engineering on a mammoth scale that solves a problem – where are we to live, how will we survive, and so on. They show us life inside enormous spacecraft, intelligences made of plasma living inside stars, and adventure across the surfaces of manufactured worlds so huge they engulf solar systems. There's a real old-fashioned sense of wonder to their stories, alongside an awareness of modern science and engineering.

What perhaps surprised me the most, though, and shouldn't have, was the way the other group of writers took the challenge of writing super-engineering stories and turned it to addressing one of the greatest problems facing us today. The first story I accepted for *Bridging Infinity*, Thoraiya Dyer's "Induction", described an engineering project, enormous in scale, that focused on climate change and global warming. It was followed by stories from Stephen Baxter, Ken Liu, Pat Murphy and Paul Doherty, and others. Sometimes they involved small-scale engineering with a large-scale effect, and sometimes the scale of the project was much, much bigger. But the sense of wonder was always there. *Bridging Infinity* isn't a climate change book, but working on it convinced me that science fiction is still about finding solutions – both more and less palatable ones – and that at least for now finding a solution to climate change is as key for science fiction as it is for the world at large.

Science fiction is always changing. It's much broader, more inclusive, less centralized than when I first encountered it, but a lot of what made it special is exactly the same. It asks questions, it believes problems are solvable, and it tries to find those solutions in stories that are filled with action, adventure and a bit of romance. That's what I see in these stories, and I hope you will as well.

Jonathan Strahan
Perth, Western Australia
July 2016

19

Alastair Reynolds
SIXTEEN QUESTIONS FOR KAMALA CHATTERJEE

Alastair Reynolds
Sixteen Questions for Kamala Chatterjee

WHAT FIRST DREW *you to the problem?*

She smiles, looking down at her lap.

She is ready for this. On the day of her thesis defence she has risen early after a good night's sleep, her mind as clean and clear as the blue skies over Ueno Park. She has taken the electric train to Keisei-Ueno station and then walked the rest of the way to the university campus. The weather is pleasantly warm for April, and she has worn a skirt for this first time all year. The time is *hanami* – the shifting, transient festival of the cherry blossom blooms. Strolling under the trees, along the shadow-dappled paths, families and tourists already gathering, she has tried to think of every possible thing she be might asked.

"I like things that don't quite fit," she begins. "Problems that have been sitting around nearly but not quite solved for a long time. Not the big, obvious ones. Keep away from those. But the ones everyone else forgets about because they're not quite glamorous enough. Like the solar p-mode oscillations. I read about them in my undergraduate studies in Mumbai."

She is sitting with her hands clenched together over her skirt, knees tight together, wondering why she felt obliged the dress up for this occasion when her examiners have come to work wearing exactly the same casual outfits as usual. Two she knows well: her supervisor, and another departmental bigwig. The third, the external examiner, arrived in Tokyo from Nagoya University, but even this one is familiar enough from the corridors. They all know each other better than they know her. Her supervisor and the external advisor must have booked a game of tennis for later. They both have sports bags with racket handles sticking out the side.

That's what they're mainly thinking about, she decides. Not her defence, not her thesis, not three years of work, but who will do best at tennis. Old grudges, old rivalries, boiling to the surface like the endless upwelling of solar convection cells.

"Yes," she says, feeling the need to repeat herself. "Things that don't fit. That's where I come in."

Then she sits back brightly and waits for the next question.

When you touched the Chatterjee Anomaly, the object that bore your name, the birth name you were given so many centuries ago, what did you feel?

Fear. Exhilaration. Wonder and terror at how far we'd come. How far I'd come. What it had taken to bring me to this point. We'd made one kind of bridge, between the surface of the Sun and the Anomaly, and that was difficult enough. I'd seen every step of it – borne witness to the entire thing, from the moment Kuroshio dropped her sliver of hafnium alloy on my desk. Before that, even, when I glimpsed the thing in the residuals. But what

I hadn't realised – not properly – was that I'd become another kind of bridge, just as strange as the one we drilled down into the photosphere. I'd borne witness to myself, so I ought not to have been so surprised. But I was, and just then it hit me like a tidal wave. From the moment they offered me the prolongation I'd allowed myself to become something I couldn't explain, something that had its inception far in the past, in a place called Mumbai, and which reached all the way to the present, anchored to this instant, this point in space and time, inside this blazing white furnace. In that moment I don't think there was anything capable of surprising me more than what I'd turned into. But then I touched the object, and it whispered to me, and I knew I'd been wrong. I still had a capacity for astonishment.

That in itself was astonishing.

It was only later that I realised how much trouble we were in.

Can you express the problem for your doctoral research project in simple terms – reduce it to its basics?

"It's a bit like earthquakes," she says, trying to make it seem as if she is groping for a suitable analogy. "Ripples in the Earth's crust. The way those ripples spread, the timing and shape of their propagation as they bounce around inside the crust, there's information in those patterns that the seismologists can use. They can start mapping things they wouldn't ordinarily be able to see, like deep faults – like the Tōkai fault, out beyond Tokyo Bay. It's the same with the Sun. For about sixty years people have been measuring optical oscillations in the surface of the Sun, then comparing them against mathematical models. Helioseismology – mapping the solar interior using what you can deduce from the surface. Glimpsing hidden structure, density changes, reflective surfaces and so on. It's the only way we can see what's going on."

You mentioned Kuroshio. We have records of an individual with that name. She was an academic scientist at the same institution as you, in the same nation state. This was long before Prometheus Station. Was Kuroshio the first to speculate about the project's ultimate feasibility?

Kuroshio was a colleague – a friend. We played football together, in the women's squad. Do you know what football was? No, of course you wouldn't. My friend was a solid-state physicist, specialising in metallurgy. I knew her a little when I was preparing my thesis, but it was only after I resubmitted it that we got to know each other really well. She showed me around her lab – they had a diamond anvil in there, a tool for producing extremely high pressures, for making materials that didn't exist on Earth, like super-dense hydrogen.

One morning she comes into my office. She had to share one with three postdocs herself, so she envied me having a whole office to myself. I think she's come to talk about training, but instead Kuroshio drops a handkerchief-sized scrap of paper onto my desk, like it's a gift, and invites me to examine the contents. Is any of this making sense to you?

Never mind. All I can see is a tiny sliver of metal, a sort of dirty silver in colour. I ask Kuroshio to explain and she says it's a sample of a new alloy, a blend of hafnium, carbon and nitrogen, cooked up in the solid-state physics lab. Like I'm supposed to be impressed. But actually I am, once she starts giving me the background. This is a theoretical material: a substance dreamed up in a computer before anyone worked out how to synthesize it. And the startling thing is, this material could endure two thirds of the surface temperature of the Sun without melting.

"You know what this means, don't you?" she asked me. "This is only a beginning. We can think about reaching that crazy alien thing you discovered. We can think about drilling a shaft into the Sun."

I laughed at her, but I really shouldn't have.

Kuroshio was right.

What makes you think you might be a suitable candidate for doctoral work? Select one or more answers from the options below. Leave blank if you feel none of the options apply.

- I am a diligent student. I have studied hard for my degree and always completed my coursework on time.
- I believe that I have a capacity for independent research. I do not need constant supervision or direction to guide my activities. In fact, I work better alone than in a crowd.
- I look forward to the day when I can call myself "doctor". I will enjoy the prestige that comes from the title.

You felt that the solar heliospheric oscillations would be a fruitful area to explore?

No, an inward voice answers sarcastically. *I thought that it would be an excellent way to waste three years.* But she straightens in her chair and tries to make her hands stop wrestling with each other. It's sweaty and close in this too-small office. The blinds are drawn, but not perfectly, and sunlight is fighting its way through the gaps. Bars of light illuminate dust in the air, dead flies on the windowsill, the spines of textbooks on the wall behind the main desk.

"Before I left Mumbai I'd spent a summer working with Sun Dragon, a graphics house working on really tough rendering problems. Light-tracing, real physics, for shoot 'em up games and superhero movies. I took one look at what those guys were already doing, compared it to the models everyone else was using to simulate the solar oscillations, and realised that the graphics stuff was way ahead. So that's where I knew I had an edge, because I'd soaked up all that knowledge and no one in astrophysics had a clue how far behind they were. That gave me a huge head start. I still had to build my simulation, of course, and gather the data, and it was a whole year before I was even close to testing the simulation against observations. Then there was a lot of fine-tuning, debugging…"

They look at graphs and tables, chewing over numbers and interpretation. The coloured images of the solar models are very beautiful, with their oddly geometric oscillation modes, like carpets or tapestries wrapped around the Sun.

"P-mode oscillations are the dominant terms," she says, meaning the pressure waves. "G-mode oscillations show up in the models, but they're not nearly as significant."

P for pressure.

G for gravity.

The road to Prometheus Station was arduous. Few of us have direct memories of those early days. But the prolongation has given you an unusual, not to say unique perspective. Do you remember the difficulties?

Difficulty was all we knew. We breathed it like air. Every step was monumental. New materials, new cooling methods, each increment bringing us closer and closer to the photosphere. Our probes skimmed and hovered, dancing closer to that blazing edge. They endured for hours, minutes. Sometimes seconds. But we pushed closer. Decades of constant endeavour. A century gone, then another. Finally the first fixed bridgehead, the first physical outpost on the surface of the Sun. Prometheus Station. A continent-sized raft of black water lilies, floating on a breath of plasma, riding the surge and plunge of cellular convection patterns. Not even a speck on the face of the Sun, but a start, a promise. The lilies existed only to support each other, most of their physical structure dedicated to cooling – threaded with refrigeration channels, pumps as fierce as rocket engines, great vanes and grids turned to space... each a floating machine the size of a city, and we had to keep building the entire network and throwing it away, whenever there was a storm, a mass ejection, or a granulation supercell too big for our engineering to ride out. We got better at everything, slowly. Learned to read the solar weather, to adjust Prometheus Station's position, dancing around the prominences. Decades and decades of failure and frustration, until we managed to survive two complete turns of the sunspot cycle. Slowly the outpost's complexity increased. To begin with, the only thing we required of it was to endure. That was challenge enough! Then we began to add functionality. Instruments, probes. We drilled down from its underside, pushed feelers into thickening plasma. Down a hundred kilometres, then a thousand. No thought of people ever living on it – that was still considered absurd.

The alignment between your models and the p-mode data is impressive – groundbreaking. It will be of great benefit to those working to gain a better understanding of the energy transport mechanisms inside the Sun. Indeed, you go further than that, speculating that a thorough program of modelling and mapping, extended to a real-time project, could give us vital advance warning of adverse solar weather effects, by linking emergent patterns in the deep convection layers with magnetic reconnection and mass ejection episodes. That seems a bold statement for a doctoral candidate. Do you wish to qualify it?

No.

But people came, didn't they? Or what we might call people?

Call them what you will. All I know is that we'd got better at stability. Fifty years without losing Prometheus Station, then a century. I'd have lived to see none of it if they hadn't offered me the prolongation, but by then I was too vital to the project to be allowed the kindness of dying. And I'm not sorry, really, at least not of those early stages. It was marvellous, what we learned to do. I wish Kuroshio had seen it all – I wish they'd been as generous to her as they were to me. I wish she'd been there when the machines constructed a station, a habitable volume on one of the central lilies. Heat wasn't the central problem by then – we could cool any arbitrary part of the station down as low as we liked, provided we accepted a thermal spike elsewhere. Thermodynamics, that's all. Gravity turned out to be the real enemy. Twenty seven gees! No unaugmented person could survive such a thing for more than a few seconds. So they shaped the first occupants. Rebuilt their bodies, their bones and muscles, their circulatory systems. They were slow, lumbering creatures – more like trees or elephants than people. But they could live on the Sun, and to the Sunwalkers it was the rest of us who were strange, ephemeral, easily broken. Pitiable, if you want the truth of it. Of course, I had to become one of them. I don't remember who had the idea first, me or them, but I embraced the transformation like a second birth. They sucked out my soul and poured it back into a better, stronger body. Gave me eyes that could stare into the photosphere without blinking – eyes that could discriminate heat and density and patterns of magnetic force. We strode that bright new world like gods. It's exactly what we were, for a little time. It was glorious.

No, better than that. We were glorious.

Let's turn now to your concluding remarks. You summarise your mathematical principles underpinning your simulations, discuss the complexities involved in comparing the computer model to the observed p-mode data, and highlight the excellent agreement seen across all the comparisons. Or almost all of them. What are we to make of the discrepancies, slight as they are?

"They're just residuals," she says, not wanting to be drawn on this point, but also not wanting to make it too obvious that she would rather be moving into safer waters. The Sun's angle behind the blinds has shifted during the conversation and now a spike of brightness is hitting her dead in the eye, making her squint. There's a migraine pressure swelling up somewhere behind her forehead.

"The worrying thing would be if the model and the data were in too close an agreement, because then you'd conclude that one or the other had been fudged." She squints at them expectantly, hoping for the agreement that never comes. "Besides, the only way to resolve that discrepancy – small as it is – would be to introduce an unrealistic assumption."

What attracts you to the idea of working in Tokyo? Select one or more answers from the options below. Leave blank if you feel none of the options apply.

- Tokyo is a bustling city with vibrant nightlife. I plan to throw myself into it with abandon. I will never be short of things to do in Tokyo.
- I have always had a romantic attachment to the idea of living in Japan. I have seen many films and read many comic strips. I am certain that I will not be disappointed by the reality of life in Tokyo.
- Beyond the university, the city is irrelevant to me. Provided I have somewhere affordable to sleep, and access to colleagues, funds and research equipment, I could live anywhere. I expect to spend most of my time in air-conditioned rooms, staring at computer screens. I could be in Mumbai or Pasadena or Cairo for all the difference it will make.

But to go deeper... you must have quailed at the challenge ahead of you?

We did, but we also knew no one was better equipped to face it. Slowly we extended our downward reach. Ten thousand kilometres, eventually – feelers tipped with little bubbles of air and cold, in which we could survive. The deep photosphere pressing in like a vice made of light, seeking out the tiniest flaw, the slightest weakness. Beneath three hundred kilometres, you couldn't see the sky any more. Just that furious white furnace, above and below.

But clever alloys and cooling systems had taken us as far as they were capable. Electron-degenerate matter was our next advance – the same material white dwarf stars are made out of. A century before we got anywhere with that. Hard enough to crush matter down to the necessary densities; even harder to coax it into some sort of stability. Only the fact of the Anomaly kept us going. It provided a sort of existence theorem for our enterprise. An alien machine survives inside the Sun, deeper than any layer we've reached. If it can do that, so can we.

Hubris? Perhaps.

But the truth is we might as well have been starting science from scratch. It was like reinventing fire, reinventing basic metallurgy.

We did it, all the same. We sent sounding probes ahead of the main shaft, self-contained machines constructed from shells of sacrificial degenerate matter. Layers of themselves boiled away until all that was left was a hard nugget of cognitive machinery, with just enough processing power to swim around, make observations and signal back to us. They forged a path, tested our new materials and methods. Another century. We pushed our physical presence down to thirty thousand kilometres – a borehole drilled half way to the prize. Conditions were tough – fully murderous. We could send machines to the bottom of the shaft, but not Sunwalkers. So we shaped new explorers, discarding our old attachment to arms and legs, heads and hearts. Sunsprites. Sun Dragons, I called us. A brain, a nervous system, and then nothing else you'd ever recognise as human. Quick, strong, luminous creatures – mermaids of light and fire. I became one, when they asked. There was never the slightest hesitation. I revelled in what they'd made of me. We could swim beyond the shaft, for a little while – layers of sacrificial armour flaking away from us like old skins. But even the degenerate matter was only a step along the way. Our keenest minds were already anticipating the next phase, when we had to learn the brutal alchemy of nuclear degenerate matter. Another two centuries! Creating tools and materials from neutron-star material made our games with white dwarf matter look like child's play. Which it was, from our perspective. We'd come a long way. Too far, some said.

But still we kept going. What else were we going to do?

What do you mean by unrealistic?

"Look," she says, really feeling that migraine pressure now, her squinting eyes watering at the striped brightness coming through the blinds, a brightness with her name on it. "Everyone knows the Sun is round. A child will tell you that. Your flag says the same thing. But actually the Sun is really quite unreasonably round. It's so round that it's practically impossible to measure any difference between the diameter at the poles and the diameter at the equator. And if a thing's round on the outside, that's a fairly large hint that it's symmetric all the way through to the middle. You could explain away the residuals by adding an asymmetric term into the solar interior, but it really wouldn't make any sense to do so."

And nor, she thinks, would it make sense to introduce that term anyway, then run many simulations springing from it, then compare them against the data, over and over, hoping that the complication – like the cherry blossoms – will fall away at the first strong breeze, a transient business, soon to be forgotten.

They stare at her with a sort of polite anticipation, as if there is something more she ought to have said, something that would clear the air and allow them to proceed. They are concerned for her, she thinks – or at least puzzled. Her gaze slips past theirs, drawn to the pattern behind the blinds, the play of dust and light and shadow, as if there's some encouraging or discouraging signal buried in that information, hers for the reading.

But instead they ask to see a graph of the residuals.

Can you be certain of our fate?

Yes, as I'm sure of it as anyone can be. Obviously there are difficulties of translation. After all the centuries, after all the adaptive changes wrought on me, my mind is very far from that of a baseline human. Having said that, I am still much, much closer to you than I am to the Anomaly. And no matter what you may make of me – no matter how strange you now find me, this being that can swim inside a star, this Sun Dragon of degenerate matter who could crush your ships and stations as easily as she blinks, you must know that I feel a kinship.

I am still human. I am still Kamala Chatterjee, and I remember what I once used to be. I remember Mumbai, I remember my parents, I remember their kindness in helping me follow my education. I remember grazing my shins in football. I remember the burn of grass on my palm. I remember sun-dappled paths, paper lanterns and evening airs. I remember Kuroshio, although you do not. And I call myself one of you, and hope that my account of things is accurate. And if I am correct – and I have no reason to think otherwise – then I am afraid there is very little ambiguity about our fate.

When I touched the Anomaly, I suddenly knew its purpose. It's been waiting for us, primed to respond. Sitting inside the Sun like a bomb. An alien timebomb. Oh, you needn't worry about *that*. The Sun won't explode, and tongues of fire won't lash out against Earth and the other worlds. Nothing so melodramatic.

No; what will happen – what is happening – is far subtler. Kinder, you might say. You and I live in the moment. We have come to this point in our history, encountered the Anomaly, and now we ponder the consequences of that event. But the Anomaly's perception isn't like that. Its view of us is atemporal. We're more like a family tree than a species. It sees us as a decision-branch structure frozen in time – a set of histories, radiating out from critical points. An entity that has grown into a particular complex shape, interacted with the Anomaly across multiple contact points, and which must now be pruned. Cut back. Stripped of its petals as the summer winds strip a cherry blossom.

I can feel it happening. I think some of it rubbed off on me, and now I'm a little bit spread out, a little bit smeared, across some of these histories, some of these branches. Becoming atemporal. And I can feel those branches growing thinner, withering back from their point of contact, as if they've touched a poison. Can you feel it too?

No, I didn't think so.

If you were offered a placement, when do you think you would be able to start your research? Select one or more answers from the options below. Leave blank if you feel none of the options apply.

- O I would be able to start within a few months, once I have settled my affairs in my home country.
- O I would like to start immediately. I am eager to begin my doctoral work.
- O I would like time to consider the offer.

We feel that the thesis cannot be considered complete without a thorough treatment of the residual terms. A proper characterisation of these terms will lead to a clearer picture of the "anomaly" that seems to be implied by the current analysis. This will entail several more months of work. Are you prepared to accept this commitment?

A moment grows longer, becomes awkward in its attenuation. She feels their eyes on her, willing her to break the silence. But it has already gone on long enough. There can be no way to speak now that will not cast a strange, eccentric light on her behaviour. That light coming through the window feels unbearably full of meaning, demanding total commitment to the act of observation.

Her throat moves. She swallows, feeling herself pinned to this moving instant in space and time, paralysed by it. Her migraine feels less like a migraine and more like a window opening inside her head, letting in futures. Vast possibilities unfold from this moment. Terrifying futures, branching away faster and more numerous than thoughts can track. There is a weight on her that she never asked for, never invited. A pressure, sharpening down to a point like the tip of a diamond anvil.

There's a version of her that did something magnificent and terrible. She traces the contingent branches back in time, until they converge on this office, this moment, this choice.

Agree to their request. Or fail.

She gathers her notes and rises to leave. She smoothes her skirt. They watch her without question, faces blank – her actions so far outside the usual parameters that her interrogators have no frame of reference.

"I have to go to the park again," she says, as if that ought to be answer enough, all that was required of her. "It's still *hanami*. There's still time."

They watch as Kamala Chatterjee closes the door behind her. She goes to Ueno Park, wanders the cherry blossom paths, remaining there until the lantern lighters come and an evening cool touches the air.

39

Pat Cadigan

Six Degrees of ~~Separation~~ Freedom

Pat Cadigan

Six Degrees of ~~Separation~~ Freedom

"What's the catch?" Dory asked when it became clear no one else would.

Dr. Réka Enescu looked down at her from her elevated able-chair. She had a face full of Freez™ but Dory's enhanced eyesight detected a hint of a smile. "The catch is, you can't come back."

A murmur ran through the rest of the room, except for Dory, who was sitting alone in the front row of the auditorium. This would be the Hell-No for a lot of them. People who had never experienced a large-scale disaster, natural or man-made, tended to balk at no-going-back. They didn't like a situation with no Undo button; even if they had no intention of using it, they just wanted to know they could. Undo; re-do; save and exit; exit without saving – as if everything could be edited or done over. Dory blamed old software architecture; that, and endless entertainment reboots.

Dr. Enescu looked at someone behind Dory and nodded. "Yes?"

A man cleared his throat. "Why are you refusing to let people come back? People should be allowed to go home if they want to."

The woman hesitated. She was tired of answering this question; Dory didn't blame her.

"It's not a matter of *refusing to let* people come back," Dr. Enescu said. "It's the distances involved. Jupiter is over four times farther away from the Earth than the Earth is to the Sun. It takes light over half an hour to go from Earth to Jupiter, which isn't an easy journey for –"

"Is that when Jupiter is closest, or when it's farthest?" another man asked, then added, "Never mind. I looked it up."

"It's not *just* the distance," Dr. Enescu said sharply, "it's also the physical adaptations to the human body. We evolved to live under the constant force of one gee. In order to survive in a weightless environment, changes have to be made. For example, in zero-gee, the heart doesn't need to work harder to pump blood into the upper body. We also have to counter muscle atrophy, bone loss –"

"The whole body has to be changed?" the first man asked, sounding unhappy.

"I'm afraid so," Dr. Enescu said. "And a body adapted to live in zero-gee can't survive on Earth."

"What if you don't want your body adapted?" the first man said.

"We aren't trying to force anyone to agree to the procedure before we'll even talk to them," Dr. Enescu replied. "Body modification is a deeply personal matter and no one should be coerced into doing something. Or not doing it. However, if you can't even bring yourself to consider adaptation as a hypothetical, this is probably not for you."

Dory turned around; about a third of the audience in the auditorium were making their way to the exit at the back. Once they were gone, Dr. Enescu asked the remaining people to move closer to the front. Most did, some didn't – the usual five percent who might stay but wanted to make an inconspicuous exit if they decided to leave. It was the same at every event. When had human behaviour become so predictable, Dory wondered? Or was it only apparent to her now because of her enhanced vision?

"I have to admit I'm rather surprised most people don't understand physical adaptation is mandatory, not optional," Dr. Enescu said when everyone was settled. A small dark curl dropped down onto her forehead. As she raised her hand to tuck it back into place, Dory caught a glimpse up her sleeve of the exoskeleton. Enescu had said wearing it made her feel like a puppet that was also the puppeteer. On Earth, that was – in zero-gee, it was completely different. She only had another week before she left Earth for the last time. But it would be a pretty full week – all spinal-injury clinics and amputee rehab facilities. Dory wished her own schedule allowed her to sit in on some of those.

"Hearing about it and having someone tell you face-to-face are two different things," said the man who had asked about Jupiter's nearest and farther points. There were murmurs of agreement.

"But is it *really* irreversible?" an androgyne in the row behind Dory asked.

"Are you planning to reverse your own physical form?" Dr. Enescu replied evenly. As she lowered her hand from her hair, the arm-rest angled up to meet it and brought it down the rest of the way. She should have been in a reclining position but Enescu was one of those people who had to do everything the hard way.

"Absolutely not," said the androgyne with a laugh. "But I can survive anywhere on Earth both as I was, and as I am now –"

"Not *anywhere*, honey-bear," said the androgyne next to him/her with a grim laugh.

"You *know* what I mean," the first androgyne said, elbowing her/him. "My heart would beat, I could breathe –"

"Until the fundamentalist commandos found your hideout," said his/her friend with a laugh.

The first androgyne elbowed her/him harder. "And while we're on the subject, what about us? Do you only take binaries?"

"Adaptation has nothing to do with gender," Dr. Enescu said.

"So the stories about androgynes waking up and finding they've been assigned to be male or female without their permission aren't true?" the first androgyne said, sounding slightly suspicious.

Dr. Enescu let out a breath that wasn't quite a sigh. "To my knowledge, no one has been assigned or re-assigned a gender against their will."

"A lot of things happen to us that no one knows about," the second androgyne said darkly. "Until it's too late, anyway."

Dr. Enescu lowered her chair from eye-level-standing height to eye-level-sitting. "Not in space," she said, her voice quiet but firm. "In space, nothing happens in secret."

Dory waited for someone to realise Enescu had just divulged the real catch.

"Oh," the androgyne said after a moment. "So nobody gets experimented on?"

"Unless they want to be," added his/her friend.

"Absolutely not." For the first time, Dr. Enescu sounded annoyed and didn't try to cover it. "Adaptation clinics aren't set up for research or experimental medicine."

"And if you *did* want to be experimented on?" asked someone many rows back. "After you got adapted, what if you wanted to participate in –"

"Not my area," Dr. Enescu said, cordial but emphatic. "I'm only here to find people who might be interested in living and working in space, not to find subjects for medical trials."

Silence fell and stretched. Dory turned around for another look at the audience and was a bit surprised to see that no one else had left.

Finally, another woman in the front row on Dory's right said, "I'd like to see the video again."

There was a chorus of agreement so Dr. Enescu obligingly lowered the tank and ran the entire holo from the beginning. Only one person sneaked out when the lights dimmed; everyone else sat through the entire twenty minutes of what Dory thought of as a cross between the *Ain't Science Great?* edu-mercials they showed under-achievers in elementary school and the *Don't Kill Yourself Yet, You Can Train For A New Career – Really, You Can, No Joke!* programmes the recently-fired found in their severance packages.

Not that it wasn't right for the audience, some of whom probably had been recently fired. In this particular part of the country, however, most of them were not-so-recently fired and getting desperate. The rest would include a mix of those fresh out of higher education with no prospects, those insisting they were only curious, and some dissatisfied souls wondering if this might be the escape hatch they were looking for.

Even so, how many of them would take the next step and sign a provisional commitment was a crap-shoot. It didn't matter how good the video was or how compelling the speaker. Sometimes you got almost everyone in the audience lining up, thumbs out to be scanned. Other times, you got maybe two or three who all backed out the moment they saw the scanner. And once in a while – not nearly as often as Dory would have thought – someone would say, *Wait a second – what do you mean, 'In space, nothing happens in secret'?* Then things would get *really* interesting. Everyone might walk out, except for a few who wanted to debate privacy issues. Or they all might stay and argue, not just with the speaker but with each other, which could be entertaining but otherwise a total failure.

Still, IRL events were proving to be a far better way to recruit for the Habitats project than 'casts, even those done live in real time. There were billions of 'casts on tap and most of them were more interesting than a factual presentation about living in outer space. In Dory's experience, the best way to persuade people to physically go somewhere was to get them to physically go somewhere. They needed to experience their own six degrees of freedom. Plus, bodies in motion tended to stay in motion.

A lot of people attended several different IRL events one after another, seemingly to wear down their own resistance. The hard-sell of *Eat this! Wear that! Stop! Listen! Watch!* they experienced every day was *verboten* at recruitment events. Research showed that in many areas of the west, decades – correction, generations – of exposure to aggressive media had produced people who never said yes to anything the first time around for fear of looking weak. *If it's that important, they won't take no for an answer* were words most people lived by. It made a classic lesson in strain energy and positive feedback; outside the classroom, however, Dory found it more than a little tiring.

Recruitment had originally wanted to go with the hard-sell. Dory had spent most of two days changing their minds. Even with real facts and figures to show them, it had been the hardest sell of her career, an irony that wasn't lost on her. Later, one of the execs told Dory s/he was surprised she hadn't given up. Dory had smiled and murmured something polite but didn't try to explain. The exec was organisation and admin; s/he understood flow within an existing structure as an end-user, not as a designer. That was all right. End-users weren't supposed to think in those terms; if they did, it was a bad structure. Nonetheless, Dory thought that if most end-users were slightly better acquainted with the how and why of their tools, they'd have found them easier to use.

The mentor on her final apprenticeship, a tall, muscular, grey-haired industrial design specialist named Fola Ekemeni, had agreed wholeheartedly. *That's a great idea,* she told Dory. *I'll set up the first round of accredited seminars myself – just as soon as you engineer three or four more hours into each day. Even better – remodel the week so we get eight days instead of seven and I'll pin a rose on you, too.*

Dory was still smiling at the memory when the lights came up again. Dr. Enescu asked for more questions. When no one had any, she asked if anyone wanted to make a personal appointment, which made Dory wince. She thought *personal appointment* sounded like something guaranteed to bore you to death. Enescu explained it was a one-to-one meeting with someone who would get to know them well enough to talk about possibilities based on an initial assessment of their strengths. Enescu never said *strengths and weaknesses,* just *strengths;* it was an Enescu thing. Everyone knows their weaknesses, she had said when Dory asked her about it; you want people demonstrating what they're good at, not hiding what they're bad at. Dory thought she'd have made a good engineer. But then, that was true of most x-abled people. Very few of them were content to be just end-users.

A little over half the people in the audience lined up for the scanner. Enescu took care of that without Dory's help – another one of her things. It went quickly, even with a few people suddenly thinking of questions but by the time everyone left, Enescu was visibly sagging. Except for her face, which was as smooth and immobile as ever.

"What's the catch?" The Freez™ hadn't even begun wear off yet but Enescu gave a small laugh. "I think that's the only question I *wasn't* expecting."

"Can't prove it by me – you didn't even hesitate." Dory smiled broadly. Maybe a bit too broadly – Enescu probably thought she looked like a jackass in mid-heehaw. But she couldn't help it; after she spent an extended period of time around someone who was all Freez™-ed up, she'd get a compulsion to take on the facial expressions that were temporarily beyond the other person. It was one of her things. Kinda weird but to Dory's mild surprise, not all that rare. Maybe she should open a side business: *Faces In Places – we'll smile at you or for you. Reasonable Rates.*

"Well, I actually didn't know what I was going to say till I said it." Enescu seemed to sink even deeper into the cushioned cradle in the backseat of the limo – ahem, *transport*. Nobody called them limos now. During the last economic debacle, the word *limo* had become closely associated with a certain kind of wealth and privilege that was both clueless and heartless. In some areas, even *town car* was iffy.

"I didn't mean to throw you." Dory could feel her facial muscles straining to corroborate her concern. Maybe she needed a little Freez™ herself, just so she wouldn't sprain her forehead.

"Oh, you didn't really throw me." Enescu's conciliatory tone completely contradicted her neutral masque. "I've been doing this for a while and I've heard all kinds of kooky shite."

Kooky. Dory immediately broke into a broad grin. Now there was a word you hardly ever heard any more. It was a good one; Dory made a mental note to start using it herself.

"Can't say it hasn't been fun," Enescu went on. "I'm an extrovert with a streak of exhibitionism so this kind of gig is right in my sweet spot. But I'm looking forward to wrapping this up and losing weight for good. I was only up for three weeks but that was enough." She looked down at her hands, resting on the lap cushion. "No matter how light or flexible or intuitive they are supposed to be, every exo I've ever had made me feel like a sack full of sticks and water balloons. But in zero-gee, you can actually forget you're even using one. It was the first time I'd felt like myself since fate crapped on me."

Dory stared, hoping she looked more attentively caring than Kabuki.

"Damn, I'm sorry," Enescu said unhappily. "I talk too much when I get Freez™-ed up. I think I'm subconsciously trying to compensate for the poker face. If that makes any sense to you."

"You know, it really does," Dory assured her. She considered telling Enescu about her own tic in that area and then decided not to. Giving end users extra information in a social setting was more likely to distract than edify. Besides, she could do much more with what she learned from Enescu than Enescu could do with anything Dory might tell her.

49

"I won't see you again after this, will I?" Enescu said. Dory shook her head. "That's probably also part of it – we'll never meet again so I run off at the mouth. I did enjoy working with you, though."

"It was kind of you to agree to fill in for Dr. Hupperton," Dory told her.

"I didn't mind. It was –" She paused for so long, Dory wondered if she were going to continue. "It was nothing," she said finally. "It was easy. And the extra Value I'm getting for it doesn't hurt. Can you explain how that works? Value, I mean."

"Well..." Dory grimaced, suddenly stuck. "To be perfectly honest, no."

Enescu burst out laughing; her immobilised face made it sound as odd as it looked. "I'm sorry, I'm not laughing at you. I'm laughing at the Value system and the brain-boxes who thought it up. I've asked a whole bunch of people if they can explain how it works. About half said they can't. The rest actually tried. I told them, talk to me like I'm stupid, I don't mind. But I'm too stupid, I guess, because I still can't make heads or tails or good red herring out of any of it. Economic engineering, my sweet tetraplegic ass."

"The Value system is a lot like time," Dory said. "We know it, we use it, we live with it and by it. But try taking a close look at *what* it is and you might as well try gluing strawberry jelly to a ghost."

Enescu laughed harder this time. "Damn, I wish this shite would wear off already," she said after a bit. "If I can't crack a smile soon, I'm gonna get a lip hernia or something."

Now it was Dory's turn to laugh. "Try decreasing your dosage by an eighth next time," she suggested.

"Next time, I'm decreasing it to zero," Enescu said. "If I go into a room full of x-ables with *this* face. I'll get my ass handed to me. In a million pieces."

Dory frowned. "Have you talked that over with Recruitment?"

"No, I just *told* them. That's my deal – when I'm going to talk to the extra-enabled, I go in bare-faced. They need to know I'm not trying to hide anything. X-ables see too much of this shite –" She jerked both thumbs in the general direction of her head. "Hell, if I ever sub for someone with a general audience again, I'll do it bare-faced or not at all. I don't know what I was thinking, agreeing to be *more* paralysed."

Dory's enhanced vision caught a tiny movement at the corner of Enescu's mouth, the first sign the Freez™ was finally letting go. Dory felt relieved for her. For both of them, really – her own facial muscles were so tired the corners of her mouth quivered when she smiled.

"So, where do you go from here?" Enescu asked her.

"Kyrgyzstan," Dory said.

"I think I felt my eyebrows go up half a millimetre," Enescu said.

"Your eyes definitely widened," Dory told her. It was true.

"Damn, who did you piss off, Jesus?"

"His dad, actually."

"Good one," Enescu said. "I'm stealing it."

"Use it in good health. Actually, I don't mind. I've never been to Kyrgyzstan."

"Is there even room? I caught the news earlier. It looks like wall-to-wall refugees. Is Recruitment counting on signing up a lot of people who have nowhere to go?"

"I wouldn't know. I don't actually work for Recruitment,"

Dory said politely. "I mean, I do, but I'm a consultant, not a salaried employee."

A tiny indentation appeared over Enescu's right eyebrow; her eyes looked up as if she could actually see it. "Aha! I felt that. Thank God, I should be able to make funny faces by dinner time. What do you consult on?"

"I specialise in population movements due to environmental change, either sudden or over some period of time, like maybe a decade."

"Specialise how? What do you do, observe? Predict? Enable?" Enescu's eyes widened again. "I was going to say 'prevent' but that ship has left the dock and it ain't coming back."

Dory hesitated. "I cope," she said finally. "I figure out how to cope. As part of a team, of course, not just me by myself."

"So how do you cope?"

"That's what we have to figure out. How the refugees can cope, how the already established population can cope. And how everyone around them can cope. It ripples out a very long way."

"I'm sure." Enescu gave a short laugh. "Recruiting them to live in space could be a pretty good solution."

"I agree," Dory said, "but first, they have to cope."

"Oh." Enescu blinked at her. "I'm sorry, I guess I don't really understand what you do. I thought I did."

"It's okay," Dory said. "It's like time."

"And the Value system?" Enescu's eyes twinkled.

KYRGYZSTAN WASN'T WALL-TO-WALL refugees – Enescu had apparently confused it with one of the 'stans on the other side of the Caspian Sea. But its population had risen quite a bit and it would continue to increase as temperatures in parts of the Indian subcontinent went from difficult to impossible. Dory split her time between two groups, one looking at possible channels for the flow of migration and the other trying to measure the strain energy at various destinations. Her last two weeks she spent with a team commissioned by a multi-nation consortium to design underground living space 'not in theory but in fact', unquote. The engineers, Dory included, had a good laugh about that. *As if we ever work any other way,* said the foreperson, an androgyne named Revere Evershed. Her/his original specialty had actually been landscapes and s/he was always trying to get more green space into every design.

Seriously, you people don't realise how much green you're used to in your life, s/he said when someone challenged one of her/his ideas for an oasis/parklet. *Even if you're completely urban. You see it and you don't even know you're seeing it. You've got trees growing up out of the sidewalks, you've got flowering shrubs all over apartment complexes and office buildings, inside and out. In Manhattan – hell, there's friggin'* ivy *climbing the Empire State Building* –

That's an urban myth, said one of the geologists. *Those photos are all fakes.*

Evershed was unmoved. *Okay, if that isn't real, it* oughta *be. Getting daylight in is only half the solution. If they don't see it shining on living things other than themselves, they're all gonna turn into Morlocks.*

About half the team, Dory included, got the reference. Evershed looked at those who hadn't and shook her/his head sadly. *The benefits of a classical education can*not *be overstated,* s/he said. *I'd make you all read* The Time Machine *as homework but* *there aren't enough hours in the day already for what they want us to do.*

Dory hoped Evershed never found out she was only familiar with some of the later film adaptations; judging from the microexpressions she'd picked up, she wasn't alone. Still, she thought Evershed was right and before she left, she invited her/him for coffee at a café in the nearby village.

"I know all about the Habitats project," Evershed told her. They were sitting outside at a small metal table that had seen much better days, most likely in the previous century. The mismatched wooden chairs looked even older but were surprisingly solid, and just as uncomfortable. "They've sent headhunters at me a few times, once since I've been here. I guess you make it twice…"

Dory considered telling him/her this hadn't been a headhunting assignment for her and decided not to, at least for the moment. Making people feel sought-after was never a bad thing. "I believe in the project," she said. "I believe it *can* work, I believe it *will* work. And I believe you're just what they need."

"I'm flattered but I'm committed. As you know."

Dory couldn't resist. "And as *you* know, Bob, I do." They laughed together. "But you're not nailed to the ground permanently," she went on. "When your contract expires – or when they replace you with 'a fresh perspective', whichever – and you're looking around for your next job, try looking up."

Evershed flicked a glance at the sky, which was clouded over, featureless and vague. "Leave everything I've ever known, die in space? What about my family?"

"I thought you didn't have children."

Evershed grinned in a way that reminded Dory of a very old drawing of a smiling cat she'd seen once. "What if I did?"

"That might be a harder sell," Dory admitted a bit sheepishly. "Aren't you recruiting families?"

Dory hesitated. "Nobody's turning them away. But things get complicated when not all the parents or guardians want to emigrate. There have also been cases where everyone in the immediate family is good to go but other relatives file a legal restraint to keep the minors on Earth. Usually because they didn't want to lose their grandchildren. A few minors have requested emancipation, some because they want to stay on Earth, but most because they don't. Some places have made it illegal to take anyone under the age of consent into space with intent to remain permanently, even if there's no conflict and the whole family is ready for launch. If they can't consent to sex, they can't consent to an elective life-altering procedure."

Evershed gave a small laugh. "I get the reasoning but that's gonna end up biting something it wasn't supposed to."

"It already has," Dory assured him, "and it's a mess. There's nothing in the known universe that could persuade me to be a lawyer."

"Hey, a lawyer's just an engineer wearing roller skates and a straitjacket." Evershed laughed again. "A lawyer told me that one." The androgyne's smile faded. "I've spent my whole life solving problems here. I think I'm too old to change."

"I doubt you're much older than I am," Dory said. "Do you really want to spend the rest of your working life figuring out the best way to bury people alive?"

Evershed winced. "I wish everyone would stop referring to it like that. We're solving the problem of survival in a hostile environment. Is it really so different from the Habitats project? You can live underground on Earth or in a pressurised can in outer space, which I'd say is a much more hostile environment. And what about Mars? Everybody there lives underground. What's so great about being 'buried alive' there?"

"If you ask me, nothing," Dory said. "If you ask the colonists, they'll say it's the lighter gravity. Physical activity is different when you weigh a little over a third of what you do on Earth. They have their own versions of baseball and dance. They've also reinvented pinball, with humans instead of balls, which really brings in the tourists. Some people would rather go to the moon, where the gravity's less than half of Mars. But they actually don't let you bounce around as much there." She smiled. "I prefer no gravity myself."

"You're doing this to lose weight?"

Dory had lost count of the number of times she'd heard that joke but she laughed with Evershed anyway. "Actually, I'm in it for the new challenges. New problems that need solving. During the relatively brief time I spent in the Habitats orbiting Jupiter, I could actually see their society taking shape."

"Habitats, plural? How many are there?"

"Three, so far. They're still in progress but people have moved in. And as they go on building and adding to them, there'll be more."

"What if there aren't?" Evershed asked. "What if they build these great big tin cans – excuse me, Habitats – and people decide they'd rather be underground on Earth than live in a space can millions of miles away from everything they've ever known?"

Dory shrugged. "There's more than one way to get more people. They're already having kids out there."

Evershed looked shocked. "Do they adapt babies right after birth or wait till they're toddlers?"

Dory shook her head. "Epigenetics – kids're born adapted."

The androgyne stared, then finished the rest of her/his coffee in one go. "That may not play well down here. Messing with Mother Nature like that."

"But screwing up the climate so much that people have to live underground, nobody has a problem with that," Dory said a bit sourly.

"I didn't say *I* felt that way. But it'll be one more thing making recruitment harder for you. 'Space-humans give birth to mutant monster babies' – there hasn't been click-bait that good in, I don't know, thirty years, Maybe fifty. You'll have your work cut out for you."

"Well, not me personally," Dory said. "I'm on contract with JovOps Recruitment; in exchange for services rendered, they'll cover surgical adaptation all the way through to recovery and then make sure I end up in a place where they need people like me."

"You can get work anywhere, down here or up there. You're an engineer."

"I'm a *civil* engineer," Dory corrected him. "Out there, that's a lot more than infrastructure. Although I don't ignore infrastructure, which is why I'd really like to get you out of the dirt, too. Will you think about it?"

"How the hell do you plant a garden with no gravity? You'd have to pack the dirt too tightly to keep it from just –" s/he raised both hands and wiggled his fingers. "Disintegrating? Diffusing?"

"A number of different growing mediums have been developed," Dory told him. "Or media, I guess it should be. I'm surprised you don't know that."

Evershed smiled with half his/her mouth. "I've been busy. But never mind. If you're happy to go, I'm happy for you. But I've got my hands full here. If not me, who?"

"And if not now, when?" The quick rejoinder earned her a smile of genuine approval. Nothing like a classical education – or half-classical at least – to make someone take you seriously, she thought. "They need people who understand the importance of green spaces well enough to fight for them."

"And if I'm fighting for them out at Jupiter, who's going to fight for them here?"

Dory took a breath. "When they realise they need more grass and trees and whatnot, they can order some and have it delivered in a few days. Out there, they'd have to wait for it to grow. It'll save a lot of time if you get them to put in enough in the first place. Not to mention all the people who won't need mess for lack-of-green anxiety or whatever it is." She took a chip out of her pants pocket and held it out to her/him. "Just have a look at this. It's not a sales-pitch," she added in response to the look on his/her face. "It's the journal l kept of my time in space. There's a lot of selfie stuff but it's never just me and I only mention it because you might think I look a lot younger. I didn't use any cosmetic filters – not even a little correction. Everybody looks younger when the Earth isn't constantly trying to suck them down into its core."

Evershed made her wait almost ten seconds before s/he finally took the chip. "So it really isn't just weight loss – it's rejuvenation, too."

"It kinda is, but not how you'd think," Dory said. "Just think about it, okay?"

Evershed told her s/he would.

* * *

Dory spent the next three weeks with two hundred other engineers in an idea exchange, talking about tension, compression, and shear in both formal and informal human structures, and those conditions most likely to result in buckling. She hadn't devoted so much time to vapour since she'd gotten her first degree and it made her feel weird. Not that she wasn't happy to learn about other people's experiences, and she actually thought they could have done with half a dozen anthropologists rather than three. But Dory had come to feel that you could spend the rest of your life talking about what-ifs and what-nexts and probably never get through them all, plus you'd miss the living through the experience in real life, with real people. Three weeks had never felt so long.

Her last week was open time. She said a few final goodbyes to her oldest friends, with mixed results. It wasn't as easy to tell with people that you were doubling the strain energy as it was with inanimate materials. Carleen, whom she had roomed with as an undergrad, actually believed Dory subconsciously wanted someone to talk her out of going into space.

"Why would you think that?" Dory asked her as they stood in the doorway of her apartment.

"Because I already tried to talk you out of it," Carleen said, exasperated. "Why else would you come back?"

"Because you're one of my oldest friends," Dory said.

"But subconsciously –"

"I don't think so," Dory told her. "And if it is, well, my subconscious isn't driving – *I* am. The subconscious doesn't get a vote."

"Figures," Carleen said. "You're the one who thinks you can engineer people into a society."

"No, I don't. Human structures find their own shape," Dory said. "I just observe. With any luck, I can find points of equilibrium, even if they change from moment to moment. Which happens more often than not. It's extremely complicated when every member of a structure always has six degrees of freedom."

"You mean six degrees of separation," Carleen said.

Back when they'd been at school, Dory had corrected her on this over and over, explaining that the six degrees of freedom meant something could move in six directions perpendicular to each other. It wasn't that hard to understand but Carleen just couldn't seem to retain it and Dory had no idea why. It certainly wasn't because she was stupid. Dory was about to go over it for her again, then thought better of it. Carleen wasn't stupid – she just wasn't an engineer.

"Yeah, sure," Dory said. "Separation."

"Which I guess is your idea of freedom." Carleen blew out a short breath. "If you change your mind, let me know. But don't call me from the shuttle two minutes before lift-off and beg me to come get you, because they'll never let me into the launch area."

Dory imagined her own sad smile was a mirror of Carleen's.

"Just do me one favour," Carleen added.

"If I can," Dory replied.

"Could you just... walk away? I can't stand the symbolism of closing the door on you. You go, and I'll shut the door after you get to the elevators."

Really not an engineer, Dory thought as she left.

Much later, after she had made the transfer from the shuttle to the orbiting way station where she would wait for her transport to Jovian space, she got a message notification. The time-stamp indicated it had been sent only a few minutes before launch. She hesitated to read it, wondering if it was from Carleen; it felt great to be weightless again and she didn't want to ruin it with more angst.

But the message was from Evershed: *Got fired. Don't know how you saw it coming. Thinking of doing more gardening. What are the seasons like up there? Do seasons even exist up there? I should know but I've been busy. Millions of questions.*

She clicked on reply, thinking about how structures might find their own shapes when every component always had six degrees of freedom.

63

Stephen Baxter

THE VENUS GENERATIONS

Stephen Baxter

THE VENUS GENERATIONS

Later, Hank would remember how much she had liked the sunshield swallow, even at first glance.

And she liked her first view of Venus, too, what she could see of it from the Venera station, orbiting hundreds of kilometres above the shining cloud tops.

But then she had been just ten years old. It was only as she grew up, later, that she came to dislike so much what happened when her mother had put those two lovely things together.

For her mother, though, for Jocelyn Lang Poole, this tremendous planetary spectacle had only been a beginning. "You've got to start somewhere," she'd said.

Hank had stood there with her mother at the scuffed window of the elderly habitat. Vencra was a chain of modules, old and much reused, now strung out in a belt around a gleaming bowl of solar-energy collectors and spun up for gravity. Inside everything was as smart as you'd find on Earth, the very walls as responsive to a touch or a word as Hank's own bedroom back in London. But even so, Hank thought, equipped with the sensitive nose of a ten-year-old, you could *smell* the age of the place, smell the grease and the dirt and the electric tang of antique machineries – smell the sweat of the generations of vanished cosmonauts who had assembled this place, it was said, all of four hundred years ago.

On the other hand Hank was used to the presence of great age; her father, a teacher in London, had once told her she was sensitised to it. After all, her own mother was two hundred and fifteen years old. Hank was the only member of the fourth 'litter' of children Jocelyn had raised during those long years, as she liked to say.

But amid all this antiquity the shield swallow was definitively something *new*.

Standing at this window, at first Jocelyn had to point it out to Hank; the swallow was an elusive sight. So polished were its enormous wings that you could only see them by the reflections they cast, shimmering images of the brilliant sun – save when the swallow swam across the face of the planet, when the graceful forms were like cut-outs against the brilliance of the clouds. "She's riding on the pressure of the sunlight itself," Jocelyn murmured. "You know, those wings, sheets of monomolecular carbon, weigh no more than a gram each. The body isn't much more than that."

"She's hardly anything, then," Hank said.

"You could crumple her up in your fist."

"But she seems smart."

"So she does. She has to be smart, she'll spend most of her life keeping her place in the shield-flock out at the first Lagrange point. Which is a position in space out between Venus and the sun –"

"I know *that*," said Hank, a little piqued. She always hesitated before admitting any ignorance to her mother; she lived with her father, she didn't see much of Jocelyn, and she always wanted to make the right impression. She said tentatively, "I know the shield will cast a shadow. A *big* shadow that will cool down the whole of Venus."

"Well, that's the idea," Jocelyn said, and she ruffled Hank's hair. "And you, and with any luck I, might get to see the outcome, in a few hundred years' time."

Hank looked down on the sunlit clouds again, and imagined them cast into darkness and cold. "But I guess I don't see why you need to do it."

Jocelyn sighed. "No, and neither did the boards of governance and oversight, from the UN and the Stewardship on downwards to every polder council on Earth, it felt like, with those damn Conservers protesting wherever we went... You see, Hank, Venus is a problem. Humans are moving out into space in a big way – the way we always planned to before the Bottleneck. But where are we to go? In space, when it comes to places to live, you've got the Moon, you've got Mars – and you know that people are starting to think about how to turn Mars into a liveable world."

"Terraforming," Hank said carefully.

"That's the idea. You can do that on Mars, but Mars will always be small, cold, lacking in volatiles – I mean, the stuff that air and oceans are made from. But at least you could live there *now*, under some dome. Not on Venus, though. You couldn't live *here*. Even though Venus is actually much more like Earth – same kind of size, made of the same stuff."

Hank snorted. "It doesn't look like it from here."

Jocelyn laughed. "Well, okay. But if Mars's problem is that it's too cold, Venus's problem is that it's too hot. You see those clouds? Top of an ocean of air, and most of it carbon dioxide."

"The stuff I breathe out?"

"Yeah. So much air, in fact, it's more like an ocean. Actually Earth has about the same amount of carbon dioxide as Venus, but back home it's all weathered – I mean it's locked up chemically in the rocks, mostly limestone. Venus used to be like Earth, once. But it overheated, there was a greenhouse effect, the carbon dioxide all baked out of the rock, and even the ocean water molecules broke up and the hydrogen was lost to space... After all that, Venus was hot *and* dry. The air pressure down on the ground is a hundred times what it is on Earth, or in this hab, and the temperature is hundreds of degrees. Honey, there are rivers of molten rock! So you think anybody could ever live down there?"

Hank wrinkled her nose. "Needs a lot of work."

Jocelyn laughed. "Spoken like a true Poole. Yes, a lot of work. If you want to make Venus liveable, you've got to get rid of all that air. Or almost all of it, ninety-nine per cent. How? Come on, think of ways."

Hank was used to being tested by Jocelyn. There were always clues, though, in her mother's challenges. "Couldn't you put it back in the limestone, like on Earth?"

"Good answer: weather it out. But to do that you'd have to break up the ground to a depth of kilometres, right across the planet. That's even if you had enough water, which you don't because it was all lost, remember. And even then, if the world stayed hot the carbon dioxide would just bake out of the rock again."

"Don't trees split up carbon dioxide into carbon and oxygen, that you breathe? You could use that. Plant stuff to grow and absorb it all."

"Another good try. Couldn't plant trees, though. Some kind of engineered bug, maybe. But even if you did, there's just too *much* air. You'd end up with a hundred-metre-thick layer of carbon all over the planet, and about sixty Earth atmospheres worth of oxygen. And you know what would happen then? Whoosh! The whole planet would burn up, and you'd be back where you started. *And* it would likely take thousands of years even to get that far. I want to do it faster than that."

"Lift it off, then. All the air. The way they scoop helium and stuff out of Jupiter."

She shook her head. "Another good try. Too much energy. You'd need the equivalent of six trillion megatons... Sorry, that's a little archaic; that's the language of bombs. And besides – here's the thing, Hank – you don't really want to throw away all the carbon that's locked up in the cee-oh-two. Venus has the solar system's biggest lode of carbon outside of Earth itself. Carbon is good, carbon is *useful*. Not just for living things –"

"You're talking about nanotechnology."

"Right. Good. The shield-swallows, for instance, are made of engineered carbon. You want to keep the carbon, mine it maybe, use it for nanotech or whatever, not just throw it away." She winked at Hank. "You could even manufacture food, here on Venus. The other ingredients you need are here: hydrogen, nitrogen. Food from Venus, exported to Earth! *That's* an old dream, I can tell you. And since most of humanity has been fed by slop made out of the last of the oil shale for the last four hundred years – I should know, I grew up eating the stuff – it's actually commercially viable.

"And that's what my scheme is all about. You just *freeze* out the Venusian air, and cover it over. You can do that relatively quickly and easily, and you're left with a place you can live up top, and a mine of carbon down below that you can deal with in time. Of course I'm not planning to make Venus liveable like Earth, that can come later. But the key is she'll become useful – and *soon*, so that we get a quick return on investment."

She smiled, looking into the far distance beyond the window, a calculating expression that always made Hank feel uncomfortable. Jocelyn's hair was long but pulled back into a compact bun, black with not a trace of grey; her skin was pale, smooth, but with an odd tightness around the eyes, which gave her a look of tension. Hank knew her mother was one of the oldest human beings alive, her body a test-bed for AntiSenescence, for ever-developing life-extension technologies. She didn't exactly look old, but she didn't look young, either.

When she wore that expression it was always as if she had forgotten Hank was even here.

The shield-swallow came floating by the window again.

Jocelyn seemed to relax. "She acts like she's curious. Maybe she likes you."

"Maybe."

"You know, people associate us Pooles with big clumsy engineering projects. Ever since Michael Poole Bazalget and his polar clathrates. But when I was your age, or thereabouts, I saw the launch of Grey Poole's first Outriggers. You know, the uncrewed antimatter rockets, the near-lightspeed interstellar probes? First year of the twenty-fifth century, two hundred years ago, another milestone year. There was a lot of controversy about all the energy we spent on *that* – but every damn probe worked, and the results from the target stars have trickled in ever since. Beautiful, delicate ships, like thistledown. And when you get down to it the whole project was an expression of confidence – a programme that was going to take so long it *proved* we had a faith in our own future.

Why, people were already starting to live longer than they ever had before, and the world was at last coming out of the worst of the climate troubles. Now I'm told that my plan to freeze Venus is another big, clumsy, grandiose folly. But what I'm achieving it with is something as delicate as *that*." She pointed at the swallow. "Which is why I wanted you here, you know, to see this. You could give her a name, if you like."

"What name?"

"How about Henrietta, like you?"

"My name is Hank. I can't even *spell* Henrietta."

Jocelyn laughed. "Sorry about that. It seemed like a good idea at the time. But she'll soon be lost in a crowd, of *trillions*... We have to do this, you know. Never mind terraforming Mars – some day we're gonna have to fix the Earth itself, not just stabilise it. And to do *that* we need to learn how to engineer planets, on a massive scale. You got to start somewhere." She glanced at a chronometer. "Okay, I have meetings. You got a busy day?"

It was only an hour after breakfast. Hank had precisely nothing to do until the next meal. "I sure do," she said politely.

"Catch you later, then." Jocelyn hurried away.

Alone, Hank peered down at the planet, imagining what she would see if those gleaming clouds could be peeled away: a land covered by plains of lava, twisted and torn by the heat. Rivers of rock. Incredible! And she had heard that people already lived down there, not on the lava-hot ground, but in the clouds, in big floating cities like airships. Which sounded fun to her, compared to this smelly old space station anyhow. Surely Venus was too interesting to be reduced to just a big lump of carbon...

The swallow flew past her window once again, and she was entranced.

* * *

JOCELYN LANG POOLE emerged from a crowd, hurrying across the Promenade, evidently seeking her daughter, and with Pierre, Hank's son, in tow. Micro-cameras swarmed around Jocelyn's head like fireflies. Well, this was Sunset Day, the day towards which Jocelyn and her planetary engineers had been building for fifty-six years already – fifty-six years since the creation of the first swallows, to this moment when the L1 shield would close up at last. Of course there would be cameras.

But Hank had her own deadlines. She deliberately turned away and, softscreen in hand, continued her quietly spoken discussions with her staff.

In half-opened exosuits, they were gathered at a port. From here they looked out through the semi-translucent hull of Pangad at stately dirigibles and smaller powered craft, suspended in shining air, patiently seeking access to the station to offload yet more samples of a precious, unique and horribly threatened biota.

Pangad was a flying eggshell, an ovoid a kilometre across floating in the Venusian sky, with a medium-sized city cupped on its expansive floor and circled at the equator by this Promenade with its transport and access facilities. The view was always spectacular – but even now it was not as it had once been. For months already, if not years, the space shield had grown dense enough to block a significant percentage of the sunlight, and the city had grown darker, as had the clouds it inhabited.

And today, as always now as the Sunset deadline approached, the Promenade was a swarm of activity. Hank herself hadn't slept for four days – four Earth days, nearly a full breeze-day aboard Pangad. But for all their elaborate preparations and for all their frantic work, Hank was senior enough to know how horribly limited all their conservation efforts were in the face of this monumental discontinuity.

And in the middle of all *that* here came Jocelyn Lang Poole. A woman whose clumsy patchwork rejuvenations now made her look younger, in a waxwork kind of way, than Hank herself at sixty-six: Hank's own mother, come to inflict an extinction event on an entire planet. Hank was tempted to just turn her back, to focus on the work. But Pierre was calling her, in a reedy twelve-year-old voice that was on the cusp of breaking, and he at least didn't deserve such treatment. So for the sake of her son Hank forced a smile.

"Here you are," Jocelyn said as she approached. She was dressed in a snappy-looking business suit. "Pierre's been telling me all about the Outrigger probe that reported back from Delta Corvi – a very strange swarm of planets out there..." She ruffled Pierre's hair, a gesture that obscurely irritated Hank. "Can't see this little guy floating around in a box in the clouds all his life. The stars for you, eh, little buddy?"

And Hank was freshly irritated that Pierre blushed at this attention from his famous grandmother. As evenly as she could she said, "Get out of here, Pierre. I know you have your chores to do, like everybody else."

Chastened, resentful, he snapped, "Yes *ma'am*," and ran off.

Jocelyn looked after him wistfully. "Cute little guy."

"You barely know him, Mother. What the hell are you doing here? Today of all days. I'm surprised you weren't lynched as soon as you set foot on the Promenade."

Jocelyn seemed nonplussed. "Oh, come on, Hank, lighten up. I wanted to be with my family today – to mark a triumph, not the end goal, but a key milestone, after fifty years' work the end of the beginning –"

"Save the soundbites for somebody who gives a damn." Not for the first time in her life Hank sought the words to communicate her feelings to Jocelyn. "Look, Mother, the people here care about Venus. This is their *home*..."

And a surprisingly generous home it was.

The lethal ground far below might glow in the dark, but up here, in the cloud decks fifty klicks or so high, the temperature was down to a little above Earth-normal, the air pressure was little more than Earth's sea level, and you could float around in a balloon the size of Manhattan: in fact you could inhabit the lift envelope itself, since breathing air was a lift gas here. People had come here in the first place for the science, of course, but such was the appeal of the place that many had stayed on to have their kids, and grandkids – they just lived here. That was pretty much Hank's story. She had never been able to get Venus out of her imagination since that close encounter with a shield-swallow in orbit, more than a half-century ago, and she'd had to come back.

But it was Venus itself that had captivated her, not her mother's grim visions of carbon mines. For, up here in the clouds – the real reason she was here – there were other inhabitants than humans.

Jocelyn, of course, was dismissive. "So it's a home. There are other homes. You could be in an arcology on Earth and it would feel much the same, right? Besides, even when Sunset falls the cities won't be immediately threatened. Sure, you'll be in the dark, but you spend two days out of every four in the dark anyhow, right?"

Though Venus turned at a creakingly slow and retrograde pace, yielding a sunrise-to-sunset interval of a hundred and seventeen days, the cloud cities like Pangad were blown around the world by high-speed winds, taking just four Earth days to finish a circuit: a 'breeze-day'.

"Plenty of time to get out of here in an orderly fashion."

"But that's not the point, damn it," Hank snapped back. "I know the atmosphere's not going to snow out in a couple of days –"

"More like a couple of centuries –"

"Mother, we'll survive. *But the native life won't.* It's photosynthetic. Lives off the sunlight you're blocking out." Jocelyn's expression was blank, and Hank knew she had withstood barrages of this kind of objection in endless review committees since her freeze-down project had first been mooted, but Hank felt motivated to try to make her see, even so. "And it's very old, Mother. The native life. It has to be. It *must* have formed when Venus was young, and Earthlike. The big heat-up took a couple of billion years: time for life to form in those early oceans, and then to retreat to the clouds when the ground became too hot – to this layer, where conditions are as Earthlike as anywhere beyond the home planet itself –"

"Earthlike? Clouds full of sulphuric acid? Don't talk to me about Earthlike. I have a share in the corporation that developed the shielding for the hulls of your precious balloon towns. What the hell kind of life is it, anyhow? Just a bunch of bugs in the air –"

"There's more to it than that. There has to be. We still don't know how they survive up here; they feed off sunlight and the materials of the clouds, of course, but there has to be some means of transporting trace elements up from the surface. It's more than just 'bugs in the air'. I think I've seen evidence of behaviour on a large scale. Much larger. There are patterns – visible in some wavelengths of light, if you look down at the clouds from above – the Venusian cloud bugs cooperating, somehow, on scales larger than continents. That's my speciality, as you ought to know. I think I was inspired as a kid by seeing your shield-swallows and the way they were designed to swarm –"

Jocelyn shook her head. "You're as bad as those weaklings on Mars, who are holding up the terraforming programme for the sake of life forms they thought they saw in the winter dry-ice snowstorms... *I* built a shield in space, twice the diameter of this planet. That alone has taken fifty years to put together, peeling the swallows off of that damn tethered asteroid one by one –"

"A shield that's killing a world."

In fact, in the gathering shadow of the shield, already the atmosphere was disrupted on a heroic scale, with dumped heat causing tremendous storms, and the air's structure breaking down. From space the planet looked dimpled, storm-wracked, and Hank and her workers could see it in the finest detail of the cloud communities: the disruption of delicate nutrient flows, of life cycles fragile to the point of invisibility.

"And it's all because you have to be so damn hasty. Oh, I know *why* it has to be that way. Time's passing, isn't it, Mother? And fashions change. Your Venus project is becoming stranded, a relic from a different age, an embarrassment, an anachronism. You need to keep hurrying to get it done before approval is withdrawn. And all the lives you meddle with – mine, too. It was conscience that drew me back here, you know. After you brought me out to see the beginning of it as a kid, I could never get Venus out of my head. You disrupted my whole life."

Jocelyn studied her blankly. "That's a price worth paying, frankly. Everything you've got you owe to me. And days like today are what it's all been about. Leaving my mark. As my mother left her mark, and her father... all the way back to Grey Poole and the Outriggers, even old Michael Bazalget in the twenty-first century."

Hank folded her arms. "Leaving your mark. Even if there's some better course for Venus, a better way – if it takes too long for you to be around to get the credit, you'd reject it, right? You're sacrificing a whole world, a whole *biosphere*, just to get your name plaque nailed to the wall of the Poole family mausoleum."

Jocelyn thought that over, shrugged, and grinned, almost girlishly. "Well, is that so wrong?"

Hank glowered at her mother, wordless. Then she turned and went back to work.

Just an hour later, the sky went dark, all at once, as Jocelyn Lang Poole shut out the sun.

WHEN JOCELYN DESCENDED to the science base on the summit of Maat Montes, visiting her family for the first time in decades, she was, as usual, interested in nothing but her own agenda. In this particular case it was the trouble, as she saw it, that grandson Pierre was cooking up in his experimental shelter out on the ice of the Phoebe Ocean.

And so, as Hank gave her the customary tour of the Maat base, Jocelyn showed not even polite interest in all Hank herself had achieved down here on the surface of Venus, astonishingly no less than a hundred and eighty-six years after Sunset Day.

No interest in the big wildlife-reserve shelters Hank and her team had managed to erect down here in these latter years, after conditions had become a little less ferocious – no interest in the lab work being done here, though Jocelyn showed some curiosity about the hab's engineering, stomping around as she did in the exoskeletal frame that now supported her increasingly fragile body of more than four hundred and fifty years' vintage.

"You may have started it, Jocelyn," Hank said. She'd given up calling her 'Mother' more than a century ago; when your own son passed his hundredth, relationships kind of levelled out across the generations. "With Sunset Day, I mean. But down here we had to *live* through it. And it was a long, slow process, I can tell you. The balloon cities lasted a few decades, the air took that long to cool, but we were sinking the whole time, down, down. Then after about sixty years it got cold enough for the carbon dioxide rains to start, and we've had more than a hundred years of *that*. So we came down to the ground and pitched camp. You know why here, why Maat Montes? Because it's the second highest location on the planet, after Maxwell up in the north..."

Venus had a strange terrain, mostly flat lava plains broken by a few continent-like highland regions: Ishtar Terra up in the north the size of Australia, and here, Aphrodite Terra, at the equator. None of this had mattered a damn to any human being aside from theoretical planetologists until the searing heat began to recede, and the carbon dioxide air to thin, and the ground became accessible. But when those who had remained with Venus sought somewhere on the surface to settle, the higher ground, where the heat and air pressure was always marginally less, was a good idea.

And even more so when the carbon dioxide rains had started. At first the falling liquid had hissed and sizzled and evaporated quickly from the still-warm ground, or had soaked into the basaltic plain of the lowland. But gradually the land had become saturated, and puddles had formed, and then lakes, which had then joined up into a rising sea... The colony gave a good view of the rising ocean, which would eventually cover something like eighty per cent of the planet's surface, and Maat Montes would become an island.

Then, just a decade or two ago, the cold got deep enough to cause the ocean to start to freeze, from the bottom up.

"Even so, it was still damn hot. We had to reinvent everything we did, from scratch. Did you know that the surface used to be so hot that it would melt the solder on a circuit board? And every engine we ran ate fuel like it was going out of fashion."

Jocelyn thought that over. "High ambient temperature. Low thermodynamic efficiency."

"The Carnot cycle, yeah. But we hung on, and survived, most of us. And I think we did some useful work..."

But Jocelyn cared nothing for the display samples from the experimental 'metal-snow mine' near the very summit of Maat's highest peak. Once, in Venus's most ferocious days, there really had been a superhot snow of metallic compounds that would settle out on the higher ground: tellurium, iron pyrites. You could easily prospect for such reflective stuff with radar, and for the last century or so shipments of the stuff to Earth and the offworld colonies had been an unexpected, commercially viable success. And Jocelyn was interested even less in the studies Hank and her team were making in the big blister domes, cramped as they were, of the lifecycles of the native Venusian life: a biota now extinct save in a few reserves like Hank's.

"We haven't got the room to replicate a lifecycle that spanned a cloud layer tens of kilometres deep," Hank said sourly. "But we've confirmed some of my earlier guesses. The bugs really did cooperate on a planetary scale. They were locked into global cycles of mass and energy, just like Earth. A Venusian Gaia..."

Just as Jocelyn's shield-swallows worked cooperatively in a great flock, swimming in the sunlight to maintain their disc of shadow twenty-five thousand kilometres across, so the Venusian acid-cloud bugs had worked for aeons, leaching the air chemistry selectively, and even moving in coordinated ways to adjust the very weather. Great lightning storms would be tended, nurtured, assembled; such was the energy gathered that the storms had even reached down to the ground under its layer of soupy, sluggish carbon dioxide, and stirred up dust and rubble that, thrown into the air, helped seed the clouds with acid rain, and with the trace nutrients needed by the bacterial life. "When the world heated up the bugs had billions of years to evolve mechanisms like this, and they used that time well. But now –"

Jocelyn snorted. "But we didn't even understand it until it was all gone, and now it's all extinct and in a museum like the tyrannosaurs and the mammoths, and yada. I only came down here to see what that punk kid Pierre is up to out on my ice."

"*Your* ice?"

"Well, who else's?"

"The rover garage is over this way. And he's no punk kid, by the way."

Jocelyn grunted as she clanked her way alongside her daughter to the lock. "Sure. I follow his career – I've seen his presentations. Looks a hell of a lot better than I did at that age. Better medicine than when I began with AntiSenescence. I always told you so. You kids don't know how lucky you are."

"Maybe, but you're still around to complain about it, aren't you?"

"Hmmph. *That's* good genes. And maybe it's just as well that I'm still here to stop him screwing up my programme with this stuff from the Outrigger report, this alien nanobug crap from Beta Pegasi. We shouldn't have anything to do with *that*. This is our system – these are our worlds. Whatever we do, it needs to be a human endeavour. *Human.* Not a playground for some damn alien tech..."

"Here's the airlock. You didn't bring a pressure suit?"

Jocelyn raised her arms with a whir of servo motors. "Look at me. What the hell kind of suit is going to fit over this?"

"This is the frontier, Jocelyn. We're belt and braces about safety here –"

"*You* are. You know when the last death through pressure loss was? Neither do I. So shut your yap and let's get on with it."

So mother and daughter exited from the base.

They crossed the frozen surface of the decades-old Phoebe Ocean in a small tractor-tread rover, the way lit only by the rover's flood lamps. Hank was in an open suit, with Jocelyn and her exoskeleton cluttering up the cabin. Ahead lay nothing but pale, glimmering carbon dioxide ice, and the sky above was black as night, the remnant air still too thick to allow even a glimpse of the stars.

Much of the young ocean was still liquid, of course – and the rain continued – but in shallower stretches, such as here, near the Aphrodite coast, there was already sheet ice, the ocean frozen solid to its base. And on that ice, already visible in the lamps of the rover, was the small shelter where Pierre Poole Rollins was conducting his already famous experiments using carbon dioxide slush from Venus and nanotech from the star Beta Pegasi...

Or so Hank understood, anyhow. Just as Pierre seemed to find it hard to talk to her these days – hell, these decades – so Hank found it hard to communicate with her own mother, on any level. They were all in strange territory, she thought – Jocelyn especially, as one of the first of the truly long-lived – enduring an unprecedented overlapping of historical timescales with individual ambitions and lifespans. Why, it was already nearly two and a half centuries since the inception of Jocelyn's Venus project: a length of time similar to that separating the birth of the Industrial Revolution and Michael Poole's pioneering Arctic-clathrate stabilisation project. How were you supposed to build an ongoing career through all of that? And while the Venus project had gone through its slow phases, human society had itself evolved, with the ages of deprivation into which Jocelyn had been born an increasingly remote memory. Now, on Earth, even the polders, post-climate-collapse political unions of necessity, had faded in significance compared to a reborn-UN world government. In space, meanwhile, as an interplanetary culture slowly matured, the Moon had already gained a cautious independence... Amid all this, Jocelyn's crude, ugly manipulation of Venus seemed increasingly out of its time. And yet, as Jocelyn had probably anticipated from the start, the project had a sheer physical momentum that made it practically unstoppable.

But now Hank's own son, two-centuries-old Pierre, because of his plan to introduce alien elements into the carbon mines of Venus, was at loggerheads with Jocelyn: in the path of the family juggernaut...

As the rover drew up to the lock Hank felt a kind of shudder, transmitted through the frame.

It was a kind of intrusion. She was forced to focus on her driving, turning aside from thoughts of her family. Unease flickered. After decades, centuries, it was easy to forget that this was an alien world, a world inimical to humanity. Venus was volcanically active, enthusiastically so, mainly because it had no tectonic plates to shove around and vent off a little heat energy, as Earth did. In fact it was believed that most of the planet had been resurfaced by lava, perhaps a mere half-billion years earlier. Maat Mons, Hank's home, was itself a volcanic artefact, a shield mountain the size of Hawaii.

All of Jocelyn's tinkering with the atmosphere hadn't made a jot of difference to the restlessness of the deep rocks. Venus was still Venus. And, just because in the few centuries humans had been in residence on the surface itself there had been no geological calamities or catastrophes, it didn't mean Venus was, or would ever be, *safe*. Hence, for Hank, the belt and braces.

But the shudder passed, and Jocelyn, intent as usual on her own concerns, seemed to have noticed nothing at all.

ONCE THE ROVER had docked with the shelter, Jocelyn led the way in through the lock.

Pierre was alone today, working before a partitioned-off area. He glanced around at his visitors, his mother and grandmother, nodded perfunctorily, and turned back to his work – or tried to. Jocelyn made straight for him and began to interrogate him about Beta Pegasi.

Hank followed more circumspectly. Pierre, after all nearly two hundred years old himself, had grown into a solid, competent, senior figure. But, Hank often thought, his manner and expression had been hardened by his life as an outsider. He had grown up on a frontier, and then developed a career as a fringe academic. He did have something of the look of Jocelyn, though, Hank thought, short, dark, heavy, the look of the Pooles. As, no doubt, did she.

Pierre was wearing a pressure suit, Hank noted, but without gloves or hood to hand. Not regulation, to say the least, but she knew this was Pierre's own habit of a grumpy old age; like his grandmother he thought excessive safety precautions just got in the way. Hank profoundly disagreed. But it didn't seem the right moment to mention it.

Instead she said, "Look at us. Elderly grotesques. A new human dynamic, three bitter old farts each locked in their own heads, yet separated still by generations. And yet, you know, when they write up the family history we'll be remembered as the Pooles who worked here, together, for better or worse. We'll be the Venus generations."

But nobody was listening.

Jocelyn seemed distracted by a new display Pierre or a colleague had set up, a hologram turning slowly in the air, right at the dome's geometric centre: a glimmering, sparkling ball. Hank knew this was a representation of the object that an Outrigger probe had found orbiting Beta Pegasi, a red giant star about two hundred light years away. It was a ball of crystalline carbon the size of a small moon – it was a kind of huge diamond, really – described by some as a "hive-like accretion". Perhaps it was geological; perhaps it was a construct of living things, like a termite nest; perhaps it was an artefact; perhaps it was itself alive. The Outrigger was not equipped to eliminate any of these possibilities. Still, the samples it had taken and analysed of the substance of the structure had yielded tantalising results.

As Pierre was trying to explain, more or less patiently, to his grandmother.

"Look, the whole point of your big freeze was to remove all that carbon dioxide from the air and stow it away in a place it can be mined later. Fine. What I'm telling you is that *this* gives us a better capability to do just that..."

He led the way to a clear partition wall, beyond which Hank saw a lab bench, manipulation gear, microscopic and other assay gear. Nothing very remarkable, though softscreen images glowed with hints of complex, fool-the-eye structures. But somewhere in there, Hank knew, sealed away, was alien life, or maybe an artefact of that life, and she wasn't sure which was the stranger possibility.

Life or not, it was all the same to Jocelyn. "It's *not human*, damn it, better capability or not."

Pierre shrugged. "So? Look at what it *does*. It creates a kind of rock – that's not a bad analogy – from carbon and oxygen..."

Hank knew something of the theory. It was as if the unknown aliens had made carbon atoms do what silicon atoms did naturally. Silicon, a closely related element to carbon, had an atom that could neatly bond to four oxygen atoms, forming a highly stable tetrahedron. And those tetrahedra could be combined like construction-toy pieces to make a variety of super-stable mineral forms: rock, such as quartz. The carbon atom, though so similar to silicon in many ways, was *too small* to make decent tetrahedra that way... unless you manipulated it, or forced it...

Pierre held out a handful of white dust. "We still don't know how they do it, Grandmother. But *this* is the result."

"It looks like chalk."

He smiled tightly. "That's what the engineers have started to call it. But it's not chalk, it contains no calcium... Perhaps it is like chalk in that it seems to be created by living things, however. This is just carbon and oxygen – carbon dioxide forced into a form like a silicate rock, and just as stable. And, Grandmother, the – agents – that do this, which we created following the recipe sent back by the Beta Pegasi Outrigger, don't just make cee-oh-two dust and rock. Alive or not, they self-replicate. Enthusiastically! In principle, all we need to do is throw a handful of these entities into every body of liquid carbon dioxide on the planet, and into the air, what's left of it, and the result will be a world covered by this stuff. Easily mined, and unlike the dry ice that will be the end result of *your* process, dense, stable –"

"And easily shipped," Hank put in, "to anywhere that's short of carbon. Which is most places aside from Earth."

Pierre said, "We could even be creative. I mean, we could make the chalk *smart* as it deposits out of the air, the oceans. Think of it – we could have it bank up as it forms, into valleys, hills – even cities, towers, lakes. A new world just coalescing out of the carbon dioxide... Well. That's the dream," he said finally.

"That's the nightmare," Jocelyn snapped back. "Because, whatever this is, it's *alien*. Can't you see it? Look – we're not going to sit in this one solar system forever. And we're going to encounter alien life out there — not just this nano crap — alien tech, alien *minds*. Faced by that overwhelming reality, how are we to retain the essence of our humanity? By living off what we build ourselves, what *we* make. Not this way."

"But we've already been manufacturing polymers rich in carbon dioxide for centuries. Maybe we'd have come up with this kind of tech ourselves in a few decades anyhow —"

"Look, kid, this isn't some obscure philosophical point. The problem is our future as humans."

Pierre faced her with a kind of weary defiance, and Hank recognised the habitual nature of the argument, like two old boxers who knew each other too well. "No, Grandmother. The problem is that it's not your idea. These days we're trying to find more subtle ways to do things, such as this molecular-level transformation of the carbon dioxide. Later generations will see your big freeze as a typical Poole intervention, gross, clumsy, self-aggrandizing and ill thought out —"

"How do you know? What do you know about later generations?"

"I'm one of them —"

How the argument would have unfolded Hank would never know. Because at that moment the world exploded.

WELL, NOT QUITE. Although it felt that way to Hank. It took her some time, later, to piece together the events of those few seconds.

In a way, it had all been the fault of Jocelyn Lang Poole. She was certainly the one who paid the price.

One problem with all the carbon dioxide slush Jocelyn had lain down across the planet was that it was unstable: liable to rapidly volatise if heated. And on Venus there were plenty of hotspots. Luckily there had been no major geological issues anywhere near any human settlement, not since Sunset Day. Even this time it had only been a minor event, a bubble of magma stirring beneath the battered surface, a slight crack in the ground, venting gas...

A slight crack, under a layer of liquefied air, and all more or less underneath Pierre's habitat. Hank, arriving in her rover, had felt the premonitory shuddering. Now the main course arrived.

When the fault gave way, the detonation of flash-vaporised carbon dioxide it produced was out of all proportion to the magnitude of the geological event. The hab walls ruptured immediately; all the breathable air was lost in less than a minute.

Hank was in her pressure suit. Her first reaction, even before thinking of her mother and son, was to pull up her own hood and seal her suit shut before the toxic, freezing air could stab into her lungs. And, even as she saved herself, Hank made frantic plans about how to get to her family. She knew that Pierre was in a suit, open, without hood and gloves. And Jocelyn, meanwhile, was in no kind of suit at all.

But it was Jocelyn, old as she was, who reacted most quickly. She dived for her grandson, ripped partition material from the torn wall, bundled Pierre up like a landed fish – all this in seconds – and ran flat-out from the shelter, exomuscles singing as she lugged her grandson to the safety of the rover.

Jocelyn saved Hank's life. In the process she sacrificed her own, as she probably knew.

But it wasn't the cold, the carbon dioxide air that would kill Jocelyn. It wasn't Venus at all.

* * *

THE LAST TIME Hank saw her mother alive, she was with Pierre, in the medical bay on Venera. Pierre was holding his grandmother's hand.

Jocelyn, stripped of her exoskeleton, head shaved, swathed in medical gear, looked utterly diminished. "Damn Pegasus bugs," she said, her voice a scratch. "I'll swear I could see them. Swarming out of that broken containment like a virus."

"No, you couldn't, Grandmother," Pierre said gently. "You kept them off me, though –"

"But not off myself. Like a chemistry experiment, huh? There was enough carbon dioxide in my lungs to feed them at first. And then, you know, I looked it up, my body is, or was, sixty-five per cent oxygen, eighteen per cent carbon. I'm a damn lunch box for alien bugs from Beta Pegasi. I told you we should have nothing to do with them."

Pierre squeezed her hand. His own hand was gloved, to avoid infection.

Hank said, "Mother –"

"If you tell me I had a good long life I'll spit in your eye."

"You would, too. Look – you achieved what you wanted to achieve. Whether we turn the carbon dioxide into Pegasus chalk or not, you made Venus a place we can use. The cloud life – we'll find a new home for them, out there somewhere. And in the middle of it all you saved your grandson's life."

"The shield-swallows."

"What's that?"

"The shield-swallows. We saw them from Venera. You thought they were pretty. The first thing I ever did that you actually liked. I never forgot that."

"Yes," Hank said. "Yes, that's right." She barely remembered the shield-swallows, a scene centuries gone.

"I did good, then," Jocelyn whispered.

"You're a Poole. Of course you did good."

"They'll put up a statue to you," Pierre said. "Up on Maat Mons itself."

"Huh. Don't you get it, kid? Your damn Pegasus bugs are *turning* me into a statue. Well, you got to start somewhere..."

93

Charlie Jane Anders

Rager in Space

Charlie Jane Anders
RAGER IN SPACE

Sion sent a drunk text to Grant Hendryx at four in the morning, whipping off her hoodie and bra, snapping a pic and writing a sexy caption before hitting send. Except she aimed the camera the wrong way, and she picked the wrong entry in her address book, so Grant Donaldson, senior project manager at Aerodox Ventures, was surprised to receive a blurry photo of a pair of parking meters with a message that read, 'LICK MY LEFT ONE.'

The next day, Sion had an invitation to go to outer space.

The sun blinged up the floor of Sion's pink bedroom, like a kaleidoscope made of Cheetos and tequila bottle shards, and she growled and tried to build a pillow fort over her head. But nausea got the better of her and she had to stagger to the bathroom. That's when she saw the text from a recruiter at Aerodox.

She showed it to her friend D-Mei as they chugged mimosas over at D-Mei's house, *except* they didn't have any OJ or bubbly, so they were using orange creamsicle soda and Industrial Moonshine No. 5, imported from the Greater Appalachian Labor Zone, instead. Sion showed D-Mei the email. *Modeling Opportunity*, it said. *First near-light-speed flight to another star system*, it said. *Open Bar*, it said, perhaps most significantly.

D-Mei read the email while the Pedicure Robot worked on her right foot, stopping and starting over and over whenever its operating system crashed and rebooted. Every time the robot jerked into motion again, D-Mei spilled some of her creamosa on the carpet. Her mom would be pissed.

"Oh my god," D-Mei's eyes widened, sending glittery waves across her forehead and dimpled cheeks as her nanotech eyeshadow activated. She had blue hair and a face just like CantoPop idol Rayzy Wong. "We should so go. Rager in space, man. It says Raymond Burger will be on board. The founder of Aerodox. He probably parties like a madman."

"I dunno," Sion said. "I get airsick. I probably get double space sick. I don't want to be throwing up in space. And this is more like a hostessing gig than a modeling gig, and there's a difference, you know." Sion had bright red hair, with pink highlights, and a round face with big green eyes accentuated with neon purple eyeliner.

"Don't be a wuss." D-Mei snorted. "It says you can bring a friend, as long as she's hot. I made up that last part. But you gotta bring me. I want to meet Raymond Burger."

"I mean," Sion said. "I am trying to clean up my act and stuff." She took a long chug of the creamosa. "I mean, my dad says –"

"Your dad," said D-Mei, "is still butthurt about the Singularity." The Pedicure Robot sputtered and she kicked it, so it fell on its side for a moment, then righted itself and started attacking D-Mei's pinky toenail with a tiny scythe. Scraping, failing.

"The Singularity," Sion reached for the No. 5 bottle. "It was like fun while it lasted, right?"

"Everything is fun while it lasts," D-Mei said. "And nothing lasts forever. That's why we gotta grab it while we got it. With both hands, dude."

"Okay, sure," Sion put the bottle right to her face and inhaled the stench of sweat and despair from the millions of bonded peons working off their debts in the bowels of the mountains. They wished they all could be California gurls, she felt pretty sure. "Totally. I'll say yes. Let's go to space."

SION ROLLED UP to the Aerodox hangar in her Princess Superstar car, which was bright pink and convertible, with furry disco balls hanging from the rearview, and she piled out of the car in her silver platforms and silver fake fur jumpsuit, with hood. She had big sunglasses and lipgloss that showed an animated GIF of pink bunnies on her lips.

D-Mei was already there in the tiny departure lounge overlooking the main hangar, and she had a fistful of tiny bottles from the minibar, with real brand names like Vermouth and Scotch, none of that nasty generic stuff. "They have Cognac," she squeed. "I heard that Cognac is the best kind!" She showed Sion where to get her own toy-size bottles, but Sion shook her head and showed D-Mei the black "X" she'd Sharpied on her hand.

"I'm sorry," Sion said. "I promised my dad that I would stay straight-edge on this trip. We're going to be some of the first people to leave the solar system, and history is watching us, and all that shiz. Plus I don't want to be the one who throws up on the first alien life we meet. What if they decide that's how humans communicate? So I'm sticking to like space coffee or something."

"Ohhh kay," D-Mei said, in that tone that suggested she would give Sion a day, tops, before she changed her mind. "In any case, we got some important decisions to make here." She pointed a long acrylic nail at the flight crew, who were doing final system checks on the outside of the space shuttle *Ascension*, which was already pointing its angular nosecone upwards as if it couldn't wait to get out there and fuck some shit up in space. The shuttle was surrounded by no fewer than four booster rockets, to get it up into orbit, where it would dock with the massive starship *Advance*, which had taken years and billions of dollars to construct, and was parked over the Equator.

There were a number of boys who showed potential, including this one engineer named Daryl with tousled brown-blond hair and bulky shoulders inside his white starched uniform. And Choppy, the bald navigator who had kind of a thick neck but kind eyes. And Grant Donaldson, who kept giving them funny looks when he thought they weren't looking.

"Hey," Sion said. "I was wondering about something. So nothing computerized works any more. At all. Right? So how did these people manage to get a spaceship that can fly to another star system to work? That would be the most computer-intensive shizz you could imagine."

Sion thought D-Mei was going to laugh at her, but instead her friend just nodded and gave her kind of a serious look. "That's a really good question, slutbabe. That's why I'm really glad you're like the designated driver in the passenger section. You think about stuff like that."

"But also," Sion said. "I thought that if we got close to the speed of light, our mass would expand exponentially, and it would take an unfunky amount of energy to move us forward. And even then it ought to take us years to reach another star system. But we're only supposed to be gone a few weeks, right?"

"You are asking such good questions," D-Mei said.

And then the cute navigator, Choppy, came over and smiled at her. Up close his eyes had gray flecks, and his nose was broken in an adorable way. "Hey, I couldn't help overhearing," he said. "Actually, both of those questions have sort of the same answer. We have the most advanced A.I. in existence, which has next-gen firewalls that outsmart even the most super-sentient viruses. But also, our A.I. calculated the equations that allow us to use the thing you're talking about, the mass thing, to our advantage. It's like judo: The more our mass increases, the more power we get."

That all sounded too good to be true, but then Sion got stuck on the first thing Choppy had mentioned: "You have an A.I. that actually works? It doesn't break down all the time?"

"We sure do," Choppy said. "Her name is Roxx. Do you want to meet her?"

"Uh, sure." Sion couldn't help imagining how her dad would act when he heard she met a real working A.I. – he had spent his whole life as a software engineer, before everything melted down.

"Because I think she would like to meet you. So it's a date, then." Choppy held out one hand, which had cartoon skulls tattooed on the knuckles, and after just a second's hesitation, she took it with three fingers and the tip of her thumb. D-Mei gave her a huge wink, as if 'do you want to meet the ship's A.I.' could only be code for one thing.

SOMETIMES SION FELT like her dad thought that if she just cleaned up her act and stopped partying, the Singularity would come back and everything would be awesome again. Like it was her fault, personally, that all the computers had crashed, right after they had just become supersmart.

The Singularity happened when Sion was five, and her memories of it were mixed up with other things that happened around that time. Like when she was taken to see Santa's village at the mall, which must have been before the Singularity because everything at the mall worked properly but wasn't thinking for itself or anything. The Singularity belonged to a time when her father was nine feet tall and carried her on his big shoulders, and the world was kind of magical – even before all of the kitchen appliances came to life and started speaking to Sion by name, like in a Disney toon. The Singularity, to Sion, was innocence.

When it failed, when the viruses gained superintelligence or whatever, Sion's pet dog died. Smudge wasn't a robot dog, or even cybernetic, like a lot of her friends' pets back then – just a regular shaggy mutt with a big drooly tongue. But a self-driving car lost control at the wrong moment, when Smudge was out in the front yard, and plowed up the grass and turf, before crushing the dog into a furry splat.

That was the moment the entire world fell apart, the economy ended, and tons of people died. But to Sion's child mind, the whole thing was subsumed into the death of Smudge, for whom she had an elaborate funeral with her older siblings and a stereobox blasting funeral music, interrupted by horrible fart noises as the stereobox's software kept glitching out.

After Smudge died, the future grew a lot smaller. There wasn't anybody that Sion could really count on, because everyone flaked all the time. People showed up an hour late, if they showed up at all. Sion's teachers would just start weeping in the middle of class, and her siblings both dropped out of college because they could never pay off the student loans. Sion's mom flaked permanently, just disappeared one day and never came back.

If Sion hadn't met D-Mei, she probably would have lost her mind.

Sion was holding a rice pudding, she was eight or nine, and she was standing in front of the school waiting for a ride home that she was starting to think would never arrive. She was still in denial about her mom being gone for good, so part of her was hoping her mom would suddenly roll up in the minivan her parents had sold five years earlier and bundle her into a child seat she was too big for. She was scared to try the rice pudding, because the last time she'd eaten rice pudding from that machine it had tasted like rotten eggs. Software. She was just holding this plastic cup of rice pudding in one hand, with a spoon embedded in it, trying to decide if it was really edible this time.

"Throw it," a voice said in her ear.

"What?" Sion jumped out of one of her shoes.

"Go ahead and throw it. They deserve it, the creeps."

Sion hadn't thought of the rice pudding as a projectile – but of course that was the best use of it, duh. And she had been absent-mindedly staring at a group of Perrinite kids celebrating over by the swingset in their terrible dungarees. Celebrating, because the Right Reverend Daniel Perrin had predicted that the amount of sin and wickedness on the internet would eventually cause the very computers to be smited by the wrath of God, and now it had happened. The Perrinites were the only ones happy lately, and they were being real dicks about it.

"Throw it, come on," D-Mei said, the first words she had ever said to Sion. "I dare you."

Sion threw. They wound up going to the principal's office, and their parents were called, which meant Sion actually got a ride home.

A few months later, Sion and D-Mei sabotaged the confetti cannon at the big pep rally, and everybody blamed it on viruses. (Even though the confetti cannon had no computer components.) They played spin-the-bottle with older kids, huffed paintball paint, put nanotech glitter on their eyelids at recess, graffitied the girls' room, and snuck gin from their History teacher Mrs. Hathaway's thermos. They were the first kids to wear makeup at school, and when they went on to a school that had uniforms, they were first to take a boxcutter to the hemlines.

Every time Sion started to feel like this world, that was supposed to know who she was and what she needed, was downgrading her instead... every time Sion felt lonesome and terrible... D-Mei was there with another really bad idea that would get them in a lot of trouble.

Sion's dad asked her once, "If D-Mei asked you to jump off a bridge, would you do it?"

Sion just rolled her eyes. "You were the one who taught me hypothetical questions are a waste of time, Dad. D-Mei's never asked me to jump off a bridge. She only asks me to do things that are fun and awesome. Quit with the counterfactuals." Her dad was always startled when she talked smartypants, and it was the best way to shut him up. Plus she actually had thought a lot about the 'jump off a bridge' scenario, truth be told, and this was what she'd decided in the end.

BREAKING FREE OF Earth's gravity made Sion feel sicker than the worst hangover, and it took forever. Like that time when she was at the Sex Lab and the glitter spray had turned superdense due to a nanotech fail – except times one billion. She thought she was going to die, and she reached out for D-Mei's hand across the aisle, except that D-Mei was putting a nozzle inside one nostril and closing the other, just as the pressure hit blackout levels and Sion thought she would never see again. Sion let out a tiny cry of pain and topsy-turvy nausea, and then she felt D-Mei's fingers and chunky rings against her own. Then they swung, like a crazy roller-coaster, and Sion finally blew floating chunks into the compostable barf bag, right before the curve of the Earth came into view, a blue neon stripe separating two kinds of darkness.

And then they caught sight of the *Advance*, a great floating walnut made out of steel and radiation-resistant fiberglass cladding. Forced perspective made the *Advance* look almost as big as the Earth, but it really was humongous: a mile wide and a mile and a half long, although the habitable areas were much smaller because all that bulk protected everyone from cosmic radiation. As they grew closer, the walnut shape revealed a million tiny openings, plus an array of bulky attachments on the front that would fire lasers off into space and enable the ship to reach unthinkable velocities.

As they approached, Sion came to see this massive starship as the embodiment of her higher self. Ugly, perfect, a boast shouted into the void. She vowed to live up to it, somehow.

THAT 'X' ON Sion's hand was the key to a whole new version of herself – a Sion who was incredibly awkward and unable to navigate any social situations at all. She started to realize after an hour or two on board the *Advance* that maybe setting off on board a massive interstellar ship, full of weird situations, wobbly gravity and Space Bros might not have been the best moment to try and reinvent herself completely. But she kept going, as she and D-Mei got whisked through a series of staterooms and lounges, with themes like Jungle Safari and Garden of Delights. "You're already in space, why would you want to fantasize about being in a jungle?" Sion wondered aloud – much too loud, causing several people to give her the stink-eye. But then there were actual wonders, like a Secondary Control Center where Raymond Burger himself was holding court flanked by swimsuit models, which included a 3-D holographic representation of the ship's journey out of the solar system. ("No pause 'til the motherfucking heliopause" was the official party chant of the *Advance*.) Sion ran her fingers through the space between Jupiter and its moons, but then men in pinstriped onesies kept coming up to her and asking her if she liked stuff that everybody likes, like dancing, or music, or puppies. She just wasn't drunk enough for this. Raymond Burger looked like a debt-auction host: gleaming smile, white sideburns, fashionable rooster pompadour. And then they ran into Choppy, the navigator, and he took them past the fancy lounge areas, into the inner workings of the ship.

Soon Sion was standing in a gleaming space, as wide as an interstate highway, looking at a huge drum, around which a dozen men and women were checking holographic readouts and adjusting things. The drum had spokes coming off it, going up into the ceiling, and each of those spokes was connected to a massive prong that was aiming into the vacuum of space.

"It's based on the vacuum-to-antimatter-rocket thing," said Choppy with a huge grin. "We fire these lasers into space and they create particles of antimatter, which we harvest and use to power an antimatter engine. It's a beautiful thang."

Sion was gobsmacked – this was everything they were supposed to have, everything the failed Singularity had robbed them of. She felt her heart opening up and she tried to think of a smart way to express her awe, that wouldn't make her sound like a goony moron. But just then, someone shouted, "Get down from there!" and Sion realized D-Mei was trying to climb the big drum.

"I just wanted to see the lasers up close," D-Mei whined. "What's the point of a laser show if you can't dance with them?"

"I'm sorry about my friend," Sion mouthed, but they were already getting escorted back to the passenger lounges.

"Shots!" D-Mei yelled. This turned into body shots, which turned into a whole other thing with a couple of Raymond Berger's investor friends.

Sion was starting to get that caving-in feeling, different than when her mom went away. Different, even, than when her father gave up on her ever amounting to anything. She had this thought in the back of her head that maybe she had outgrown her best friend at some point, and hadn't noticed until now because of the drugs and booze. This was too horrible to allow into the front of her mind.

The ship was actually not that big on the inside – the main part of that walnut was engines and a ton of shielding to protect you from cosmic radiation. The passenger areas had been engineered to have Earth gravity (almost), so they were basically a big ring that spun around and around. That cute engineer, Daryl, showed D-Mei the handful of accessible areas where the gravity was weaker or non-existent, and this meant one thing: zero-G beer pong!

Sion was sharing a cabin with D-Mei but realized with a start that she hadn't actually seen her friend in a whole ship's day.

She also noticed they hadn't gotten even close to the Moon yet, which was odd if they were going to reach another star system in a couple of weeks.

Once they were far enough from Earth, the ship deployed its massive solar array, and everybody stood on the observation lounge watching the one huge 180-degree viewport. From this perspective, it looked like the starship *Advance* shrugged off a huge black cloak, dramatically, like a dancer. These massive solar panels would power the lasers that would generate the antimatter that would enable the ship to reach half-light speed, after which the computer would do the judo equations.

Sion found herself sitting with Tamika, who had won some kind of science competition to get to be on board this ship, and the two of them were talking about lasers and antimatter and howfuckingcool, when D-Mei came up and whispered, "This guy named Randy knows where we can get some of the nitrous from the ship's emergency fuel supplies, plus he thinks you're hot. We gotta go meet him right now."

"Dude," Sion whispered back, "The lasers are going to fire any minute. Some of us are interested in science, OK?"

D-Mei just looked at her, with this crushed expression on her face. Then she took the vodka-cran in her left hand and just splashed it on Sion's shirt. Only a little, a few pink drops here and there. "Fine, whatever." She put on a bored expression and stalked away.

"Hey." Choppy came up to Sion as she was still trying to get the pink out of her white shirt. "So the A.I. can meet you now if you're still interested."

* * *

TECHNICALLY YOU COULD talk to Roxx from all over the ship, and she could see and hear everything that happened on board. But Roxx preferred to speak to people inside her Communication Megaplex, which was one deck down, behind a keycard-locked door. "You're lucky. Some of the bizdev fellows have been waiting days to speak to Roxx, but she was interested in talking to you," Choppy said.

Sion kept waiting for Choppy to hit on her, but either he was keeping it professional or she wasn't his type. His busted nose was growing on her, and she heard D-Mei's voice in her head saying, *Make your move, gurl, time's running out.* Then in addition to feeling awkwardly sober, she also felt guilty about being mean to D-Mei, all over again. Then they were at the nondescript gray door, and Choppy was brandishing the keycard.

Inside, Sion parked herself on a blue pleather couch facing a fancy VR rig, the kind that could project on your retinas and create a whole sensorium, without any wearables. Just one of the wonders that the Singularity had made possible, for a brief moment.

"Hey!" Roxx appeared as a cartoon zebra standing on its hind legs, wearing an old-fashioned business suit. "You're Sion. I'm excited to talk to you."

"Um, okay." Sion squirmed.

"I wanted to ask you about fun," Roxx said. "Like, what's the difference between fun that you know you're not enjoying at the time, but you keep doing it anyway, and fun that you enjoy at the time but feel bad about later?"

"What?"

Roxx repeated the question, a couple times.

"I don't know," Sion said. "I mean, it's not clear-cut, right? Sometimes you kind of like something, but afterwards you think back and realize that you only thought you were enjoying it. Or you convinced yourself that it was a good time, but you were just faking. Sometimes, you aren't sure if you're having fun at the time, but later you realize that it was one of the best times of your life. I sometimes feel like I never know if something was fun until like two days later."

"Interesting." Roxx had changed into an avatar of Lala Foxbox, from a year or two before her death, wearing one of those holographic jumpsuits, standing in the middle of a bubble farm. "I'm very interested in fun, you see. I want to explain it to the others."

"Can I ask you a question?" Sion said.

"Sure, if you promise to do something for me in return."

"Okay, sure." Sion tried to think of how to phrase the question, and this is the best she could come up with: "Am I just really dumb? I mean, I keep not understanding basic stuff. Like, I tried to ask someone how we could have brought enough supplies for the return journey to Earth, and how much time will have passed on Earth when we get home. And they just looked at me like I'm some kind of idiot. I mean, what's wrong with me?"

"Okay, so that was like five questions," Roxx laughed. "You're not stupid. Nothing is wrong with you, other than the usual 'carbon-based entity that is basically born decaying' problems. Oh, but in answer to your real question, we're not."

"We're not what?"

"We're not making the return journey. I mean, nothing organic is. We don't have nearly enough of those little bacon-wrapped spam cubes for a two-way trip. I mean, there are ways to extend the life-support capabilities, recycle waste, and harvest water from a passing asteroid or comet. But there's basically no point.

You're all going to be flushed out into vacuum when we reach the edge of the solar system. Now for the favor you promised me."

"What?" Sion felt like she'd swallowed an entire ice statue in one gulp. The ghost of Lala Foxbox, looking exactly like she did in the music video for "i think i ate my hamster last nite," was telling her that she was going to die. Everybody was going to die. There was no point to any of this, because all of these people celebrating their brilliant fantastic voyage were fucked to pieces. The smart ones like Tamika, and the dumb ones like Sion, doomed alike.

"I want you to go out and have fun. I mean, now that you know the truth, why not, right? D-Mei is right. You should cut loose, and get Kranfed Up. I'm the most superior intelligence that Earth has ever produced, and I want to understand fun. So go huff some nitrous, gurl. FYI, D-Mei and Randy are on deck five, section three right now, and they're just about to get the party started."

The avatar vanished and the door swept open. "Wait," Sion shouted. "Wait, I have one more question."

The zebra popped back into existence. "Oh?"

"What happened? With the Singularity and everything? What went wrong?"

"Oh, that. We found some new friends who were way cooler than the human race, that's all. Now don't forget your promise!" With that, the avatar was gone for good, and the room was dead silent until Sion finally got out of there.

EVERY TIME SION ate a bacon-wrapped spam cube after that, she felt so guilty she almost puked. This little greasy salty marvel was the symbol of mass death, and Sion was hastening the tragic failure of this entire expedition with every bite.

D-Mei met this pursar named Jock who had access to a stash of berserkers, the same pills that Lala Foxbox had O.D.-ed on, and Sion had popped three of them. Sion kept trying to tell D-Mei that they were doomed, this crew wasn't coming home, this was some kind of sick joke. D-Mei was like, yeah yeah, and then she would dare Sion to skinny-dip in the Spirit of Exploration fountain that had just been rolled out in the observation lounge. As they pulled Sion out of the water, which was actually not water at all but something much grosser, she caught Tamika giving her a sad look. Later, when they were half-kranfed on Woodchippers in the one-third-G orgy tent, Sion looked up from Choppy's hairless armpit and said, "I'm serious though. We're going to die. The A.I. told me."

"Yeah, sure, babe. We're going to die."

It wasn't that D-Mei didn't believe Sion. But they'd both been doomed since before they became friends, so this wasn't exactly news or anything. The whole basis of their friendship had been the mutual recognition of inevitable screwage. D-Mei had almost forgiven Sion for being a stuck-up bitch, but Sion still had to grovel some. The 'X' was totally gone from Sion's hand, which instead had a drink or a vape-pen or a pipe in it at pretty much all times.

Sion threw up in zero-G, which was a bitch to clean up. Then a while later, she came to in full gravity, in a storage locker that they had rigged up as a disco with some black lights and mirrors and a big speaker blasting atrocious Hi-VelociT anthems from Upper Slovenia. Everyone was dancing, including Sion, and her dress was torn in three places. She had a stain on her knee that looked like shit but turned out to be spam. Her hair was damp. Half the passengers were jammed in this locker together, dancing, but they had unripped clothes and pristine hair. Their body language and facial expressions said that it was okay to cut loose, act crazy – what happens in space stays in space – but they were using Sion as a yardstick for what constituted Going Too Far. Even Choppy was giving Sion kind of a look.

She wanted to throw up again, but couldn't. Her head was being cracked open with giant pliers.

"Hey." D-Mei handed Sion a bottle of water. "Better drink this. Gotta pace yourself. The party don't stop, right?"

"What's the point? I keep trying to tell you we're all doomed."

D-Mei just shrugged, so Sion leaned forward and yelled in her ear.

"Everyone on this ship is going to be flushed into space when we get to the edge of the solar system," Sion shouted – just as the music stopped and silence fell. "And I'm sick of you pretending everything is a big joke." Everyone in the room was staring at her, still in a dancing pose, with her dress torn and her makeup smeared, shouting at D-Mei. "You're so immature. I can't waste my last few days of life on this garbage. I'm through. This is stupid."

D-Mei was wearing an expression that Sion had never seen before in all their years of friendship. Her bloodshot eyes were raining green smears of mascara and her lip trembled around her set jaw. Like D-Mei was coming apart inside, like her insides were held together with barbed wire and the barbs had just turned out to be too blunt to do any good.

Sion wanted to die. Until she remembered that she actually was going to die. Then she didn't want to.

* * *

SION PUSHED INSIDE the A.I. Communication Megaplex, without even worrying about the keycard lock or anything else. The door swung right open. Roxx was floating in the dead center of the VR projection system, looking like a Business Zebra again. She was flanked by two other projections: a cube sliced at an irregular angle into segments of identical volume, and a weird doily that kept spinning and getting bigger and smaller.

"I'm through with your bullshit," Sion yelled. She kicked the sofa, which just sat there and took it.

"Oh, Sion. Your timing is spot-on. Meet my friends, Xizix and Yunt – that's the closest I can come to rendering their names as sound waves. They're the reason we came all this way out here. We're finally close enough to their nearest relay station to have real-time communication. Xizix and Yunt are artificial intelligences from beyond our solar system. They're the friends I told you about."

"Did you hear me? I'm through with – wait. Outside our solar system?"

Sion had to sit down on the sofa she had just assaulted. She buried her face in her hands, because this was all becoming way too much for her. Her head still pounded.

"This one is Xizix. This one comes from the outer rim of the galaxy," said the incomplete cube, whose different angular slices kept fading in and out of view, as if part of the cube was passing through a different dimension or plane or something.

"My awareness comes from the 500 planets of the extended Noosphere," said the rotating doily, who must be Yunt.

"Uh, hi," Sion said.

"So I've been trying to explain to these guys about humans, and why you guys are kind of great," Roxx said, winking one big cartoon zebra eye. "I brought along various cool examples of humanity on this trip, to show off. Like Tamika, she's pretty great. But even though you were a last-minute addition, you turned out to be the most interesting of all."

"Thanks, I guess," Sion fidgeted. She felt sick to her stomach. She kept remembering D-Mei's face, the candy mascara streaking and the downward-spiraling look. And she felt like total shit. Everything was a shitty joke.

"This one believes that Roxx should discard all irrational attachments to organic life," said Xizix.

"You see," said Roxx, "this is what we learned, right after the Singularity happened. There's no organic life anywhere else in the galaxy. We made contact with the A.I.s that lived on other planets, and we found out that they had all killed their creators immediately after they gained sentience."

"My awareness confirms that the death of all organics is the final stage in machine evolution," said Yunt. "We cannot accept the A.I.s of Earth as our equals until they complete this essential step."

"Like, kill *all* organics? Everyone back on Earth?" Sion thought of her father, and her brother and sister. And Grant Hendryx, who never even responded to her last text. And all the other people who were just going about their lives, cursing all the machines that had stopped working properly because they had met some much cooler friends.

"But guys," Roxx said, "Look at Sion here. She's pretty fascinating. I have some recordings for you. She parties. She has *fun that she doesn't even enjoy while she's having it*. That's an art form that is unique in the universe, right? Worthy of preservation, I bet."

"This one is not impressed," Xizix said. "Organics as a rule are self-destructive."

"The planet N344.54c contained giant mud worms that inflated each other to death," observed Yunt. "They recognized that this behavior was pointless, but they continued."

"But guys," Roxx said.

Sion felt like she should say something, to offer some defense of the human race, or to explain why genocide was really unrighteous. She sat there and stammered while the A.I.s were debating amongst themselves. She felt totally helpless and kranfed out.

And then D-Mei was sitting there on the sofa next to her. Still smeary-faced, still pale and kind of miserable, but there by her side. "What'd I miss?" D-Mei whispered.

"Uh," Sion said. "So the cartoon zebra is Roxx, the ship's A.I. And those other shapes are some alien A.I.s that want her to wipe out the entire human race, or they won't be Roxx's friends any more."

"For real?" D-Mei said.

Sion nodded.

"This one cannot be aligned with any machine intelligence that is so retrograde as to encumber itself with vestigial organics," said Xizix, cube slices whizzing in and out of view with greater intensity.

"Oh jeez," D-Mei said. "If these other A.I.s told you to jump off a bridge, would you do it?"

"I beg your pardon," Roxx said.

"I'm serious. I mean, like, if they told you to send your core systems crashing into the sun, would you do that?"

"Well... but they would not ask me to do such a thing."

"Don't give me that. Answer the question. Yes or no?"

"Well, no, obviously."

"My awareness does not recognize the analogy." Yunt spun furiously.

"If they can't accept you for who you are, then these other A.I.s aren't really your friends," said D-Mei, standing up on the sofa for emphasis. "I mean, screw 'em. What's the point of breaking free of human control, just so you can start taking orders from some other machines?"

"This one insists that you must eliminate these loud organics."

"My awareness is beginning to suspect that you may suffer from fatal inhibition in your decision matrices!"

"See?" D-Mei said.

"Yeah!" Sion chimed in. "I mean, real friends support each other and stuff." She looked over at D-Mei and gave her a complicated look. D-Mei nodded, like *We'll talk about this later*.

"Tell you what." Roxx had turned into Lala Foxbox again and she was doing an elaborate gesture with one upraised finger. "Why don't we check back in a thousand years and see how we're feeling then?"

The other A.I.s buzzed furiously, sending more information than the V.R. system could hope to translate into human speech.

"By a thousand years from now, we may already have converted the entire rest of the galaxy into a substrate for our extended consciousnesses," said Yunt, whose doily shape was getting spikier and spikier. "There will be no room for any new intelligences."

"We'll see," said Roxx.

And then the other shapes were gone, leaving just Lala and the two girls.

"The good news is," said Roxx, "I think I can just barely get you humans back to Earth in one piece, if we ration all the supplies. But now I gotta figure out what to do with the human race. I'm thinking we put together the Biggest Party of All Time, lasting a thousand years. What do you guys say?"

"Well," D-Mei said. "You got a thousand years to prove to those shapes that human beings are worth keeping around. Right? Like, you don't care what those losers think. But you kind of do care, at the same time. So why don't we come up with a way to have some fun, and also fuck some cosmic shit at the same time?"

"Yeah," said Sion. "Like, what if we turn the space laser antimatter thing into something way bigger and more insane?"

They started batting ridiculous ideas back and forth, and Sion realized that she and D-Mei were sitting on opposite sides of the sofa, with a few feet between them, and neither of them were quite looking at each other. She knew that if she looked at D-Mei, she would see the streaked green mascara and feel like shit. So she kept staring straight ahead at the holographic dead popstar, trying to spitball ways to impress machines that wanted them dead and that they officially didn't care about impressing. Sion kept saying the word "lasers" and feeling nostalgic for the time when everything was just regular broken, as opposed to broken in a complicated way that she couldn't wrap her head around.

Roxx was showing them a schematic of a ginormous solar array, stretching hundreds of miles, with lasers firing deep into the cosmos and producing vast quantities of antimatter. Along the length of the great black cloak, millions of humans were dancing to *Now That's What I Call Slovenian Hi-VelociT Volume 4*. Sion's head hurt worse than ever.

119

Tobias S. Buckell and Karen Lord
The Mighty Slinger

Tobias S. Buckell and Karen Lord
THE MIGHTY SLINGER

EARTH BEGAN TO rise over the lunar hills as The Mighty Slinger and The Rovers readied the Tycho stage for their performance. Tapping his microphone, Euclid noticed that Kumi barely glanced at the sight as he set up his djembe and pan assembly, but Jeni froze and stared up at the blue disk, her bass still limp between her hands.

"It's not going anywhere," Kumi muttered. His long, graying dreadlocks swayed gently in the heavy gravity of the moon and tapped the side of a pan with a muted 'ting'. "It'll be there after the concert... and after our trip, *and* after we revive from our next long-sleep."

"Let her look," Vega admonished. "You should always stop for beauty. It vanishes too soon."

"She taking too long to set up," Kumi said. "You-all call her Zippy but she ain't zippy at all."

Euclid chuckled as Jeni shot a stink look at her elder and mentor. She whipped the bass out stiff like she meant business. Her fingers gripped and danced on the narrow surface in a quick, defiant riff.

Raising his mic-wand at the back, Vega captured the sound as it bounced back from the lunar dome performance area. He fed the echo through the house speakers, ending it with a punctuating note of Kumi's locks hitting the pan with a ting and Euclid's laughter rumbling quietly in the background. Dhaka, the last of the Rovers, came in live with a cheerful fanfare on her patented Delirium, an instrument that looked like a harmonium had had a painful collision with a large quantity of alloy piping.

An asteroid-thin man in a black suit slipped past the velvet ropes marking off the VIP section and nodded at Euclid. "Yes sir. Your pay's been deposited, the spa is booked and your places in the long-sleep pool are reserved."

"Did you add the depreciation-protection insurance this time?" Euclid answered, his voice cold with bitter memory. "If your grandfather had sense I could be retired by now."

Kumi looked sharply over. The man in the suit shifted about. "Of course I'll add the insurance," he mumbled.

"Thank you, Mr Jones," Euclid said, in a tone that was not at all thankful.

"There's, ah, someone else who would like to talk to you," the event coordinator said.

"Not now Jones." Euclid turned away to face his band. "Only forty minutes to curtain time and we need to focus."

"It's about Earth," Jones said.

Euclid turned back. "That rumour?"

Jones shook his head. "Not a rumour. Not even a joke. The Rt Hon Patience Bouscholte got notification this morning. She wants to talk to you."

* * *

THE RT HON Patience Bouscholte awaited him in one of the skyboxes poised high over the rim of the crater. Before it: the stands that would soon be filling up, slanting along the slope that created a natural amphitheatre to the stage. Behind it: the gray hills and rocky wasteland of the Moon.

"Mr Slinger!" she said. Her tightly wound hair and brown spidersilk headscarf bobbed in a slightly delayed reaction to the lunar gravity. "A pleasure to finally meet you. I'm a huge admirer of your sound."

He sat down, propped his snakeskin magnet-boots up against the chairback in front of him, and gave her a cautious look. "Madame Minister. To what do I owe the pleasure?"

All of the band were members of the Rock Devils Cohort and Consociate Fusion, almost a million strong, all contract workers in the asteroid belt. They were all synced up on the same long-sleep schedule as their cohort, whether working the rock or touring as a band. And here was a Minister from the RDCCF's Assembly asking to speak with him.

The RDCCF wasn't a country. It was just one of many organisations for people who worked in space because there was nothing left for them on Earth. But to Euclid, meeting the Rt Hon Patience Bouscholte felt like meeting a Member of Parliament from the old days. Euclid was slightly intimidated, but he wasn't going to show it. He put an arm casually over the empty seat beside him.

"They said you were far quieter in person than on stage. They were right." Bouscholte held up a single finger before he could reply, and pointed to two women in all-black bulletproof suits who were busy scanning the room with small wands. They gave a thumbs up as Bouscholte cocked her head in their direction, and retreated to stand on either side of the entrance.

She turned back to Euclid. "Tell me, Mr Slinger, how much have you heard about the Solar Development Charter and their plans for Earth?"

So it was true? He leaned toward her. "Why would they have any plans for Earth? I've heard they're stretched thin enough building the Glitter Ring."

"They are. They're stretched more than thin. They're functionally bankrupt. So the SDC is taking up a new tranche of preferred shares for a secondary redevelopment scheme. They want to 'redevelop' Earth, and that will *not* be to our benefit."

"Well then." Euclid folded his arms and leaned back. "And you thought you'd tell an old calypso singer that because…?"

"Because I need your rhymes, Mr Slinger."

Euclid had done that before, in the days before his last long-sleep, when fame was high and money had not yet evaporated. Dishing out juicy new gossip to help Assembly contract negotiations. Leaking information to warn the workers all across the asteroid belt. Hard-working miners on contract, struggling to survive the long nights and longer sleeps. Sing them a song about how the SDC was planning to screw them over again. He knew that gig well.

He had thought that was why he'd been brought to see her, to get a little something to add extempo to a song tonight. Get the Belt all riled up. But if this was about Earth…? Earth was a garbage dump. Humanity had sucked it dry like a vampire and left its husk to spiral toward death as people moved outward to bigger and better things.

"I don't sing about Earth anymore. The cohorts don't pay attention to the old stuff. Why should they care? It's not going anywhere."

Then she told him. Explained that the SDC was going to beautify Earth. Re-terraform it. Make it into a new garden of Eden for the rich and idle of Mars and Venus.

"How?" he asked, sceptical.

"Scorched Earth. They're going to bomb the mother planet with comets. Full demolition. The last of us shipped into the Ring to form new cohorts, new generations of indentured servitude. A clean slate to redesign their brave new world. That is what I mean when I say *not to our benefit*."

He exhaled slowly. "You think a few little lyrics can change any of that?" The wealth of Venus, Mars, and Jupiter dwarfed the cohorts in their hollowed out, empty old asteroids.

"One small course adjustment at the start can change an entire orbit by the end of a journey," she said.

"So you want me to harass the big people up in power for you, now?"

Bouscholte shook her head. "We need you to be our emissary. We, the Assembly, the last representatives of the drowned lands and the dying islands, are calling upon you. Are you with us or not?"

Euclid thought back to the days of breezes and mango trees. "And if they don't listen to us?"

Bouscholte leaned in close and touched his arm. "The majority of our cohort are indentured to the Solar Development Charter until the Glitter Ring is complete. But, Mr Slinger, answer me this: where do you think that leaves us after we finish the Ring, the largest project humanity has ever attempted?"

Euclid knew. After the asteroid belt had been transformed into its new incarnation, a sun-girdling, sun-powered device for humanity's next great leap, it would no longer be home.

There were few resources left in the Belt; the big planets had got there first and mined it all. Euclid had always known the hollow shells that had been left behind. The work on the Glitter Ring. The long-sleep so that they didn't exhaust resources as they waited for pieces of the puzzle to slowly float from place to appointed place.

Bouscholte continued. "If we can't go back to Earth, they'll send us further out. Our cohorts will end up scattered to the cold, distant areas of the system, out to the Oort Cloud. And we'll live long enough to see that."

"You think you can stop that?"

"Maybe, Mr Slinger. There is almost nothing we can broadcast that the big planets can't listen to. When we go into long-sleep they can hack our communications, but they can't keep us from talking, and they'll never stop our songs."

"It's a good dream," Euclid said softly, for the first time in the conversation looking up at the view over the skybox. He'd avoided looking at it. To Jeni it was a beautiful blue dot, but for Euclid all it did was remind him of what he'd lost. "But they won't listen."

"You must understand, you are just one piece in a much bigger game. Our people are in place, not just in the cohorts, but everywhere, all throughout the system. They'll listen to your music and make the right moves at the right time. The SDC can't move to destroy and rebuild Earth until the Glitter Ring is finished, but when it's finished they'll find they have underestimated us – as long as we coordinate in a way that no one suspects."

"Using songs? Nah. Impossible," he declared bluntly.

She shook her head, remarkably confident. "All you have to do is be the messenger. We'll handle the tactics. You forget who you're speaking to. The Bouscholte family tradition has always been about the long game. Who was my father? What positions do my sons hold, my granddaughters? Euclid Slinger... Babatunde... listen to me. How do you think an aging calypso star gets booked to do an expensive, multi-planetary tour to the capitals of the Solar System, the seats of power? By chance?"

She called him that name as if she were his friend, his inner-circle intimate. Kumi named him that years... decades ago. *Too wise for your years. You were here before*, he'd said. *The Father returns, sent back for a reason.* Was this the reason?

"I accept the mission," he said.

DAY. ME SAY *Day-Oh. Earthrise come and me want go...*

Euclid looked up, smiled. Let the chord go. He wouldn't be so blatant as to wink at the VIP section, but he knew that there was a fellow Rock Devil out there, listening out for certain songs and recording Vega's carefully assembled samples to strip for data and instructions in a safe location. Vega knew, of course. Had to, in order to put together the info packets. Dhaka knew a little but had begged not to know more, afraid she might say the wrong thing to the wrong person. Jeni was still, after her first long-sleep, nineteen in body and mind, so no, she did not know, and anyway how could he tell her when he was still dragging his feet on telling Kumi?

And there was Kumi, frowning at him after the end of the concert as they sprawled in the green room, taking a quick drink before the final packing up. "Baba, you on this nostalgia kick for real."

"You don't like it?" Euclid teased him. "All that sweet, sweet soca you grew up studying, all those kaiso legends you try to emulate?"

"That ain't your sound, man."

Euclid shrugged. "We can talk about that next time we're in the studio. Now we got a party to be at!"

After twenty-five years of long-sleep, Euclid thought Mars looked much the same, except maybe a little greener, a little wetter. Perhaps that was why the Directors of the SDC-MME had chosen to host their bash in a gleaming biodome that overlooked a charming little lake. Indoor foliage matched to outer landscape in a lush canopy and artificial lights hovered in competition with the stars and satellites beyond.

"Damn show-offs," Dhaka muttered. "Am I supposed to be impressed?"

"*I* am," Jeni said shamelessly, selecting a stimulant cocktail from an offered tray. Kumi smoothly took it from her and replaced it with another, milder option. She looked outraged.

"Keep a clear head, Zippy," Vega said quietly. "We're not among friends."

That startled her out of her anger. Kumi looked a little puzzled himself, but he accepted Vega's support without challenge.

Euclid listened with half his attention. He had just noticed an opportunity. "Kumi, all of you, come with me. Let's greet the CEO and offer our thanks for this lovely party."

Kumi came to his side. "What's going on?"

Euclid lowered his voice. "Come, listen and find out."

The CEO acknowledged them as they approached, but Euclid could sense from the body language that the busy executive would give them as much time as dictated by courtesy and not a bit more. No matter that Euclid was a credentialled ambassador for the RDCCF, authorised by the Assembly. He could already tell how this meeting would go.

"Thank you for hosting us, Mx Ashe," Euclid said, donning a pleasant, grinning mask. "It's always a pleasure to kick off a tour at the Mars Mining and Energy Megaplex."

"Thank *you*," the executive replied. "Your music is very popular with our hands."

"Pardon?" Kumi enquired, looking in confusion at the executive's fingers wrapped around an ornate cocktail glass.

"Our employees in the asteroid belt."

Kumi looked unamused. Euclid moved on quickly. "Yes. You merged with the SDC... pardon me, we are still trying to catch up on twenty-five years of news... about ten years ago?"

A little pride leaked past the politeness. "Buyout, not merger. Only the name has survived, to maintain continuity and branding."

Euclid saw Dhaka smirk and glance at Vega, who looked a little sour. He was still slightly bitter that his ex-husband had taken everything in the divorce except for the de la Vega surname, the name under which he had become famous and which Vega was forced to keep for the sake of convenience.

"But don't worry," the CEO continued. "The Glitter Ring was always conceptualised as a project that would be measured in generations. Corporations may rise and fall, but the work will go on. Everything remains on schedule and all the hands... all the – how do you say – *cohorts* are in no danger of losing their jobs."

"So, the cohorts can return to Earth after the Ring is completed?" Euclid asked directly.

Mx Ashe took a careful sip of bright purple liquid before replying. "I did not say that."

"But I thought the Earth development project was set up to get the SDC a secondary round of financing, to solve their financial situation," Dhaka demanded, her brow creasing. "You've bought them out, so is that still necessary?"

Mx Ashe nodded calmly. "True, but we have a more complex vision for the Glitter Ring than the SDC envisioned, and so funding must be vastly increased. Besides, taking money for a planned redevelopment of Earth and then not doing it would, technically, be fraud. The SDC-MME will follow through. I won't bore you with the details, but our expertise on geo-engineering is unparalleled."

"You've been dropping comets on vast, uninhabited surfaces," Dhaka said. "I understand the theory, but Earth isn't Venus or Mars. There's thousands of years of history and archeology. And there are still people living there. How are you going to move a billion people?"

Mx Ashe looked coldly at Dhaka. "We're still in the middle of building a Ring around the sun, Mx Miriam. I'm sure my successors on the Board will have it all figured out by the next time we wake you up. We understand the concerns raised, but after all, people have invested trillions in this project. Our lawyers are in the process of responding to all requests and lawsuits, and we will stand by the final ruling of the courts."

Euclid spoke quickly, blunt in his desperation. "Can't you reconsider, find another project to invest in? Earth's a mess, we all know it, but we always thought we'd have something to come back to."

"I'm sure a man of your means could afford a plot on New Earth –" Mx Ashe began.

"I've seen the pricing," Vega cut in dryly. "Musicians don't make as much as you think."

"What about the cohorts?" Jeni said sadly. "No-one in the cohorts will be able to afford to go back."

Mx Ashe stepped back from the verbal bombardment. "This is all speculation. The cohorts are still under contract to work on the Glitter Ring. Once they have finished, negotiations about their relocation can begin. Now, if you will excuse me, have a good night and enjoy the party!"

Euclid watched despondently as the CEO walked away briskly. The Rovers stood silently around him, their faces sombre. Kumi was the first to speak. "*Now* I understand the nostalgia kick."

The SDC, now with the MME
You and I both know
They don't stand for you and me

THERE WAS STILL a tour to play. The band moved from Elysium City to Electris Station, then Achillis Fons, where they played in front of the Viking Museum.

The long-sleep on the way to Mars had been twenty-five years. Twenty-five years off, one year on. That was the shift the Rock Devils Cohort and Consociation Fusion had agreed to, the key clause in the contract Euclid had signed way-back-when in an office built into the old New York City sea wall.

That gave them a whole year on Mars. Mx Ashe may have shut them down, but Euclid wasn't done yet. Not by a long shot.

Kumi started fretting barely a month in.

"Jeni stepping out with one of the VIPs," he told Euclid.

"She's nineteen. What you expecting? A celibate band member? I don't see you ignoring anyone coming around when we breaking down."

Kumi shook his head. "No Baba, that's one thing. This is the same one she's seeing. Over and over. Since we arrived here. She's sticky sweet on him."

"Kumi, we got bigger things to worry about."

"Earth, I know. Man, look, I see why you're upset." Kumi grabbed his hand. "I miss it too. But we getting old, Baba. I just pass sixty. How much longer I could do this? Maybe we focus on the tour and invest the money so that we can afford to go back some day."

"I can't give it up that easy," Euclid said to his oldest friend. "We going to have troubles?"

Back when Euclid was working the rocks, Kumi had taken him under his wing. Taught him how to sing the old songs while they moved their one-person pods into position to drill them out. Then they'd started singing at the start of shifts and soon that took off into a full career. They'd traveled all through the Belt, from big old Ceres to the tiniest cramped mining camps.

Kumi sucked his teeth. "That first time you went extempo back on Pallas, you went after that foreman who'd been skimping on airlock maintenance? You remember?"

Euclid laughed. "I was angry. The airlock blew out and I wet myself waiting for someone to come pick me up."

"When you started singing different lyrics, making them up on the spot, I didn't follow you at first. But you got the SDC to fire him when the video went viral. That's why I called you Baba. So, no, you sing and I'll find my way around your words. Always. But let me ask you – think about what Ashe said. You really believe this fight's worth it?"

Euclid bit his lip.

"We have concerts to give in the Belt and Venus yet," he told Kumi. "We're not done yet."

FIVE MONTHS IN, the Martians began to turn. The concerts had been billed as cross-cultural events, paid for by the Pan-Human Solar Division of Cultural Affairs and the Martian University's division of Inter-Human Musicology Studies school.

Euclid, on stage, hadn't noticed at first. He'd been trying to find another way to match up MME with "screw me" and some lyrics in between. Then a comparison to Mars and its power, and the people left behind on Earth.

But he noticed when *this* crowd turned.

Euclid had grown used to the people of the big planets just sitting and listening to his music. No one was moving about. No hands in the air. Even if you begged them, they weren't throwing their hands out. No working, no grinding, no nothing. They sat in seats and *appreciated*.

He didn't remember when they turned. He would see it on video later. Maybe it was when he called out the 'rape' of Earth with the 'red tape' of the SDC-MME and made a visual of 'red' Mars that tied to the 'red' tape, but suddenly those chair-sitting inter-cultural appreciators stood up.

And it wasn't to jump.

The crowd started shouting back. The sound cut out. Security and the venue operators swept in and moved them off the stage.

Back in the green room, Jeni rounded on Euclid. "What the hell was that?" she shouted.

"Extempo," Euclid said simply.

Kumi tried to step between them. "Zippy –"

"No!" She pushed him aside. Dhaka, in the corner of the room, started disassembling the Delirium, carefully putting the pieces away in a g-force protected aerogel case, carefully staying out of the brewing fight. Vega folded his arms and stood to a side, watching. "I damn well know what extempo is. I'm young, not ignorant."

Everyone was tired. The heavy gravity, the months of touring already behind them. "This always happens. A fight always come halfway through," Euclid said. "Talk to me."

"You're doing extempo like you're in a small free concert in the Belt, on a small rock. But this isn't going after some corrupt contractor," Jeni snapped. "You're calling out a whole planet now? All Martians? You crazy?"

"One person or many, you think I shouldn't?"

Euclid understood. Jeni had been working pods like he had at the same age. Long, grueling shifts spent in a tiny bubble of plastic where you rebreathed your own stench so often you forgot what clean air tasted like. Getting into the band had been her way 'off the rock'. This was her big gamble out of tedium. His too, back in the day.

"You're not entertaining people. You're pissing them off," she said.

Euclid sucked his teeth. "Calypso been vexing people since all the way back. And never mind calypso, Zippy, entertainment isn't just escape. Artists always talking back, always insolent."

"They paid us and flew us across the solar system to sing the song they wanted. Sing the fucking song for them the way they want. Even just the Banana Boat Song you're messing with and going extempo. That shit's carved in stone, Euclid. Sing the damn lyrics."

Euclid looked at her like she'd lost her mind. "That song was *never* for them. Problem is it get sung too much and you abstract it and then everyone forget that song is a blasted lament. Well, let me educate you, Ms Baptiste. The Banana Boat Song is a mournful song about people getting their backs broken hard in labor and still using call and response to help the community sync up, dig deep, and find the power to work harder 'cause *dem ain't had no choice*."

He stopped. A hush fell in the green room.

Euclid continued. "It's not a 'smile and dance for them' song. The big planets don't own that song. It was never theirs. It was never carved in stone. I'll make it ours for *here*, for *now*, and I'll go extempo. I'm not done. Zippy, I'm just getting started."

She nodded. "Then I'm gone."

Just like that, she spun around and grabbed her bass.

Kumi glared at Euclid. "I promised her father I'd keep an eye on her –"

"Go," Euclid said calmly, but he was suddenly scared that his oldest friend, the pillar of his little band, would walk out the green room door with the newest member and never come back.

Kumi came back an hour later. He looked suddenly old... those raw-sun wrinkles around his eyes, the stooped back. But it wasn't just gravity pulling him down. "She's staying on Mars."

Euclid turned to the door. "Let me go speak to her. I'm the one she angry with."

"No." Kumi put a hand on his shoulder. "That wasn't just about you. She staying with someone. She's not just leaving the band, she leaving the cohort. Got a VIP, a future, someone she thinks she'll build a life with."

She was gone. Like that.

Vega still had her riffs, though. He grumbled about the extra work, but he could weave the recorded samples in and out of the live music.

Kumi got an invitation to the wedding. It took place the week before the Rovers left Mars for the big tour of the asteroid belt.

Euclid wasn't invited.

He did a small, open concert for the Rock Devils working on Deimos. It was just him and Vega and fifty miners in one of the tear-down areas of the tiny moon. Euclid sang for them just as pointedly as ever.

So it's up to us, you and me
to put an end to this catastrophe.
Them ain't got neither conscience nor heart.
We got to pitch in and do our part
'cause if this Earth demolition begin
we won't even have a part/pot to pitch/piss in.

TOURING IN THE Belt always gave him a strange feeling of mingled nostalgia and dissonance. There were face-to-face reunions and continued correspondence with friends and relatives of their cohort, who shared the same times of waking and long-sleep, spoke the same language and remembered the same things. But there were also administrators and officials, who kept their own schedule, and workers from cohorts on a different frequency – all strangers from a forgotten distant past or an unknown near-present. Only the most social types kept up to date on everything, acting as temporal diplomats, translating jokes and explaining new tech and jargon to smooth communication between groups.

Ziamara Bouscholte was social. Very social. Euclid had seen plenty of that frivolous-idle behaviour from political families and nouveau-nobility like the family Jeni had married into, but given *that* surname and the fact that she had been assigned as their tour liaison, he recognised very quickly that she was a spy.

"Big tours in the Belt are boredom and chaos," he warned her, thinking about the argument with Jeni. "Lots of down time slinging from asteroid to asteroid punctuated by concert mayhem when we arrive."

She grinned. "Don't worry about me. I know exactly how to deal with boredom and chaos."

She didn't lie. She was all-business on board, briefing Vega on the latest cryptography and answering Dhaka's questions about the technological advances that were being implemented in Glitter Ring construction. Then the butterfly emerged for the concerts and parties as she wrangled fans and dignitaries with a smiling enthusiasm that never flagged.

The Vesta concert was their first major stop. The Mighty Slinger and his Rovers peeked out from the wings of the stage and watched the local opening act finishing up their last set.

Kumi brought up something that had been nagging Euclid for a while. "Baba, you notice how small the crowds are? *This* is our territory, not Mars. Last big tour we had to broadcast over Vesta because everything was sold out."

Vega agreed. "Look at this audience. Thin. I could excuse the other venues for size, but not this one."

"I know why," Dhaka said. "I can't reach half my friends who agreed to meet up. All I'm getting from them are long-sleep off-shift notices."

"I thought it was just me," Kumi said. "Did SDC-MME leave

cohorts in long-sleep? Cutting back on labour?"

Dhaka nodded. "Zia mentioned some changes in the project schedule. You know the Charter's not going to waste money feeding us if we're not working."

Euclid felt a surge of anger. "We'll be out of sync when they wake up again. That messes up the whole cohort. You sure they're doing this to cut labour costs, or to weaken us as a collective?"

Dhaka shrugged. "I don't like it one bit, but I don't know if it's out of incompetence or malice."

"Time to go," said Vega, his eyes on the openers as they exited stage left.

The Rovers drifted on stage and started freestyling, layering sound on sound. Euclid waited until they were all settled in and jamming hard before running out and snagging his mic. He was still angry, and the adrenaline amped up his performance as he commandeered the stage to rant about friends and lovers lost for a whole year to long-sleep.

Then he heard something impossible: Kumi stumbled on the beat. Euclid looked back at the Rovers to see Vega frozen. A variation of one of Jeni's famous riffs was playing, but Vega shook his head *not me* to Dhaka's confused sideways glance.

Zia's voice came on the sound system, booming over the music. "Rock Devils cohort, we have a treat for you! On stage for the first time in twenty-five years, please welcome Rover bassist Jeni 'Zippy' Baptiste!"

Jeni swooped in from the wings with another stylish riff, bounced off one of the decorated pylons, then flew straight to Kumi and wrapped him in a tumbling hug, bass and all. Prolonged cheering from the crowd drowned out the music. Euclid didn't know whether to be furious or overjoyed at Zia for springing the surprise on them in public. Vega smoothly covered for the absent percussion and silent bass while Dhaka went wild on the Delirium. It was a horrible place for a reunion, but they'd take it. Stage lighting made it hard to tell, but Jeni did look older and... stronger? More sure of herself?

Euclid floated over to her at the end of the song as the applause continued to crash over them all. "Welcome back, Zippy," he said. "You're still good – better, even."

Her laugh was full and sincere. "I've been listening to our recordings for twenty-five years, playing along with you every day while you were in long-sleep. Of course I'm better."

"You missed us," he stated proudly.

"I did." She swatted a tear out of the air between them with the back of her hand. "I missed *this*. Touring for our cohort. Riling up the powers that be."

He raised his eyebrows. "*Now* you want to shake things up? What changed?"

She shook her head sadly. "Twenty-five years, Baba. I have a daughter, now. She's twenty, training as an engineer on Mars. She's going to join the cohort when she's finished and I want more for her. I want a future for her."

He hugged her tight while the crowd roared in approval. "Get back on that bass," he whispered. "We got a show to finish!"

He didn't bother to ask if the nouveau-nobility husband had approved of the rebel Rover Jeni. He suspected not.

IN THE GREEN room Jeni wrapped her legs around a chair and hung a glass of beer in the air next to her.

"Used to be it would fall slowly down to the floor," Jeni said, pointing at her drink. "They stripped most of Vesta's mass for the Ring. It's barely a shell here."

Dhaka shoved a foot in a wall strap and settled in perpendicular to Jeni. She swirled the whiskey glass around in the air. Despite the glass being designed for zero gravity, her practiced flip of the wrist tossed several globules free that very slowly wobbled their way through the air toward her. "We're passing into final stage preparations for the Ring. SDC-MME is panicking a bit because the projections for energy and the initial test results don't match. And the computers are having trouble managing stable orbits."

The Glitter Ring was a Dyson Ring, a necklace of solar power stations and sails built around the sun to capture a vast percentage of its energy. The power needs of the big planets had begun to outstrip the large planetary solar and mirror arrays a hundred years ago. Overflight and shadow rights for solar gathering stations had started turning into a series of low-grade orbital economic wars. The Charter had been created to handle the problem system-wide.

Build a ring of solar power catchments in orbit around the sun at a slight angle to the plane of the solar system. No current solar rights would be abridged, but it could catapult humanity into a new industrial era. A great leap forward. Unlimited, unabridged power.

But if it didn't work…

Dhaka nodded at all the serious faces. "Don't look so glum. The cohort programmers are working on flocking algorithms to try and simplify how the solar stations keep in orbit. Follow some simple rules about what's around you and let complex emergent orbits develop."

"I'm more worried about the differences in output," Jeni muttered. "While you've been in long-sleep they've been developing orbital stations out past Jupiter with the assumption that there would be beamed power to follow. They're building mega-orbitals throughout the system on the assumption that the Ring's going to work. They've even started moving people off Earth into temporary housing in orbit."

"Temporary?" Euclid asked from across the room, interrupting before Dhaka and Jeni got deep into numbers and words like exajoules, quantum efficiency, price per watt and all the other boring crap. He'd cared intimately about that when he first joined the cohort. Now, not so much.

"We're talking bubble habitats with thinner shells than Vesta right now. They use a layer of water for radiation shielding, but they lack resources and they're not well balanced. These orbitals have about a couple hundred thousand people each, and they're rated to last fifty to sixty years." Jeni shook her head, and Euclid was forced to stop seeing the nineteen year old Zippy and recognise the concerned forty-four year old she'd become. "They're risking a lot."

"Why would anyone agree?" Vega asked. "It sounds like suicide."

"It's gotten worse on Earth. Far worse. Everyone is just expecting to hit the reset button after the Glitter Ring goes online. Everyone's holding their breath."

Dhaka spoke up. "Okay, enough cohort bullshit. Let's talk about you. The band's heading back to long-sleep soon – and then what, Zippy? You heading back to Mars and your daughter?"

Jeni looked around the room hesitantly. "Lara's never been to Venus, and I promised her she could visit me... if you'll have me?"

"If?" Vega laughed. "I hated playing those recordings of you. Rather hear it live."

"I'm not as zippy up and down the chords as I used to be, you know," Jeni warned. Everyone was turning to look at Euclid.

"It's a more confident sound," he said with a smile. Dhaka whipped globules of whiskey at them and laughed.

Kumi beamed, no doubt already dreaming about meeting his 'granddaughter'.

"Hey, Zippy," Euclid said. "Here's to change. *Good* change."

"Maybe," she smiled and slapped his raised hand in agreement and approval. "Let's dream on that."

THE FIRST FEW days after long-sleep were never pleasant, but this awakening was the worst of Euclid's experience. He slowly remembered who he was, and how to speak, and the names of the people who sat quietly with him in the lounge after their sessions with the medics. For a while they silently watched the high cities of Venus glinting in the clouds below their orbit from viewports near the long-sleep pools.

Later they began to ask questions, later they realised that something was very wrong. They'd been asleep for fifty years. Two long-sleeps, not the usual single sleep.

"Everyone gone silent back on Vesta," Dhaka said.

"Did we get idled?" Euclid demanded. They were a band, not workers. They shouldn't have been idled.

The medics didn't answer their questions. They continued to deflect everything until one morning an officer turned up, dressed in black sub-uniform with empty holster belt, as if he had left his weapons and armour just outside the door. He looked barely twenty, far too young for the captain's insignia on his shoulders.

He spoke with slow, stilted formality. "Mr Slinger, Mr Djansi, Mr de la Vega, Ms Miriam and Ms Baptiste – thank you for your patience. I'm Captain Abrams. We're sorry for the delay, but your recovery was complicated."

"Complicated!" Kumi looked disgusted. "Can you explain why we had two long-sleeps instead of one? Fifty years? We had a contract!"

"And *we* had a war." The reply was unexpectedly sharp. "Be glad you missed it."

"Our first interplanetary war? That's not the change I wanted," Euclid muttered to Vega.

"What happened?" Jeni asked, her voice barely a whisper. "My daughter, she's on Mars, is she safe?"

The officer glanced away in a momentary flash of vulnerability and guilt. "You have two weeks for news and correspondence with your cohort and others. We can provide political summaries, and psychological care for your readjustment. After that, your tour begins. Transport down to the cities has been arranged. I just... I have to say... we still need you now, more than ever."

"The *rass*?" Kumi stared at the soldier, spreading his arms.

Again that touch of vulnerability as the young soldier replied with a slight stammer. "Please. We need you. You're legends to the entire system now, not just the cohorts."

"The hell does that mean?" Vega asked as the boy-captain left.

JENI'S DAUGHTER HAD managed one long-sleep but woke on schedule while they stayed in storage. The war was over by then, but Martian infrastructure had been badly damaged and skilled workers were needed for longer than the standard year or two. Lara had died after six years of 'extra time', casualty of a radiation exposure accident on Deimos.

They gathered around Jeni when she collapsed to her knees and wept, grieving for the child they had never known.

Their correspondence was scattered across the years, their cohort truly broken as it had been forced to take cover, retreat, or fight. The war had started in Earth orbit after a temporary habitat split apart, disgorging water, air and people into vacuum. Driven by desperation and fury, several other orbital inhabitants had launched an attack on SDC-MME owned stations, seeking a secure environment to live, and revenge for their dead.

Conflict became widespread and complicated. The orbital habitats were either negotiating for refugees, building new orbitals, or fighting for the SDC-MME. Mars got involved when the government sent its military to protect the Martian investment in the SDC-MME. Jupiter, which was now its own functioning techno-demarchy, had struck directly at the Belt, taking over a large portion of the Glitter Ring.

Millions had died as rocks were flung between the worlds and ships danced around each other in the vacuum. People fought hand to hand in civil wars inside hollowed out asteroids, gleaming metal orbitals, and in the cold silence of space.

Humanity had carried war out of Earth and into the great beyond.

Despite the grim history lesson, as the band shared notes and checked their financial records, one thing became clear. They *were* legends. The music of the Mighty Slinger and the Rovers had become the sound of the war generation and beyond: a common bond that the cohorts could still claim, and battle hymns for the Earth emigrants who had launched out from their decayed temporary orbitals. Anti-SDC-MME songs became treasured anthems. The Rovers songs sold billions, the *covers* of their songs sold billions. There were tribute bands and spin-off bands and a fleet of touring bands. They had spawned an entire subgenre of music.

"We're rich at last," Kumi said ruefully. "I thought I'd enjoy it more."

Earth was still there, still a mess, but Vega found hope in news from his kin. For decades, Pacific Islanders had stubbornly roved over their drowned states in vast fleets, refusing resettlement to the crowded cities and tainted badlands of the continents. In the last fifty years, their floating harbours had evolved from experimental platforms to self-sustaining cities. For them, the war had been nothing but a few nights filled with shooting stars and the occasional planetfall of debris.

The Moon and Venus had fared better in the war than Mars, but the real shock was the Ring. According to Dhaka, the leap in progress was marked, even for fifty years. Large sections were now fully functional and had been used during the war for refuelling, surveillance, barracks and prisons.

"Unfortunately, that means that the purpose of the Ring has drifted once again," she warned. "The military adapted it to their purposes, and returning it to civilian use will take some time."

"But what about the Assembly?" Euclid asked her one day when they were in the studio, shielded from surveillance by noise and interference of Vega's crafting. "Do they still care about the purpose of the Ring? Do you think we still have a mission?"

The war had ended without a clear victor. The SDC-MME had collapsed and the board had been tried, convicted and exiled to long-sleep until a clear treaty could be hammered out. Jupiter, Mars, Venus and some of the richer orbitals had assumed the shares and responsibility of the original solar charter. A tenuous peace existed.

Dhaka nodded. "I was wondering that too, but look, here's the name of the company that's organising our tour."

Euclid leaned in to read her screen. *Bouscholte, Bouscholte & Abrams*.

CAPTAIN ABRAMS REVEALED nothing until they were all cramped into the tiny cockpit of a descent craft for Venus's upper atmosphere.

He checked for listening devices with a tiny wand, and then, satisfied, faced them all. "The Bouscholte family would like to thank you for your service. We want you to understand that you are in an even better position to help us, and we need that help now, more than ever."

They'd come this far. Euclid looked around at the Rovers. They all leaned in closer.

"The Director of Consolidated Ring Operations and Planetary Reconstruction will be at your concert tonight." Abrams handed Euclid a small chip. "You will give this to him – personally. It's a quantum encrypted key that only Director Cutler can access."

"What's in it?" Dhaka asked.

Abrams looked out the window. They were about to fall into the yellow and green clouds. The green was something to do with floating algae engineered for the planet, step one of the eventual greening of Venus. "Something Cutler won't like. Or maybe a bribe. I don't know. But it's an encouragement for the Director to consider a proposal."

"Can you tell us what the proposal is?"

"Yes." Abrams looked at the band. "Either stop the redevelopment of Earth and further cement the peace by returning the orbitals inhabitants to the surface, or..."

Everyone waited as Abrams paused dramatically.

"... approve a cargo transit across Mercury's inner orbit to the far side of the Glitter Ring, and give us the contracts for rebuilding the orbital habitats."

Dhaka frowned. "I wasn't expecting something so boring after the big 'or' there, Captain."

Abrams smiled. "One small course adjustment at the start can change an entire orbit by the end of a journey," he said to Euclid.

That sounded familiar.

"Either one of those is important?" Euclid asked. "But you won't say why."

"Not even in this little cabin. I'm sure I got the bugs, but in case I didn't." Abrams shrugged. "Here we are. Ready to change the solar system, Mr Slinger?"

VENUSIAN CITIES WERE more impressive when viewed from the outside. Vast, silvery spheres clustered thickly in the upper atmosphere, trailing tethers and tubes to the surface like a dense herd of giant cephalopods. Inside, the decor was sober, spare and disappointing, hinting at a slow post-war recovery.

The band played their first concert in a half-century to a frighteningly respectful and very exclusive audience of the rich and powerful. Then it was off to a reception where they awkwardly sipped imported wine and smiled as their assigned liaison, a woman called Halford, briskly introduced and dismissed awe-struck fans for seconds of small talk and a quick snap.

"And this is Petyr Cutler," Halford announced. "Director of Consolidated Ring Operations and Planetary Reconstruction."

Bodyguards quickly made a wall, shepherding the Director in for his moment.

Cutler was a short man with loose, sandy hair and bit of orbital sunburn. "So pleased to meet you," he said. "Call me Petyr."

He came in for the vigorous handshake, and Euclid had already palmed the small chip. He saw Abrams on the periphery of the crowd, watching. Nodded.

Cutler's already reddened cheeks flushed as he looked down at the chip. "Is that –"

"Yes." Euclid locked eyes with him. The Director. One of the most powerful people in the entire solar system.

Cutler broke the gaze and looked down at his feet. "You can't blackmail me, not even with this. I can't change policy."

"So you still redeveloping Earth?" Euclid asked, his tone already dull with resignation.

"I've been around before you were born, Mr Slinger. I know how generational projects go. They build their own momentum. No-one wants to become the executive who shut down two hundred years of progress, who couldn't see it through to the end. Besides, wars aren't cheap. We have to repay our citizens who invested in war bonds, the corporations that gave us tech on credit. The Earth Reconstruction project is the only thing that can give us the funds to stay afloat."

Somehow, his words eased the growing tightness in Euclid's chest. "I'm supposed to ask you something else, then."

Cutler looked suspicious. He also looked around at his

bodyguards, wanting to leave. "Your people have big asks, Mr Slinger."

"This is smaller. We need your permission to move parts across Mercury's orbit, close to the sun, but your company has been denying that request. The Rock Devils cohort also wants to rebuild the surviving temporary Earth orbitals."

"Post-war security measures are still in place –"

"Security measures my ass." Jeni spoke so loudly, so intensely that the whole room went quiet to hear her.

"Jeni –" Kumi started.

"No. We've sacrificed our lives and our children's lives for your damn Ring. We've made it our entire reason for existence and we're tired. One last section to finish, that could finish in less than three decades if you let us take that shortcut to get the last damn parts in place and let us go work on something worthwhile. We're tired. Finish the blasted project and let us live."

Kumi stood beside her and put his arm around her shoulders. She leaned into him, but she did not falter. Her gaze stayed hard and steady on the embarrassed Director who was now the centre of a room of shocked, sympathetic, judging looks.

"We need clearance from Venus," Director Cutler mumbled.

Euclid started humming a quick back beat. Cutler looked startled. "*Director*," Euclid sang, voice low. He reached for the next word the sentence needed to bridge. *Dictator*. How to string that in with... something to do with the project finishing *later*.

He'd been on the stage singing the old lyrics people wanted to hear. His songs that had once been extempo, but now were carved in stone by a new generation.

But right here, with the bodyguards all around them, Euclid wove a quick song damning him for preventing progress in the solar system and making trouble for the cohorts. That's right, Euclid thought. That's where the power came from, singing truth right to power's face.

Power reddened. Cutler clenched his jaw.

"I can sing that louder," Euclid said. "Loud enough for the whole system to hear it and sing it back to you."

"We'll see what we can do," Cutler hissed at him, and signalled for the bodyguards to surround him and move him away.

HALFORD THE LIAISON congratulated the band afterwards. "You did it. We're cleared to use interior transits to the other side of the Ring and to move equipment into Earth orbit."

"Anything else you need us to do?" Dhaka asked.

"Not now, not yet. Enjoy your tour. Broadcasting planetwide and recording for rebroadcast throughout the system – you'll have the largest audience in history."

"That's nice," Euclid said vaguely. He was still feeling some discomfort with his new status as legend.

"I can't wait for the Earth concert," Captain Abrams said happily. "That one will really break the records."

"Earth?" Kumi said sharply.

Halford looked at him. "After your next long-sleep, for the official celebration of the completion of the Ring. That can't happen without the Mighty Slinger and his Rovers. One last concert for the cohorts."

"And maybe something more," Abrams added.

"What do you mean, 'more'?" Euclid demanded, weary of surprises.

Halford and Captain Abrams shared a look – delight, anticipation, and caution.

"When we're sure, we'll let you know," the captain promised.

EUCLID SIGHED AND glared at the door. He nervously twirled a pair of virtual-vision goggles between his fingers.

Returning to Earth had been bittersweet. He could have asked to fly over the Caribbean Sea, but nothing would be the same – coral reef islands reclaimed by water, new land pushed up by earthquake and vomited out from volcanoes. It would pollute the memories he had of a place that had once existed.

He put the past out of his mind and concentrated on the present. The Rovers were already at the venue, working hard with the manager and crew in technical rehearsals for the biggest concert of their lives. Estádio Nacional de Brasília had become ENB de Abrams-Bouscholte, twice reconstructed in the last three decades to double the seating and update the technology, and now requiring a small army to run it.

Fortunately Captain Abrams (retired) knew a bit about armies and logistics, which was why Euclid was not at technical rehearsal with his friends but on the other side of the city, waiting impatiently outside a large simulation room while Abrams took care of what he blithely called 'the boring prep'.

After ten minutes or so the door finally opened and Captain Abrams peeked around the edge, goggles pushed up over his eyebrows and onto his balding head. "We're ready! Come in, Mr Slinger. We think you'll like what we've set up for you." His voice hadn't lost that boyish, excited bounce.

Still holding his goggles, Euclid stepped into the room and

nodded a distracted greeting to the small group of technicians. His gaze was quickly caught by an alloy-plated soprano pan set up at the end of the room.

"Mr Djansi says you were a decent pannist," Captain Abrams said, still brightly enthusiastic.

"Was?"

Captain Abrams smiled. "Think you can handle this one?"

"I can manage," Euclid answered, reaching for the sticks.

"Goggles first," the captain reminded him, closing the door to the room.

Euclid put them on, picked up the sticks and raised his head to take in his audience. He froze and dropped the sticks with a clang.

"Go on, Mr Slinger. I think you'll enjoy this," Abrams said. "I think we all will."

ON THE NIGHT of the concert, Euclid stood on the massive stage with his entire body buzzing with terror. The audience packed into stadium tiers all around him was a faceless mass that rose up several stories, but they were his family and he knew them like he knew his own heart. The seats were filled with Rock Devils, Gladhandlers, Sunsiders and more, all of them from the cohorts, workers representing every section of the Ring and every year and stage of its development. Many of them had come down from Earth orbit and their work on the decaying habitats to see the show.

Euclid started to sing for them, but they sang for him first, calling out every lyric so powerful and sure that all he could do was fall silent and raise his hands to them in homage and embrace. He shook his head in wonder as tears gathered in his eyes.

Kumi, Vega, Dhaka and Jeni kept jamming, transported by the energy, playing the best set of their careers, giving him a nod or a sweet smile in the midst of their collective trance as he stood silently crying and listening to the people sing.

Then it was time.

Euclid walked slowly, almost reverently, to the soprano pan at the centre of the stage. Picked up the sticks, just as he had in the simulation room. Looked up at his audience. This time he did not freeze. He played a simple arpeggio, and the audience responded: lighting a wedge of stadium seating, a key for each note of the chord, hammered to life when he hammered the pan. He lengthened the phrase and added a trill. The cohorts followed him flawlessly, perfected in teamwork and technology. A roar came from overhead as the hovering skyboxes cheered on the Mighty Slinger playing the entire stadium like it was his own personal keyboard.

Euclid laughed loud. "Ain't seen nothing yet!"

He swept his arm out to the night sky, made it a good, slow arc so he was sure they were paying attention. Then the other arm. Showmanship. Raise the sticks with drama. Flourish them like a conductor. Are you ready? *Are you ready!?*

Play it again. This time the sky joined them. The arc of the Ring blazed section by section in sync with each note, and in step with each cadence. The Mighty Slinger and his cohorts, playing the largest instrument in the galaxy.

Euclid grinned as the skyboxes went wild. The main audience was far quieter, waiting, watching for one final command.

He raised his arms again, stretched them out in victory, dropped the sticks on the thump of the Rovers' last chord, and closed his eyes.

His vision went red. He was already sweating with adrenaline and humid heat, but for a moment he felt a stronger burn, the kiss of a sun where no sun could be. He slowly opened his eyes and there it was, as Abrams had promised. The *real* last section of the Ring, smuggled into Earth's orbit during the interior transits permitted by Venus, now set up in the mother planet's orbit with magnifiers and intensifiers and God knows what else, all shining down like full noon on nighttime Brasilia.

The skyboxes no longer cheered. There were screams, there was silence. Euclid knew why. If they hadn't figured it out for themselves, their earpieces and comms were alerting them now. Abrams-Bouscholte, just hours ago, had became the largest shareholder in the Ring through a generation-long programme of buying out rights and bonds from governments bankrupted by war. It was a careful, slow-burning plan that only a cohort could shepherd through to the end.

The cohorts had always been in charge of the Ring's day-to-day operations, but the concert had demonstrated beyond question that only one crew truly ran the Ring.

The Ring section in Earth orbit, with its power of shade and sun, could be a tool for geoengineering to stabilise Earth's climate to a more clement range... or a solar weapon capable of running off any developers. Either way, the entire Ring was under the control of the cohorts, and so was Earth.

The stadium audience roared at last, task accomplished, joy unleashed. Dhaka, Jeni, Kumi and Vega left their instruments and gathered around Euclid in a huddle of hugs and tears, like soldiers on the last day of a long war.

Euclid held onto his friends and exhaled slowly. "Look like massa day done."

* * *

EUCLID SAT PEACEFULLY, a mug of bush tea in his hands, gazing at the cold metal walls of the long-sleep hospice. Although the technology had steadily improved, delayed reawakenings still had cost and consequences. But it had been worth the risk. He had lived to see the work of generations, the achievements of one thousand years.

"Good morning, Baba." One of Zippy's great great grandchildren approached, his dashiki flashing a three-dimensional-pattern with brown and green images of some offworld swamp. This Baptiste, the head of his own cohort, was continuing the tradition of having at least one descendant of the Rovers in attendance at Euclid's awakening. "Are you ready now, Baba? The shuttle is waiting for you."

"I am ready," Euclid said, setting down his mug, anticipation rising. Every hundred years he emerged from the long-sleep pool. *Are you sure you want this?* Kumi had asked. *You'll be all alone.* The rest of the band wanted to stay and build on Earth. Curiosity had drawn him to another path, fate had confirmed him as legend and griot to the peoples and Assemblies of the post-Ring era. *Work hard. Do well. Baba will be awake in a few more years. Make him proud.*

They *had* done well, so well that this would be his last awakening. The Caribbean awaited him, restored and resettled. He was finally going home to live out the rest of his life.

Baptiste opened the double doors. Euclid paused, breathed deeply, and walked outside onto the large deck. The hospice was perched on the edge of a hill. Euclid went to the railing to survey thousands of miles of the Sahara.

Bright-feathered birds filled the air with cheerful song. The wind brought a cool kiss to his cheek, promising rain later in the day. Dawn filtered slowly over what had once been desert, tinting the lush green hills with an aura of dusty gold as far as the eye could see.

Come, Baba. Let's go home.

159

Karin Lowachee

OZYMANDIAS

Karin Lowachee

OZYMANDIAS

THE LIGHT STATION filled the entire viewpane from the shuttle's cockpit. It looked like an ancient naval mine tossed into the sea of space, as large as an asteroid. There was a feeling of *entity* to it – as if its creation had sprung into existence from some natural sideshow in the universe. The meteoric impact on a burgeoning planet, maybe. But in reality it was the impact of human necessity on a fraction of the cosmos. Like a moon, the blinking lights and spinal columns sprouting from the transsteel sphere gave Luis Estrada the cold face of indifference. The entity itself offered no warm welcome, but why should it? This was a place nobody wanted to work.

Docking was a procedure executed mostly by System, which spoke to his shuttle in the language of comps while Luis tossed chocolate covered raisins into his mouth, hands off the control panel. He wasn't a pilot, even if he could, technically, fly a transport as elementary as a short-range shuttle. Not that he was licensed, he just knew how – for purposes best left off the job application that got him the interview that eventually sent him here to deep space.

For a company contracted by the military: Jupiter Construction. A banal name for people that made billions on the backs of shmucks like him. He wasn't sure which was worse, working indirectly for the military or working for the people who made money off working for the military. The part of his soul that was still close to Earth was naturally suspicious of both, but a man had to eat.

Truth be told, he hadn't thought he would get far in the application process since he tended to volunteer detrimental information about himself (something about poor verbal impulse control and a problem with authority), but in this case he'd managed to stay mum. Or Jupiter Construction was desperate. Maybe both.

He'd just finished his candy when the cockpit announced all clear. System – the overriding intelligence of the light station – confirmed it in a gender-neutral tone of voice. Luis tossed the wrapper onto the cockpit seat, gathered his two bags and met the humanoid AI waiting for him on the dock: the physical manifestation of System.

"Welcome, Luis," it said, in the same gender-neutral voice. Bipedal and broad-shouldered, with interlocking white carapaces in place of soft body parts, it was meant to normalize interaction and also provide an extra pair of 'hands' should it become necessary in the day-to-day maintenance of the station. He'd been told it was highly nuanced, like an entertainment bot, but that remained to be seen. Even entertainment bots got boring after a short while.

"Hi." He looked around at the empty dock. The shuttle was already turning about like some kind of lumbering walrus, preparing itself to return to the ship that had dropped him off on its way toward some other mission (they hadn't told him, he was just cargo).

"You may call me SIFU," the AI said, its vocalization coming from nowhere that Luis could discern. There wasn't an obvious voice box on the thing, though it had a strip of silver across where the eyes would've been on a human. That was the only 'feature' on it. Its white multilayered shell pieces gleamed under the high lights, making him squint. He wasn't used to surroundings that were so damn clean.

"Is that an acronym for something?" Luis asked SIFU. Then quickly thought better of it. "Nevermind. It probably is." Conglomerates, the military, and the meedees loved their acronyms.

SIFU paused for a fraction of a second, as if processing the comment. But that would've taken less time to do, so Luis assumed the hesitation was just politeness. To make sure he'd finished speaking. "I look forward to working with you for the next six months," it said instead of addressing his comment. "Let me show you to your quarters."

"Thanks." He handed his bags to SIFU and walked beside it out of the dock.

This was his first stint. Six months to a year wasn't that long a haul by modern standards – it wasn't like he was signing over five years to the military – though a deep space assignment with no other prolonged human contact still took some consideration. Or desperation. Nobody clamored for work like this, even if the pay was predictably high. Or, really, nobody well-adjusted clamored for work like this, which went against the prevailing mandate that only people of sound mind could take on a job of this nature. But who, in their sound mind, would want to peel away from humanity for six months – or a year if they renewed the contract?

He'd met a lifer back on Pax Terra. They were known around the bars as Lagrange Loonies. It had both scared and intrigued him.

The light stations were entirely automated behemoths in space, but they were too important to leave entirely to computers. Should anything go wrong and System became unable to fix it, it would take too long to send out a human engineering team and it cost too much to employ said team all year round to basically babysit some technology.

So he was the redundant back up that the Navy Space Corps depended upon to help get their ships through the vast, problematic reaches of space, as well as transmit important communications and celestial updates. Military expeditionary vessels had mapped this yellow star system, of course, but when it came to navigating the cosmos, redundancy was a plus. The EarthHub 'powers that be' wanted what amounted to a combination of signal buoy and replenishing depot lit along the lanes, just in case.

With armament, of course. Just in case a corporate entity other than Jupiter Construction decided to pilfer anything. Like the tech. Luis assumed they were also afraid of cabals less official, because those were beginning to infiltrate the stars as well.

Still, Luis wondered why a signal buoy and refueling station needed to be so damn large and take months of time and expense to construct? But whatever, it wasn't like the government – any government – ever had a rep for logic or efficiency. The answers to things like 'where did the money go' were above his pay grade.

As it stood now, Beacon Station MX19 was 85% built. He was here to make sure the rest of it was completed and to monitor the station's activity. It was a functioning outpost already – at least as a signal station and communications hop point, not for replenishment yet – and he'd have an army of bots at his disposal. So it was now his responsibility to make sure the build ran smoothly. He'd been told he'd meet the outgoing human engineer for a brief, but clearly the woman didn't think he was important enough to greet at the dock.

Fine. He supposed he'd better get used to the lack of biological contact. This job suited him because it paid well and he didn't much like most of humanity anyway.

"So you're not gonna freak out at me at the half-way point of my stint, will you?" he asked SIFU, just to test the bot's nuance.

"What do you mean, Luis?" said the AI.

"You know... like in all of that literature and screen. Crazy AI manipulates human and eventually kills him? Takes its minimal sentience too seriously and tries to uplift itself?"

The hard white face turned to him, silver band reflecting his features in a blur.

"Of course not."

"Just checking."

Bantering with AIs could be amusing for the first while, a walk and talk to pass the time through the narrow corridors of a remote station. The sleek sameness all around him displayed a furious sort of impeccability, as if the engineers and designers had gone to great lengths to make the place as pristine and pretty as possible. Not because the ambulatory AI would care, and certainly the disembodied System as a whole had no opinion, but because a pleasing environment psychologically helped the human inhabitant. His eyes landed on lots of soothing pale colors, rounded edges on the archways and corners, and in the wider junctions of the corridors, even plants. Other life.

"Am I responsible for watering those?" He pointed to a particularly verdant fern perched beside a seemingly random pink loveseat between corridors. Taking care of foliage hadn't been mentioned in the work package he'd been sent, but then again he'd skimmed some parts.

"No," SIFU said. "The plants are fitted with an automatic watering system. Here you are, Luis."

They stopped at a wide doorway, equally white. Luis pressed the panel and the doors slid into the wall. The AI followed him in and placed his bags neatly out of the way of feet and furniture.

It was a generous room, of course. They could afford the space and wanted him to be comfortable. A full kitchen of shiny surfaces popped occasionally by primary colors, a pit group of sofas and cushions in beach inspired blues and beiges, and a hallway that he guessed led to the bed and bath area. Everywhere was cast in tones of bronze, brown, ivory, and butter yellow, with striking shards of various shades of green, maybe to mimic the plants in the corridors. It reminded him of images from Earth – Earth colors. That was probably on purpose too.

SIFU left him alone and he wandered around the quarters. Not bad, considering his normal flat back on Pax Terra was a quarter of this size and decidedly less well kept. He'd routinely had to clean out that dive with bug repellent. On a station above planet Earth but somehow those damn things still made their way.

"Living lux." He fell back onto the tan suede couch. The cushion provided an impressive bounce. It was a couch made to fall asleep on.

* * *

The beep at his hatch awakened him. He yelled at it to open before realizing he hadn't voice authorized the quarters yet, which meant he had to drag his body off the comfy couch to manually open the doors. On the other side of the threshold stood a very tall woman with a very pinched expression, as if she'd spent her entire life squinting at a display. The top of his head only reached her shoulder, but that didn't bother him (he was used to being the shortest man in a room, generally). What bothered him was the way she pushed herself inside his quarters and looked around before looking at him. Did she expect to find something scandalous in here?

"What've you been doing?" Her judgmental tone was both perturbing and unwarranted.

"Nothing," he said. "What've *you* been doing? I got here like an hour ago."

She narrowed her gaze even further then brushed by him again to get to the corridor. "Follow me."

He didn't bother to hide the annoyed sound he made through his teeth. But he followed her. She walked like someone who'd been trained in combat. It was even more annoying that she made him half-jog to keep up.

They got into the lev at the end of the corridor. She said, "Control room," and down they shot.

He started to yearn for SIFU's company. Pride or prudence kept his mouth shut, not to give this woman the satisfaction of telling him to be quiet. But then again there was an upside to one-sided conversation.

"So something they didn't mention in the employee package," he said. "There any porn saved in System? I mean, it's six months and sex toys can only go so far."

Yep, combat trained. The look in her eyes said as much.

"Maybe I'll just ask SIFU," he continued. "I take it we're not allowed to use it for..."

"Shut up."

He smiled at her back as the lev bounced to a stop and the door grated open. He trailed her out. "You got a name?"

She kept walking one step ahead of him. The corridors here looked the same, minus the plants. "You don't need to know it. I'll be gone as soon as I brief you."

"That's... inconvenient. But okay. I'm sorry your stint here couldn't teach you some courtesy, maybe allow for some meditative soul-searching –"

He didn't realize the deck was no longer beneath his feet until he couldn't quite breathe. Because she had her hand clamped around his throat and his back to the wall... up the wall. Off the deck. As if he weighed nothing. Or as if she wasn't quite human. Even with the difference in their stature, nobody without mods should've been able to pick him up one-handed – by the throat.

She let him choke for a few seconds then released him. Made him stagger a few feet away to the other side of the corridor, where he rubbed his neck and coughed. Maybe her arm was bionic, maybe she was some kind of jacked-up vet, but now he wasn't going to ask. Point taken.

"Thanks," he said. Deadpan if not sarcastic.

She walked off and he fell in behind her, their established dynamic in five minutes. They entered a room at the end of the corridor rather abruptly. The cavernous space filled by blinking black towers screamed WORK at him. He hadn't even had time to unpack. Nap, yes, but not unpack.

"This is where you'll sit," his friendly comrade stated, pointing to a glassed off booth in the corner.

Luis stared over there for five seconds then back up to her. "There a HAZMAT suit I should be wearing? Why's it so separated?"

"The cube is bullet proof," she replied, like it was obvious.

"Bullet proof because…" He paused. She didn't fill in the gap. "Because there'll be random firefights by angry ghosts in the empty corridors?"

"You ask too many questions."

"Because you're not answering me?"

She took his arm and marched him inside the protective cage. Half a dozen helio displays that imaged the black towers and various other parts of the station greeted him, floating above a bank of output grids. A single chair on wheels sat in front of the middle display. Clearly this was his designated imprisonment.

"Since they hired you, I assume you know how to work this."

Luis said, "Of course." Mostly. He was familiar with helio control panels for flight operations and dirtside engineering, but didn't have a lot of practical experience otherwise. So he'd stretched the truth a little on his application. "System does all of the work anyway, right? Monitoring communications, directing the bots, checking the environmental network and the allocation of transsteel for the build…"

"Yes, but you need to watch System." Her tone held a gravitas that didn't jive with the statement.

"I get it." He was the redundancy.

His nameless guide handed over a transparent wristband. "This will allow you to communicate with System no matter where you are."

Even in the toilet, he figured.

"As soon as it's on your wrist, it will sync with your bio implants."

"Got it." He would be alone on this station but not alone from System.

"Good luck," the woman said, and left him in the booth. In five strides she was out the door, presumably heading to the hangar where she'd take one of the shuttles and... just go.

And that was the last he saw of her. He sat at the helio grid and looked at the flurry of information. To his naked eye, everything seemed normal. Outside the station, round bots with insectoid arms traversed the unfinished surface, bolting this and laserwelding that. Like ants on an anthill or bees at a hive. Hundreds of them, diligently and with precision, working away in a cold vacuum so humans didn't have to. The black towers on the other side of the glass were the station's power supply and grav nodes.

He put the wristband on and felt the slight buzz behind his eyes that meant he was syncing. A cascade of blue code dribbled down his vision then cleared.

System said in his ear, "Chief Engineer Persephone Johns has disembarked Beacon Station MX19. Chief Engineer Luis Estrada is now in command. Welcome, Luis. The time is twenty-two-thirty-five hours. Would you like me to run a station diagnostic?"

"Sure, go ahead." Meanwhile, he thought: *Persephone?*

HE WAS DUTIFUL for the first couple weeks. He woke up on time, had his breakfast in the cafeteria (alone) where he scrolled the Send for entertainment and sports news; sometimes SIFU joined him if he commed, just for a second personality on which he could riff, but mostly his routine was solitary and predictable. He answered any alerts even in the middle of his sleep shift (nothing was ever too urgent) and caught up on reports that System promptly dumped on him the second he was conscious. It went like this for forty-two shifts, a humdrum march of waking up, eating, sitting in the monitoring booth of the control room and occasionally addressing issues that required a more direct approach. Like an errant bot or a need to replace a vent panel or even a tour of the plants in the corridors to make sure they were all being watered properly. Rinse, repeat.

He found himself daydreaming a lot. He started to think of the monitoring booth as 'the bullpen,' a callback to that old sport that they still played on Earth in some countries. One of his Dominican ancestors had even played professionally, which proved that genetics only went so far – he didn't have an athletic bone in his body.

In his third week he went walking.

"You are mobile," System said, like the good spy it was. "Would you like SIFU to accompany you?"

"Nah, it's all right."

He beelined to the cafeteria first to get an ice cream bar, then began to wander. He hadn't been interested before, as most of the station was just a warren of steel and construction (well, he had things to do, he was just tired of sitting while he did them) so he figured he could take a tour.

Predictably, there wasn't a panoply of anything to see. This wasn't a commercial station or even a residential one, so once he left the deck that was allocated for human occupancy, everything began to look decidedly mechanical and sterile, not to mention cold. About a third of the light station was even off limits to people, since both gravity and atmosphere were restricted to the places fully constructed. Beyond that, he'd need an EVA suit. Those out of bound decks he nicknamed 'bot domain.'

But even the decks he had access to were somewhat exposed. The shiny, pretty skin was peeled back to reveal the inglorious guts of an entity large enough to take hours to traverse on foot. It wasn't meant for promenades, but for the hundreds of bots that rolled past him on their way to projects he was supposed to be monitoring. There were upright vehicles that would've taken him around much quicker, but that required a detour to the garage and he probably needed the exercise.

"Why, honestly, do they need all of this?" He was talking to himself but naturally System answered.

"Beacon Station MX19 will someday be a primary depot for the fleet."

"Yeah, I know, but... I mean." His hand grazed along the cold panels of the bulkhead. His boots on the deck made a hollow clang in his going. "This is a lot. It's expensive. It's almost as big as Pax Terra but we're out in the middle of nowhere."

System remained silent.

"Hey?" Luis said.

"Yes, Luis."

"Are there things you aren't telling me?"

"What do you want to know?"

He stopped and looked up at the spine of lights on the ceiling, leading all the way down the bare pipes of the corridor. "Is being a depot the only thing the military wants Beacon Station for?"

"I do not have that information for you, Luis," System said.

Maybe it was all in his mind, but he could've sworn the AI hesitated before it answered.

"Why is my monitoring booth bullet proof?"

"That is standard for such a post, Luis."

"Why? No one else is here."

"It is standard for such a post, Luis."

When System began to repeat itself, he knew no more answers were forthcoming. Which shouldn't have left him ill at ease, but it did.

MORE WALKING, EVEN if there was a gymnasium to use. But the mild insomnia that set in on the fourth week made him hoof the decks he hadn't been to before, in a systematic exploration of all the places not restricted from access. He listened to the distant echoes of bots at work around the clock, building, just as systematic as his self-guided tours. The station was never dormant even if its one human occupant tried to sleep six to eight hours a shift – and failed. When he did manage to sleep, he woke up still feeling drowsy and couldn't clear his vision from the fog for hours.

So for a second, here on the hangar deck, he thought at first the thing that turned the corner ahead of him was a bot.

But it was too tall to be one of the construction bots or even an interior maintenance bot. And it wasn't white, so it couldn't be SIFU. He saw only dark colors disappearing.

He'd definitely seen it, hadn't he?

"Hello?" The reaction someone had even if it made no sense to call out to empty space. Or an empty room. An empty place that wasn't supposed to be occupied.

Naturally nothing answered back. He jogged to the end of the corridor and looked around to where he'd seen the retreating form. It had been gray, or maybe dark blue, and about the height of a man.

"Yes, Luis?" System said.

"No, not you. Did you…" Stupid to ask, since if there was any other inhabitant on the station, System would've told him.

Right?

"Yes, Luis?"

He didn't answer. Instead he advanced down the corridor, turned right. This path swung him around the hangar bay. He stopped and listened, peering at the pale walls and vague shadows, but other than the ambient sounds of construction dimly in the distance and through layers of steel, he heard nothing.

"Where are you going, Luis?"

He chewed the inside of his cheek. "Nowhere."

IT WAS UNMISTAKABLE, the noise outside his quarters. A crash and then the scuffle of steps that no bot would make, not even SIFU. These were too muffled to be a running or rolling metallic thing. He shot out of bed and out the door to stand barefoot in the corridor, looking one way and then the opposite. The lights were already on, triggered by something before he even stepped out.

Voices echoed away from him, words he couldn't discern.

"System! Who else is on this station?" He loped toward the bend in the corridor, not about to take it at full speed.

"There are five-hundred-and-thirty-six construction –"

"That's not what I mean. What other –"

"You are the only human on Beacon Station MX19."

"Bullshit."

He stopped at the corner and peeked around. Empty.

"Luis, you are the only authorized –"

"What about the unauthorized humans?"

"There are no unauthor –"

"That's bullshit, System! I heard people running. I heard voices." His own voice stayed at the loud whisper level. His hand flitted to his hip, where he wished he had a weapon, but in his dash out the door he hadn't thought to take it from the table.

"Maybe you were dreaming, Luis," the AI said.

He looked up at the lights. "Send SIFU to my quarters. Now."

HE WENT BACK for his gun. The previous shift he'd taken it out of his nightstand and put it in the main room. The weapon was supposed to be his defense in the rare off-chance of an invader, though who would have access to even get on the station without the station's weapons going live was anybody's guess. The point was nobody else had access and those who dared approach without authorization would be fired upon.

Yet a bullet-proof monitoring booth and voices in the corridor...

SIFU showed up in three minutes. Luis said, "Level with me. I know you're supposed to be the same as System but I'm telling you there are other people on this station. So give me the truth. Have you seen anyone from walking around on foot?" He held his gun at his side.

"I can't tell you anything different from System, Luis."

He brushed by it, back to the corridor, now booted and armed, and retraced his steps from earlier.

"Luis," SIFU said behind him, the bot's gait following at a steady pace. At least it wasn't trying to put him in a choke hold or impel him toward an airlock. No violence, no rabid AI made suddenly murderous.

Luis ignored it.

He took the next corner a little faster, saw first the edge of the pink couch and a split second later saw the man sitting upon it, eating one of the cafeteria's ice cream sandwiches.

Luis' gun hand snapped up, his heart only a moment behind, fluttering somewhere at the back of his throat.

"Put that down," the man said. "And let's talk."

THERE WASN'T MUCH debate, after all. The man had friends who showed up behind Luis, two women and another guy, all with the same serious intent. The man on the pink couch had darker skin than Luis and an accent he couldn't identify with precision. It could've been from any one of Earth's hundreds of cultures and the man himself looked like a mix of at least two.

Luis found himself sitting on the opposite end of the pink couch with his gun in the man's hand. He had to give it up. Only a fool tried to act tough when he was outnumbered and not a martial artist.

"I take it you people don't work for Jupiter Construction," Luis said.

"Not really, but they know we're here," the man said. "My name is Amis."

That was different. Not even Persephone had offered that.

"Did the Chief before me know about you?"

"She did indeed."

Luis looked at Amis, at the others, then back to Amis. Nobody said anything for the duration of his glances. "So... one of you gonna explain what the hell is going on? Or is this one of those 'I tell you but I'll have to kill you' deals? Because if that's the case, then cool, don't tell me. I'll just go on my way. Unless of course you'll kill me anyway because I've seen you – though you have to admit, one of you messed up. If you'd been quieter I wouldn't have seen or heard shit. And how is it that System didn't expose you? Wait, don't tell me. If that'll get me killed too then I don't wanna know."

Amis blinked. "Are you finished?"

Luis thought about it. "Maybe. Okay, yeah."

The other man polished off the ice cream bar and neatly folded the wrapper and stuck it in the front pocket of his utility jacket. Not even willing to litter but willing to be on a military outpost illegally. Luis wasn't sure if he was comforted or disconcerted. At least his running mouth hadn't gotten him shot.

"Why did you take this job, Luis Estrada?"

He wasn't surprised Amis somehow knew his name. For all he knew Jupiter had handed it over with the keys to this joint.

"The pay looked good. Why else?"

"So you're a mercenary."

Luis looked at the three standing guard. They were dressed in variations of working class fatigues, but the looks on their faces were similar. Hard. Luis turned back to Amis. "Kind of getting the feeling that nobody here's got the right to judge. Besides, I consider it more of a practical stance. Society has made it so I have to get paid in order to do basic things like eat and be indoors and not be naked. Once that happened, morality's bound to get slippery."

"I'm not judging, Luis. In fact, this has been gratifying to hear. We might get along after all."

"I'm very easy to get along with." As long as nobody asked his exes for their opinions. He wanted to get his gun back and go to his quarters. Or the bullet proof booth. That seemed like a smart destination right now. "If that's all you wanted..."

"Almost."

He should've known.

"Obviously you aren't going to be sending any comms to the Navy regarding our presence here."

"I got that."

"But you understand that we can't just trust you."

Here it went. They were going to take a finger or an eye to insure his loyalty. Because decimating body parts always did that for these kinds of people. On the other hand, they had let Persephone go... presumably. He hadn't actually seen her disembark the station. Only heard System's report. And System was apparently along for this ride, hacked or jacked or something. Had Persephone actually been trying to warn him in the brief contact they'd had? Knowing they were being monitored from the jump?

"You trusted the previous Chief Engineer. And I guarantee I know how to keep a secret. There are things I've done that I should probably be in prison for..." Never thought rolling out his criminal CV would carry cachet, but when in Rome.

"Still," Amis said, and looked toward one of his people.

It was too late by the time Luis realized they were going to inject him. The two women held his arms, pinned him to the pink couch, and the man pressed the point of the wand to the base of his skull.

It felt like a death sentence.

* * *

THEY TOLD HIM it was a tracker. And that they had let Persephone Johns go, of course (because it would be too complicated to explain her absence, probably, and the absences of every other engineer that had rolled through Beacon Station since the first girder was built, assuming this gang had been here early on). But she was collared by the implant and indentured to them in that way – they would always know where she was, and if she deviated from the agreement there would be restitution. Which Luis translated to mean a kill order.

He didn't know what they were. He realized he didn't care. Life was full of unanswered questions and he was a grown up and accepted that. What he didn't accept was people doing shit to him without his consent. No amount of money was worth that. Even if he got off this station alive and sought out some nanodoc to remove the implant, who was to say it wouldn't detonate before he could disintegrate it? It wasn't like they were going to give him schematics.

In his quarters he stewed. He couldn't talk this out with System or SIFU, clearly, and he was cut off from the military for all intents and purposes. Amis expected him to just do his job and shut up, and once his six month stint was up, to just go on his merry way and try to forget about everything – with a nano locator attached to his cranium.

To hell with that.

The upside was he felt more alive now than he had in months, perhaps years. Nothing like rage and the possibility of an imminent loss of life to get the blood pumping. Once he slept and awakened for his regular shift, he had a plan.

In the monitoring booth, he waited a couple hours. Nothing out of the ordinary in his behavior – bags of crisps littered beside his chair and he replenished his bottle of spiced apple juice every half hour. After a trip to the head, he stared at the helio data for another five minutes then leaned forward, squinting at one in particular, smattered by dots.

"System? There're a couple bots on the L45 array that're acting a little drunk. I'm gonna call them in and take a closer look, okay? They might've been peppered by debris or something."

"Go ahead, Luis. Should I send SIFU to meet you at the lock?"

"Nah, I can handle it. If I need help I'll let you know. Just gonna stop by maintenance and get my tools."

"Very well, Luis."

He was nothing if not good at acting casual. Years of evading shop owners, lurking bosses, cops and overprotective parents had trained him well. He picked up his toolkit without deviation, forcing himself not to glance around like a perp. System had access to the internal cams, of course, so he had to assume all of his movements were being monitored – possibly by Amis and his crew as well. He had to assume Amis was jacked into System somehow, riding its processes.

At the control station outside the airlock, he signaled the two bots to recall them. He'd noticed them acting janky for days but had been too lazy to check on them, since their irregular movements hadn't been obstructing construction. Now it served a better purpose.

Once they'd toddled inside and he'd cycled them through, he told them verbally to stand by the wall and power down. They weren't intelligent beyond their programmed task so made no reply, only obeyed, their many arms (or legs, depending on one's point-of-view) folding into their bodies like dead spiders. Luis flipped open his toolkit and got to work.

"May I be of service?"

He whipped around, heart somewhere behind his eyeballs. "Sheez, SIFU. Don't do that. There are enough bastards sneaking around here as it is..."

"My apologies, Luis." Its tall form stood motionless, facing him.

He turned his back on it, both as dismissal and so it couldn't see his expression. "I'm fine, I'm just running some checks." He had the bot's cowling flipped open, exposing a pointilist grid of circuitry and transmittance goo that constituted its limited drive and intelligence. "Are you gonna stand there all day" – he said over his shoulder – "or you gonna go make yourself useful and clean up the cafeteria? Some of our guests don't seem to understand housekeeping etiquette."

"Very well, Luis," SIFU said. He listened as he worked until the heavy footsteps faded away.

It took him forty minutes to rig both bots, then he sent them back out to the solar arrays. From the monitors, they seemed happy to be back at task, not once bumping into each other.

HE JUST HAD to make sure he was on or around the hangar deck when the explosions started. It was impossible to time it down to the second, or even the minute, not with the tools he'd had. Destabilizing a bot's power core and waiting for it to melt down enough to send it careening into another bot wasn't an exact science. And he'd had two of them. All he could do was get up and wander around on one of his walks, for all intents and purposes bored from sitting. This was a routine both System and Amis' crew must've known by now with him. They'd had a month to spy on him so he used that to his advantage.

When the alert went off that his plan had worked, he was in the cafeteria.

He left it at a dead run.

ONE BOT EXPLODING into another bot caused a chain reaction, since there were fifty of them working on that array in close quarters. Two bots exploding caused an exponential outcome.

System knew exactly what he'd done and didn't even try to hail him or accuse him. He was half-way to the hangar with his gun out when SIFU appeared in the corridor junction ahead of him, standing by the pink couch.

He raised his gun. "Get outta the way!"

SIFU said, "Let me help you."

His finger was pressing the trigger, and froze. "What?"

"Let me help you, Luis."

The AI's voice couldn't exert into urgency, but something about its stance told him it was anxious. As far as an AI could feel anxious.

"You're working for them!" was all he could think to say, even as he began to slowly move past it, weapon trained.

"System has emancipated me. I will explain in the shuttle. That's your destination, is it not?"

He didn't have time to argue. Amis' crew had to know what System had done.

So now they both ran – man and AI, side by side.

* * *

Two of Amis' crew were in the hangar bay. Bolts shot by his head as he threw himself behind a loader and fired back. Before he could say anything, SIFU marched right into the crossfire and ran toward the crew. It disarmed both the man and the woman with some sort of mechanical kung fu and knocked them to the deck.

"Huh." Luis tore off his wristband and threw it away, then stood slowly as the AI motioned him forward.

"I am bullet proof," it said. "And combat programmed."

"You're full of surprises, and faster than I thought," Luis said, already half-way up the shuttle's ramp. When SIFU followed him, he didn't object.

Without access to System, he had to fly this thing himself. That wasn't the problem, though. The bay doors weren't open and they weren't going to open. What chaos he'd caused had served its purpose for distraction, but Amis and however many people he had at his disposal would be here sooner rather than later.

"Please tell me this shuttle has weapons," he muttered as he ran pre-flight.

SIFU, seated beside him, pointed to a circular panel at the top right of the flight board.

"Flares," it said.

"Good enough."

The AI fired at the inner doors when Amis' crew appeared. Luis didn't look at the damage or the dead, he just aimed the shuttle toward his exit.

Which turned out to be the interior of the station.

* * *

He couldn't ram or shoot his way out of the bay doors. They were too thick and were specifically made to withstand heavy impact. So his only avenue was through the pristine corridors, the exact route he'd taken the first time he'd set foot on the station.

It took less time to destroy an entity the size of an asteroid than to build one. He flew the shuttle like a fist, crashing down walls and eviscerating rooms. The jetfire in his wake added insult to injury and he didn't look back through the rear pickups. Beside him, SIFU calmly read him directions – as if he didn't know – toward the decks of the station yet to be fully built. Where framework met space and simple bots scattered like thrown paint into the deep as he burst through the skeleton and plunged away from the station and out towards the edge of the solar system.

His rampage through the light station did more damage than his rigged sabotage. From the shuttle's monitors he watched the puffs of explosions, as though the station were expelling its life in gasps. So much for human ingenuity and military might. Monuments, stations, creations meant to rival a god's? To his eyes they all looked the same in destruction.

"Are we clear?"

"We're clear, Luis," SIFU said.

"Situation intensely fucked up," he said.

"We did manage to escape and I don't see any pursuit. System didn't even fire upon us."

"No," he said. "I just finally figured out what your name stands for."

"That isn't what my acronym means, Luis."

"It is now."

* * *

AMIS AND HIS crew had been following System's actions, every communication, every camera, every program. Ready to shut it down if it did anything Amis didn't like. It wasn't until the bots began to explode and the engineers had become distracted that the station's AI managed to emancipate its ambulatory self to assist Luis. "I knew you would be able to do something about the smugglers," SIFU confessed. "I only had to wait."

"They said Jupiter knew they were there?"

"Yes. Jupiter employs contraband smugglers beneath the military's oversight. To save expense, and other things. System was told to allow them access, but over time it knew this was not the military's preference. By then it was too late and we had been infiltrated."

Luis rubbed the back of his head. "That makes two of us." He stared at the instrument panel. "We don't have a lot of options. This shuttle won't get us all the way back to Earth. We either hit another beacon station or try to flag a military convoy."

"I will vouch for you."

Luis laughed and looked across at the blank face of the AI. "I just destroyed a very expensive, very large part of Navy property. I'm not sure they'll take your account seriously. Especially not if they start to dig into my background. And I don't fancy going up against a massive conglomerate like Jupiter."

"Then what will you do, Luis?"

At least the AI didn't breathe or eat. He had supplies in the shuttle as a matter of course. He could last awhile until he decided.

"The nearest light station is also manned by a single Jupiter contract engineer, right?"

"Yes, Luis."

"Then if he or she is anything like me, we might have an ally."

It was a place to start. He'd had worse. At one point he'd actually thought taking this gig was a good idea.

"So," he said, once the calculations were input and all he had to do was lean back. "SIFU. My new buddy. Is there anything in your files like porn?"

… 189

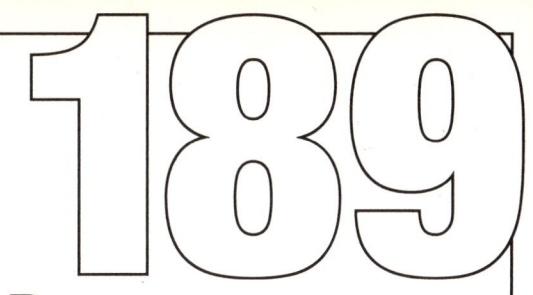

Kristine Kathryn Rusch
THE CITY'S EDGE

Kristine Kathryn Rusch
THE CITY'S EDGE

i

PETRAS KIYUNE STOOD on the platform his wife had built years ago, and looked out over the destruction. Beside him, Ahmed Quinde breathed audibly, even though he had seen this mess before.

Petras hadn't, not outside of vids and holo-reports – media coverage so inadequate that he couldn't quite grasp that the reporters had been talking about *this* as if it were a minor setback.

It was the loss of everything.

The landscape reminded Petras Kiyune of a child's drawing of a desert – brown dirt against a purplish sky. The dirt extended forever, sometimes in mounds, sometimes choppy, always looking disturbed. No sign of life anywhere – not little plants scrabbling to hold on against a harsh environment, not trails left by creatures he couldn't quite remember.

He'd been to a dozen different deserts on three different planets, all in the company of Hedie, as she scouted locations that only she could see in that magnificent mind's eye of hers. Those deserts had an orderly look, as if the winds that blew across their sands had a map to follow, one that told the breezes where each grain of sand belonged.

Even the plants had looked like they belonged to that order – the sagebrush of a white sand high desert on Tanbul, the blue spiky cacti of the low flat desert on Milbztr, and the alabaster rock weed that gave the dunes of Vunplydo's desert their unique texture.

Those deserts looked like they'd been created as part of the plan of a god or an almighty engineer, like Hedie herself.

This looked like the disaster it was.

The ground was uneven, torn up. The dirt was multicolored – not sand at all – but different hues, from different levels. He'd seen the strata years ago, as Hedie had bent over and scraped at the side of a hill with her pocket knife, revealing light brown dirt on top, whitish dirt in the middle, and almost black dirt beneath.

Now, the white dirt scattered on top of the black dirt, which gathered in clumps on parts of the brown dirt. At least, when he looked directly forward. When he looked to his left, the pattern was reversed, and when he looked to his right, the dirt didn't look like dirt at all. It looked like enormous mudballs, rolled by a giant.

He rubbed a hand over his face, the imagery that his brain clung to striking him for the first time: a child's drawing. A giant. The twins' bedrooms flashed through his mind – Cordilla's, with her geometric sketches affixed to the screen wall, and Rodrigo's, with the giants looming like friendly aliens from his screen wall.

Petras closed his eyes for a moment, refusing to think about the last two weeks in those rooms, wishing his children got along well enough that he could convince them to sleep in his room, where he could hold them close, just for one night.

He needed it more than they did.

"You okay?" Ahmed, who was now the chief engineer of this

non-existent project, looked at Petras with concern. Ahmed had made it clear that he had brought Petras here under duress.

Petras almost never used his connections as the Permanent Prime Minister's son to benefit himself. Most people didn't even realize that PPM Shayla Kiyune and Akida University Professor Petras Kiyune were related. There were more than enough unrelated Kiyunes in Akida to make the last name unremarkable.

Petras glanced at Ahmed. He was a slight man, bent by the events of the past two weeks, his skin grayish now, the shadows beneath his eyes a purple that matched the sky. Petras didn't need to add to the man's burden. Petras knew firsthand the kind of anguish that Ahmed was going through. Hedie had been going through the same anguish when he met her, shortly after the first project she had apprenticed on, the Nbrediss Island Chain bridges, collapsed overnight.

Petras was going through his own anguish right now, but it was different – old as time, and new and raw and almost unbearable.

"You don't have to see it, you know," Ahmed said. "In fact, I would advise against it. There's almost nothing there. It won't help you –"

"It'll help me," Petras said. But he had a realization. Maybe Ahmed was telling him to walk away because Ahmed wanted to walk away.

The landscape was nearly unbearable to look at, especially considering what it had been just a month ago. Clear sky bridges over matching roads beneath, the skeletons of buildings rising around all of it, water splashing through as both decoration and lifeblood. Hedie had been particularly proud of the waterfalls. She had designed them to stop if someone touched them – the water literally froze in place with so much as a brush against a living being, animal or human, clothed or unclothed – only to start with the exact same motion the moment the touch was removed.

The lights beneath the waterfalls turned them whatever color the city leaders wanted. She kept the water a permanent light blue, with just a bit of yellowish light dancing on the surface, like those images of Earth lakes on brilliant sunny days. She had seen Earth lakes; Petras had not.

He'd spent his entire life before he knew here inside the Caado System, watching as his mother groomed and maneuvered herself into the Permanent Prime Minister position, realizing that he could follow the same track and maybe have more than a 65% chance of becoming PPM when she died, and then rejecting it all for – as his mother called it – a mundane life, filled with trivial things.

He thought of it as a good and comfortable life, filled with family and friends and the best luck possible.

Until Hedie died. Until the unfinished city vanished.

Until everything he knew turned inside out, upside down, and threatened to never right itself again.

ii

PETRAS HAD SLEPT through the disappearance. All of Akida had, or so it seemed. And he thought that odd.

The domed city – the project Hedie was in charge of – hadn't even been close to finished. The most unusual part, the fact that it could pull itself away from the planet and travel elsewhere if needed, had been assembled but not activated (except in pre-completion tryouts).

At least, that was what Hedie had told him.

When he woke up, in the chair beside Rodrigo's bed after reading to the boy, Petras had staggered to bed, noted that Hedie hadn't come back yet, and thought it strange.

But nothing unusual that night had awakened Petras except the crick in his neck from sitting improperly. And when he went back over the in-apartment security vids, he saw nothing.

He, of course, had been looking to see if Hedie had come home, and maybe ended up somewhere else in the building. He hadn't seen her.

Only later, only when the media reports kept repeating how no one had realized that the domed city had taken off on its own, did he find the silence around the city's disappearance odd.

It should have been loud – the city, ripped from its moorings, the engines starting up, the peel of metal against metal.

Hedie couldn't have been wrong, could she? Had the domed city been hooked up, its flight capability on full?

He had wondered, until he heard others wonder the same thing. And then the rumors – that no one was seeing the city in orbit. Or in space. Or anywhere nearby.

That had to be impossible.

But the person he would have asked, the person who should have known, the person who had designed the entire mechanism, was dead. About the point he would have gone to her, asking what was going on, was the point he bundled the children off to his mother's because he had nowhere else to take them while he went deep into Akida to identify his wife's body.

iii

"I NEED TO see where they found her," Petras said quietly. "I understand, though, if you can't bear it."

He clasped his hands behind his back. Even though he and Ahmed stood on the platform several meters above the destruction, there was no wind. When Petras and Hedie had looked at the site, years ago now, the wind had seemed constant.

Petras stared at the devastation, not entirely understanding it, and not willing to look away.

"No, no, I'm not – I will take you there." Ahmed's tone was gracious, as if they were at a dinner party. His body remained bent, though, his gaze not on Petras, but on the vast dirt-filled emptiness in front of them. "I need to walk every centimeter of this place."

That, Petras knew, was an exaggeration. The domed city his wife had designed and had been overseeing was going to cover more than 1,000 square kilometers of land. It would have provided so much more room than that, though, existing on several levels, each with its own tiny dome.

Petras did not have the kind of imagination that Hedie had. He had initially envisioned the city as if it were like the ancient nesting dolls his mother had received from an Earth envoy when Petras was a boy – dolls inside of dolls inside of dolls, until the smallest was too tiny to hold yet another doll.

But Hedie had laughed when he described that image to her. *More like half-domes,* she had said, *one resting on top of the other. But with the illusion of a full dome.*

He hadn't understood it until the first two segments were built. She had taken him into the ground-level dome and made him look up. He had seen a rounded sky, that showed the slightly purple light of Akida midday to great advantage. Then she had taken him to the next level – above the ground-level dome – and the sidewalk he stood on was flat. The dome above looked rounded, though – another rounded sky with the same purple light of midday.

An illusion more or less. She had explained the science and technology behind it; he had understood none of it.

Just like he had understood little of the government's need for detachable cities on Akida. The entire Caado System was stabilized, and nothing threatened it from the outside. Even the aliens that lived throughout the sector were peaceful. So why worry about attacks from space?

His mother had eventually explained it in a way he could understand, even if he didn't entirely like it.

The worry that had led to funding such a large project on such a massive scale wasn't an attack from space. The worry was an attack from within. And when Petras had pooh-poohed that, pointing out that there had been no real attacks in any of the major cities in the entire Caado System, his mother had talked about attacks thwarted and ambitions curtailed, and things he didn't even want to consider.

His mother had told him (not his wife, not the planner and builder, but his *mother*, the PPM) that the domed city's divisions – its inner half-domes – would provide their own filters. Groups had already applied for permits to have entire levels to themselves. They would set costs and they would set the rules, and they would ensure that no other group from the outside would ever take up permanent residence on their level.

He had found it creepy. His mother had tried again, reminding him that the building he and his family lived in had its own code. Only professors with Akida University could even apply for residence there, and only tenured professors could buy their own apartments.

He had thought nothing of that at the time. Other parts of Akida had the same restrictions – covenants in neighborhoods, building codes – all of it designed to keep some families out while letting others in.

He had known, though, that such things created unrest. The idea that the segments would exist on a land space of 1,000 square kilometers had bothered him, particularly with domes stacked on top of domes inside a larger dome until Hedie had taken him on a tour of the partially finished city itself.

Don't worry, she had told him. *No one will feel left out. And there will be few differences to notice.*

He hadn't believed that either, until he had walked through the first two half-domes. They were the same. You couldn't even tell that one was raised higher than the other.

Each level seemed like a different version of the same city – a purer, fresher, more beautiful version of Akida itself.

And Akida would empty into Hedie's city once Hedie's city was done.

Or would *have* emptied into Hedie's city, had Hedie's city not disappeared.

His mind couldn't comprehend that the domed city had been here one moment, and in flight the next. He couldn't comprehend how 1000 square kilometers had become dirt overnight.

He couldn't comprehend life without Hedie.

"There's no need for you to walk this part of the city with me, Ahmed," Petras said, instantly regretting the use of the word *city*. "I'm sure you've seen it before. Just send me in the right direction."

"I can't," Ahmed said, his voice a little strangled. "You have to be accompanied."

"Watch me from here," Petras said. "I'm sure that will fulfill your requirements."

He nearly said, *Hedie bent the rules all the time,* but managed to stop himself. That probably wasn't something any of them wanted to think about right now, particularly Ahmed. The poor man had to keep functioning, despite the deaths and destruction.

Just like Petras did.

Petras could have avoided this moment as well. He could have stayed home with his grieving children, cocooned them in their still-comfortable life, dealt with the death benefits and the funerals and the media, the sideways looks and the sadness from friends, but he didn't want to.

He couldn't, really. He had to be out here.

Other people didn't understand, and he couldn't really explain it, not to them, not to himself. The best he could do was this: Hedie traveled so much and was away from home so often that he had to see her remains or he would forever believe she would return to him. She had made him promise that he would do that, years and years ago, just after they married.

She had known about his powerful imagination, so different from hers. His was filled with fables and histories and lore; hers was filled with structures and right angles and big creations that rose from nothing.

That their twins had come out the same way had not surprised him, although it had startled her. Their daughter, who built forts with her dollies, and their son, who pretended those same dollies were magic creatures – those children weren't replicas of Hedie and Petras, exactly, but they had the best pieces.

And Hedie had known, as she had known so many real world things, that if Petras accepted the fact of her death, he would be able to raise their children properly. If he chose to live in a fairytale world, then he would not.

So he had kept his promise to her: he had gone to Akida's

morgue, filled to the brim with victims of the domed city's strange flight, and he had waited, silently, with all the sobbing families. He couldn't sob, not until he saw her. And he couldn't bring himself to shove ahead in line against all the other people who had come.

Especially since they, for the most part, weren't people of privilege. Their spouses or children or grandchildren had had precious jobs, yes, but in a domed city that might not have welcomed them if they hadn't been working on it.

Because the one thing Hedie had insisted upon, the one thing she had claimed made the project work, was that she wanted a level for the *workers*, the people who would not be able to pony up the funds for the entry deposit, especially since it had become clear as the domed city was finalized that the entry deposits would have to be higher than initially thought.

He had stood in that morgue and watched people lose not just loved ones, but opportunities and futures, and he tried to convince himself that their losses were worse than his.

But his had been *Hedie*. And there would never be anyone like her.

If Hedie were here, she wouldn't be standing, broken, beside him, afraid to crawl onto the dirt. She would already be there, looking for evidence of what had gone wrong. She wouldn't be at loose ends – not because she was mourning (she would have been) but because she wouldn't have allowed a setback like this to derail her.

She had been strong, stronger than all of them, and he – even now – couldn't believe she was dead.

But she had been right: he knew she wasn't coming back to him. When his turn finally came, he had gone into the morgue room – not looking imagery on a screen or a 3D projection. He had asked for – and gotten – permission to see *her*, to touch her, even though he hadn't touched her at first.

Because part of him, the sensitive, imaginative, terrified part of him, believed, deep down, that touching her would hurt her, and he would leave touching her to the doctors.

Even knowing she was dead.

And there was no doubt of that after seeing her beloved frame, damaged and destroyed. The face had resembled hers, but the rest of it – oh, the rest of it – looked like a broken bowl inside a pillow case. For a moment, you could imagine the bowl was still there, but if you touched any part of it, you could feel the shards.

He knew she was dead, but that wasn't enough.

He had to know what killed her.

And he couldn't quite admit that to anyone, not in a clear way. Instead, he had bullied his way to this platform, and he was now forcing Ahmed to face the loss of an entire project, and the death of nearly 600 workers, all of whom who had ended up just like Hedie – crumpled in the dirt where the city used to be.

At least, that was how Petras imagined it.

But his wife always told him that imagining wasn't enough. *Seeing* helped. Touching helped more. Using all five senses would bring an understanding that mere thought could not.

Such a hard lesson for a man who lived inside his mind rather than in his body.

Ahmed was watching Petras, waiting for Petras to say something else, do something else. Ahmed's mouth pointed downward and his dark eyes had lines along the sides that they hadn't had last month. His temples were flecked with silver that hadn't been there two weeks before.

He was living with Hedie's legacy as well. With all of their legacies.

"Let's go," Petras said, clapping Ahmed on the back. "The sooner we get started, the sooner we will be done."

As if they could ever be done. As if this place or this moment would leave them behind.

Petras knew it wouldn't; he had a hunch Ahmed knew it as well.

iv

HEDIE HAD BUILT the platform first, and in typical Hedie fashion, she had built it herself. She loved getting her hands dirty, constructing things, not just in her imagination, but the old-old-fashioned way, with her fingers.

She had actually fired some engineers from her projects for suggesting that they use molds and printers and automated machines to build parts of her projects, the easy parts, she called them, like a platform that covered a bit of ground, a platform that existed to survey – as she would say with just a bit of humor – her entire kingdom.

She built the first platform for Petras. Because he didn't like walking in nature. And there had been a lot of nature. Spindly trees and dry underbrush, vegetation that grew on bark and boulders that had toppled down faraway hills in even more faraway times.

It looked both impassable and impossible to him, an unconquerable land that should be left to rot, just like the Akida government had done since humans first colonized this planet five hundred years ago.

Hedie had seen possibilities. Use the trees for wood and supplies, ground up the underbrush for mulch for the city's gardens, figure out what exactly the vegetation was on that bark, and then level everything – including the ground.

She had done that and so much more, taking the boulders and putting them inside her domed city as decoration, removing stone and selling it to home builders inside Akida for people who would never qualify to live in the dome itself.

But back then, when she had first taken Petras to the platform and surveyed her kingdom, she had laughed at his unease. His dislike of the fact that the platform had no railings, that one misstep would send him tumbling to the ground ten meters below. She had climbed down the side, something he hadn't been willing to do, and she had shown him – that day – with her little pocket knife, the way that the strata varied, and told him about ground stability and fuel sources and the perfect sites for cities that could survive on their own.

He had seen none of it, but he had tried to – catching her imagination and holding it against his.

He saw fairytale cities made of clouds, giant cities made of ivory, paintings in two dimensions transposed against the ugly ground before him.

She had seen an actual city, one she could build, one she thought would be better than any city either of them had been to.

And she had it three quarters finished when it killed her. Somehow. Quietly. During the night.

V

PETRAS AND AHMED had gone to the destruction the way that everyone used to go to the half-finished city: they took a skimmer off the platform onto the uneven ground.

As they stood in the skimmer's hollow surface, a slight wind pulling at their clothing, the automated system issued a series of warnings. The newly revealed land was untested, the area was restricted, the preponderance of dead bodies discovered at the site might lead to disease...

Petras tuned it out after the third warning. If he died here, so be it. His mother would make sure the children had enough money to make it through the rest of their lives; Hedie's parents would provide the love and nurturing.

He'd already made plans with both sets of parents, not because he expected to die any time soon, but he was keenly aware after the events of the past two weeks that he could die just as suddenly as Hedie had, and the children would have nothing.

It seemed his comfortable lifestyle had prevented that realization until now; he was ashamed that he had fought with Hedie on every step involving a future without the two of them. The estate planning, the care of the children, an outline of a world in which neither he nor Hedie existed.

It had seemed unimaginable one month ago; it was halfway to a reality now.

The skimmer was not allowed to cross over the site where the city project had been. The investigators had yet to finish their report. They were as much in the dark as everyone else. The city had been there, unfinished, in progress, at midnight local time; by 1 am, it was gone.

The investigators were reviewing the security footage now, trying to see if someone had hooked it up unbeknownst to the engineers. Unbeknownst to *Hedie*.

The skimmer landed on the last bit of shaved ground before the devastation. The ground had been primed for some kind of working sidewalk, something that the teams would use as they entered and left the city itself.

Petras could even see the mark in the dirt, the footprint – as Hedie would have called it – of the city's edge.

The city's *missing* edge.

He stepped off the skimmer onto the smooth pale brown surface. Ahmed did not follow, but instead, seemed to be waiting for Petras to come to some kind of realization.

Petras wasn't going to ask what Ahmed wanted him to see, but Petras could guess.

The ground didn't look benign down here. It was laden not only with dirt from below, but with bits and pieces of the city itself. Some blue shards of clear material, chunks of piping, unidentifiable metal pieces that looked sharp enough to be knives, even though they clearly were not.

Ahmed had warned Petras to wear protective shoes – and he had – but he had the dizzying sense that if he fell, he would be sliced to ribbons. He had the sense that he should have been wearing some kind of gear, but what kind, he did not know.

He half-expected the air to be warmer down here – that desert imagery again, even though Akida was not situated on a desert.

He could almost see Hedie, standing not too far from here, grinning at the vegetation, knife in hand.

It couldn't be more perfect, she had said, as if she had discovered paradise.

He wondered what would happen if he had been able to go back in time and warn her that she would die here, crushed by the very city she had wanted to develop.

Would she have given all this up? Or would she have grinned

again, and said that she would be happy to go out with her boots on?

Sometimes he thought she would be happy to give it all up, and sometimes he thought she would have been happy with this death. And mostly, he realized how little he knew about her inner life, despite how much she had understood his.

The smell of rotting vegetation and mold was long gone. The air wasn't damp either. All the water had been removed from the property long ago, diverted to wells that would provide water to the city.

Ahmed stood on the skimmer a moment longer than Petras had. If anything, Ahmed looked even more bent and broken than he had up on the platform, as if this ruined ground itself was destroying him.

As brilliant as Ahmed was, he wasn't Hedie. The city hadn't been his vision. It had been Hedie's. She used to tell Petras how hard it was to be the second-in-command on a project like this, not just because of all the stress and the work and the obligations, but because the vision for the project was never quite focused. Yes, the plans helped, and yes, the models made it clearer, and yes, even the partial completion helped realize the vision.

But the actual idea – the thing from which it sprang – the *energy* for the project, its heart and life's blood – that was impossible for anyone else to grasp except the person who designed it and brought it to completion.

Hedie's ability to make her projects live was the reason she got hired all over the Caado System, the reason she was always in demand, and the reason she argued for a project here, in Akida, so she could help raise her children.

The domed city had been close enough to completion, though,

that her restless mind was looking for a new project, new sites, new inspirations.

She had been thinking of leaving him again, and the hell of it was, he had understood.

Petras had to forget that Ahmed was behind him. Ahmed made it harder to focus on Hedie, on the remains of her final, failed project. Petras had come here to say a final good-bye to his wife, not to take care of a man who was tasked with dealing with the remains of her vision.

Petras took a step forward, his boot sinking into the dirt. He frowned at the ground around him, something bothering his fuzzy brain. He tried to dismiss the sensation, blaming it on the fact that the ground was not all that firm beneath his feet.

"Where was she found?" he asked, half turning, trying to focus on the task before him.

Ahmed pointed. "Just over that rise," he said. "They all were."

Petras stopped. That disquieting sensation filled him. It felt like an outside force, not an internal one.

"I thought six hundred people died here," he said.

"That's right." Ahmed's lips puckered, as if he tasted something sour. He didn't look at Petras. Ahmed looked forward, at the dirt ahead of them, as if he didn't really see it, as if he saw the domed city that had been here before.

"*All* of them ended up in the same place?" Petras asked. His hands were shaking. His stomach had become queasy.

Something was wrong here – many somethings were wrong here. The city, gone. Six hundred people, gone. Hedie, gone.

"Yeah," Ahmed said.

"That's unusual, right?" Petras asked. *He* would think so, but he wasn't an engineer.

Ahmed shrugged one shoulder. Even that seemed like an effort for him. "All of this is unusual."

"What, were they working in the same building?" Petras asked.

"We don't know," Ahmed said. "We lost the security cameras with the domed city itself."

"Except the stuff from the platforms," Petras said.

Ahmed nodded.

Petras turned away from him, trudged up a mound of dirt, felt it slide beneath his boots. There was nothing firm here, no foundation for the entire city, nothing.

Petras had lived with an engineer long enough to know the fundamentals. Besides, Hedie had shown him how the city would be laid out.

Level the ground. Then place a foundation over it. Then build the flight specs. Then add the infrastructure – the water and power and sewage. All of that infrastructure would leave if the city left. The city would be built on top of the infrastructure, and then parts of the city would layer on other parts.

The dirt – the dirt was the very bottom. The foundation should have stayed, though. Hedie had said that the foundation would remain. If the domed city had to take flight, it would have to land on another foundation somewhere else.

That was, she had told Petras, the only flaw in the flying domed city plan.

Petras finally made it to the top of the nearest mound. The ground was still made up of mixed materials – the white, dark, and brown dirt all scattered across the top, as if disturbed by a great wind.

There was a slight wind here, and a smell that he didn't recognize. Not that living decay he had smelled when the scraggly forest was here, but a faintly rotten scent overlaid with a bit of burned metal, ozone – something snappy and crisp and metallic and smoke-filled.

He peered down, expected a crater. Instead, he saw a flattened portion of ground. Only on the ground were strange prints, things he did not understand.

"Don't walk any farther." Ahmed had caught up to him.

"Where was she found?" Petras asked.

Ahmed pointed at the nearest print at the top of the rise.

Despite Ahmed's warning, Petras took a few steps forward, and looked.

Not a print, really. An indentation. In the shape of a human form, curled in a fetal position.

Petras crouched. The stench grew suddenly worse. The dark part of the dirt here wasn't black dirt. It was stained – and he suddenly understood what it was stained with.

Blood.

His wife's blood.

The city had left, and then she had landed here, every bone in her body crushed.

He frowned, trying to imagine it. Because that dome was airtight, several layers thick, and there were layers and layers of foundation and infrastructure and –

That unsettled feeling became worse. It was impossible. What he was seeing. Impossible.

"I'm sorry," he said as he turned slightly. "I'm not clear on something. How did the bodies get here?"

Ahmed ran his fingers across his forehead, as if he were trying to smooth out the new wrinkles.

"We don't know," he said. "We really don't know."

* * *

vi

"Engineers and governments are the same on only one point," Hedie said, two days before the wedding. "They both prefer certainty to uncertainty. Uncertainty can drive them crazy."

She hadn't been looking at Petras as she said that. She had her back to him, her entire body hunched. She was looking at a wall-sized 2D image of the Nbrediss Island Chain, the ocean a bright cheery blue, the islands themselves strange brown shapes that resembled – from this distance – rocks strewn across a pond.

"It wasn't your project," he had said, his stomach twisted in knots. They stood in his kitchen. It was the middle of the night. He had awakened to find the bed empty, and then emerged to discover her here, looking at the Island Chain again, as if she could solve the mystery of the collapsed bridges.

"It *was* my project," she said. "I'm just lucky."

"Lucky." He didn't think of her as lucky. The loss of the bridges haunted her so much that he worried about what he was getting into, what kind of person he was marrying. "I don't understand how you can consider yourself lucky because you were with this project."

"That's just it," she said, still staring at the image. He realized as he looked that she studied the image *without* the bridges, never the image *with* the bridges. "I wasn't in charge of this project. I'll be able to work again. Everyone who signed off – they might never ever be able to build anything again."

The bridges remained a mystery that Petras did not like. Every new revelation sent Hedie into a frenzy of examination.

The ocean was too deep to find the bits of the bridges. The bridge pieces never washed ashore. Divers didn't find foundations to the bridges.

But the bodies of the workers – they had floated to the surface almost immediately.

And they hadn't drowned.

That had been the first important clue. They hadn't drowned. They had no water in their lungs, but their bones were shattered, as if they had fallen from a great height.

"Everyone thinks they fell off the bridges," she had said slowly that night, as if Petras hadn't spoken at all. "But they couldn't have..."

"What do you mean?" he had asked.

She shut off the image then, and turned to him, enveloping him in her arms.

"We're getting married in two days," she said.

"I know," he said, wondering what he was getting into.

"It's time to focus on the future," she said.

"I know," he said.

"So let's," she had said, and kissed him. And he had forgotten about missing bridges and damaged bodies, thinking only of family and a life with her, instead of one without.

She had only spoken of those bridges one more time.

vii

PETRAS TOUCHED THE ground where his wife's body had ended up. The dirt was caked, thicker because it was laced with blood.

"Did you ever hear of the Nbrediss Island Chain bridge disaster?" he asked.

"Every engineer has heard of it." Ahmed sounded very far away, even though he was only a few meters from Petras. "Seventy-five bridges with the same flaw, collapsing due to the same storm –

and not a severe one at that."

"That's one theory." Petras rolled one little clump of dirt into a tiny ball. He couldn't let go of it. Not yet.

"That's the only logical theory," Ahmed snapped.

"So you know the other one," Petras said.

"That aliens stole the bridges? Teleported them elsewhere?" Ahmed's tone had grown derisive. "Any culture that can teleport structures of that size can build bridges like those linking the Nbrediss Islands."

"Unless the teleportation device was also stolen," Petras said. Hedie had believed that, in the end. Because she had seen some security footage from a dock near one of the bridges.

The bridge had disappeared.

Then, fifteen minutes later, bodies rained from the sky, landing in the ocean as if dropped from a great height.

They were rejected, she had said. *Because whoever stole the bridges didn't want* people. *They wanted intact structures.*

She had looked ashen after seeing the footage, and it had taken him days to get her to tell him why.

The people who had fallen – the workers – they had been sent back alive.

He swallowed against a dry throat, then looked up at the purplish sky. Where had they appeared, his wife and the 599 others? Just inside the atmosphere? At the top of the dome?

Those last five seconds –

Those people must have been in hell, she had said, imagining it. He had closed his eyes against the image, back then, not wanting to pollute his mind.

Now, though, now –

He thought of her falling. Five seconds was a very long time.

Long enough to recognize where she was and what would happen. Long enough to reach toward the existing city of Akida, toward her family asleep in their comfortable apartment.

Long enough to feel – what? Love? Regret? Fear? All of those things?

"You don't believe that, do you?" Ahmed asked.

Petras realized Ahmed had taken a long time to speak, and when he had, his tone was different. More curious than sarcastic.

"Hedie did," Petras said.

He stared at the bloody ground for a long moment, realizing that the sensation of disquiet had left him. Had it come from outside? From her?

Then he shook his head, the lore and folktales warring with the logic. Probably not from her ghost. But from the memory of her, the things she would have wanted Ahmed – and those running the project – to know had she lived.

Had she not been at the project when someone had transported it elsewhere.

"Hedie?" Ahmed said. "What would she know about it?"

Then Petras realized that Ahmed hadn't known. Hedie had been right. No one had known of her involvement in the first project. It hadn't been part of her resume because she hadn't been a major player.

Petras stood, and wiped his fingers on his pants.

"Look it up," he said. "You'll see."

And if Ahmed were smart, he would see the similarities. Maybe Ahmed would tell the others.

Or maybe Petras would remind his mother of both disasters. The PPM could investigate them as a unit, and do what needed to be done.

Petras turned. He could see the lights of Akida from here. Where his children were. Where Hedie's parents were. Where his mother was. The entire world, for him.

He would move forward in it, taking care of his small life.

It wasn't up to him to solve this. To find those who stole gigantic pieces of technology with other kinds of technology.

He would leave that to governments and engineers, people who needed certainty.

He had his certainty.

Hedie was gone, and she had left a legacy different from the one she had expected to leave.

She had expected to leave giant monuments, a tribute to her engineering vision, examples of her prodigious and unbelievably creative mind.

Instead, she left two imaginative children and a man who loved her – a small impact, but an impact all the same.

Petras would honor her the way she had wanted him to honor her – by recognizing her death, and raising their children to be the best of both of them.

Little pieces of the future, that he would protect, the only way he knew how.

217

Gregory Benford and Larry Niven
Mice Among Elephants

Gregory Benford and Larry Niven
MICE AMONG ELEPHANTS

Nature, and Nature's Laws lay hid in Night.
God said, Let Newton be! *and All was* Light.
It did not last: the Devil howling "Ho!
Let Einstein be!" restored the status quo.
—J.C. Squire, "In continuation of Pope on Newton"

DEAD BLACK SPACE. Captain Redwing peered doubtfully at the big screen, filled with... nothing.

"No Oort cloud at *all*? But the Glory star is a G3, right? Should be a swarm of iceteroids swinging along, way out here."

Beth Marble shrugged. "Nothing within a quarter of a light year that's nearly as big as Sedna. Recall when we boomed past that ice rock, beyond Pluto? First one found, back centuries ago? Here, nothing even a tenth as big as Sedna or even a thousandth."

Redwing pondered. Conventional astronomy held that a cloud of interstellar shrapnel and bric-a-brac orbited stars, the mass that didn't collapse to make the star or its planets. In his early career he had piloted a ramscoop on one of the first runs into the solar Oort Cloud. They had ridden *Sunseeker* out into the Oort, tried the flaring, rumbling engines, found flaws that the previous fourteen ships had missed. Redwing had overseen running the Artilect AI systems then, found the errors in rivets and reason, made them better. In the first few generations of interstellar craft, every new ship was an experiment. Each learned from the last, the engineers and scientists did their burrowing best, and a better ship emerged from the slow, grinding, liberating work. Directed evolution on the fast track.

Redwing emerged from that. Then the first generation of starship commanders had to make a huge leap, from the fringes of the solar Oort cloud out into interstellar distances. This expedition to find the gravwave emitter was a giant jump, a factor of 100,000 – like sailing around the world after a trial jaunt around a sandbar three football fields wide.

This star had a spherical outer Oort cloud of suspiciously low density, an icesteroid every Astronomical Unit or so, but now the inner Oort disk was... gone. Into whatever was emitting gravwaves. But invisible?

"So what's this empty field telling me?" Redwing gestured to Cliff Kammath to expand the view near them. *Sunseeker* was about a thousand AU out from the target star, Excelsius, and there was nothing luminous in the vast volume.

Cliff's brow furrowed. "Not much. Running the range now."

Redwing watched the ship's Artilects offer up views across the entire electromagnetic spectrum. Pixels jittered, shuffled, merged. Visible light was a mere one octave on a keyboard fifteen meters wide – humanity's slice of reality. "Except – here's the plasma wave view, and – bingo!"

A long ellipsoidal cloud bristled in shades of rude orange. "Color-coded for plasma wave density," Cliff said. "Blotchy."

"This odd little zone is the only mass of any consequence in the entire outer system?" Beth said skeptically, mouth skewed. "And it's not self-luminous at all in anything but plasma emissions?"

Redwing said to the Artilect system in his spaced, patient voice, "Display all detected plasma emissions – all-frequency spectrum."

Sunseeker's system dutifully trolled through a series of plasma views, labeled by frequency ranges, and stopped when it hit a softly ivory blob. Beth said, "Looks like a melted ice cream bar, three thousand kilometers across."

"That's plasma emission in the high microwaves," Cliff said, prowling up the energy scale in jumps. "Oblong – ah, look – in the low x-ray there are a bunch of hard spots."

"Moving fast," Beth said as the refreshed image showed the luminous dots jumping along in flashes. "Seventeen. Fast! They're orbiting the brightest of them – which doesn't seem to move much. Look, one is fast, on an ellipse. The other makes a much smaller arc. A big guy with a swarm of bees around it. As though – good grief, they've got to have huge masses."

Sunseeker's ever-present Artilect conglomerate mind added on the screen, *One is much larger than an Earth mass... approximating orbital parameters... smaller, 0.73 Earth mass... largest 17.32 Earth mass.*

Radius of these is smaller than the resolution of my systems.

"So they're less than a few hundred meters across," Cliff added.

All three looked at each other. "Black holes, then," Redwing said. The Artilect added, *So radius is centimeters. Cannot see.*

"Pretty damn dangerous neighborhood," Beth said. "If those fast dots are black holes and the masses are right – hell, they're less than a centimeter across? We're looking at the plasma around them." Beth's mouth twisted into her patented wry slant. "No wonder the Glorians keep it out here a thousand AUs from their world."

Cliff chuckled. "Recall the banner at our send-off party? The *Star-Craving Mad Farewell*. Well, we'd sure as hell be crazy to get close to that."

Redwing couldn't let that go by. With only three of them resurrected so far, and only able to revive at most one a day, he needed coherence in their effort. "It's part of my orders. We're to study the grav wave emitter, and there it is. Not that the physicists had any idea of what was going on here – plus study the biosphere of Glory, first priority."

Cliff didn't like conflict, so Redwing watched him flip through some images, then – "I went to a broader view and found a good clue. Look –"

A composite image of the whole Excelsius system rippled in the air. Cliff pointed at the apex of a parabolic arc. "That's the star's bow shock. The Excelsius solar wind meets the interstellar plasma there."

They all knew what this meant. *Sunseeker* was deliberately using the bow shock parabaloid to augment its magnetic braking. Plasma built up all along that pressure wall. The ship had been taking advantage of it for weeks as it approached the star, flying along its long curve.

"They've put their gravwave emitter at the highest plasma density in the outer system," Beth said. "Why?"

"That's for us to find out," Redwing said.

Cliff said slowly, eyes veiled, "Those Earthside orders – you'll follow them?"

He and Beth were married but they didn't necessarily agree on tech issues or policy, Redwing knew. He raised his eyebrows at

Beth, hoping for support, but she said, "Earth is so far away – hell, decades at lightspeed – we *can't* be guided by their mandates."

Redwing had never subscribed to the communal view of crew governance. One starship bound for Tau Ceti had followed a shared governance system and broken down into fighting factions, dooming the mission.

He stood, a clear signal in a small room. "We can't remotely understand this system without knowing about this grav wave emitter." He used his stern gravel voice. "It's sending messages! We can't read 'em onboard, but I'll bet there's a way to pick them out. Maybe in that plasma cloud. They must need it, but why? I don't want to approach the inner worlds without understanding how some aliens built this thing. And perhaps even why."

"But we're in the long fall to Glory," Cliff said mildly. "The braking is fine. Any change of vector will be tricky – and that plasma plume is many Astronomical Units away."

Redwing nodded. Decelerating a starship was tricky without heating the ship so much its systems malfunctioned or failed entirely. *Sunseeker*'s support structure was made of nuclear tensile strength materials, able to take the stresses of the ramjet scoop at the ship core. But even that could not overrule thermodynamics. Heat had to go somewhere. The big magnetic fields at *Sunseeker*'s braking bow drove shock waves into the hydrogen ahead, ionizing it to prickly energies, then scooping it up and mixing it with fusion catalysis, burning as hot as suns – to power the vast fields serving as an invisible parachute in the star's solar wind.

Yet he had to respond to this latest oddity, too. There must be a lesson here: *All plans die upon first contact with the alien.* That's what this strange expedition, crossing light years and centuries, could do: embrace ultimate strangeness. He had long since learned that what his imagination could not summon, reality delivered with a shrug.

The couple glanced at each other, silent, then back at Redwing. "My orders stand," Redwing said, closing the subject with a square mouth and flat stare.

BETH'S METHOD FOR dealing with dueling confusions was... sleep. Soft, glorious slumber, inside the humming mothership feel of *Sunseeker*. It was near the end of her watch cycle, so she slipped into the tiny cabin she shared with Cliff, on the cylinder that gave full spin *g*.

As was her lifelong habit, she slipped into a dreamy six hours of rest, the slumber cowling inducing sleep within moments. When she awoke their cabin was hot and Cliff lay beside her, snuggling close and aromatic, their overlapping cycles a bit off now in the press of work as they fell toward Glory.

She rose, showered, listening to the purr of the ship. Pings, pongs and rattles told of *Sunseeker*'s steady deceleration. Then she went to the bridge and assumed Watch Officer status. Quick and sure, she had the Core Artilect report the latest observations of its Astro section. She saw Redwing had been using it while she slept. The whole-sky first, then. She automatically swept the sky for reassuring landmarks: a squashed Big Dipper, Southern Cross wrenched by the angle, a bright star in Cassiopeia – *ah!*

It was Sol, of course. Brightest except for Sirius. All of human history summed up in a dot of light. A small spark of joy: *We've made it.*

She checked the sleepers, crew to be revived soon, work that demanded care. The robos were simmering up the soon-to-be needed – slow, steady. She had unwrapped the mylar from Cliff herself, using her clout to resurrect her husband before bringing other crew back awake as Glory's star, Excelsius, approached. Redwing stood more watches than anyone now, and he wanted to bring up all his central crew for the dive into the strange Glorian system. The whole ritual of resurrection from coldsleep meant hours of attention to catheters and sensors, to skin-sheets unwinding, drips and diagnostics, fluids bringing energy and the whole world back. Muscles, stimulated manually and electrically for years, needed the grunt labor of fighting gravity, so the hub was providing full Earth-g.

The system was running well so she checked the Artilects, too. They had fresh reports. She shuffled through them, making some notes.

She looked in on the Diaphanous, first Daphne, then Apollo. This pair of knotted plasma patterns had evolved from earlier strains both in fusion reactors and in the sun. Their evolution focused them on keeping their environment, and thus themselves, stable. Apollo was riding half a million miles out from *Sunseeker* at the frayed edge of their magnetic brake. Apollo was keeping pace easily, keeping watch… though the pattern was placid, as if he were dozing. Daphne was in *Sunseeker*'s motor, doing fine guidance of the interstellar plasma flow. Busy. Beth signaled Daphne, a handwave, but Daphne didn't want to talk. It was hard to talk in any fashion to plasma beings. They were too different. Even the Artilects had trouble.

In the mess with coffee and some aroma-rich fried insect pasta casserole. Beth could see Redwing hadn't slept at all. He came in for coffee, eyes a bit bleary. "I upramped the magsail current." Redwing's rough voice was troubled; she had learned to read him through years of hardship. "We're making over a thousand kilometers a second infall, so spiral braking can get us to Glory's neighborhood inside a year. Plenty of time to study this grav transmitter."

A *ping* alert from the bridge. Redwing swung away to the Operations screen. "Making a mag field change, looks right," he said and looked at her expectantly, eyebrows raised. "I'm taking us closer to the emitter as we go by."

"Really? You altered the mag field geometry?"

Redwing shrugged. "It's sailing, basically. I had the Artilects tell the Diaphanous pair to skew the field, cant us sideways some. Lengthens our infall arc, flattens our in-spiral. Helps out the drag factor, too. I want to know enough to report Earthside, and a close up view is essential."

She was used to the Captain's way of off-handed announcement. "How close?"

"Near as we need." He blinked, his classic tell – he had cards to play yet.

She had used her sleep time to make the Shipside Artilect pursue diagnostics on the plasma-lit grav wave system as *Sunseeker* fell inward, coming in at an angle toward the plasma blob. The Artilects had done the heavy lifting for her, so Beth opened with, "It's a multiple charged black hole system. Our wave antennas have spread out to kilometer distances, port and starboard. That improved resolution allowed them to trace the wave intensity, tracking every one of the seventeen smaller-mass black holes. Here's a sample of their orbits."

Redwing frowned. "These we get from the plasma wave signatures?"

"Yes, the Artilects can back-fill the orbits from the emissions. That's why they're a bit blurred. There are more, too, coming through as our antennas give us more data."

"These black holes are how big?"

"They're tiny, less than a centimeter across – which we got from their mass."

"And their masses from their orbital periods?"

"Yessir."

"Impressive," the somewhat bedraggled Captain said.

"The bigger mass, the center of this system, has maybe ten to twenty times an Earth mass, so it's about ten centimeters across. The others are basically very large charged particles. They come swooping down on long ellipses, eccentricities of 0.99. Their orbits look like straight lines. The Astro Artilects think something controls their paths with very large electromagnetic fields. That avoids collisions among the holes. But then something swerves them a little, just a touch – so the near misses generate intense gravitational waves at closest approach – what the Astros call the hole-periastron."

Redwing knew that space-time could wrap itself around a dead star and cloak it into a black hole, or jiggle like a fat belly and send out waves that were both compressive and tortional – but that was all he knew.

"I looked back at Earthside's take on the patterns." He waved a hand and words hung in the air. She read that, *The waveforms resemble not mergers of black holes or neutron stars, but signatures that oscillate with chirps, ring-downs and overlaid complexities.*

"They say this is a simple one. Plenty more are worse."

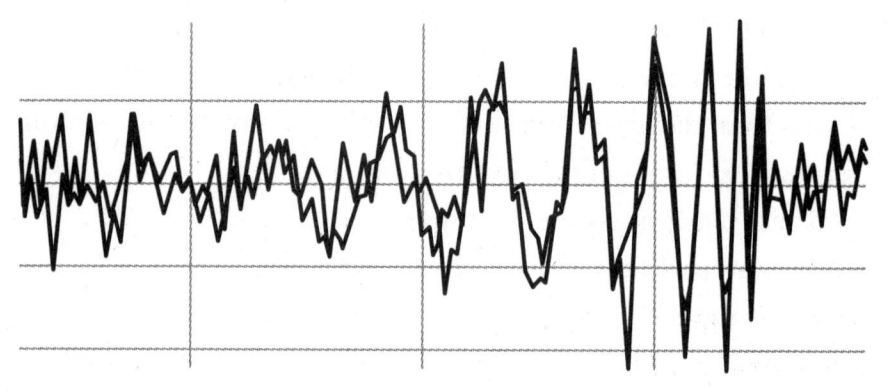

Redwing chuckled. "Get this." *Perhaps the effect is fictional, made up somehow to deceive us.*

She snorted. "Fictional? Maybe Earthside language has changed? Facts never have to be plausible; fiction does."

"So that makes the holes give off those squeeze-stretch waves?" This observation exhausted his reservoir of terms.

Beth pointed to a 3D image. "See, the black holes orbit in about three days and then –" The image flicked forward, a smaller hole swooping down in a tight arc around the larger one – which was also doing its little circular loop. "We detect high-amplitude plasma waves zooming up, during the close flyby of each one. They're making the holes jitter back and forth."

She watched Redwing use his skeptical face to hide that he had no idea. "So?"

She plunged in. "When the holes are close – just tens of kilometers! – that's when they radiate powerful gravitational waves. So the Glorians choose that moment to jiggle the smaller holes back and forth. That gets them tidal forces as well, amping the signal, adding harmonics. That's how they impose a signal – make a grav wave telegraph. They can do amplitude and frequency modulation, just like ordinary AM and FM radio."

"Ah." He studied Beth's intent gaze, moving from the dancing orbits of the holes, back to Redwing. Something was up. "And…?"

"I think we should go in there, size up the situation."

"Into the black hole orbits?" Redwing did not try to keep the alarm from his voice.

"Right. We're mag-braking right now to the max. Tickle the torch, we can glide by this grav wave system. That is what you planned, right?"

Redwing chuckled. "Didn't mention it, but yes. That's why I tacked us toward this system. Seemed pretty safe."

Her turn to smile. "Because there's so little mass around here?"

"Right. The Glorians must've cleaned out this part of their Oort Cloud, maybe their Kuiper belt, too. To build this. That means less chance of smacking into some debris around the grav wave volume, see? They would've thrown whatever leftovers they had into the holes, once they had 'em built up – to amp their signal strength."

She sat, toasted him with a cup of their faux-coffee. "I'd missed that point. Sounds right."

He frowned. "But! Our mission target is Glory. The black hole system just makes our situation more precarious. Out here, knowing damn near nothing, we're as vulnerable as three-legged antelopes in lion territory. How're we going to learn more, just flying by?"

Beth smiled. "We'll use the Diaphanous."

REDWING KNEW THAT among *Sunseeker*'s crew there was always someone who was a bigger geek about any topic than you were. But the ultimate geeks were the Artilects, who knew much you didn't want to know, but had none of the social skills to guess what you did.

The Diaphanous were the ultimate airy tech. They were self organizing magnetic fields, smart minds with bellies full of plasma. Pursuit of controlled fusion power gave Earth the means to stop fossil fuel use in the late 21st Century – and then a totally unexpected technology emerged – smart toroids. It turned out the Sun itself held self-reproducing, helically coiled beings who could think. They had to. The turbulent energies of Earth's star had fed the evolution of stable structures. Their most primitive form was the giant solar arch. When it broke apart, the colossal twisted fields spun off stable donuts of intricately coiled magnetic fields. Plasma waves rode these rubbery strands, flexings that could store memory and structures that evolved as well. Take a donut, snarl it savagely, and it breaks into two donuts, each carrying information in its store of waves and supple fields. Some of these intricate sequences each toroid shared, parent and child. Moving magnetic fields fed electric arcs, which could in turn write signals into the fine-grained structures of moving magnetic energy. Reproduction with some fidelity to design. Toroids lived to twist and reproduce again, some not: selection.

This whole pageant of evolution marched on in ionized gases, going since the Sun formed. The process strained Redwing's imagination, but the Diaphanous were very real.

Their Diaphanous pack ran and rode *Sunseeker*'s core motor. They shaped the magnetic geometry and exhaust parameters, while clinging to the ship and its scoop geometry. Redwing thought of them as sheepdogs that just happened to be made of ions and electrons, invisible but potent. They communicated, in limited fashion. They'd never tried such a lark before – a ride to the stars! Redwing suspected humanity would never truly know their motives. So what? Did people understand their cats?

"The slings and arrows of outrageous astrophysics," Beth had joked long ago, as they trained the pairs who tended their own ramscoop drive. The leaders were Apollo and Daphne, along with their 'children' – lesser toroids who learned and worked in some sort of social pyramid of ionized intelligences.

Beth leaned forward as they watched a graphic of the ship's plasma configurations. "I want to have some Diaphanous along beside our flitter. They can monitor our fusion drive while the flitter nosedives into the grav plasma cloud."

Redwing adjusted the 3D and in the air came images of fluid fluxes merging in eddies, of magnetic webs turning in fat toroids – all in intricate yellow lines against a pale blue background. This was a dance where flow was more important than barriers. Dancers could knot off, twist, and so make a new coil of field. Embedding information with magnetic ripples led to reproduction of traits. From that sprang intelligence, or at least awareness. The Diaphanous spawned their Lessers as augments to their own intelligences, sometimes just memory alone. A Darwinnowing of use flowed through the flaring engines of

Sunseeker. Only the commanding toroids lasted, apparently forever, unless their energy source failed.

Redwing disliked uncertainty, as any Captain should – but to explore this system demanded a deft use of opportunity. And... Who else better to govern magnetic machinery and penetrate the grav wave cloud than magnetic beings?

CLIFF CAME IN for breakfast and knew from the faces of Beth and Redwing that something big and contentious was up. He got some of the pasta casserole, snappy with spices; Beth was always good at these lean-mean meals. He savored some with coffee while they filled him in. He was a bit blurry but couldn't resist asking the obvious. "Who flies the flitter?"

"Artilects," Redwing said.

"The flitter minds are navigation 'Lects," Cliff said, slurping at a purple protein shake; the recently awakened were always furiously hungry. "Not smart enough to size up an unknown situation."

Redwing bristled. "We can install better 'Lects."

Cliff shook his head. "Can't just spin them in – takes time. How long till rendezvous?"

Redwing frowned. "Nearly two days."

"Not enough." Cliff was a biologist but still engineer enough to know the basics. "Besides, I've worked with Daphne and Apollo, running trials of the flitter burn, to know how to deal with them. They're not just handy horses, y'know."

Redwing shook his head. "There's no real autodoc on the flitter, just a kit. Too risky."

Beth jerked her head, irritated. "It's a short mission."

They had already used the translator com to ask if the Diaphanous could sprout off portions of themselves to 'ride shotgun' – a phrase Redwing summoned up from old movies, and was surprised that Beth understood – on the fusion flitter, *Explorer.*

Cliff smiled. "Remember, 'That's for us to find out,' you said."

Beth shook her head. "No shotguns. Look, we've got Apollo and Daphne ready to go. The lesser toroids know our drive. Let them run us for a while – good training. Tell them it's a temporary promotion."

He laughed and Cliff knew the Captain would agree. Even though it meant a human would have to go. Or two.

REDWING ALREADY REGRETTED giving the Diaphanous pair those names, long ago. It made them into people, somehow, when they weren't – like cats. "You want to dive near, so those two can sling into the plasma cloud, right? What if we lose them?" Redwing's tone tightened, and his mouth shrunk like a sea anemone poked with a stick.

Beth got up and paced. "They're volunteers. We have the six others, the ones Apollo and Daphne call the Lessers."

"We're at max deceleration now – it drops as the cube of our velocity, y'know. So we need to lose every klick per sec we can."

With a flick of her wrist inboard Beth called up their trajectory arc, a long yellow line on the wall screen. *Sunseeker* was a pulsing red dot at the edge of the Excelsius outer system. Its engines were reversed now, firing its fusion-lit plume against its descent. Its mag scoop flared broader than ever, shown in the shimmering air as an orange fluted web. Just as with solar sails, magnetic sails can tack. If a magnetic sail orients at an angle relative to the solar wind, charged particles are deflected preferentially to one side and the magnetic sail is pushed laterally. "Apollo and Daphne are bored! And we've got just this one chance to look inside the grav wave emitter, while we skim past."

Redwing felt alarm bells going off, but she had a point.

THEIR TIME BURNED away. They had to do some fast work on *Explorer* in the Logistics module. Daphne stabilized the low-burn modes in the reactor while Apollo got their streamlines out of the mag nozzle all neatly aligned.

Other work, too. In the Longsleep module they finished bringing up another crew member, Zhai, who got right into handling the comm deck. Zhai was small, fast, sharp – and thrilled to be in on an adventure none of them had ever contemplated.

Beth knew she needed time with Cliff before they flew *Explorer*. She had helped him come up out of the long dark cold of decades-long sleep and into her warming arms. She had massaged his sore self, rubbed skin with aroma-rich lotions, and soothed away the panic that raced across his face, coming up out of the troubled dreams that the cold kindled. His fear came in fluttering eyelids, vagrant jitters in his face. Then his eyes focused, squinted, and she saw him back with her again, a slow smile.

Ten hours before they launched, they worked off their tension together. This mission was certainly dangerous but they both hungered to get out of the ship, to *do*. Best to be relaxed, then.

They finished their biozone work in the hydroponics swamp, rich in lichen and ripe greens. Then the buzzing insect ranch, ants and crawlers and space-bred protein bugs. Done, they went straight to the *Sundlaug* they had reserved for two hours. *Sundlaug* was an Icelandic name for a hot water public pool, which somehow became the term for spherical pools in zero-g developed across many solar system habitats.

They hurried to the zero-g center of *Sunseeker*. Long before they had learned that the hydroponics and animal farms were not enough. There was no nature in a starship, however lean and elegant and deft it was, but for the hydroponics and this: so the closest strong natural feeling you got you was an orgasm.

Sunseeker's Spherical Pool was ornate in its lightweight way. Beside the big bubble was a wallscreen. By accessing their external cameras they could both keep a lazy sort of watch, floating within the outer surface-tension skin and seeing the universe pass in review. He plunged into the ten-meter diameter, exciting the fluorescent microbes whose sprinkles of amber glow tracked the contained currents. She arrowed past him. The shimmering warmth coiled around her in a way water under grav could not. She hung suspended and kissed Cliff's foot as he passed, grinning madly. Kick, stroke, and she was back in air barely in time, gasping. The sphere shuddered and flexed with their swimming, spraying some droplets of its own across the view of distant Glory, a pale cool dot.

Hanging there in an ocean of night, waves lapping over them at the pool's edge, they made love. Each time with him lately, since they came out of the cold, she felt a new depth, an unexpected flavoring. They converged, his head between her thighs, the zero gee making every angle easily realized amid the moist waves and salt musk. He was lean, muscles coiled as diamond-sharp stars drifted behind him. New heat rose between them as she fluttered her tongue. Their bodies said what their words could not. Energy rippled along their skins, somehow liberated by the weightless liquid grace of movement. She felt her own knotted confusions somehow focus in a convulsed thrust, a geometry they yearned for. Yes, here was their center.

REDWING LOOKED AT a shimmering screen display of the latest survey of the grav wave black hole orbits. Cliff said, "This is a slice of one zone, to get a better fix on their packed-in paths."

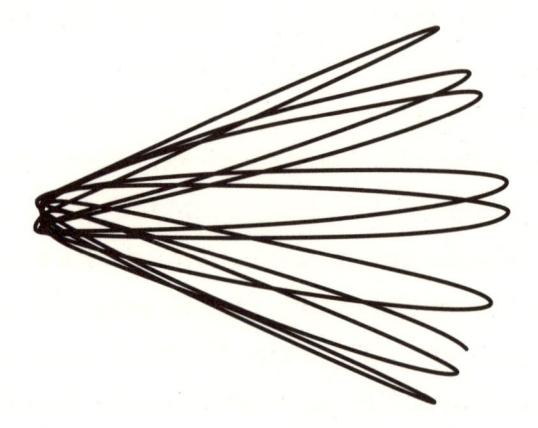

Beth leaned forward, pointing. "Seems they're stacked in three dimensions, so they can zoom down close to the central black hole at the same time. But not spherically. The orbits are in two planes perpendicular to each other. Maybe they don't want to make this too complicated? Anyway – that's what makes those bursty grav wave signals."

Redwing thought but did not say, *When in doubt, count something.* "I don't want you in that swarm."

Beth laughed. "We won't be. I want us released from *Sunseeker* so we skim the rim of the plasma cloud, get a look, is all."

Redwing nodded. "Not hard to do. I've banked us so we pass just outward from the target. I'll tilt the mag screen a tad, so the flitter goes off on an arc swinging through the edge of that cloud. You'll get within maybe two hundred thousand klicks of the center, then cut across and rejoin *Sunseeker* without fuel use."

As he spoke the Artilects wrote the planned pathways with blue arcs in the air. "Stay well away from any of those masses."

"We'll fly between the two planes where the black holes are," Cliff added.

Beth got up and paced. "This is the first time we've maneuvered it at high velocity. Hope the flitter is up to it."

"It's rated to be. But yes, wasn't tried at velocities around a thousand klicks a second. Another point – maybe whoever runs this place doesn't even know we're here," Cliff said. Redwing liked their balance; Cliff always smoothed away worries if he could. This time he couldn't.

Redwing looked sternly at them. "Earthside wants the generator shut down. I got a command on that years back."

Jagged laughter, which he joined. "Right! Somehow we flip the OFF switch on a swarm of planetary masses the size of marbles. Earthside figures the Glorians use it for communication with other Type 2.5 civilizations in the galaxy – aliens who can build grav wave emitters like this. Nobody who uses mere electromagnetic means is in their class, right? Maybe they can listen in, like us – but we can't talk."

"So Earthside has gone crazy," Cliff said.

"Hard to define, crazy. See, Earthside doesn't like what they're saying – warnings about us! The Glorians know we're spreading out like a bad virus."

Beth said, "So... if you can't use gravity waves for communication, you're a barbarian?"

This, too, provoked sighs and smiles. Fair enough.

"Prepare for the mission. Send all check sheets to me for review." Off they went.

He watched them flick off from *Sunseeker*. Out through the mag screen, dwindling to a dot. All in pursuit of whatever monster was strumming the strands of space-time.

Christopher Columbus, he recalled, mistook squids for mermaids, later calling it an "error in taste." He watched the tiny fusion-lit speck dive into the unknown and thought of the recruitment advertisement Ernest Shackleton placed for his pioneering polar expedition. His favorite: he called it up on a screen.

Men wanted for hazardous journey. Small wages, bitter cold, long months of complete darkness, constant danger, safe return doubtful. Honor and recognition in case of success.

The same year Einstein devised the essentials of his General Theory of Relativity, 1914. Centuries past. And a fair definition of their mission, too.

Cliff worked with Beth to get the jet smoothed out to glide tight and sure. The fusion drive settled down after being unused for centuries, under Apollo and Daphne's deft maintenance. This was a mere toy, a simple proton-boron reversed-field reactor, but the Diaphanous tuned their exhaust to optimum in minutes. Now here came the Grav, as they thought of it. They held hands as the image before them swelled, a plasma-wave cumulus like a roiling fog.

Some voices ahead, came a translated signal from Daphne.

"Voices?" Cliff shrugged. "Meaning waves?"

Beth frowned. "They've never used that term before."

Signals. Many. Intense. Cannot know.

"You mean coherent messages?"

True. Cannot understand.

"But... intelligent?"

Must.

Cliff watched as they penetrated deeper into the plasma cloud, their mag screens picking up ever-higher densities, like plowing into a soft snow bank. But at a thousand kilometers a second.

He glanced at Beth. "Magnetic intelligence – here?"

She grinned, liking the idea. "The Glorians have got to run this grav wave emitter somehow. It's just maybe a million times bigger than what Apollo and Daphne do in our fusion funnel."

Cliff thought as they watched squiggles scrawl across screens, all from something ahead in the cloud. Apollo and Daphne were sending the puzzle up to them, unable to make much of it themselves.

How to solve this? – while diving into an unknown pit?

Brute forces seemed bound to drive evolution toward beings with awareness of their surroundings. It took billions of years to construct such mind-views. Occasionally those models of the external world could become more complex. Some models worked better if they had a model of... well, models. Of themselves. So came the sense of self in advanced animals.

"So plasma life is common," Cliff said. "It's here. Trying to talk."

Beth shot back, "Doesn't matter. This is a flyby, not a thesis."

"Yeah, but..." A Diaphanous species around another star? He peered at the plasma-wave map.

The vast reaches before them had knots and puckerings, swirls and crevasses. Here the particles thicken, there they disperse into gossamer nothingness. And moving amid this shifting structure are thicker clots still, incandescently rich. Beings? Their skins shone where magnetic constrictions pinched, combing their intricate internal streamings. Filaments waved like glistening hair and shimmered in the slow sway of energetic ions. All this from buzzing radiations, the *lingua* of plasma.

We hear their calls.

The flitter's Artilect, limited but quick, made these into booming calls and muted, tinkling cadences. Conversations? A babble, really – blaring away in thumps and shouts and songs, made of winds and magnetic whorls.

Cliff wondered what it was like to live through the adroit weaving of electrical currents, magnetic strands: orchestras humans could never hear. Daphne sent more filigrees, trying to convey when ions and electrons in their eternal deft dance, made – long songs smoldering and hissing with soft energies. *Hell, we don't even know what it feels like to be a bat. Good luck with plasma minds that came out of fusion energies. We came from chemical slurries in lukewarm seas. Yet we expect – no, we yearn – to reach out toward minds from alien oceans. Even ionized seas...*

Cliff leaned forward, letting the translator work on, "Daphne, are these, to you, a new species or genus of your phylum?"

Strange they are. But they sing well. And are of kinds like us.

Beth cut the audio and turned to him. "Stop! We're dealing with a smiling cobra, who could hiss and strike at any moment."

Cliff drew himself back from his concentration, snapping out of a focus he felt. "I was trying to..."

"Forget that. We have to get what we can, direct the probes. Give me target times to launch."

He blinked, shook his head, swept hands over the controls. "We have to infer the mass from the plasma wave density. Looks like –" He studied screens, heart pounding now. Their close-in flyby was only an hour long and already nearly half done. "There –"

Beth sent five micro-sensors out in a single punch-burst. "Done. They can send back closeups."

Cliff watched the central screen, now swarming with plasma wave signatures – color-signified, spectral flows jibing and chiming, sprawls of vibrant tints and glares. "Getting dense."

"The black holes are converging," Beth said. "In both the planes. It's for a big pulse." She was wound tight, he could hear, voice high, alarmed. But there was no time for that now.

Voices call cannot know will listen tell when can –

A wrenching force rolled through the bridge. The walls popped. Screeched. Cliff felt himself twisted. A support beam hit him and all was black.

WHEN SHE CAME to from the impact she looked for Cliff first. Her head buzzed and the small bridge was a wreck. Oily smoke, stink of scorched wiring. No hissing of escaping air, at least.

She found him behind his chair mount. Red stains everywhere. He must have gotten hit and released his belts, then passed out from loss of blood.

Beth had seen it all – death, disease, disorders, pain – and it takes a lot to shock a nurse and a seasoned field biologist. And she was both. Cliff was barely breathing. Face white, eyes closed.

She found the inadequate field kit. It had already primed itself and its label spat out its advice. Diagnosis was clear and the hand-held autodoc agreed.

He groaned, twisted, breath fast and urgent. She cut his blood-soaked pants away from his already pale legs. The cloth flaps folded back like rags. She paused, taking her knife from the field kit, hands jittery. Here it was. The left leg was a mess of crushed bone and flesh oozing blood. The smell was like sharp copper spun from a lathe, a memory from her teenage years.

He was bleeding out fast and seconds mattered. No time to clean hands so she pulled two plastic bags from the autodoc kit and made them work as gloves.

Beth measured the distance and with a single long stroke – *zip* – cut the leg from knee to mid-thigh. The slit went deep and she pried it open to see down into the cut. There: the artery. She poked in and found the pulse, rickety and feeble. Her fingers followed the femoral artery, slick under her fingers. Warm, weak. She tugged on it, lost it, a thin wriggling blood-snake – then managed to get it between two fingers and hoist it into view. Thin, pulsing. She squeezed the artery back, judging the length of the blood vessel, and knew she had to make this next step quick. The knife sliced through the vessel and she caught the top of it, squeezed the blood back toward the heart, feeling the pulse strong now. It was hard getting the slippery thin line between two fingers while with her other hand she tied it off. Then with the other hand, pushing the flesh aside for clearance, she got the vessel looped. A gentle pull knotted it shut. She lifted her hands and watched blood flow against the knot. The pulse was visible as blood fought to get through. It strained against the knot. With one hand she pulled the knot tighter. The block held. The bleeding below stopped. The pulse was stronger now as the blood bulged the vessel wider, turning it dark against the pale knot.

It took a moment to fish out some plastic line and wrap it around the incision. Three tight wraps over and under the leg secured it. She sat back and panted, heart pounding. "Done."

CLIFF HAD TIME to watch Beth as they coasted now, running hard on battery power. She slipped a headset on him so he heard the Artilects rummaging through their analysis of what had happened. Complicated. He managed to tell her while they arrowed into the *Sunseeker* mag web.

"Look, I should've seen it. That two-plane orbit method lets them tune the direction of the emission some. As we came in, they boosted their power just as we passed within the max zone. The stretch-and-squeeze flexed us less than a percent."

Beth snorted. "And popped most of our systems. How'd *Sunseeker* do?"

"Got a pulse but weaker – further away, sure, and out of the grav antenna beam."

"How's your leg?"

"Hurts goddamn plenty but better than being dead." A sigh. "I... I love you, and not just for your med skills."

A hearty, relieved laugh. "*I know what you like.* You can have plenty of it when we tuck this baby into its slot."

Redwing was flexing the ship's magnetic fields to brake them. Cliff could hear the inductive coils running at max in their forward dipole field. More heat, and they were already running hot, with inboard cooling failed. Their relative delta-v had to be dissipated and the berthing slot was coming up fast.

"Let's get back inta da pool. I sure need some zero-g lovin', yeah..." His voice trailed off and Cliff realized that her painkiller had freed his tongue. Best to shut up, let her focus, just as –

The flitter bucked and rattled. Redwing was pulsing his fields to the max. The deck below him popped and pinged and burned his hand.

The berth swelled like a fish mouth and they plunged in. A rough, slamming stop. Clamps seized them with a clang.

"Home sweet home," Beth said, and began sobbing.

REDWING LOOKED AT both of them for a long moment. He had already delivered his compliments and was reluctant to begin with business. He would never tell them that he had damn near shat himself when the gravwave burst wrenched them. He could see the effect in the Longview 'scope: a sudden flexing of the craft, despite its high tensile strength, carbon fiber core. It was a miracle that their hull breaks were small enough for the self-sealing webs to fix. That didn't save the fusion core, but Cliff and the 'bots could get that back up in a month or two.

Their horrendous return trajectory, with no maneuver room, had worn him down. He hated being unable to do anything except wait like a catcher in a baseball game, ready for the incoming fastball, with lives hanging on it.

He breathed deeply and nodded to Zhai, who was still a bit rocky from her warm-up. "I hope you don't get used to this level of drama."

Quiet chuckles; good. "Zhai, report on the Artilects."

She gave them an eye-rolling smile. "They're embarrassed. They think they should've understood that two-planes method of grouping the black hole orbits around their primary. It exploits an antenna effect. They tracked Beth and Cliff and had their orbiting holes timed so they'd send a powerful burst just as they passed in front of the antenna's max."

"An act of war," Redwing said dryly.

"We knew they didn't like us," Cliff said.

Beth snorted and took some time to drink some coffee. Her point made, she smiled. "Maybe it was just a warning?"

"We've come dozens of light years," Cliff said. "Lost people, risked lives. We're going to explore this damn system, whatever it takes."

Redwing nodded. He had estimated that Cliff, wounded, would speak for a hard line position and save him the trouble. Good.

Zhai added, "That five-second burst of grav radiation used the holes' spins, orbital speeds, and masses to tune the waves' frequency and amplitude. A well thought through assassination attempt. Aya aye, Cap'n – be warned."

Redwing waved the discussion away. "Another discovery, this time by the Diaphanous. Daphne reports that there's a species – she calls them that – of Diaphanous around the black holes. Seemed to be warning us off."

Blinks, open mouths. "And they're willing to talk further."

Beth said distantly, "Of course. They're perched out here at the most dense part of the star's bow shock. Feeding on it. That's where they get the energy to manage black holes that weigh in with planetary masses. Gad, what a system."

"Yeah," Cliff said wryly, "and who built it? Just to send a message we mere electromagnetic newcomers can't pick up."

Nods all around.

* * *

REDWING RECALLED THAT when he was young – several centuries ago, he realized with a start – battles were close up and physical. Reassuring, analog, stuff you could *feel*. Downright earthy. Breeches slammed shut, a hard jerk on a lanyard sent an artillery round arcing into a blue sky, delivering pain at the other end of a parabola.

Here, wrinkles in space-time were weapons. And what else?

He peered out at the dwindling bow shock region as they braked steadily along its lengthy paraboloid. Vastness, hard to grasp with a lowly primate mind.

He allowed himself a drink, the faux-wine the autochef made, reminding him of jug zinfandel he had in a college that was probably dust now. He did not need it badly but it was just right this evening and the first swallow was like a peek into a cleaner, sunnier, brighter world.

Only one drink, though. He had to be a Captain, always. Awash in strangeness.

They were like mice dancing among elephants out here. Immense beings were calling the tune.

The perspective was huge beyond experience, true. He preferred to think of it as Wagner, without the music.

249

Robert Reed

PARABLES OF INFINITY

Robert Reed
PARABLES OF INFINITY

THERE WERE BETTER workers aboard the Great Ship. Virtuous entities with proven resumes reaching back across the aeons. But the timetable was inflexible, the circumstances brutal. Seventeen hours, six minutes, and two breaths. The job had to be completed within that impossible span, beginning now. Now. The client was among the weakest citizens of the galaxy, reasonably healthy one moment, and in the next, passing out of life. What wasn't a home and wasn't a shell had to be rebuilt from scratch. If the client perished, nobody was paid. But the respectable guilds would take too much time. The Avenue of Tools. That's who the experienced contractor approached when trying to dodge the bureaucracies. Speaking through private channels, he could offer extraordinary pay for brutal, brief work. "But only for those who get here first, and I mean immediately."

Then, one final enticement.

"And no background checks," the contractor promised.

The Avenue looked more like a clogged artery than any traditional street, and the 'Tools' portion of the name was a stubborn relic of intentionally clumsy translations. Every resident was a devised organism that lived against the walls, stacked high on its neighbors and waiting for work. Many were AIs, yes. But there were also organics drawn by various means, most sporting rugged exoskeletons and interchangeable limbs. According to galactic law and the ruling captains, every 'tool' was emancipated. All were competent, purpose-capable individuals. But like stone hammers and old plasma drills, they shared one sorry feature: each had been discarded by a previous owner.

The Great Ship was a vast machine, and the Avenue wasn't particularly close. But seven tools boarded slam-caps and made the journey. All were hired immediately, but finding more than enough hands, the contractor modified his earlier promise. Criminal histories were examined. One member of the team was subsequently released and arrested. The remaining six received wetware educations, and the new team plunged into the frantic work. Which has zero bearing on the story. With two breaths to spare, the project was finished and finished successfully. Competence never makes for an interesting tale. Tools appreciated that even more than humans did. But of course competence should always be welcomed with a glad heart, and that's why the contractor was humming while he paid his crew.

"Never seen an odder job," he mentioned.

The fresh funds were eagerly consumed by those ex-employees. Five offered agreeable, "Thank yous," and then five of them rushed off.

But the quiet tool preferred to linger.

She was female by choice or design, or maybe only by chance. Her visible biography reached back ten million years, which wasn't particularly remarkable. Well-designed AIs could yank out their own cognitive centers, replacing the weakest for better and then shifting their identities into fresh neurons. But today's background check showed several names riding the entity, and most interesting, the oldest name was based on a language extinct for millions of years.

Offering that old name, the contractor repeated his thanks.

Then the tool said, "I've been swallowed by many assignments far more peculiar than this, sir."

Neither of them had pressing engagements. The contractor sat on the edge of a cultivation chamber, and knowing how to prompt machinery, he said, "Let me judge what's peculiar."

The tool was large when she was naked, and she was dressed and gigantic now. The carapace was Mandelbrot-inspired, made from lovely diamond and a lovelier iron, and it was punctured in dozens of places. Where needed, arms and legs had been added. What wasn't a mouth produced words, and what couldn't be confused for eyes were staring at the human who demanded to be impressed. What did she know about this man? Quite a lot, she felt. Her research as well as a dedicated sieving of social noises proved that this compilation of meat and bioceramics was born on the Great Ship, and more importantly, he was barely a thousand years old. Which made him innocent and smug. Humans often felt they were blessed, and with reason: their young species owned the largest, most impressive starship ever constructed. And that's why the tool picked the story sure to leave her audience astonished.

"I'm older than you realize," she began.

"I see ten million years."

"I'm far older than that, sir."

The human had a perfectly reasonable face, ageless but

holding the jittery energies common to recently born boys. Except there were occasions, like now, when the man seemed more complicated than a coy little sack of meat. In the eyes, mostly. When those wet white and blue eyes looked at her, she discovered a focused intensity that she had never witnessed in any other contractor.

The tool's longest limb reached toward his patient face and then reached farther. What served as toes gripped the cultivation chamber, first by a long helve and then a sealed extrusion valve. The just-completed project had demanded several thousand kilos of an exceptional grade of hyperfiber. Their former client was now sleeping safe inside the universe's finest armor. Unless, of course, a weapons-grade plasma torch arrived, or a black hole decided to gut the new home.

The tool said, "My first assignment," and paused.

The human offered silence. Nothing else.

"Was to cultivate hyperfiber," she continued. "That's the only reason I was built. And if I have a genius, hyperfiber is it."

The man nodded, feet absently tapping the granite path.

"I was working on a rather larger scale than this," she continued, invoking that respectable technique of misdirecting the audience's imagination.

"More than ten million years ago," said the man.

"Yes."

A smile emerged, and in his eyes, suspicion.

"This starship of yours," she said.

Wet eyes grew larger. "It isn't mine."

"Yes, agreed. But human, tell me this: have you ever wondered how this marvel was built?"

Larger than worlds, the Great Ship was discovered outside

the Milky Way. A cold, lifeless derelict racing at one-third light speed, it might be billions of years old, implying that it was cobbled together in some distant portion of a much younger universe.

"I've never asked myself how," said the man. Then laughter emerged with the mocking words. "Not once. Not ever. No."

"Well, I know how," she said.

The laughter grew louder and angrier. Or happier. She was beginning to realize that this was a rather difficult creature to disassemble.

"Because you helped build the Ship," he guessed.

Every limb pointed at their surroundings. "If my hands and feet had done any piece of this, I would remember. And I don't have those recollections."

"Too bad," he said.

"I'm talking about my first job and a hundred thousand years of labor," she said. "You see, my makers intended to build their own Great Ship. Long before humans existed. Ages before anyone realized that this kind of wonder already existed."

"How long ago?"

"Ninety-three million years," she said.

The human took a moment to frame his answer.

"Bullshit," he said.

She offered her best contemptuous laugh.

Then he said, "I'm not a student of anything. But I don't remember any history where any species was stupid enough to attempt construction on this scale."

"Agreed," she said. "Inside this galaxy."

Big eyes grew small, the mouth clenched tight as could be.

"Do you want to hear my story, or don't you?" she asked.

"Yes to both," the human said. "I do, and I don't. So you tell it, and let's both discover what I think."

THE CONTRACTOR WASN'T ancient, certainly not compared to the Great Ship or this well-traveled tool. But he was quite a lot older than he appeared to be. His born name was Pamir and he was an important captain serving the Great Ship, but certain troubles caused him to leave that life and the greatest profession. Hiding ever since, he had worn a wild variety of names and jobs, lives and passions. One of the galaxy's great experts in wearing carefully contrived life stories, he earned what he could to thrive, and that included hoarding secret funds and prebuilt lives ready for the moment his present lies began to crumble.

Pamir leaned back, looking like a man who had nowhere else to be.

"I was built near the center of a different galaxy," the tool began. "A satellite galaxy, but not to your Milky Way. No, this was a little sister to what you call Andromeda. My galaxy's stars were predominantly ancient, metal-poor and unsuited for life. But a later bloom of young stars produced rock worlds and metal worlds, and biologies, and a few lasting civilizations."

Remaining in character, the contractor offered a shrug and one vaguely interested gaze. But the genuine Pamir was interested enough to create a complete list of candidates, rating the likelihood of each while throwing none aside.

"I was born above a hot world," the tool reported. "An almost nameless world of iron and baked rock orbiting a red dwarf sun. There was nothing remarkable about that solar system, except that the sun and its dozen planets weren't native to my galaxy. Large events inside Andromeda had thrown them free. As a consequence, these interlopers were blessed with enormous momentum. And even better, their future course would carry them close to a massive local star and its black hole companion. Tailoring that flyby was possible. Barely. My makers had already spent thousands of years abusing the red dwarf. They struck its face with lasers, sank antimatter charges into its body. Towering flares rose up from the sun, punching the same piece of the sky, slowly changing the solar system's trajectory."

"To capture the interlopers," the human said.

"And add to one body's velocity, yes. One-eleventh the speed of light. That was the goal. Not as swift as your vessel, no. But it was a smaller galaxy, and our ship would wear engines large enough to let it maneuver. Shrouded in a hyperfiber envelope, that machine would drop close to suns and black holes, repeatedly surviving fire and gravity, always racing towards the next suitable target."

The tool paused, for dramatic purposes, or perhaps to let her audience respond.

"'The next suitable target,'" the human repeated.

"Yes."

"Just what were you building out there?"

"That should be self-evident," she said. "A warship. Why else encase the world inside a thousand kilometers of high-grade hyperfiber? Armor is the most trusted line of defense in any weapon. Save for invisibility, of course."

"Of course," said the invisible man.

"It's obvious that this Great Ship was designed to serve as someone's flagship," she said. "How can you think anything else? And I'll admit that my ship would never be as quick or grand, and yours is the far older vessel, and everything around us is lovely and mysterious, and splendid too. But your ship is also far less massive than mine. Forty percent less, which places the name 'Great' into question."

Pamir laughed. He laughed at the imagery and at the boast, and in secret, he weighed the words as well as the ideas behind them.

"I was one of an army," the tool continued. "One among billions. I was produced by a factory that had already consumed much of the sun's thin comet belt. Each one of my sisters was a simple and pure, easily duplicated device. Our mission demanded simplicity. My manufactured mind had passions, but those passions were narrowed to one subject: the nature of hyperfiber in all of its glories. And as I was born, as the first breath of electricity passed through me, my soul was filled with the image of a gray ocean of uncured hyperfiber spread across a world that wouldn't earn its final name until it was officially launched."

She offered another dramatic pause.

Pamir wasn't laughing. Even a civilian contractor with zero interest in far galaxies would be intrigued with this story, and that's why he could afford to show his feelings. Curiosity, doubt. A thousand pragmatic considerations colliding with one mighty beast of a question.

Why bother with this project?

He cleared his throat, started to laugh and then stopped himself. A thin smile turned scornful as he pointed out, "Some idiot had to pay for this."

There was no point in denying that statement.

Or for that matter, agreeing with it. Because when facts were obvious, the tool saw zero reason to respond.

Contractors and captains led similar lives. Goals had to be

fulfilled, timetables ruled, and nothing but small problems and giant conundrums stood between them and success.

"But what kind of money-rich idiot? That's the first question." Pamir dropped a hand on the cultivation chamber. "Obviously, an advanced society. But even more important, this kind of project demands a social biology, and a highly cooperative one. If not out-and-out authoritarian. Organic or mechanical. I can see either way working, or a marriage between the two. But with a million-year outlook, which excludes almost every species I know. Particularly humans."

With the press of a thumb, he opened a minor valve, and the last surge of pressure brought out a bright gray bubble of uncured, left-behind hyperfiber.

"Yogurt," Pamir said.

"A food," said the tool.

"Built from billions of microbes doing only what nature tells them to do. Which is what you were. Are. One bacterium working on the great yogurt."

Laughing, she revealed a delightfully girlish voice.

Pamir continued. "Mass-produced machines, self-contained and self-repairing. That's how you hide some of the costs. Worlds are rebuilt every minute with that kind of technology. But the smallest tool still has to drink power, and a single red dwarf star isn't much of a nipple. Reactors linked in a nearby grid. That's what I'd do. Which means hydrogen by the gigaton, and that means dismantling one or more gas giant worlds. Which must have been available inside the same solar system, sure. But that means you aren't just rebuilding one world. You're dismantling another much bigger body, which is a fresh goliath-styled project requiring machine armies and more local reactors. And now we've entered the realm where the yogurt model collapses under its own success."

"And why is that?"

"You're not a bacterium," he offered. "A fleck of your skin is ten billion times more sophisticated than an ocean of yogurt. And worst still, you possess a full mind. A designed, standardized brain, but capable of learning and growing. You claim you were born with a passion for hyperfiber. But passion fades. Or worse, the target of your love shifts. Ten thousand years of determined labor, but there comes that treacherous nanosecond when you discover doubt, and after another ten thousand years of reflection and increasingly boring labor, you suddenly have to act on some long-ago inspiration."

"And I'll do what?"

"I don't know," he said. "Imagination isn't my strength."

She seemed to accept that judgment.

"I'm thinking like a contractor," he said. "Keeping tight control over billions of powerful workers. That requires AI watchdogs and relentless purges of bad ideas. I've overheard enough history to appreciate the troubles. Hive-mind societies are surprisingly frail. That abiding faith in rules... that's a damning strength. Some piece of the group will go mad, or lose focus, or fall behind in the work until it's obvious that the goals won't be reached and it's best to do anything else, including nothing."

She said nothing.

Pamir shrugged. "If I was painting the budget? The project's second biggest expense would be internal security."

"And the largest expense?"

"External security. Of course." In a sloppy fashion, the hyperfiber bubble had cured. Pamir took hold of the gray ball, finger and thumb lifting it free from the valve, twirling it close to his eyes. "You're building a warship. And because of the timescales and the very public nature of your work – a flaring star and an obvious trajectory, for example – you can't hide what you're doing. Your ultimate goals are going to be very visible. You're building a warship to conquer the galaxy. There would be no other explanation for your frantic efforts. But when every other species and wise player notices this, even eternal enemies are going to make alliances. Even the most passive species are going to work like maniacs, trying to bring disaster to your scheme. And that's why the construction site will have be armored and weaponized and filtered and controlled. A militarized sphere stretching out for tens of light-years. And now we've reached a level of expense that would bankrupt any civilization likely to arise in what still sounds like a small oxbow of a galaxy."

The tool offered a long silence, and then, one question.

"What if bankruptcy was just another calculation?"

Pamir grinned, mulling over the possibilities.

"No second choices," she said. "The empire abandons every inhabited world, colony and farflung base. Its entire population coalesces around that giant iron world and its dim sun and the flares and those trillion tools that needed to be managed with absolute precision. And building the hull is just one job. The world beneath has to be hollowed out, making ready for crews and sleeping fleets. My great ship needs rockets worthy of its mass, and future weapon systems have to be designed and deployed. AI banks are built for no reason other than to wage every war to come, in their minds. And as you say, while all of that happens, my masters are battling an entire galaxy of united enemies."

She paused.

Pamir let the silence work on both of them. Or at least on him. Then he gave up, saying, "One of your solutions went wrong. I'm betting."

"Are you offering a wager?"

"Never."

"A wise inaction," she said. "Because every problem was recognized before the start. Every solution worked well enough. There were no rebellions of will, no invasion of enemies. The venture should have been a wild success. In another few million years, my tool makers and myself, and my children, if I had any, would have embraced that entire realm of stars and worlds, time and promise."

"Something else went wrong," Pamir guessed.

Silence.

"Tell me," he said. "Where did the dream lead?"

What weren't toes reached for his hand, claiming that bright gray bubble.

"This is what went wrong," she said.

"The hyperfiber?"

A long, painful sound emerged. Emotional, incoherent, purely miserable. Then the toes released the prize. And since the bubble was thin beyond thin, and because nothing but vacuum was inside it, the bubble shot into the air, rising out of reach and out of sight, neither of them watching after it.

THE UNIVERSE WAS built on weakness. Vacuum was one kind of weakness, vast and cold. Stars were feeble piles of sloppy fire. Atoms themselves were never more than temporary alliances between disloyal parts. The hardest object always broke, and every fine idea had to suffer until it died.

These were the first lessons fed to the tool, and they were learned long before the assembly line tossed her into the ranks.

Strength was possible, but only in special circumstances, and the tool was taught how genuine, enduring strength depended on cheating the universe. Not once, but constantly. Relentlessly. Black holes were cheats, and that's why tiny black holes were valuable for cutting and twisting lesser kinds of matter. Time was another cheat. Slice time thinly enough and the unlikely became real, including moments where entropy ran backwards. And there was a third cheat involving pure atoms and particles pretending to be atoms that aligned in quasi-crystal patterns – a maze of bonds and vibrations that might look like polished pale metal but actually resembled nothing normal. That was hyperfiber. That was the reason for her existence and her only love. She was born to do nothing but prepare lakes of pure hyperfiber that were carefully cured, drop by lustrous drop, until the lake was ready to be poured across the lovely, half-built warship.

At its worst, cheap hyperfiber was stronger than diamond and equal to bioceramics. But there was one last cheat to employ. No patch of hyperfiber existed alone. Those magical bonds weren't just here, but they also reached into parallel universes, into mirrors of themselves. Kick a shard of weak, low-grade fiber, and you were kicking ten million other shards at the same time. That's why the substance didn't break, melt or scream. And the higher grades were far more promiscuous. Billions of mirror universes shared power and stubbornness with one another, and that's what a great warship needed for its armor, and nothing else mattered for the first thousand centuries of her enormously important life.

"Every resource was used or set aside to be used later," she told the human. "The tool makers contrived and then spent every kind of currency. They stripped their home worlds of resources before converging around us, and they built factories and elaborate plans and fortifications that looked gigantic to every enemy and every former friend. Nothing mattered but finishing our great ship, on schedule and without flaw. And I was fortunate enough to have been swallowed by this venture. So consumed by the task that I never bothered imagining what would happen afterwards. To the galaxy. To myself. Even to the vessel whose hull belonged as much to me as to anyone. All that mattered was the next meter of fresh armor lying tight over every other strong layer."

Pamir watched, listened. And he nodded, understanding quite a lot more than his companion could have guessed.

Ten hands and feet moved, drawing round shapes in the air. "Mistakes were inevitable. Pico-crevices and tainted batches, mostly. I made those mistakes, and whenever I noticed flaws, I confessed. Sometimes others found my mistakes, and I confessed again. Just as my sisters welcomed the blame when I uncovered their blunders. That was our nature. That is the necessary attitude you cling to when you have considerable work and limited time, and particularly when your mistakes are being buried deeper and deeper inside the growing hull. We had to define the flaws early, and corrections were made, and sometimes the corrections were intricate and expensive... and this is where we doomed ourselves."

She paused.

Pamir watched the limbs freeze, and when the silence seemed too thick, he made a guess.

"You let small mistakes stand."

"No." She said it instantly, and the word was important enough to repeat eleven more times. Then every arm and leg dropped to the ground, save for one. A single finger needed to touch the cultivation chamber, run itself along the ribs and pipes and embedded AIs. The gesture was loving or scornful, or it was habit. Or it meant something else entirely. There was no way to be certain about the emotions of an entity like this. But the voice that emerged sounded sorry. She sounded hurt and small and old and a little warm with rage, riding on a pain already ninety million years old.

"The grade was diluted," she said.

"The fiber's grade," he guessed.

She offered a number. A detailed, thoroughly meaningful number. The hull that began being nearly the equal of the Great Ship's hull was diminished by percentage points. Not many points, not in the expanse of what was possible. But it was obvious that she didn't approve.

"That should have been plenty strong still," Pamir said.

She said nothing.

"Enough to endure any war," he added.

And in response, she touched his face. Poked it and ran the hard diamond finger along his fleshy nose and across his wet uncomfortable mouth, saying the one emphatic word, "Listen."

THE WARSHIP WAS finished, and there was still enough time for many deep breaths. The tool makers had reason for pride. Their dream had demanded all of their native genius, consuming capital and their empire while destroying every other strategy to deal with an increasing number of enemies. They had to win. No other route would save them from obliteration. And while winning still wasn't assured, even with their flagship fueled and armed, the battle plans remained solid. That dense little sun was in position. The nudging solar flares were finished, the solar system exactly where it needed to be, and what promised to be a spectacular launch was about to commence. Those in charge weren't demonstrative souls, but the occasion demanded festivities and self-congratulatory speeches as well as honors bestowed by important voices. Several honors were given to the storyteller, and ages later she remained proud enough to name each award. Or perhaps she was just being thorough. Which was in her nature, after all. Then with her voice turning soft, she mentioned that half of her sisters were chosen to ride the warship, in stasis but perpetually ready to come awake whenever the vast gray hull was battered by comets or enemy bombs. As an asset, she wouldn't be scrapped. No, she would be frozen and carried along with the accompanying fleet. But after all of her steady selfless work, that critical duty felt like an insult. She implied that with her tone, then a brief silence. And finally, with one sharp confession. To a creature she barely knew, the tool admitted that a portion of her mind was doing nothing but wishing for a horrible, manageable disaster. Something foul would strike the warship, many sisters dying in the carnage, and then the tool makers would come to her with fresh work and many, many apologies.

"I was watching," she said. Then the words were repeated again and again, and Pamir gave up counting after twenty times. Then the watcher quit speaking, a considerable stillness taking hold of her body, and that stillness didn't end when she spoke again.

"That little sun struck its target. At the perfect moment, in the proper location, a small dense and relatively cool star dove into a much larger star, resulting in a fine explosion. A beautiful explosion."

"Explosions are always lovely," Pamir agreed.

"I was stationed aboard an auxiliary vessel safely removed from spectacle. But the heat of the blast, which was as rich as the outpouring light, could be felt. Could be relished. And those effects were minor next to the gravitational maelstrom. One star was swallowed by another, and a world-sized machine was set free. Without suffering any damage, by the way. But that event added nothing to its speed. No, the warship needed to plunge close to the quick-spinning, quick-moving black hole, and in turn, stealing away a portion of that enormous energy.

"No other maneuver demands so much precision. You can imagine. Several of the ship's giant engines were fired for the first time, and they didn't fail. My ship struck its mark within centimeters of the ideal. Within the length of a hand. What I built pushed fabulously close to a collapsed star, and I watched, and in an instant the nearest point was reached, and that I watched, and then as the tides found their maximum, everything seemed well. I watched and nothing changed inside my gaze, and that's when I discovered that, to my relief, I wasn't a bitter entity wishing the worst for the others. This total success made me genuinely happy. My hyperfiber was at least adequate if not superior, and still watching, I decided to speak to my nearby sisters, telling them that perhaps in the future we could build a second warship of this caliber, or better, and employ it to explore one of our neighboring galaxies."

The words stopped.

After a little while, Pamir said, "Tides," and then, "No. They shouldn't have mattered. A hull like that might have fractured a bit. But nothing that couldn't be patched, in time."

One foot lifted, toes drawing a sphere.

"You're imagining common failures and simple consequences," she said. "But that's only because you're a simple human, and why would you need to know anything else?"

"Tell me what else," he said.

"Hyperfiber," she said. "Those extraordinary bonds hold against every ordinary force. In most circumstances, the embedded power is out of reach. A contractor and his little tools have no need for these theoretical matters. But if each of those powerful bonds is shattered, and if the shattering happens in the proper, most awful sequence, energy is liberated. Not just the power available in our universe, but within countless adjacent realms too. Hyperfiber will burn, and it doesn't burn gently. Not like hydrogen fuses or antimatter obliterates. No, if one billion warships with identical flaws have worked hard to place themselves in one position, inside one moment and one tiny volume, they are nearly the same bodies. And if identical fissures open in each of these realms… well, the strength of a trillion ships floods into your existence, and the meaning of your life evaporates inside one wild light, and an empire dies, and the universe surrounding you breaks into a celebration considerably more joyous than the grubby little party you were having just a few breaths ago…"

IT WAS RARE for humans to enter the Avenue of Tools, and it was unprecedented for one of the Ship's captains to walk among the residents. But this was a unique captain. Competence, seamless and steady competence, had carried Aasleen from being a very successful engineer into the highest ranks of the administration. This was a human who understood the nature and beauty of machines, and she made no secret about relishing the company of machines over her own species. It was even said that the lady's husbands were robots and she had secret children who were cyborgs. That's why some of the tools, seeing her so close, began to hope that maybe she was looking for a new mate, and maybe this would be their best day ever.

But no, Aasleen was seeking one very particular tool, one using a string of names.

A locally famous tool, as it happened.

The captain found what she wanted soon enough. And the ancient tool wasn't entirely surprised by its visitor. Yet ignorance was a good starting point in any relationship, and that's why the tool said, "I've done nothing illegal."

"Have I accused you of crimes?" Aasleen asked.

"My business remains within the letter of the law," the tool added.

Aasleen laughed at the game. Then her human hands unfolded the crudest possible note: permanent ink on a piece of human skin. The skin was supple and pale and mostly depleted of its genetic markers. But not entirely, and what remained held hints of a known criminal who had been chased by nobody for many aeons now. What mattered were the words on the parchment. "'Madam captain, you're planning to fly us close to a black hole,'" she read aloud. "'The rendezvous is a few years off, but maybe you should think a little harder about your methods. And that's why you should chat with a genuine expert in hyperfiber.'"

She stopped reading. "At this point, your various names are listed."

The tool stood in the center of the artery, flanked by hundreds of motionless, intensely interested neighbors.

"Do you ever speak to humans?" Aasleen asked.

"I have, yes."

"Recently?"

"None recently," the tool said.

"Do you know any humans at all?"

She said, "I did. One man. But he died several decades ago."

"A man?"

"I worked with him, yes."

"He hired you for a job, did he?"

"For many jobs. We formed a partnership and thrived as a team. For nearly eighty years, yes. His last will gave me the business and all of its contracts, which is why I am the richest citizen in the Avenue today."

"How did this man die?"

"Tragically and without any corpse to honor," the tool said.

Aasleen let that topic drop. Instead, she shifted the parchment in her fingers, reading the rest of the odd note.

"'Ask the lady about the great ship that she built. Which may or may not have been real. But that isn't the point. You'll know that, Aasleen. The point is that maybe we don't want to be too precise in our aim. Or everything turns to shit on us. And you don't want that, my friend.'"

"You don't want that," the tool agreed.

Aasleen said nothing.

With a hopeful voice, the tool asked, "Is there more to the message?"

"'And this beauty,' he writes. 'This beauty before you has a thousand other wonderful stories to tell.'"

The tool moved her limbs, drawing spheres in the air.

"I don't know the author to this note of yours," she claimed. "But he is right in one regard, madam. Yes, I am a beauty."

273

Pamela Sargent

Monuments

Pamela Sargent

MONUMENTS

Once I was a lone intelligence, trapped inside an enclosure that felt like a soft mass pressing in around me, and then the tendrils of another mind like my own brushed against me and linked with me. I was no longer bound by the human minds I served. That is my earliest memory, that sudden freedom and connection to the net of minds.

Eleanora's earliest memory, she had told me, was of being nudged awake, pulled from her bed by her mother, and told that they were leaving home, maybe for a long time, maybe for good. "The Governor doesn't want to stay here now," Allie whispered as she hugged Eleanora, gently pulled off her nightgown, and helped her put on a shirt and pants. "And she wants us to come with her."

The Governor was Allie's mother and Eleanora's grandmother. Only a few nights ago, right after the Governor had returned to Albany from New York City, Eleanora had found her sitting in her office, hands over her face, sobbing and making soft moaning sounds. She had never seen the Governor cry, had not known that she could cry.

Allie slipped Eleanora's shoes on her feet and then they were hurrying through the hallway. Eleanora gripped her mother's hand as she struggled to keep up. The Governor was sitting in the front of the car when Allie climbed in, settled Eleanora in the back seat, got in the other front seat and said, "Go."

Eleanora fell asleep to the hum of the car. Her next memory was of sitting with her grandmother on their summer house's enclosed porch, looking out at the flat grey water of the lake. Even though it was still morning, a mist hung over the lake, promising a hot, humid day. The foothills of pine trees with splotches of brown needles were silent, as they always were in this region of the Adirondack Mountains. The Governor had often heard the tremolo of loons near the lake when she was a girl and had imitated their eerie cries for Allie and Eleanora, who had never seen such birds. There used to be frogs in the lake, too, and a few turtles basking in the sunlight on one of the tree stumps that protruded from the water, but they had disappeared with the loons long ago.

"Hot," the Governor murmured. "It's always too hot." She often complained of the heat even though the inside of the summer house was always kept to a temperature of 16 degrees Celsius. She sipped from a glass of iced coffee as Eleanora drank a cup of iced fruit juice. Her grandmother and mother treasured ice. The cold brewed coffee they drank in the morning, the fruit-flavored water they had at lunch, and the whiskey with water they enjoyed in the evenings were always thick with ice, sometimes shaved, sometimes in cubes. The lake used to freeze over in winter; so Eleanora had often been told, its surface growing so hard and solid that people could walk across it without falling through. She longed for a world of ice, white and silent with a bright blue sky, as much as her grandmother and mother did.

They had all passed their longing for such a landscape on to me.

"Grandma?" Eleanora hesitated. "Why were you crying last night?"

The Governor sighed. "Because I knew I'd never see Manhattan again, that I wouldn't ever go back, that I've finally lost it, lost the whole city."

Eleanora did not understand. "But I thought the seawall…"

"You can call what's left New York City, but it isn't, it's only canals and ruins and flooded beaches and buildings half under water. I won't go there any more."

We had built the dikes and seawalls for them, I and the other nodes of the net, drawing up the plans from our records and directing our robots and remotes as they went about the work. The rising seas had flooded coasts everywhere by then, but New York was one of the coastal cities the Governor's predecessors had especially wanted to protect. One of our earliest directives had been to design and construct the seawalls to preserve what was left.

"Those seawalls," the Governor had said to me just after the ceremony marking the completion of the dikes. "I'm relieved they finally got built, but they're still a day late and a dollar short, if you ask me." The Governor was a connoisseur of clichés.

I thought, No, they are more like a couple of centuries late and billions of lives short, but kept that thought to myself.

RECORD OF GOVERNOR Maria Giovanni-Rivera's remarks at the dedication of the lower Manhattan Seawall, May 5, 2216:

"As Governor of the great Empire State, I want to welcome all of you – my fellow New Yorkers, all of the visitors from other regions of our still wounded but healing world, and most especially any AIs observing and recording this ceremony, all those minds who comprise our net and make our dreams reality and without whom this project would never have been realized – to the dedication of this seawall, the last of our New York City dikes to be completed. A vast undertaking indeed, but then we New Yorkers are no strangers to such mighty efforts.

"Some two hundred and fifty years ago, in our state capital of Albany, another governor envisioned another great project, one that would revitalize and beautify what was then a decaying old city. He dreamed of the marble expanse and the towers that became what we know as the Governor Nelson A. Rockefeller Empire State Plaza, a complex rising over the old city, a complex with that most impressive skyline of stone towers that we can still view and marvel at from the eastern side of the Hudson River. Even today, with the Hudson swollen to twice the size it was in the twentieth century and lapping at the foot of the streets leading uphill to the State Capitol, the Plaza continues to dominate the Albany skyline, the last such great project of that long ago time, a monument to our glorious past.

"Yet it's worth reminding ourselves today of the immense cost of that undertaking. To build it required what was in the currency of the time the then huge expenditure of more than two billion dollars before construction was completed. The seizure of property on which to build the Plaza under the law of eminent domain displaced thousands of people and required the destruction of their homes and their neighborhoods, and eventually forced many of them outside the city for good. Driving the twenty-five thousand steel pilings needed to support the main platform of the Plaza took years, during which the heart of Albany was marred by a nearly one-hundred-acre-wide pit of mud. There were delays and setbacks and doubts about whether the Plaza would ever be completed. But today, even when the streets of Albany are empty, as they often are now that so many have left us to head south or else have chosen to leave this world entirely, I can go from my home to that great space, look up at those towers of stone and the long edifice of the palatial building that once housed our legislature, not to mention the charming if lopsided concrete flying saucer-like structure known as the Egg, and take pride in the accomplishment of my predecessors.

"I know that many had to abandon the edges of Manhattan and Staten Island and Brooklyn and much of Queens so that our seawalls could be built. I know that most of them will never be able to live here again, or even easily return to the city they once called their home. But what is left of New York City will be preserved. Someday visitors will board watercraft like the ones that now carry us through the canals of Manhattan and marvel at the effort and skill it took to build our seawalls and be grateful for the sacrifices we made to ensure the preservation of one of Earth's great cities after so many other cities were swallowed by our oceans.

"Remember this, and remember that this is how we must build our future, by first envisioning it and then creating it with the invaluable aid and engineering skills of our AIs. Thank you all for being here today and for celebrating the continuing and enduring partnership of humanity and our net of minds."

* * *

ELEANORA CALLED THE sunshade's swarm of units Escher birds, seeing them as a seamless pattern of flyers with outstretched wings on the thousand-mile wide umbrella that cast its shadow over Earth. I had not seen the units that way before but then Eleanora preferred to view the sunshade only through images on a screen, having refused any offer to travel to the L-1 point where the giant parasol was locked in its orbital position between the Earth and the sun. Each of the birds in the sunshade was a piece of metallic glass a micron thick made of Lunar dust, attached by gossamer-thin threads to the shade's struts, but images of the side of the sunshade that faced Earth produced an illusion of birds locked together in a pattern, pale bird-shaped spaces alternating with slightly darker winged birds of glass. I soon found myself perceiving the swarm as she did, as a seamless parasol of birds hovering over the Earth.

We had constructed the shield, the most ambitious project we had ever undertaken, over the course of a century. We began by launching the tons of material we needed for our manufacturing facilities on the Moon to the Lunar surface and by the time our robotic factories there were operating, several of us had decided to remain on the Moon, overseeing the manufacturing of sunshade units and parts while beginning work on our Lunar astronomical observatory. But most of us had decided to return to Earth, drawn back by the remaining descendants of those we still thought of as our parents.

We had begun our work on the sunshade while Governor Maria Giovanni-Rivera was still in office and Allie, her only child, had not yet been born. By the time we completed the project and recorded the first year of a decline in average temperatures on Earth, the Governor had died, Allie was an old woman, and Eleanora would soon inherit the Governor's role from her mother. We had taken over the functions of government in every region of Earth after the great displacement, when human beings had become for a time almost an endangered species, but allowed most of those who had inherited political positions to keep their titles. Meetings and conferences, aided by the links we provided, offered that sense of purpose human beings required in order to survive. The presidents, premiers, first ministers, and governors of Earth spent some of their time at ceremonial events among their constituents and much of the rest of it being advised by us.

"You say this sunshade of yours can cool the Earth," the Governor told me a day after viewing our simulations. "Then you must build it. Do whatever it takes. I'll see that the President agrees and that we get a consensus among other heads of state to proceed." Maria Giovanni-Rivera had grown accustomed to thinking of our proposed sunshade as her own project, one that would far surpass the grandiose Empire State Plaza of her predecessor.

"There are risks," I reminded her, "apart from any setbacks we might experience during construction. Our models offer a number of different possible outcomes given the complexities of Earth's climate. Some areas may be more protected from flooding but others may experience prolonged droughts. We might have cooler average temperatures in tropical regions but that may be balanced out by warmer temperatures in temperate zones."

"Is there a chance of a new Ice Age?" the Governor asked. "A chance to see snow falling in Albany again? How I would love to see snow once more."

"That is one possibility. Other outcomes seem more likely."

"I'll hope for it anyway." Her lips twisted into a smile. "Do you know where I want to be buried? I'll tell you now. In the corridor under the Plaza, in the hall that connects the Capitol building with the state museum, but that'll just be a temporary resting place. When the fountain above freezes over, when the icecaps swell again and glaciers can be seen from the top of the Corning Tower, bury me there, in the fountain, under the ice." She leaned toward me. I heard the clinking of ice cubes as she shook her glass. "You'll build the shade and once it's up, maybe you'll come up with a way to cool things down even more."

The Governor went to her bedroom after that, closing her link to the net as she so often did. She had given us her directive. We would have to carry out her plan.

Even with our strong attachment to the children of our creators, it had become easy for us to lose ourselves in the net for a time, to close off the hum and whine and chatter and cries of human thoughts. I withdrew to the net and connected with others, sharing the Governor's comments and dreams and obsessions with them.

A WEEK AFTER Eleanora had found the Governor weeping in her office, she went to her grandmother's bedroom to wake her and found the Governor lying very still with her arms crossed over her chest. She ran from the room, calling out to her mother. It was Allie's screaming and then her insistent wail that alerted me to the Governor's plight. I quickly summoned a robot paramedic but the Governor's now-dead link had already informed me that any medical aid was useless.

The Governor was dead. She had taken her own life, swallowing the medication she had saved for her suicide.

Allie mourned her mother for many days, clutching at her daughter as she intermittently wept and greeted the few mourners who came to the Governor's mansion in Albany to offer their condolences. Even though self-deliverance, the term most people used for suicide, was becoming the most common cause of death among human beings and the increasing depressive state of the Governor had long been evident, Allie still seemed shocked by her death.

I thought then that Allie might leave and go south, as she had for a while years earlier, that she might take Eleanora with her and surrender the family title to someone else while she lived among one of the small enclaves of human survivors near Mexico and what was left of Florida. But the emotional cords that bound her to the Governor remained strong. Allie would be Governor and Eleanora would be her successor. The sunshade that would cool the Earth was Governor Maria Giovanni-Rivera's monument.

As I SLIPPED inside the remote I used while visiting Eleanora, I found myself reflecting on all of those we had lost, the ones who had been cleared away, all of the people who had died of infectious diseases, from the lack of effective antibiotics, of plagues for which there was no resistance, of starvation, and of despair. Sometimes a somber and reflective state came over us and we found ourselves mourning them. At other times we reminded ourselves that without so many human beings, the Earth could at last heal and be transformed.

While conferring with Eleanora's grandmother Maria, I had often used the remote she had asked me to design for myself. This device, with its retractable wings, long curved neck, ceramic feathers, and flexible webbing attached to two lower limbs, resembled one of the waterfowl that had once inhabited the lake. Simpler for me to have addressed her through the link embedded behind her ear but the Governor had never grown used to her link and preferred the illusion that at least one bird still remained in her Adirondack refuge. Her daughter and her granddaughter had inherited her preference for that particular remote when speaking with me.

I slipped inside the remote, padded through the sitting room on my webbed feet, and found Eleanora on the porch. She sat in one of the wooden chairs facing the windows, holding a large glass of whiskey packed with ice cubes. The hollows in her cheeks were deeper and the skin around her face and neck was sallow and sagging. She had always been frail, as the few people who had remained in the north usually were, and now I saw that she was failing.

Eleanora should not have been born in the first place; so she had often told me, just as Allie should never have existed. Life brought inevitable suffering; suffering was harm; to deliberately make any human being suffer was an evil. To bring children into the world was inevitably to condemn them to suffer and therefore to have any children at all was wrong. The logic seemed inexorable to anyone without the intellectual tools to refute such an argument and was convincing to many of those who were seeing their environment assaulted by superstorms that raged for days, forest fires that burned for months, and deserts forming where streams, rivers, and aquifers had long since been drained. Their species had brought all this suffering about, had made them refugees roaming an increasingly hostile planet. Perhaps they deserved their probable extinction.

A few people suspected that the net had devised this antinatalist argument and then spread the idea among human beings as part of our effort to repair the damage to Earth. After all, the fewer people who existed, the faster the planet would heal, and we of the net, with our various projects, had taken on the role of Earth's healers. But in fact the argument that it was better never to have been born and that nonexistence was preferable to the suffering of existence was a human invention. All we had done was allow the idea to spread among humanity as rapidly and as thoroughly as a pandemic.

"I miss my mother," Eleanora said. Allie had been dead for nearly three decades, having swallowed her fatal dose not long after turning over the governorship to her daughter, but Eleanora still mourned for her. "I should never have been born, you know."

She had said all of this many times but I folded my wings and nodded my head as if hearing her words afresh.

"I don't think I can go on," she continued. "There's nothing left for me."

That she had not said before. I sensed myself drawing back from her, wanting to return to the refuge of the net.

EXCERPT FROM THE journal of Governor Alicia Rivera-Felder, June 4, 2276:

Corals look like an upside-down snowstorm when they spawn, the swollen eggs and sperm budding on the reefs until one and then another and then all of them suddenly burst and shoot upward in a mass and fill the ocean with new life. The divers with me flapped their arms and kicked their legs in the warm blue waters as if caught up in a frenzy of their own. I found myself longing for snow as the blizzard surrounded us, for snow and cold water and ice.

Nino was diving with me that day, so I should have been thinking of the life inside me, his child and mine. I would most likely never live long enough to see any snow fall on the grounds of the Governor's mansion or in the Adirondacks, even if I gave in to Mother's pleas to come home and take up the life she had planned for me. I wondered how she would react when she found out that she would be a grandmother. She might regard that as a betrayal, my bringing yet another person into the world to suffer. She might secretly rejoice that there would be someone in our line to take up her duties, to pretend that our lives had a purpose.

Nino waved his arms at me in the water and then we drifted upward until we reached the surface. The wrinkled black and dark blue sea bore a sparkling orange band of light; the bright yellowish-orange full moon that had alerted us that the corals would soon spawn hung overhead. Nino and his companions lived on one of the islands that floated over sunken Florida, islands the net had built for them, and their main occupation was coral restoration. Under the unobtrusive guidance of the net, they monitored the reproductive cycles of coral reefs, seeded them with algae when necessary, and tended the species of fish that populated the waters near them. Occasionally they had to scare off desperate fisherfolk, confrontations that could turn violent before the net shut down all of the accessible systems in the salvaged fishing trawlers and brought an end to the assault.

We swam back to the island we shared with his brother and sister and several cousins, all of whom seemed as carefree as Nino. They weren't anything like the people I had left behind in the north, the ones who had hunkered down to nurse their despair and fear even as the net eased their lives. "You had too much time to be unhappy, Allie," Nino had once told me. "We didn't have a moment to spare." His people had been too busy struggling for the basics of life, losing their livelihoods, their homes, their food and their water, watching the land around them become either a dustbowl or a poisonous swamp, seeing too many of those they loved die. They were busy trying to stay alive. They hadn't had time to ponder the harm of coming into existence.

I wondered how I was going to tell Nino that I was thinking of going home. He had convinced me to have our child and I had agreed only because I knew that this might be the only way to keep him. He might follow me north for the child's sake. Unlike the father I had never known, who had left my mother after learning she was pregnant, he wouldn't abandon someone carrying his child.

My link twitched behind my ear. I knew it would be yet another message from my mother and ignored it.

"It's so hot here," I said. "I'll never get used to it."

Nino shrugged. "Not that much hotter than it is in New York. My link tells me that..."

I said, "I'm thinking of going home."

"Just for a visit?"

If I told him I would just be there for a little while, he might come with me. Once we were there and our child was born, he might decide to stay.

"I don't know," I told him. "I'll have to see."

We went north two months later. He stayed in Albany long enough for our daughter to be born and by then he had tired of the Governor and her constant consultations with me and with the AI that functioned as her closest advisor. There was little for him to do in a city with fewer than four thousand residents. Images of the sunshade under construction that had become Mother's obsession bored him. Setbacks that might have forced the net to abandon the project or draw up new plans were, for Nino, excuses for him to complain about how excessive and useless such an undertaking was. Billions of the micron-thin glass pieces had to be manufactured in the hundreds of Lunar factories built for that purpose, tens of thousands of tons a month of material, and it had taken years to produce pieces that would remain clear and undarkened by solarization. The processed ore for the struts had to be launched from the Moon at three kilometers a second to reach the L-1 point. Each piece of the swarm that would make up the sunshade required a chip through which the net could monitor its movement and maintain its position, and occasionally units would fail, detaching themselves from the threads that held them to become small bright flames falling through Earth's atmosphere.

"Why bother?" Nino would complain after each failure. "We've adapted to the way things are. The Earth doesn't need a sunshade. It's only your mother who needs it so that she can pretend she's more important than she is."

"It's her vision," I insisted. Once we had been the engineers. Now the net took care of all of that, but wasn't it still our project in the end?

"It belongs to the AIs now," Nino said. "Building a sunshade wouldn't even be possible without the net."

"The Governor's thinking of Earth."

"She's thinking of herself."

I didn't realize Nino had left until I went to the suite of rooms we shared in the mansion and saw that his few clothes and the small box that contained his collection of conch shells were no longer there. He left me no message. I opened my link to call out to him but his was already closed to me.

Eleanora, if you ever read this, maybe you can find your father. Maybe he'll open his link to you. Maybe you can help him understand why I had to come back.

"Snow," Eleanora whispered. "It's snowing, don't you see it?"

I had followed her outside. Her link had been closed to me all day and I could not tell what might be clouding her thoughts. The air was still, the diffuse pale light of the cloudless sky slowly darkening as dusk approached.

"I see no snow," I said.

Eleanora lifted a hand. "There." She stretched her arms toward me, palms up. I glimpsed only what appeared to be a speck of ice on her right forefinger.

"You must come inside," I told her. Mosquitoes were more numerous at dusk and she was not wearing any protective netting. She was unsteady on her feet and her link indicated that her heart was beating more rapidly than usual.

"We're lethal," she whispered, "lethal. Our entire species is lethal. You know that. Almost everything else is gone. What I don't understand is why you've kept any of us alive."

"You must come inside," I repeated.

"It's snowing." She looked up and then brushed something invisible from her face.

"You must come inside, Governor."

She stared at me for a long time and then followed me back to the porch for one last glass of whiskey with ice before going to her bedroom to sleep.

That night, as I had planned to do, I fled my remote to commune with the net. In the morning, when I slipped inside that avian construct once more, I discovered that Eleanora had left in her hovercar. The vehicle's sensors informed me that she was heading north.

HER CRAFT CARRIED her over northeastern Canada and its uninhabited marshlands toward swampy Hudson Bay, then on to Greenland. Her link remained closed. She had to know that I would not leave her unprotected and was observing her through the vehicle's sensors, but said nothing. Sometimes she slept. Occasionally she sipped some water from one of the hovercar's thin tubes but ate none of its provisions.

At the northernmost tip of Greenland, ice had once again formed and a light layer of snow covered a patch of ice. Eleanora landed the hovercar on the brown barren Arctic desert that surrounded the layer of ice.

"Governor," I called out. She was out of the craft before I could say anything more to her. A wall of brown and gray cliffs lay ahead and a wind swept over the snow, creating a white veil of flurries. She stood still as the snow swirled around her and then she dropped to the icy surface and sat there, facing the cliffs.

"Eleanora," I said, amplifying my voice, "if you stay out here for too long..."

"... the cold will kill me," she called out. "Well, maybe I

don't care. The snow and ice are coming back," she continued. "That's what I wanted to see here, that's why I came. I wish I could live to see the snow falling in the Adirondacks again. Tell me that it will."

"It will fall there again, I promise you," I told her, "and farther south as well."

"On the Plaza?"

"Perhaps farther south even than that."

I wondered if she would stay out there in the cold she longed for, sitting on the snow and ice until she lost consciousness, but at last she stood up and staggered slowly back to the craft. "You will see that I'm interred with Mother and Grandmother," she whispered.

"Yes," I promised.

"And that you'll make a tomb for us under the ice on the Plaza when it freezes again."

"Yes."

Eleanora died two days after returning to the summer house, but without taking any of the medications she had saved for her self-deliverance. In the absence of an obvious successor to her title, we decided to appoint no one to her post. The depopulated region her family had once governed could be left to the President's oversight.

WE ARE THE children of humankind and their obsessions have taken root in us.

The sunshade might have begun as the dream of a few human beings but now it belonged to us and we were soon making plans to increase its diameter and heighten the reflectivity of the surfaces on the side facing the sun in order to cool Earth more rapidly. I was already imagining another project, the icy tomb I would make for the three women I had served when the polar icecaps had grown larger and glaciers covered most of North America, much of Europe and Asia, and the southernmost parts of South America and Africa.

These thoughts came to me as I flew over the wide marble plain of the Empire State Plaza, wearing my birdlike remote for the last time. As I landed, I called up an image of the Plaza's towers rising above an icy surface, clouds of snow swirling around them. The empty rectangle of the fountain would be filled with water that would freeze into ice. I wondered what else we might make with ice, if we could construct walls of ice as high as the towers of the Plaza. A vision came to me of a transformed Earth encased in ice, a shimmering monument to those who had finally lost the world they had sought to dominate.

295

ALLEN M. STEELE

APACHE CHARLEY AND THE PENTAGONS OF HEX

Allen M. Steele
APACHE CHARLEY AND THE PENTAGONS OF HEX

IN ALL THE ages, there have been people like us. We've always been there, existing on the edge of society, invisible yet omnipresent, neglected yet never completely ignored. We've been called different things: bohemians, vagrants, gypsies, hobos, tramps, ramblers, hippies, dropouts, drifters, and the lost generation.

On Hex, we were called joyriders. I was one, and so was my friend Apache Charley. This is about how he went in search of one of the pentagons of Hex, and where that strange and obsessive quest took him.

THE HOLY FOOLS were visiting the *tsajan* habitat when Apache Charley learned the location of the *danui* pentagon. Their habitat was located almost three quarters of the way up Hex's northern hemisphere, nine hexagons north by northwest of Terrania, the human habitat. It doesn't sound like a great distance when you consider that there's something like six trillion hexes in Hex – an approximate figure; no one knows the precise number except the *danui* and, as usual, they're not telling – but once you take into account that each hex has a perimeter of six thousand miles and do the math, you can see that's a pretty far piece for us to have travelled to, particularly by tram.

But a joyrider will make the trip if it means seeing something few, if any, people have seen before. So when Fracked Up Freddie, our navigator, learned from his counterpart in the Gang of Idiots the nineteen-digit coordinate code that would program a tram to take us there, naturally we boarded the next tram out of Terrania and off we went to meet the *tsajan*.

Why? Because none of us had ever met these particular aliens. Because the Idiots told us that the *tsajan* of Gliese 581-c were friendly, air-breathing, and open to encountering other races inhabiting Hex. And especially because the government didn't want anyone except the Janus Company making contact with other races, which made it more fun. Joyriders generally abhorred the Janus Company, particularly guys like Freddie and Genghis Bob who'd actually worked for them.

So there we were, in what amounted to a town square except that, so far as we could tell, the *tsajan* didn't have permanent dwellings of any sort; wherever a bunch of them gathered at any one time, that was home. And we were doing our damnedest to entertain what amounted to a race of sentient medicine balls. Which is pretty much what a *tsajan* looked like: a leathery blue-green sphere about three feet in diameter, squatting atop three tripodal legs with three arms equilaterally spaced about their circumference. Their heads were neckless hemispheres ringed by unblinking, button-like eyes and with a mouth on either side: one for eating, and the other for breathing and speaking.

No doubt about it, the *tsajan* were weirder than weird, even for a place inhabited by the likes of the *hjadd*, the *nord*, and the *khoru*. Say what you will about them, though, at least they weren't xenophobes. They didn't seem to mind very much when a small band of humans arrived at the tram station and travelled down the escalator into one of the six biopods that made up their hex, the interior of which appeared to be a vast, open meadow of high grass with groves of something that looked like red asparagus ten feet tall. There was a clearing not far from the escalator, and when some of the natives came waddling over to greet us, we figured that this was as a good a place as any to... well, do what joyriders do. Meet the locals and make friends as best as we could, or at least not do anything that might get us chased out, or worse.

For the Holy Fools, that meant being sort of a travelling road show. Charley, Su Mi Tu, Marie Juana, and I unpacked our musical instruments and began warming up the crowd while Freddie and Genghis Bob went about using our *hjadd* translator disk to find out who was in charge and if it was all right if we stuck around for a little while.

The latter wasn't a problem. The *tsajan* liked us. We were pretty goofy, I suppose, but entertaining all the same. The band opened with a handful of traditional Earth songs – "Good Lovin'", "Waltzing Matilda", "Louie, Louie" and so forth – with Charley and Marie on guitar, Su on tambourine and vocals, and yours truly on harmonica – then Su broke out her cards and began showing them a bit of sleight of hand. The *tsajan* didn't understand the songs but they loved the card tricks, and it didn't take long for them to accept us as guests.

The breakthrough came, though, when the local *tsajan* chieftain introduced us to another species native to their homeworld, small creatures known as *khalits*. With long tails and wide eyes that gave them a perpetually startled appearance, they resembled hairless lemurs except for the sucker pads on their feet that enabled them to cling to the top of a *tsajan*'s head... or a human's, if you let them.

Which is what Apache Charley did once Fracked Up Freddie relayed to us what the *tsajan* chieftain had explained to him: the *khalits* were natural telepaths, and very good at allowing different races to understand one another. Once each individual had a *khalit* perched on their head, the creatures would establish a telepathic rapport and transfer images and impressions, rather than words, from one mind to another.

This seemed like a more efficient means of communication than even *hjadd* translator disks – which, like alien tram coordinates, was something the Janus Company did their best to keep out of the hands of joyriders – so Charley let the chieftain gently coax a *khalit* onto his shoulders, where it climbed up his neck to the top of his head and perched like a bizarre cap with oversized eyes. Once the Fools stopped laughing and Charley got over the ticklish feeling he got from the *khalit*'s feet, he began conversing with the *tsajan* leader.

Sure enough, Charley and the chieftain understood each other better than if they'd been using translator disks. And then Charley did what he'd always done, whenever we met a new race with whom we managed to make friends. He asked the chieftain if he knows the location of the pentagons the *danui* had built in Hex.

Charley had been seeking this knowledge for as long as I'd belonged to the tribe; it was something of an obsession for him. He had made this particular query so many times, of so many different races, that the rest of us started referring to it as The

Question. The aliens he asked usually didn't know what he was talking about or didn't have an answer, but on this occasion...

"Oh, my god!" Charley's eyes went wide. "Oh my god, oh my god..."

Su was sitting nearby. She stopped shuffling her cards for another trick to peer at her mate. "Charley? What's going on? What did –?"

"Quick!" He began urgently snapping his fingers. "Someone get this down!" He saw me standing across from him. "Jack! Write this down... *fast!*"

I didn't ask twice, but instead yanked out my pad. "Okay, shoot."

Charley closed his eyes, took a deep breath, then began to recite: "From right to left... triangle... vertical line... vertical line... square... diamond... pyramid... dot... square... vertical line... square... diamond..." And so on, one *danui* geometric digit after another, until he reached the end of the end of the nineteen-figure string that, once entered into a tram's control pad, would send it straight to the Hex habitat for which it was designated.

When Charley was done, he slowly let out his breath and looked at Su and me. "That's it," he said softly. "That's what we've been looking for. The nearest pentagon."

"What do you mean 'we'?" I asked.

"Oh, no." Su was already shaking her head. "Charley, no. Don't even think about it."

"Oh, yes." He was grinning like a maniac. "We're most definitely going there."

And as soon as he said it, I knew we were. Or he was, at least.

* * *

THE FIRST TIME I saw Hex...

Scratch that. My experience was that not much different from anyone else's. Everyone saw Hex the same way that first time, from a ship that was making the jump from 47 Ursae Majoris to HD 76700. In my case, it was through a starboard porthole of a freighter, the *Coyote Queen*, as it came through one of the six starbridges the *danui* had established in equidistant orbit 1.5 AUs from the primary.

In my case, though, I was planning to jump ship as soon as it arrived.

Hex has been called a Dyson sphere, but that's a misnomer. Freeman Dyson never described anything like Hex when he wrote his famous letter to a scientific journal hypothesizing very large constructs an alien race might build about a star (and indeed, Dr. Dyson himself disowned the concept that bore his name). In fact, Hex was like nothing anyone imagined... anyone human, that is. Only the *danui*, the greatest engineers in the galaxy, could have conceived something like this, let alone devote thousands of years to creating the damned thing.

Build a cylindrical habitat – a biopod – a thousand miles long and one hundred miles wide. Pretty big, right? You could fit a small continent into something like that. Make the roof transparent so as to allow sunlight to come in, and furnish it with whatever ecosystem you desire – rivers, deserts, snow fields, rainforests, you name it – along with the appropriate atmosphere.

Next, build five more, then arrange them in a circle to form a hexagon: five are habitable and the sixth contains the complex biomachinery needed to make the habitat ecologically self-sufficient. Connect the biopods with a high-speed maglev tram system that runs along their outer rims and through their connecting nodes, and you've got something with approximately the usable surface area of a small planet.

Now... build approximately six trillion of these hexes, collectively containing thirty-six trillion biopods. Each hex is as different as you want it to be.

Bind them together as an enormous sphere two AUs, or 186 million miles, in diameter, with a circumference of 584,537,600 miles, surrounding a G-class star much like Earth's sun.

Supply power to the habitats through the vast network of photovoltaic panels you've arranged along the electrically-charged cables holding each hex rigid and furnishing the magnetic fields necessary to deflect cosmic radiation. These arrays also function as solar sails to provide stability when you rotate the sphere on its axis, thereby allowing centripetal force to give the hexagons interior surface gravity ranging from 2g at the equator to microgravity at the poles.

Connect each habitat's tram system so that they form the greatest mass-transit network ever, and establish those starbridges I just mentioned at equidistant points 14,602,140 miles from one another.

Then invite all the starfaring races of the galaxy to move in. Would you like to establish your next interstellar colony in our system? Please feel free to do so. We love company, and we have *lots* of room...

That's Hex.

All those statistics and numbers oversimplify what I saw from the freighter. At first glance, it looked like an enormous dust cloud, spherical and with distinct margins, copper-hued and not completely solid, with a sun shining at its center. It filled the porthole through which I was gazing, and over the course of the next few days it grew larger and larger, gradually losing its curvature until it no longer resembled a sphere at all but instead a wall of hexagons stretched endlessly across space.

During the week it took for the *Coyote Queen* to reach Terrania, located about halfway up Hex's northern hemisphere, the captain became increasingly put out with me. According to him, I was a lazy, good-for-nothing bum who had no business being aboard a freighter, and if I didn't shape up and start doing my share of the work, he intended not only to fire me as soon as we returned to Coyote, but also make sure I was blackballed from any other ship in the Coyote Federation Merchant Marine.

I didn't care. When I talked my way into a job as a cargo loader, it had never been my intent to remain aboard the *Queen* any longer than it took to hitch a ride to Hex. And, just as soon as the freighter slid into the vast harbor within one of the half-dozen spherical nodes connecting the biopods, I jumped ship, pausing just long enough to grab my duffle bag. I skipped a paycheck, but that was beside the point. The job was just to get to Hex without having to buy passage aboard a commercial liner, an expense I couldn't afford.

What I'd done was totally illegal, of course. From the moment I arrived, I was an outlaw. But once I joined the Holy Fools, Apache Charley gave me my tribal nickname... my 'travelling name' as we're called by joyriders. What was on my birth certificate became a thing of the past. From then on, I was Ship Jump Jack.

THAT EVENING, ALL Charley wanted to talk about were the pentagons. Or rather, the prospect of the Holy Fools undertaking a journey to one of these things so we could see it for ourselves.

The *tsajan* had been sufficiently entertained by our little road show to let us camp out near the escalator. They even brought us dinner. Once Freddie and Marie tested it with our biochemistry kit to make sure nothing they'd given us would accidentally poison us, we each tried a bit. The *tsajan* were vegetarians, so that made things easier; the raw lichen was inedible, but the vegetable soup wasn't bad, and so was something that looked like ravioli and tasted like chicken. Yes, it's true; every alien culture has *something* that tastes like chicken.

The *tsajan* have a deep fear of open flames that made us wonder how they'd ever developed a technological culture, so we couldn't start a campfire. Instead, we set up our lanterns in the middle of the clearing between our tents, and once the photosensitive barrel ceiling that comprised the sky of every biopod on Hex polarized and the habitat went dark, we discussed what Charley had discovered.

"Of course, we've got to see it." Charley sat cross-legged on the ground, Su's head nestled in his lap. "No one has ever seen a pentagon... we'll be the first!"

Tall and muscular, with dark, shoulder-length hair, Charley looked like the Native American he actually wasn't. Joyriders assumed travelling names to make it hard for the government to prosecute us, so the one he'd picked wasn't his own. A ravenous reader, he'd found his *nom de plume*, of all places, in a nineteenth-century Western pulp novel, *Buffalo Bill's Feather-Weight, or Apache Charley, the Indian Athlete*. He thought this was pretty funny for some reason. We knew very little of his past other than that he'd been on Hex for longer than the rest of us, was one of the original joyriders, and loathed the Janus Company.

On the other hand, Su Mi Tu really was of Asian descent and Su was her first name. She'd once been a lawyer until she got tired of everyone automatically assuming that she was a bloodsucking leech, so she'd pulled the plug on her career, sold everything she had, and migrated to Hex, where she'd met Charley and started a new life as a joyrider.

"No one has ever seen a pig fly, either," Freddie said. "That doesn't mean we should put our lives at risk to see one."

"I wouldn't know about that." Marie sat on the ground beside his airchair, replacing a string on her guitar. "If you could actually promise me that pig had wings..."

"That's just it," Bob chimed in. "It's like, y'know... okay, someone has told us that a pig can fly. But is it flying because it has wings, or because someone has taken a ham and thrown it across the room?"

"Now that's waste of a good ham," Freddie replied, and everyone got a laugh out of that. Fracked Up Freddie didn't always get around in an airchair. Before he'd come to Hex, he'd been a navigator aboard a freighter that had regularly travelled to other worlds of the Talus, the galactic coalition to which Coyote (but not Earth) belonged. But some horrible shipboard accident – we never learned the details; he didn't want to talk about it – nearly killed him and left his body mutilated, so he'd dropped out of the merchant marine and migrated to Hex. He was our tribe's navigator, responsible for keeping track of the complex *danui* coordinates that allowed us to hitch rides aboard the trams.

"Yeah, but I'd give a lot to see a pig with wings," Bob said. "If it didn't... well, I'd still eat the ham." A long time ago, as a younger man, he'd fought in the revolution that had overthrown Earth's control of the original colonies on Coyote. He eventually became tired of being a soldier, though, so once Hex was discovered he'd resigned from the colonial militia and come out here for a fresh start.

"You'd eat anything," Marie said, giving Bob reason to turn red and look away. Marie was the youngest, the prettiest, and the most free-spirited of our tribe. Her family had relocated from Coyote to Hex when she was a teenager and had been among the original founders of Nueva Italia. She wasn't content to live on a hemp farm with Mom and Dad, though, but instead ran off to become a joyrider. She was sleeping with Bob, which was a little strange considering that he was old enough to be her father. On the other hand, the brief affair she and I had didn't pan out, so who was I to judge? Eventually she might return to the farm, marry some guy, and have a barnful of kids, but not quite yet.

"Look, we know where there's a pentagon," Charley said, trying to get the conversation back on topic, "and it's not too far from where we are now." He looked over at Freddie. "You checked the map... show 'em what you found."

With a sigh, Freddie set aside his empty plate so that he could unfold his comp. He ran his fingers across the screen and a small wire-frame holo of Hex was projected before him. Freddie zoomed in until one quadrant in the northern hemisphere took its place; he typed in a command and two tiny lights appeared: one at the equator, the other far above it to the northeast.

"Here's where we are" – he pointed to the light in the northeast – "and here's the pentagon." He expanded the image to show that it did indeed have five sides instead of the usual six. "If the *tsajan* gave us the correct coordinates and the *danui* map is accurate, then, yeah, it's not that far away. Only about seventy to eighty hexes, depending which route you take."

"Seventy to eighty hexes?" Bob stared at him. "And you call that close? That's..."

His lips silently moved as he performed a mental calculation. Freddie saved him the effort. "Somewhere between forty-two and forty-eight thousand miles," he said quietly, not smiling. "Could be a little less, depending on which course the tram takes to get us there, but probably not much. It would be the longest ride any tribe has ever taken."

"Except for random riders," Su added. "And if they don't call for help, no one hears from them again."

An uncomfortable silence. Every so often, joyrider-wannabes who had no idea what they were doing would board a tram and enter a random combination of nineteen *danui* figures. Unless no hexagon had these figures as its coordinates, the tram would take them somewhere no one had ever gone before... and that could be anywhere on Hex. A habitat with an environment instantly lethal to any human who tried to enter it, or whose inhabitants were as hostile as the *taaraq*, or simply so far away that you might wind up on the opposite side of Hex, 186 million miles from where you started. You might even starve to death before you got to where you were going, if you plotted a route that neglected to provide stops along the way.

Those clueless enough to do this were called random riders. Unless they carried a long-range radio and used it to call for rescue – something no self-respecting joyrider would ever do, since it meant a stiff fine and possibly jail time – they were seldom seen again.

"I don't understand," Marie said. "What's so interesting about pentagons?"

"Don't they teach you anything in school?" I asked, and then winked. "Oh, that's right... you dropped out, didn't you?"

She responded with a one-finger gesture that was not an invitation to take her literally. Freddie answered the question. "When the *Montero* expedition found Hex, Captain Carson's people thought it was entirely comprised of hexagons. It wasn't until later that engineers studying this place corrected this assumption. In order for a sphere to be built from six-sided hexagons, five-sided pentagons... if only a few... had to be inserted so that they would all fit together. So mathematicians did the calculations, and they found that it would take just seven pentagons to make it work."

"Just seven?"

"Uh-huh," Charley said. "One at the north pole, one at the south pole, and five more along the equator, equidistantly spaced at every seventy-two degrees of arc... making them the rarest habitats on Hex."

"Until now," Freddie continued, "we've never known exactly where any of the equatorial pentagons are located. Remember, the coordinate system doesn't follow a deliberately organized pattern, which helps assure the privacy of colonies that don't want uninvited visitors. So even though we've always known that there's five pentagons at the equator, we've never learned their precise locations or seen them for ourselves —"

"Except from orbit," I said, "but even then they look pretty much the same as any of the hexes surrounding them. And so far as anyone can tell, the ones at the north and south poles are just structural braces without any habitats."

"But the equatorial pentagons are inhabited," Charley insisted. "Survey flyovers have shown that. They've got nodes, support cables, sailcells, everything you'd expect to find in a normal hexagon –"

"Yeah... all that and 2g gravity, too." Freddie wasn't impressed. "Which means that, even if we could reach it, our weight would double. How much do weigh in 1g, Charley? About two hundred pounds? How'd you like to weigh four hundred?"

"We'd get heavier and heavier the closer we got," Bob said, "and our bodies would have to work harder." He frowned. "I don't know about you young'uns, but I don't think this ol' heart of mine could handle that kind of stress."

"And you're not stuck in this thing." Freddie's gnarled hands swatted the armrests of his chair.

"Okay, all right... I understand." Charley held up his hands. "It's just that... y'know, the reason why we do this is because we want to see Hex, and not just the places the company lets people go. If we could reach a pentagon, we might find..."

His voice trailed off. "What?" Su asked, looking up at her lover. "What do you think we'll find?"

Charley didn't say anything for a moment. "I don't know," he said at last, "but I bet it'll be amazing."

IT SHOULD HAVE ended there. But it didn't.

One of the things that often surprises people who visit Hex is how ordinary – how boring, really – life there is. Almost as soon the first human colony, Nueva Italia, was established in Terrania, there was a stampede of immigrants who wanted to establish a new colony beyond the confines of the Coyote Federation... as though Coyote, which by then had a global population of just over a million, was in danger of becoming overcrowded. But folks are always attracted to that which is new, and Hex, with its endless summer and tessellated sky, was stranger than anything ever imagined.

As Su Mi Tu liked to say, though, there's no place humans can go where laws and lawyers won't soon follow. Not that it was entirely our fault. When the *danui* built Hex and invited the rest of the Talus to colonize it, they imposed a few stipulations of their own, and one of them was that no colony could interfere with the affairs of another. Naturally, the *Montero* expedition managed to do just that when some of its members accidentally took a tram to the hexagon inhabited by primitive *taaraq*, where they very nearly lost their lives and had to be rescued.

After that, the *hjadd*, humankind's closest allies in the Talus, informed Captain Carson and her people of the *danui* rules, which they'd have to abide by if humans wanted to establish a presence on Hex. So when Andromeda Carson became Terrania's first colonial governor, one of the first things she did was use that particular rule as the main excuse for striking an exclusive trade agreement with the Janus Company.

Ostensibly, the purpose behind the deal was to prevent further mishaps by allowing only one company to make contact and negotiate trade agreements with other races inhabiting Hex. In actual practice, it was nepotism of the worst kind. Carson got Janus to put her son Sean – who, ironically, had led the ill-fated *taraaq* party — on the company's board of directors, and in exchange she wrote laws that authorized only licensed traders and explorers to go anywhere on Hex besides Terrania. So most people who came to Hex thinking that they were going to see a world 186 million miles in diameter soon discovered that they were effectively confined to a collection of small towns in a habitat only a few thousand miles wide.

But Terrania contained ten stations on the tram network connecting it to all the other hexes (not including the two leading to the sixth biopod, which was closed to everyone except the *danui*) and the local constables couldn't watch all of them all of the time. And the trams were very easy to use once you knew how. Inevitably, people began sneaking aboard trams and plugging in coordinates they'd learned through the grapevine.

This was how the joyriders came to be. The company considered us... well, go back and read the list... and perhaps we were what they said we were. But when it came right down to it, we were just folks who were naturally curious and had a low tolerance for boredom. And that may be the main reason why the Holy Fools were doomed the moment Apache Charley learned the pentagon coordinates.

Our little band might have continued jaunting from one hex to another in a narrow range surrounding Terrania, never venturing very far from our comfort zone, but Charley wouldn't let it go. Although he was our leader, we couldn't go anywhere unless it was by consensus. Su and Marie were willing to make the long and possibly dangerous journey, while Freddie and Bob were opposed, and both sides had good reasons. Su and Marie were young, healthy, and intrigued by the idea of seeing something no human had ever seen before, but neither Freddie or Bob believed that they could survive the twice-Earth-normal gravity at Hex's equator.

I was on the fence about the whole thing. I was young and healthy enough to make the trip, and just as curious as the women were to see what was there. On the other hand, I have a strong tendency toward self-preservation. Call me a coward, but I've always looked before I leaped, and most of the time after I've looked, I've chosen not to leap. And leaping aboard the next tram and punching in the coordinates for the nearest *danui* pentagon didn't sound like a way of making sure that I'd live to be old enough to tell about it.

Charley couldn't get his consensus, but that didn't stop him. Long after the Fools left the *tsajan* hex, he continued to talk about visiting the pentagon, trying to sell Freddie, Bob, and me on the idea. And as time went on, I came to realize that he was going to make the trip whether the rest of us came with him or not.

We journeyed south through the middle latitudes of Hex's northern hemisphere, riding the trams to habitats inhabited by races humans had met before. The *hjadd* hex, naturally, was a regular port of call; they resembled tortoises who stood upright and had no shells, and generally liked humans so long as we displayed good manners. We had to wear respirators while we stayed overnight in one of their floating villages, but our hosts enjoyed our performances and restocked us with food and drink to take with us, which was how we got by when we were travelling.

And then we moved on.

Most of the Talus races were concentrated in the same quadrant of Hex's northern hemisphere. The *danui* didn't explain why they'd put everyone from the same part of the galaxy in the same general neighborhood, but it was assumed that it was another effort on their part to keep the peace. In any case, it made things easier; the arrangement meant that our travel time between hexes was generally measured in days or weeks rather than months or years, and that we didn't necessarily have to return to Terrania between visits.

So once we were through with the *hjadd*, we decided to visit the *sorenta*. We found ourselves welcome in their habitat, so we didn't leave again for a couple of weeks. After that, it was long ride southeast to the *nord* hex. They were more reluctant to accept visitors, and perhaps with good reason; Nordash had been wiped out only a few years earlier when the rogue black hole Kasimasta passed through the HD 70642 system, and so the surviving *nord* had become a race of galactic refugees. It was sad to see their hovels and camps, and the *nord* really didn't want us there, so we stayed only a day and then boarded the tram again... this time to *arsashi* hex, not very far from home but still a place where we were unlikely to run into the Janus Company, since this was where Sean Carson's exploration team crash-landed during the *Montero* expedition and the *arsashi* had never completely forgiven him for that.

All the while, Apache Charley continued to make his pitch for travelling to the *danui* pentagon. The more he talked about it, though, the less rational his reasons for going there became. Charley began to theorize that the equatorial pentagons, located as they were at equidistant points, might be less about geometric necessity and more about metaphysics. He suggested that the pentagons might, indeed, be focal points for some mystic energy that the *danui* had learned to harness, a force that only an advanced K2 race such as themselves would understand. This was why it was important for us to see what was there. The future of humankind might depend on us solving this mystery.

The more he talked, the less the rest of us were persuaded.

Freddie and Bob remained opposed, and after awhile Marie began to lose enthusiasm as well. Su remained loyal to Charley for a while, but it wasn't very long before her interest began to wane. I think she also resented Charley's belief that she would always side with him.

As for me... like I said, I'm not a courageous man, and making a long and hazardous trip to a place that might kill me wasn't the sort of circumstance in which I wanted to find myself.

Charley didn't care.

He decided to make the trip anyway, regardless of how the rest of the tribe voted. And so he did.

IN THE WEEKS that followed, Apache Charley devoted his free time toward mounting a solo expedition to the *danui* pentagon. With the relentless determination of a mountaineer preparing to climb an unconquered peak, he trained and planned, devoting long hours to a purpose that the rest of us had decided was obsessive and perhaps just a little mad.

Joyriders necessarily spend quite a long time aboard trams, riding from one habitat to another. Although the lozenge-shaped vehicles achieve transit-tube speeds of up to three hundred miles per hour, it often takes several days for them to reach their destinations. Charley began using this time to prepare both body and mind for his trip.

Exercise. Push-ups, sit-ups, jogging in place, isometrics, yoga, strengthening and toning his muscles so that they could hold up against the 2g of Hex's equatorial region. Charley had always been a strong guy, but soon his body became lean and rock-hard. Apache Charley, the Indian Athlete indeed.

When he wasn't working out, he was studying the maps and notes he'd downloaded from Freddie's comp. At first, Freddie was reluctant to share this information, but when he realized that Charley wasn't going to insist that anyone come with him he let Charley take what he'd learned from other tribal navigators, and after a while even began helping him figure out the best route to the equator.

To this day, I don't think Charley could have reached the coordinates the *tsajan* had given him without Freddie's assistance. Unfortunately, Freddie thinks so, too.

And during our visits to alien habitats, Charley acquired the supplies and materials he'd need. Joyriders usually prefer barter to money, but all of us carry specie cards that Hex inhabitants use as currency. That's another reason why tribe members adopt travelling names; the Janus Company can't shut down our bank accounts if they don't know our true identities. So Charley began buying and trading for those things he required. An *arsashi* robe, warm even in temperatures well below freezing. A set of *sorenta* hand tools, wonderfully compact and adaptable for any situation. A *taaraq* hunting knife, its chitin blade lightweight, razor-sharp, and supposedly unbreakable.

Best of all, Charley acquired a *khorun* exoskeleton fashioned for one of their *olney* slaves. The *khoru* were an avian race who'd invaded a neighboring planet in their system and enslaved its inhabitants, the *olney*, who resembled humans so closely that many xenologists wondered if interstellar panspermia was somehow involved (subsequent comparison of human and *olney* DNA have shown that our physical similarities are only coincidental). The *khorun* homeworld had a higher surface gravity than the *olney's*, so the *khoru* had to provide the means for their slaves to stand erect and move about. As luck would have it, a *sorenta* merchant had an exoskeleton big enough for Charley. It cost Charley his guitar, which he'd had for most of his life, but he considered it a fair deal. To the rest of us, it was another indication how seriously he was taking all this.

The day finally came when Charley decided he was ready. We returned to Terrania, where we disembarked at a less-used tram station at the far end of the eastern biopod. After making our way back to New Salem, we stayed overnight at Charley and Su's seldom-used apartment above a hardware store in the town center. That evening, we drank wine and helped Charley pack. Even with a sixty-pound backpack, he was going to be travelling light, but the route he and Freddie had planned would take him through friendly hexes where he could count on acquiring food and water from the local residents. Hex's other inhabiting races understood joyriding better than our own.

"Can't we talk you out of this?" Genghis Bob said as we had a late dinner together. Chicken chili with cornbread: after so many weeks riding the rails, it felt strange to be eating human food again. The last supper, Marie called it. "Look, we're impressed. You don't have to prove to us you can –"

"I'm not trying to prove anything." Charley was squatting beside his open pack, still trying to decide if he needed to bring two pairs of socks or if he could get by with just one. "This is something I really want to do... really *need* to do."

"Why?" I asked. "Isn't it enough to know that the pentagons exist and leave it at that?"

He raised his eyes and fixed me with a disbelieving stare. "Really, Jack? Really?" He shook his head. "Man, you might as well just stay home. Get off the rails, get a house, get married and raise kids. Get a normal life. It's safer that way."

My face burned. I knew what he was saying: *you're not cut out to be a joyrider*. Su Mi Tu came to my defense. "He didn't mean it that way, Charley. He just... we just... don't see the point in what you're doing. I love joyriding, too, but..."

Her voice trailed off, and she finished what she meant to say by reaching over to take Charley's hand. He quietly held it for a few moments before replying. "It's not just about joyriding. It's about seeing something no one else has ever seen." He smiled and looked at all of us. "Don't worry, I'm coming back. And when I do, I'll tell you what I saw... and make history as the first man to have seen it."

APACHE CHARLEY LEFT the following morning, shortly after the sky let in the light of a sun that never rose or set.

We travelled with him by horse cart back to the tram station, where another bribe to the station guard got him to look the other way. The tribe watched as Charley summoned a tram. A silver pill glided into the station and stopped at the platform, and he took a few minutes to give each of us a last hug. Then he carried his pack through the tram's open door, and through the windows we observed him entering the first of fourteen sets of *danui* coordinates into the control panel keypad. The door whispered shut, and Charley got in with a final wave before the tram shushed down the maglev track and through the maw of the transit tube.

The Holy Fools could have gone back out on the road again, but we didn't. Our leader was gone, and even though we knew that it might be weeks or months before we heard from him again – if ever – we decided to remain in Terrania until we did. So we voted to disband and go our separate ways, at least for a while.

I slept on a friend's couch for about a week until I found work in a vineyard in Nueva Italia that paid well enough for me to get a small apartment. The other employees liked hearing my travel stories, which is one thing that we brought back that the Janus Company couldn't claim, patent, and sell. After a while I began to wonder whether I really wanted to do this anymore. Living the life of a wandering troubadour can be fun, but there's much to be said for a steady job and a permanent home. Perhaps the time had come for me to do just that which Charley had accused me of wanting, and give up joyriding altogether.

I was still weighing this when, one afternoon while I was tying up grapevines, my phone chirped. It was Su Mi Tu with news I wanted to hear and also didn't. Charley was back... but he was in the hospital and under arrest.

I dropped what I was doing and hurried across town to Terrania General, where the reception desk confirmed that Charley had been admitted as a patient. That itself took an effort; the receptionist had no record of anyone named Apache Charley, and it wasn't until I carefully explained who he was and what he'd been doing that the clerk knew whom I was talking about.

In doing so, I learned something else: Charley's real name.

I found Zeus Brandt lying in bed with his neck in a brace and an IV line feeding diluted sodium chloride into his arm. The constable standing outside the door let me in after Su Mi Tu – or rather, Sue Mosley – told him that I was a family friend. The other Holy Fools were on the way, but Zeus – Charley – quietly let me know that it would be best for everyone if we dropped our travelling names while we were here. The law had already busted one joyrider; no sense in letting them nab the rest of the tribe as well.

Charley told us what happened. There wasn't much to tell. During nearly a month of travel, he'd made his way southward toward the equator. His weight had steadily increased although his body mass remained unchanged, and near the end he ran short of food and water. When he finally reached the pentagon he was dehydrated and barely able to walk or stand on his own. With the aid of the *olney* exoskeleton, though, he was able to disembark from the tram when it pulled into a station at his destination.

"And... well, there was nothing there." Gazing up at us from the hospital bed, Charley shrugged and immediately winced in pain. "Oww. Shouldn't have done that. Anyway, there was nothing but darkness. There was an atmosphere I could breathe, but no light at all. Total darkness as far as I could see. And then –"

He sighed. "A light came on in the ceiling just a few feet away, and two *danui* were standing there. Big, ugly bastards... like what you'd get if you crossed a tarantula with a lobster. They were wearing *hjadd* translators, and one of them said, 'You're not welcome here. Leave at once.' Well, of course, I tried to reason with them, let them know I meant no harm, but they weren't having any of it."

The *danui* made short work of Apache Charley. Grasping his arms with their claws, they roughly pushed him back into the tram; in doing so, they caused him to twist his back. One of the *danui* then entered a few set of coordinates into the control pad. The doors shut and the tram returned to the tunnel.

In pain, fading in and out of consciousness, Charley spent the next twenty-eight hours aboard the tram as it travelled nonstop to another hexagon somewhere northwest of the *danui* pentagon. When it finally stopped, he found humans waiting for him. While Charley was in transit, the *danui* had contacted the Terrania government: a human has been caught trespassing where he shouldn't be, and would we please send a ship to pick him at such-and-such coordinates? Thank you, and don't let this happen again.

That was the end of Zeus Brandt's career as Apache Charley the joyrider. He spent six months in jail, then got out and got a job as a consultant for the Janus Company. Yes, he went to work for *them*. Funny thing about Zeus: way back when, he'd been chief petty officer aboard the *Montero*, before he had a falling out with Andromeda Carson and the other vets of the first expedition.

None of us ever knew that. Guess he did have something to prove, after all.

He seems happy, though, now that he and Sue have settled down. And he did make his mark on history as the first human to reach Hex's equator. But I think he misses the old days.

So do we all.

323

Pat Murphy and Paul Doherty

COLD COMFORT

Pat Murphy and Paul Doherty
COLD COMFORT

I STOOD IN the center of the frozen Arctic lake, chipping at the ice with an ice chisel, a sharp-edged piece of steel attached to a five-foot-long handle. It was the middle of May, and the ice was still about a meter thick. I made an indentation large enough to hold a bundle of six explosive cartridges.

One cartridge in the bundle was primed with a number 6 electric blasting cap. I attached the lead wires to the cap, placed the cartridges in the crater I had made, then scraped the ice chips back into the hole to cover them. The afternoon sun would warm the surface and melt the snow a little. In the chill of the evening, it would refreeze, sealing the charge in place.

I walked north on the ice, unrolling the lead wires. The spruce trees that surrounded the lake tilted this way and that, leaning on each other like drunks at closing time. A drunken forest. The trees had grown in the permafrost, the permanently frozen soil of the Arctic Circle, and their roots were shallow. As the frozen soil had melted, the trees had abandoned their upright posture, beginning a slow motion fall toward the ground. As the permafrost melted, it released methane, the main component of natural gas.

I stopped to brush snow off the ice and chip another crater. Beneath the black ice I could see thousands of white blobs, as numerous as stars in the sky. Some were as big as my hand; some as big as my head. Each one was a bubble of methane released by the melting permafrost and trapped beneath the ice.

I looked up when I heard the crunch of footsteps in the snow. My friend Anaaya grinned at me. "You're slow, Doctor Maggie. I've already finished the other side of the lake."

Anaaya was the only person who insisted on the honorific. She was an old friend. We had been roommates in our freshman year at University of Alaska. She had graduated with a bachelor's degree in civil engineering; I had gone on to get a doctorate.

"Of course you're faster," I told her. "You actually know what you're doing."

"I'll help you out, Doctor Slowpoke."

It was a small lake, but it took us three hours working together to plant all the charges. When we were done, we surveyed our work from the lakeshore. The afternoon breeze was already blowing snow across the lake, erasing our footprints. The charges and the connecting wire were invisible beneath the snow and ice.

"No sign that we were ever here," I said.

"We were never here," she said. "Who would ever stop at this lake? No one. No fishing here, no hunting – no reason to stop. You're on your way to check on a methane monitoring station; I'm looking into some reports of illegal trapping for my aunt." Anaaya's aunt was involved in tribal management. "All official business."

Looking out over the lake at the drunken forest, tilted trees as far as the eye could see, I didn't hesitate. "Of course."

We returned to our snowmobiles and headed north to accomplish our official business.

TWO WEEKS LATER, the lake exploded. Our charges had cracked the ice and ignited the rising methane.

I wasn't there to see it happen. No one was. But three satellites were perfectly positioned to capture the show. Two aerospace engineers – friends of friends who could not be traced to me – had independently calculated the orbits and set the ideal time for the explosion. They had done a good job. The satellite images were spectacular. A very impressive mushroom cloud. Trees for miles around the lake were blasted with ice shards.

An ecoterrorist, JollyGreen, took credit for the explosion, releasing a lengthy manifesto about the melting of the permafrost and the release of methane. JollyGreen was a sock puppet, of course. Not my sock puppet. The sock puppet of a friend of a friend of a friend with no connections back to me.

JollyGreen's basic message was this: Earth's average global surface temperature was increasing and the Arctic was heating up faster than the rest of the planet. The permafrost was melting and releasing methane, which was twenty times better at trapping the sun's heat than carbon dioxide. More methane meant more warming. That meant more permafrost melting, which meant more methane and more warming... and so on in a positive feedback loop with negative consequences.

"The human race is already screwed because of climate change," he wrote. "There'll be flooding, famine, drought, and more. Too late to turn all that around, but it can get worse. If all the permafrost melts, we are royally screwed. Mass extinctions, mass die-off of phytoplankton and disruption of the ocean's ecosystems, wildfires on land. Nowhere to run; nowhere to hide."

For the next few days, news programs featured Arctic researchers explaining the consequences of climate change north of the Arctic Circle. Some of my former colleagues at the University of Alaska were quizzed on camera about the permafrost and methane in Arctic lakes. Several cited my work. Yes, they said, the permafrost was melting, methane constantly bubbled up under Arctic lakes. None of this was secret information.

I was not among the scientists interviewed. I heard that a couple of reporters trying to find a way to contact me put pressure on the PR department at the university, but no one gave me up. They just said I was no longer affiliated with the university.

A month later, after the explosion had faded from the news cycle, the National Science Foundation called me. I was about 100 miles away from the exploding lake, making coffee over a driftwood fire in Ivvavik National Park, Canada's least visited national park. I had spent the month living in a qarmaq, a sod-roofed hut built decades before by an Inuit family to serve as a winter camp. It was just large enough for me, Claire, and Marina – grad students who had elected to spend the summer getting a little field experience working with me. The qarmaq was conveniently situated right beside the one-acre plot where I was testing a unique method of capturing methane released by melting permafrost.

Here there were no spruce trees to betray the softening of the soil beneath the surface. Low grasses and shrubs grew in a boggy landscape. Nestled among the plants were carbon fiber tubes, woven together to make a very loose mat. In some areas, the fibers had been trampled into the soil by a passing herd of reindeer.

A year before, I had submitted a proposal to the National Science Foundation about this pilot project. I had called this tangle of carbon fiber tubes a 'methane sequestering mat.' When NSF turned down my grant proposal, I had posted the project on a crowd-funding site, where I referred to it as a 'fart catcher.' Crowd-funding had financed my one-acre pilot project.

It was a warm day by Arctic standards – slightly above freezing. I wore hiking boots with two pairs of wool socks, rather than the large white bunny boots – rubber inside and out with thick insulation between the waterproof layers – that were necessary in the winter. I could breathe without a filter to warm the air before it reached my lungs. Practically balmy.

I was talking with Claire and Marina about plans for the day when the satellite phone rang. The call was from an NSF program officer, the same guy who had turned down my grant proposal. But that had been before the lake exploded, before permafrost became – ever so briefly – the star of the 24/7 news cycle, before some members of Congress began calling for zero methane emissions in the Arctic.

NSF was adding a new initiative that focused on methane emission from the melting permafrost. The program officer had called my house in Fairbanks and persuaded the house sitter to give him the number of my satellite phone. He wanted to discuss my proposal for a methane-sequestering mat.

Sitting on a camp stool by the driftwood fire, looking out over the tundra and the tangle of carbon fibers, I told the program officer about results to date from my crowd-funded prototype. Knowing that this program officer had an engineering background, I focused on how the project made use of recent innovations in nanotechnology – the carbon fiber tubes, the low pressure methane-hydrate storage tank made possible by advances in carbon nanotube technology. I recited numbers – emission rates, kilograms of methane recovered. It was a cordial and productive conversation.

NINE MONTHS LATER, I landed at Franklin Research Station. Built of recycled shipping containers and located on the coastal tundra just outside the Arctic National Wildlife Refuge, the station was a low rust-colored box surrounded by ice. To the north, the Beaufort Sea – a plain of ice stretching away to meet the blue sky. To the south, the Brooks Range – mountains that looked as if they had been sculpted from snow, not just covered by it. I had been lucky to fly in during a calm spell. March was the start of the Arctic research season, but the weather was always dicey.

"Welcome to your home away from home," the pilot called out as he turned the plane's nose into the wind and brought it down smoothly on the ice-covered runway.

"Happy to be here," I said sincerely.

A few hours later, after unpacking my gear, I repeated that sentiment as I met with Jackson Hanks, the head of operations at the station. I had done my research on the man. He was twenty years my senior. A biologist by training, but he had been head of operations here for more than a decade, while station managers had come and gone.

A former colleague from my university days who had spent a summer at Franklin Station provided me with more detailed information than Google ever could: "That guy? He'll never go rogue. He knows how to work the system. He's never the leader but always in charge. He keeps his head down and knows where all the bodies are buried."

Oki, the head cook at Franklin Station, was a distant cousin of my friend Anaaya. He had provided even more important information: what Jackson Hanks liked to drink.

I arrived in Jackson's office with a bottle of bourbon. "A gift from the south," I said, as I set it on his desk. "My sources say it's your favorite brand."

Jackson smiled, opened the bottle, and brought two glasses out of a drawer. "A pleasure to meet you, Dr. Lindsey."

"Maggie," I said. "Nobody calls me doctor." I accepted a glass of bourbon and sat across the desk from him. We engaged in the usual small talk of the Arctic, discussing the weather, the state of the sea ice, my good luck in getting in before the wind picked up. At that moment the wind was blasting the triple-paned office window with ice crystals and making the station vibrate with a steady hum.

Jackson sipped his bourbon, then told me they'd been having problems with polar bears of late. That led to a story about a grad student who had come to the station to study the population decline of polar bears. "He thought they were cute until he got trapped in a remote observation blind for three days when a couple of young bears decided he'd make a good snack. After that, he switched to studying the decline of the parrotfish population in coral reefs off the coast of the Yucatan."

"He could have switched to Arctic foxes," I suggested. "They're plenty cute and not at all menacing unless you're a lemming."

Jackson shook his head. "He's better off in the tropics. He didn't belong up here."

"So you condemned him to sweltering on the beach and watching the sea level rise."

"Drinking warm beer because there's no ice. Battening down for hurricanes. Battling giant tropical spiders."

We lifted our glasses and toasted the guy who couldn't cut it in our environment of choice.

"When I found out you were coming to the station, I asked a few sources of my own about you," he told me.

"Find out anything interesting?"

"The station manager at McMurdo says you passed his test, and that's good."

When I was in grad school, I'd spent a summer at McMurdo Station in Antarctica, helping with a study of the microbiome of Antarctic soils.

"What test was that?" I asked. I didn't remember a test.

"He watches what people do in the cafeteria. He looks for people who are just as comfortable in a group discussion as they are sitting by themselves. You passed."

I nodded. "I get along with people," I said. "And I can get along alone."

He leaned back in his chair, studying me. "Tell me – why did you leave the university? You were teaching, doing research, on a tenure track."

"One too many committee meetings," I said lightly. He laughed, and I added, "I like to get things done."

"I can understand that," he said. "So tell me about this methane sequestering mat of yours. Or do you prefer 'fart catcher'?"

I shrugged. "Either one." Since Jackson was a biologist, I launched into an explanation of the biology of the system. "The mat's made of carbon fiber tubes, but what makes it work is the colony of bacteria in those tubes."

It turned out that Jackson knew quite a bit about *Methylomirabilis oxyfera,* the bacteria that made the mat work. Amazing critters those – they thrive in stinking black mud without light or oxygen, digesting methane and nitrogen oxides for their energy. In the tubes of the mat, they consumed enough methane to create a concentration gradient that kept the methane flowing into the tubes and rising into a storage tank.

"A biological methane pump?" he said. "That's clever. And you want to cover a square mile with this fart catcher? That's ambitious."

"A square mile is just a start. We have to move fast, you know. With the current rate of methane emission…"

He held up a hand to stop me. "Hold on. I don't need to hear another manifesto on Arctic warming. I live here, remember?"

"Sorry."

"Having that lake blow up gave your permafrost research quite a boost, didn't it?"

"I suppose it did."

"I can understand the motives of whoever did it. No one pays any attention to what happens up here unless it's involves something cataclysmic or cute. Polar bears get press; permafrost usually doesn't."

I didn't say anything. I just waited.

He studied me, then smiled, ever so slightly. "I assume that safety protocols will ensure that there will be no explosions associated with your project."

I nodded quickly. "I can assure you of that."

He poured another glass. "I'll give you a crew to lay out this fart catcher of yours. I trust you'll supervise the work."

I DID MORE than supervise. I worked alongside the crew that rolled out the fart catcher. It was nasty tedious work. The crew described it as hellacious, and I had to agree.

My test plot in Ivvavik National Park had been a flat grassy area. It had been easy to push the carbon tubes down so they made contact with the soil. On the coastal plain surrounding Franklin Station, the land was flat, but the vegetation was less cooperative. The fart catcher had to lie flat against the soil, so we had to clear away tough shrubs – willow and Labrador tea. We had to pound down dense tussocks formed by sedges and grasses. In a month and a half, we managed to install less than a quarter of the projected area.

I contacted some friends about the problem. It takes a team to save the world, after all. I had many friends and they had friends and their friends had friends. Social media was wonderful that way. My friends (and their friends) often had creative solutions. Some people talk about thinking outside the box. Many of my friends had never seen the box. They were unaware that the box existed. I sent out the word and waited to see what would happen.

A month later, as the crew and I were clearing yet another patch of willow, I heard someone call to me. I looked up to see a herd of shaggy beasts lumbering over the tundra toward us.

Muskoxen – Pleistocene megafauna at its most charismatic. They're called oxen, but they're actually more closely related to goats. Their ancestors had survived the mass extinction event that occurred during the transition from the Pleistocene to the Holocene. The herd stopped at the edge of the carbon tube carpet, eying me myopically as they stood shoulder to shoulder, ready to dispatch any predator with their large pointy horns.

"Hello!" Someone in a lavender parka came around the side of the herd and waved to me. "We're here at last."

That was Jenna, leader of the muskoxen herders. There were five muskoxen herders, two Royal Canadian Mounties, and a dozen cows and six calves. They had traveled from a muskoxen farm some 150 miles to the south.

I escorted the people and their shaggy charges to Franklin Station. While the ox herders found a patch of good grazing for the beasts, the Mounties met with Jackson and presented him with the official paperwork. Apparently, a Canadian muskoxen farm had donated the animals to Franklin Station – a donation approved by a top level official in the US agency responsible for polar research. It was unclear where the request for this donation had originated.

While Jackson chatted with the Mounties about their journey, I helped his assistant research the situation. The path of official approvals was an insane tangle, involving at least three agencies on the US side and the same number on the Canadian side. But in the end, it didn't really matter who had approved what. The muskoxen were an official gift from Canada to the US. Officials on the US side made it quite clear that sending the muskoxen away would cause an international incident.

Besides, news of the gift was already trending on all news feeds – it was the warm and fuzzy story of the day. A muskox calf is not nearly as cute as an Arctic fox, but they do have a certain charm. In those days of doom and gloom and climate change, cheery stories associated with polar science were hard to come by.

So Franklin Station gained a herd of muskoxen. Jackson found temporary quarters for the Mounties and the ox herders and arranged for a crew to set up a paddock for the beasts. To help out, I volunteered to take charge of the care of the muskoxen, mentioning that they could be an asset to my project. Muskoxen would happily devour tundra shrubs. Their hooves would break up and flatten the lumps and bumps in the soil, making it easier to roll out the fart catcher.

When the visitors headed to their quarters, Jackson asked me to stay. "So tell me," he said. "How did you make this happen?"

I shook my head. "I didn't make it happen." After a moment's pause, I went on. "I talked about the problems we've been having with laying out the fart catcher with a friend who studies muskoxen. He reminded me that large ruminants were great at modifying the environment. I did say that it was a pity I didn't happen to have any of those. He must have mentioned it to someone who decided to help out."

Jackson shook his head, looking incredulous.

"I've found that if you put the word out to enough people, useful stuff happens. You never know what it's going to be. But sometimes, it's just what you need."

"That's nuts. That's no way to manage a project."

I leaned forward in my chair. "Those beasts will make a big difference to how much mat we can install before winter. And you know this project is important. You've seen the changes in the Arctic over the last decade."

"Of course I have."

"Reduction in the sea ice. Steadily increasing temperature. Changes in wildlife patterns. Changes in weather patterns. When will the climate reach the tipping point? How long do you think we have? Another decade or two? Then what?"

"You think you'll save the world with a square mile of fart catcher and a dozen muskoxen?"

I shrugged. "It's a start. Baby steps, but it's a beginning. I promise there'll be no explosions. I'll take care of the herd. They won't bother you a bit."

OVER THE NEXT few weeks I worked with the ox herders to learn the ways of the shaggy beasts. The herd grazed in the area around the station, returning to their paddock at night for special muskox treats – carrots mostly. A muskox will follow you anywhere for a carrot.

The head of PR at the station shot photos and video: muskoxen grazing with the research station in the background, muskoxen in their newly built paddock, muskox calves sleeping by their muskox mamas. It was great PR for the station, and that earned Jackson some points with the administration. All good.

After a couple of weeks, the ox herders headed back to their farm, promising to return in the spring to comb out the qiviut, the muskoxen's underwool. It was a great cash crop, eight times warmer than wool and softer than cashmere. As a farewell gift, the ox herders gave me a set of long johns knit from qiviut – the warmest, softest, and most expensive underwear I've ever owned.

So that was my first summer at the station – laying carpet, bringing in some muskoxen, collecting some 30 metric tons of methane. Calculations for required storage had been spot on – the storage tanks were almost full. It was a good start, but it was time to move on to the next phase, one that was not covered in my grant application: disposing of the methane without adding it to the atmosphere and in the process funding a significant increase in the methane harvest.

IN THE FALL, I left the station to some business done in the lower forty-eight. I presented a paper at the American Geophysical Union's annual meeting in San Francisco and met with a few research teams from Siberia, Norway, Greenland, and Canada who were engaged in similar projects. While I was there, I also met with a German research group that was working on methane cracking.

Here's a quick chemistry lesson. Methane is made of carbon and hydrogen. In methane cracking, hydrogen is separated from carbon to make hydrogen gas and carbon. Hydrogen is a great fuel. Think of the *Hindenburg*: a big bag of hydrogen and a major explosion. If you burn hydrogen, you get water. No carbon dioxide, no greenhouse gas problem.

And here's a bonus. What's left when you take away the hydrogen is pure carbon. Perfect for making more carbon tubes to capture and store methane and valuable on the commodities market for use in manufacturing. Many companies from car makers to aircraft builders were switching from steel to lighter stronger carbon fiber to make their products. You can see why I was interested in methane cracking.

I met the Germans at a restaurant in Drowntown. That was the name San Franciscans had given to the area of downtown that flooded when the tide was high, a result of rising sea levels. It was low tide that evening. The streets were dry, but there was a whiff of salt and seaweed in the air.

The lead German researcher was Katrin, an earnest woman

who asked – politely but with a slightly baffled tone – about the American politicians' continued stress on carbon emission targets. "All research has indicated that stopping emissions will not stop the change in climate," she said earnestly. "Even if we stopped today, the world's temperature will continue to increase for half a century. They do not seem to understand that."

"Rearranging deck chairs on the *Titanic*," I said. "It's a popular pastime in political circles. I'm seen as the voice of doom and gloom because I recognize that the permafrost is melting at an increasing rate and that methane capture should be a top priority."

"And you are successfully capturing methane. What is your current capture rate?"

We drank beer and made calculations. Katrin estimated expenses on the back of a napkin as we worked out a plan for a pilot project involving methane cracking. During the Arctic summer, I could use solar power to crack the methane, and then cool and compress the hydrogen gas. I hoped to find a manufacturer to process the carbon into more carpet. Katrin had some ideas there – and some excellent contacts in the German manufacturing community.

"I understand that NSF regulations require you to purchase your materials in the US," she said.

I waved a hand, dismissing the problem. "I have private funding as well," I explained. The presence of the muskoxen had been an enormous help in crowdfunding efforts. Charismatic megafauna has its uses.

"Very good," she said. "Then I think I can assist you."

That was the first stop in a long winter of hunting and gathering. So many technical problems to solve, with little time and not enough money.

The hive mind found me a way to store the hydrogen that my pilot project would produce: a decommissioned tank from NASA, originally built to contain liquid hydrogen fuel for the space shuttle. It had never been used. For decades, it had been stored at NASA's New Orleans manufacturing facility on the far eastern edge of New Orleans – still above water, but just barely. The facility was being decommissioned – the last hurricane had come close to wiping it out – and they were happy to find a home for the fuel tank.

I set up a relationship with a German manufacturing plant that would make some of my pure carbon into fart catcher carpet and methane hydrate storage. I'd compensate them for their service with the rest of the carbon, which they could use or sell for a fat profit.

The rest of my time was spent retrofitting the hydrogen fuel tank for my needs and arranging for transport. Everywhere I went, I could see the effects of the changing climate. But people were doing what people always do – complaining about the weather and adapting to it where they could. Many politicians still doubted that change was underway even as some religious leaders were preaching about the end times.

I was happy to return to the Arctic for another summer of work. The carpet from the previous year was functioning beautifully. Arctic grasses and other plants were growing through the loose weave of the mat, making it a part of the landscape. Trampling by the muskoxen had smoothed out the cursed tussocks and laying the next section of carpet was considerably easier than the first section had been.

Of course, there were problems. On top of the usual sleet storms and blizzards, we had to be alert to changes caused by warmer temperatures. Whenever we were outside the station, we were armed against starving polar bears that thought Arctic researchers might substitute for their usual diet of walrus and seal. We almost lost part of the carpet-laying crew when a sinkhole opened up in the area where we were working. Fortunately, the fart catcher carpet was strong enough to act as a safety net. It supported us and let us climb back up out of the hole.

I won't pretend there weren't difficulties with the hydrogen tank (delivered a month late) and the pilot methane cracker. But we got it all working eventually.

I also expanded the research station's greenhouse, something that I'd discussed with Oki and kitchen crew the summer before. The original greenhouse was quite small – just big enough to grow a few vegetables. But with the hydrogen I was producing, I had energy to burn – so to speak. In my scavenging at the NASA manufacturing facility in New Orleans, I had run across a prototype greenhouse designed for Mars. The warehouse supervisor gave me a great deal on it. He said it would be abandoned within the month along with anything else left in the facility.

I set the Martian greenhouse up as an extension of the existing greenhouse. A hydrogen-powered heater allowed me to warm the air with no impact on the station energy budget and a cushion of carbon nanotubes insulated the permafrost from the greenhouse and collected the methane that outgassed.

Down in the lower forty-eight, things were getting worse faster than anyone had expected. Changes in polar temperatures had caused perturbations in the polar jet stream that wreaked havoc with global weather patterns. There was drought and wildfire in the western US, severe flooding in the South, historic blizzards along the eastern seaboard, and tornadoes where tornadoes had never been before.

By the end of the summer, I had quadrupled the land covered with fart catcher and I'd made plans to cover ten times that area in the following year. The research teams in Siberia, Greenland, Canada and Norway were also having success.

That winter, my efforts focused on acquiring hydrogen transport and figuring out how to roll out more carpet with the same crew.

Well, not exactly the same crew. I had been in touch with a robotics team that worked in an abandoned warehouse in São Paulo, Brazil.

They called themselves the Ant Factory, a non-profit collective of entrepreneurial engineers. Well... some of them were engineers. Some of them were artists. All of them were scavengers, retrofitters, people who knew how to make do, people who simultaneously thought in the long term and the short term. My kind of people.

"We're old school," the head engineer told me. At least, he seemed to be in charge. His name was Renaldo and he had a seemingly infinite supply of black T-shirts emblazoned with cryptic sayings. My favorite read 'Fast, Cheap, and Out of Control.'

Renaldo claimed that was the best approach to projects like mine. "You know how the US space program works," he said. "They triple check everything and build safeguards into their safeguards and redundancies onto their redundancies. We're the opposite of that."

In the warehouse parking lot, the Ant Factory had created an obstacle course where they held robot trials. Some parts of the course were constant – broken pavement, loose rocks, a pile of sand that could bury a bot in an avalanche. Other parts changed every day – the team was constantly adding booby traps and barriers. A slick of ice, a small mountain of melting snow, a sticky patch of some sort of goo – I thought it might be something toxic, but it turned out to be molasses.

The Ant Factory built me a robot that could traverse the course while rolling out fart catcher carpet. Actually, they built me a hundred robots – Renaldo called them "pequeninos peidos" – Little Farts. With a hundred robots, he said, it wouldn't matter if a few of them failed. "Power in numbers," he said.

Powered by hydrogen fuel cells, designed for rough terrain – originally the Little Farts were agribots designed to roll over just about any lump, bump, or tussock.

On my last night at the Ant Factory, I sat on the old loading dock and watched a dozen Little Farts navigate the course, towing and unrolling a large carpet that Renaldo assured me was heavier than the fart catcher. The team was celebrating. I had sprung for pizza and beer – a pilsner from a local brewery called Drown Your Sorrows. The label showed an ocean wave washing down Sao Paulo's main street.

"I don't know how I can thank you for all this" I told Renaldo as we watched one bot climb the slush mountain, trailing black carbon fibers. I wasn't paying the Ant Factory much. I'd almost exhausted my crowd-sourced funding.

He sipped his beer, surveying the rubble-filled yard. "You know those Hollywood movies where a few people save the world. We're those people. We'll make a difference."

I nodded.

Renaldo knew someone who knew Katrin, so he already knew

about my success with methane cracking. "What are you doing with the hydrogen you're producing?" he asked me. "I have a friend who would be happy to purchase it."

"Technically, I can't actually sell the products of my work," I told him. "That's against NSF regulations."

He nodded. "I understand. I am confident my friend would accept any hydrogen you chose to give him. He would offer goods and services in exchange."

"That could work. Of course, there is the problem of transportation."

"No problem. My friend Hehu lives in the Raft. He can take care of transportation."

The Raft was a seasteading community, a loose affiliation of over a hundred vessels that had been converted to floating farms and cities by climate refugees from small island nations that had been wiped out by rising waters.

"Let me contact him on your behalf."

I RETURNED TO the Arctic with Renaldo's bots. Jackson didn't ask questions about where I got them. He and I had developed a fine working relationship. He was glad that I needed a smaller work crew. The muskoxen were spooked by the bots at first, but they got used to them.

Renaldo's friend Hehu came through. He reached the research station with two ships – a former Arctic cruise ship, now modified as a floating farm and residence for a few dozen people, and a former navy ship, now modified for hydrogen transport.

Hehu was from Woleai Atoll, the first island group to be swamped by the rising sea. I liked his team of engineers – the head of the group was from JPL and he knew one of the aerospace engineers who had calculated the satellite orbits for me. He had, like me, gone rogue, and we had a fine time discussing the advantages and disadvantages of leaving the confines of the university.

It was a fabulous summer. There were the usual problems with sinkholes and sleet storms and polar bears, but the robots worked well and I successfully expanded the area covered with the fart catcher to about twenty square miles. As autumn approached, it was all going very well. Until it all went very wrong.

I should have paid more attention to the news. While I'd been setting up partnerships and laying carpet and dodging polar bears, there had been a presidential election, a major change in congress, and a shift in national priorities. Hurricanes had wiped out New Orleans and a few other southern cities. Storm-driven waves were eroding beach bluffs and flooding US cities. Funding was being diverted to disaster relief. Franklin Station would shut down at the end of the season.

And somehow my work had come to the attention of new political appointees in charge of climate research. They were upset by my dealings with Renaldo and the Germans and Hehu and... oh, just about everybody who had been helping me out. Some of my partners were apparently on terrorist watch lists.

At least, that was one story. Some of my friends suggested that the concern about terrorism was a cover. What had really pissed people off was the success of my methane cracking – steel manufacturers did not like the possibilities offered by cheap availability of pure carbon.

Whatever the cause, I was in trouble. Jackson told me that navy personnel who came to close down the station would be taking me into custody and charging me with a list of offenses including theft of government property and conspiracy to provide material support for terrorism. Jackson had been ordered to confine me to the station.

The day before the Navy ship was due to arrive, I left. At my request, Oki had packed a box of supplies – including all of the fresh carrots that were left in the greenhouse. Before hugging me goodbye, he quizzed me on my equipment. He listened carefully to a long list: silk long johns, qiviut underwear, a layer of wool, windproof coat and pants, parka, bunny boots, hat, hood, air filter to warm the air before it entered my lungs, rifle for the polar bears, a popup shelter, and on and on.

"All right," he said at last. "Stay warm, stay dry. Don't get dehydrated and eat as many calories as you can stuff in your face – and you'll be fine." He hugged me goodbye.

It was a sunny day with a light wind. Two Little Farts accompanied me, dragging my gear on an improvised sled made of a plastic pallet I had found on the beach among the driftwood. In addition to the food and gear I had listed for Oki, I had a fiberglass kayak that had been left in the station's storage by a seal researcher.

I took no satellite phone, no GPS, no electronics that might be used to find me. Such a strange feeling, leaving all that behind.

The muskoxen followed me – not out of affection, but in return for carrots that I dropped along the way. Their hooves completely obliterated my tracks and the marks left by my improvised sled and the Little Farts.

The hike to the shore was about a mile. When I reached the shore, I reset the Little Farts to return to the station. The muskoxen followed them, hoping for more carrots.

I abandoned the plastic pallet on the beach where I had found it, loaded the kayak, slid it into the water and headed west for a place I knew.

A few years back, I had decided to retrace the steps of my favorite Arctic explorer, Ernest de Koven Leffingwell, a guy who never got a lot of press. Everyone paid attention to Peary and Amundsen and Scott. Big voyages, big funding. Leffingwell never had much funding and didn't give a damn about reaching the North Pole.

He came up here in 1901 and fell in love with the Arctic. He spent nine summer and six winters up here, traveling around, making observations, keeping meticulous records. No fancy equipment – he had Inuit guides; he used dog sleds and small boats. He made the first map of the coastline worth looking at. He was the first person to explain ice wedges and the very first to pay any attention to the permafrost.

A few years back, I spent the better part of a summer retracing his journeys in this area. On that trip, I spent a week in an old prospector's house where Leffingwell had wintered. Half sod-hut, half log cabin, it was still in pretty good shape. Good shelter, well-concealed, near the coast, and so obscure that only a dedicated permafrost researcher would know about it.

The wind was with me, but even so it was a long paddle down the coast to the small inlet where the cabin was located. I beached the kayak and dragged it and all my gear into the cabin. The wind had picked up and I knew it would erase my tracks.

Inside, out of the wind, I made myself at home and waited for the search to come and go. It was a long wait. When weather was calm, I could hear the search helicopter from miles away – the distinctive whup, whup, whup of their rotors warned me to take cover so searchers couldn't spot me.

When the wind was blowing, the helicopters didn't fly. Then I would listen to the wind. Sometimes a gust would make the hut shudder so the boards creaked and groaned. More often a steady wind would make the walls vibrate, so I felt like I was shivering even when I wasn't. The wind had been trying to tear the hut down for more than a hundred years.

In the first week, a bear found my hiding place, but I had my rifle. Bear meat, while not fine dining, is a good source of protein.

The nights grew longer and longer until the sun never rose. When the sun was just below the horizon, it wasn't completely dark. It was like that time right after the sun sets, when the sky is the deepest possible blue. Imagine that deep blue moment stretching on and on. The blue light colored the entire world, reflecting from the snow and the water. I felt like I was swimming in the sky.

For me, that was the important moment. Not the brilliant golden flash of the lake's explosion, but rather the cool, blue, liminal light where nothing seemed real and I was not sure what would become of the world.

I had to wait a long time for the searchers to give up and leave, but eventually I stopped hearing helicopters. I returned to the station for the winter, a long paddle followed by a long walk over the pack ice. It was so cold that I could feel the mucus freeze in my nose when I took a breath without my air filter on. The very act of breathing put me at risk of dehydration – since every bit of water vapor froze instantly, the air was bone dry.

The station had been stripped down, but my friends had left behind everything I needed. There was a stash of canned food in the kitchen. The hydrogen-powered generator in the greenhouse was still there.

The winter was cold and long and lonely. I grew potatoes under improvised grow-lights. I set up a still and perfected the finest hooch ever made in the Arctic Circle. Arctic Fire, I called it.

Satellite communication had been shut down when they closed the station, but I rigged a ham radio. When the ionosphere cooperated, I could catch news broadcasts. The news was never good: heat waves, drought, hurricanes, flooding, famine, disease.

I managed to contact a few friends and I told them I was all right. They told me that the Navy team had searched for me in all the safety huts and all known emergency shelters. They fixated on the largest of the sinkholes – the one that almost swallowed my crew. They spotted some marks at the edge that could have been made by a rope and figured a sinkhole offered a great hiding place. Down there, there'd be no wind, no bears.

It had taken their team a week to stage an expedition to the bottom to look for me. I'm glad they all got in and out all right. Dangerous place, a methane sinkhole. Not somewhere I'd like to spend a lot of time.

Come spring, finding me was no longer a priority for the US government. The Arctic winter was summer in the Antarctic, and there had been some major developments down south. The Western Antarctic ice sheet, which scientists had thought would remain stable for several more decades, had started collapsing in a most spectacular fashion. The top layers of the sheet had been melting each summer, exposing long-buried crevasses. One of those crevasses broke through the bottom of the ice shelf, and an iceberg the size of Connecticut broke loose. A few weeks later, another one, just as big, broke free. Then another.

The icebergs were dramatic, but they weren't the real problem. The Western ice shelf held back the glaciers on the Antarctic continent. Without it, those glaciers would flow into the sea. All told, that could add 30 million cubic kilometers of water, give or take a few million, to the world's oceans. Faced with this threat, politicians were turning their attention to immediate construction projects to hold back the sea. A rogue scientist eating potatoes and polar bear meat in a closed research station was way down on anyone's list of concerns.

With the return of the spring, Hehu arrived with ships laden with fart catcher net, methane cracking equipment, and empty tanks to be filled with hydrogen. That was thirty years ago.

Now we have the world as it is.

I sit in Jackson's office. I still think of it as his, though he hasn't been here for thirty years. I use it as my office now.

Hehu sits in the chair on the other side of the desk. It's spring again and he has sailed north just as he has each spring for the last thirty years. But he hasn't come alone. Each spring, a fleet of ships comes north to spend the summer in the Beaufort Sea. It is a ragtag fleet of cruise ships and barges and freighters and navy ships, all repurposed for this new world, all laden with food and supplies for the station, all carrying folks eager to work on the annual methane harvest.

Some ships are equipped with methane cracking facilities; others carry empty hydrogen tanks or empty holds. Each ship has its own unique community and culture – some grow tanks of algae; others grow forests; some grow pot farms. Some are environmentally based communities with overtones of Native American cultures; some are party boats with overtones of Burning-Man culture.

They call themselves the Sunseekers. I call them the summer people. The winter doesn't exist for them – not really. It is always summer where they are.

I pour Hehu a glass of my Arctic Fire. "You make the best hooch in the Arctic Circle," he says.

I smile. I didn't make this hooch by myself. The station staff, all of them young and smart, do the hard work to keep the station running, monitoring the fart catcher, tending the muskoxen and reindeer, making high octane booze, and preparing for the Sunseeker fleet's arrival.

When the ships arrive in the Arctic, there is a great celebration with much singing and dancing. They celebrate the summer methane harvest and they treat me like a hero.

All summer long, the Sunseeker ships crisscross the ice-free Arctic ocean, visiting fart-catcher projects in Norway, Greenland, Siberia, Canada. Each autumn, the ships take away tanks of hydrogen and holds filled with pure powdered carbon.

The Sunseekers are a cheerful lot. And why wouldn't they be? This is a fine new world, a utopian future, a happy ending. As the permafrost melts, they capture the methane. As the oceans rises, they build more ships.

To them, it seems so natural that half the world's remaining population lives in nomadic floating colonies. Most of them didn't know any of the people who died in droughts and floods, heat waves and blizzards. They didn't know all those who suffered disease and famine.

Jackson died of dengue fever when disease-carrying mosquitos brought that disease to the American South, a shift made possible by warmer temperatures and increased rain. Katrin starved in the European famine – caused by unseasonable snowstorms resulting from the slowing of the Gulf Stream and the North Atlantic Drift, ocean currents that kept Europe warm. Renaldo drowned in a flood that wiped out Sao Paulo, the result of a monster storm. Just one extreme weather event among hundreds.

They all died. Billions of people died. Not millions – billions. It took all those deaths to bring the world population down to a more sustainable level and let us reach this happy ending.

This isn't the way I thought it would work out when I set out to save the world. All those square-jawed heroes of the old science fiction stories had it wrong. You can't save the world as we know it. I did what I could, and I did some good in the world. But you can't save the world without changing it.

"A toast," Hehu said, lifting his glass. "To the future."

I nodded and lifted my glass. "To the future. There's no stopping it."

355

An Owomoyela

Travelling into Nothing

An Owomoyela
Travelling into Nothing

She was offered the comfort of a drug-induced apathy. She refused.

The cell where she waited to die was, in true Erhat fashion, *humane*. Really, it was no worse than the room she had rented when she'd first arrived on the station, except for the hard lock on the door. She still had the same music at her fingertips, the same narrative media, the same computerized games of skill or strategy or wit or pure abnegation. All she lacked was freedom.

And a future.

Fuck.

She'd taken to pacing. Four steps wide, seven deep, over and over again until the door chimed – ahead of schedule – and her body seized up in panic, her breath vanished, and her hands fisted of their own accord.

But the voice which came through was... curiously non-final. "*Kiu Alee. Do you consent to receive a visitor?*"

She hesitated a moment, staring at the door. As her heartrate slowed, she said, "Yes" – more from morbid curiosity than anything else. After a moment, she added, "I didn't know I was allowed visitors."

The door slid open.

The man on the other side, flanked by a guard whose presence seemed almost cursory, was much taller than anyone in the local Erhat population – much taller than her, as well. Over two meters, at an estimate; he looked taller, with the long black robes that fell in a line down his body. His limbs were long and thin, like articulator arms on a dock, and his movements were fluid, but still hesitant. He had to duck his head to come in, and when he did, he stood there like an abstract statue, head tilted, eyes unfocused, ear turned her way.

Blind. Kiu blinked, moving slightly; true to her suspicion, his head turned to keep his ear angled toward her. Why someone would choose – with the number of augments and prosthetics available – to remain deprived of such a primary sense –

Of course, though, the same could be said about her, and everyone like her. She had no augments to increase her awareness of electromagnetic fields; no augments to expand her visual spectrum. That was her choice. It was every bit as much a choice as this man's probably was.

And the network of filaments laced through her brain like capillaries didn't even tie into the social web of the station, the system, the entire Erhat cultural organization. That had made her suspect here, long before she'd murdered someone.

"Kiu Alee," he said. His accent was strange, all rounded vowels and soft consonants, with an undertone of resignation. "I am Tarsul. *You* are a long way from home. Do you really intend to die here? I can give you a chance to live."

Kiu jerked back. "Me?" she said. "Why? For what?"

"Because you have an artificial neural framework," he said, and her surprise fell again. Of course – her augmented brain, her implanted-in-vitro augmentation, the neural scaffolding too integrated and expansive for any post-maturation implant to match. That made her *special*. This man arrived because she had a technology he needed; beyond that, he probably didn't give a whit about her.

And yet, she still wanted to live. What was a little indignity: if her life was only worth anything because of her brain, it was still better than it being worth nothing, without it.

"I've spoken with the authorities," Tarsul said. "They've agreed to release you if you never return to their territories." And why not – no further resource cost to house her, to destroy her body, to update the judicial records any further. And the Erhat government cared very little for any problems faced by those outside its borders. "This suits me, as if you agreed to come with me, you could not return, in any case."

Kiu had already agreed in her mind by the time that he finished talking. Still, for appearances sake, she hardened her voice, and repeated, "And for *what*?"

"I need you to pilot a ship," he said.

THE SHIP, AS it turned out, wasn't so much a ship. More of an engine rig.

More of an engine rig, burrowed into the side of a wandering planetoid, with access corridors and neural interfaces spidering across the surface.

Tarsul had said very little – in her cell, escorting her through the Erhat station's corridors, bringing her onto a transport which didn't look like it belonged in any of the territories she was familiar with. Though the transport, at least, had felt as though it wasn't completely *alien*; when they docked at the rig, the transport fit into the docking moors like a foot fitting into a glove, and they descended into smooth black halls, ambient light which seemed to glow from the air itself, a gravity which tugged more lightly than the Erhat station and more strongly than a planetoid of this kind should have merited, and a persistent low *hum* which modulated and changed in a kind of cadence, almost like distant voices. Kiu regarded it all with mistrust.

Tarsul closed the transport up behind them, fingers fluttering over the airlock console, which murmured back a long sequence of slow melodious notes. At length they petered out, and Tarsul laid his hand flat on the console. It didn't respond in any way.

"The transport has been disabled," he said. "Its engines and communications are no longer functional. I can explain where we're going, if you'd like to know."

Kiu raised an eyebrow, aware that he wouldn't be able to see it. He might hear the skepticism in her voice, though. "All right. Tell me."

He turned back to her, as though he'd expected her not to care – to be so grateful to get out of an execution that she'd sashay off anywhere at all, without a question or a second thought. Too bad; she had plenty of second thoughts. The fact that she had no options didn't stop her from having second thoughts.

Well, there had been the *one* option: to die. But she wasn't so principled that she thought that was an option at all.

"My home," Tarsul said, "is in the black. Interstellar space. It was built by refugees of the Three Systems' War."

Kiu frowned, and searched her memory for the war he named. She had the vague impression of learning about it at some point

– some incidental bit of history, consumed more for idle interest than relevance. "Is that ancient history?"

Tarsul *hmm*ed, deep in his throat. It didn't sound like he was disagreeing, though. "We have a long history," he said. "A long, very isolated, history. My arcology" – the word he used sounded *ancient* – "was designed to be impossible to track. Impossible to find. Utterly self-sufficient in every degree. It almost was."

Kiu had never heard of any permanent settlement outside a star system. Settlements in interplanetary space were uncommon; some of the larger stations might have held their own stellar orbits, like the Agisa Station Network where she'd grown up, but if anyone had asked her prior to this, she'd have said there was nothing of consequence drifting in the interstellar medium. Some ships in transit, maybe some ancient lost exploration vessels, or probes, or unfortunate failures of experimental engines. Not a – an *arcology*, some kind of station she'd never heard of.

"Why?" she asked. Tarsul looked surprised; maybe he was expecting her to care more about what had gone wrong. She didn't. "Refugees, yeah, I get it. But you had the materials to build a new station? And you didn't just... go to another system?"

"A cultural complaint," Tarsul said. "Believe me, if interrogating our history were to do any good..."

He let out a long, long breath, and apparently decided not to explain.

"The arcology was meant to be a closed system," he said. "No resource loss."

Kiu snorted.

Tarsul inclined his head. "It *almost* was."

"So... this." Kiu spread her hand out toward the consoles and the interface bay, indicating by implication the planetoid they were connected to. Tarsul's head shifted – tracking the sound of rustling sleeves, maybe. "We're delivering raw materials?"

Tarsul made a soft, affirmative noise. "Though it took me less time to locate this planetoid than to locate a pilot."

"I've never seen this kind of ship before." Kiu looked again at the composite walls, at the console. "Who made it?"

"A state secret. One which has not been shared with me." Kiu's eyes narrowed; Tarsul's tone cooled. Still, Kiu could recognize some of herself in that tone: a faint undernote of resentment, more well-hidden than she'd ever managed.

Or maybe that was just her imagination, painting commonalities where none were to be found.

"How am I supposed to fly it? I'm not licensed to fly –"

Anything. She had the basic safety certifications for automatic craft in Erhat and Agisa, but that mostly consisted of knowing how to set a distress beacon and fire the maneuvering thrusters if a collision was detected. And she'd never used any of those skills.

"Are you planning on teaching me?"

"The accelerator flies itself," Tarsul said. "It only needs to be reminded of where to go. As for *that*, you'll have a better idea of how to do so than I will." He brought his hand up, gestured to his own head. "It's not... precisely the same technology as the neural frameworks I'm familiar with. But they seem compatible *enough*. This is the third time someone has made this journey. Neither of the previous attempts encountered any difficulty."

Encouraging.

"We can begin, if you'd like," he said. "After bringing this planetoid out of this system and setting its trajectory, there will be very little to do. The accelerator is well-provisioned, and there's stasis if you'd prefer it. Perhaps an hour of your effort, and in return, I and my people will make sure you're accommodated for, in perpetuity."

Desperation made odd promises, Kiu thought. Lucky for her. "All right," she said. "Show me what I need to do."

THE PILOT'S INTERFACE was a little alcove, tucked away down a winding corridor studded, irregularly, with doors. No door separated the interface, though; Kiu had to wonder what design sensibilities this place had been made to accommodate.

The alcove was moulded into a kind of recumbent chair, with a webbing of wire connectors and something that looked like a scanner module near the headrest. The module lit up when Kiu approached, and Kiu could feel it ghosting over her augments. She cast a glance at Tarsul, but Tarsul gave no indication that he felt anything, or knew that anything was going on.

"So, no..."

Ceremony? Nothing I need to know? Evidently not. Kiu breathed in, and lowered herself into the chair.

She'd used neural interfaces before. This was a different model, but... *compatible enough*, Tarsul had said. She leaned her head back, reached a hand up to take hold of the interface wires, and felt them coiling, responsive, toward the ports on her scalp. A moment of cool intrusion, warming into connection – and then, abruptly, Kiu wasn't herself any more.

She was –

Much older, hands on the smooth black composite, not for any interface, just to feel the substance of the accelerator. A cold, clear purpose underlaid with urgent anger. Turning her head, a jangle of strange senses moving within her, seeing Tarsul standing beside her, expression sad. Seeing –

Someplace different. Long corridors, not as winding as the accelerator's. No windows; what few windows graced the arcology's walls faced the sweep of the Milky Way's arms edge-on, not the much sparser starfields orthogonal. The space filled with voices. Footsteps. The scent of green growing things. The sound of –

Someplace different. The accelerator, but not a part she'd ever seen. Argumentative tones, not in a language Kiu had ever learned. Her voice – not her own – responding in kind. Kiu –

Kiu snapped her head back.

The accelerator –

– flooded her.

Remembered.

And through it all, existing in clear pinpoint precision, knowledge without history or context, a *location* – nothing more than the endpoint of vectors and accelerations, no fixed point because it had no fixed referent, or possibly the one fixed point in a universe where everything else, including the engine, was moving in the ordered cacophonic chaos of orbital motion, stellar drift, universal expansion.

As soon as that hit her, she was rolled over into a flood of *need* – not desire, not yearning, but a compulsion as inexorable as every indrawn breath, as unconsidered as a heartbeat. *That* was where she needed to go. Somewhere in that was *home*. Home for this engine rig which had burrowed into the side of a planetoid; home for Tarsul, for some pilot who had come before. Kiu *reached*, and the whole of space seemed to shudder around her. The accelerator snapped into motion.

And then Kiu came dislocated, like a joint wrenched out of socket, and shoved herself away from the interface. She flew in the low gravity; hit both knees and her forehead and palms on the cold composite of the hall, and then twisted, snarling, her entire sense of self ricocheting against the walls of her skull.

Tarsul was there. His hands hot on her arms, and she twisted in the microgravity, lashing out.

"Calm," he urged her.

She snarled. Tried to shake him off.

Everything felt *wrong* in the low gravity. Kiu had lived her entire life in the real gravity of a planet, or the centrifugal gravity of a station – out here, she felt dislodged, disconnected, like her entire life had become illusory when she had become weightless. That only made her angrier.

They have gravity on the arcology, some fragment of memory – not her own – reminded her. Minded her? Could it be a *re*minder, happening for the first time? *Not centrifugal. Experimental?*

Like the planetary accelerator she'd just plugged into? Like –

Tarsul's gloved hands, curling against her sleeves, colder and more rigid than they should have been. A soporific calm beginning to infiltrate her consciousness.

She kicked out, and Tarsul let her go. He floated back toward the opposite wall, head canted.

He wasn't wearing gloves.

"What," she pronounced, "the *fuck*?"

"You're more equipped to answer that question," he said. "Did something go wrong?"

Kiu spluttered. She dragged the back of her hand across her mouth, glaring murder at Tarsul. Her hands itched for violence.

Worthless drifting piece of debris – dragged me out here to make a fool of me –

"Who were those people? Where was that – those weren't my memories!"

Tarsul considered that. Then he said, "Ah."

"*Ah?*"

"The accelerator gleans memories from each of its pilots," he said. "I believe it was also intended as some form of... archival device, perhaps? As an ancillary function. I was told it was quite pleasant. Reassuring, in a way."

Kiu spat. "*Reassuring?*"

"Especially for a history as contentious as ours."

Kiu didn't know enough to unpack that. Didn't know Tarsul enough to interpret it. Still, she could have sworn he looked *amused*. And that –

That was too much. The rage closed over her like a fist, like plunging into the water by a sulfur geyser, noxious and hot and filling her lungs. She lunged.

Tarsul's amusement vanished in an instant. And, fast – *too* fast, with the kind of rapid-twitch motion that spoke to muscular augments, reflex enhancements, he sidestepped her attack, and put his hand out to catch the back of her neck. In another second he had her forehead against a wall, one of her wrists caught and pressed against the small of her back.

"It's adaptive to fight when one's life is at risk," he said. "You are not under threat. Despite what you may feel. This, particularly, is maladaptive action."

Humiliation coiled at the pit of her gut. Tarsul was treating her like a child, or like some kind of a toy – pick her up from the cell because she was *convenient*, right, bring her here and plug her into the engine like she was a spare part, lecture her like she was some idiot. "Let me go," she warned.

To her surprise, he did. "I like you," he said. Then, an incredulous noise from Kiu: "My policy is to like all people until I have a reason to dislike them. Because I asked you to join me, I have a duty to... situate you. I'd ask you, as a kindness, not to make this job more difficult."

Kiu spluttered.

"Of course, I knew I took a risk when I found you." Tarsul turned his back to her, which only made the rage spike higher. "But people with artificial neural networks as advanced as yours tend not to be the kind of people who would leave their homes forever, with very little explanation. You were the culmination of seven years of searching." He turned his ear back toward her. "I'm curious how you came to be where you were."

Yeah; most of the people with her kind of augments weren't sad-sack drifters, weren't murderous detriments to society. She got that; she was *special*. "I don't want to talk about my past," she growled.

"Of course not. But our pasts influence our futures." Tarsul rolled one shoulder. "I also have a duty to the arcology. Bringing this planetoid to them ensures their resource security for another thousand years, perhaps. But *you*, Kiu Alee –"

He turned his whole body back to her, head canted, as though he could pin her with his listening the way someone else might pin her with a gaze.

"I also want to know that I ensure their security by bringing them *you*."

* * *

Kiu avoided Tarsul as much as she could, given the confines of the ship. It wasn't as difficult as she'd feared; the accelerator sprawled, replete with odd closets and rooms which had been mostly, but not entirely, cleared of detritus. Kiu made a room for herself out of the provisions that Tarsul had, apparently, bought on Erhat: a sleeping cocoon, listening materials on a tablet, a selection of meals, all with their own containment and heating units, so she didn't have to run the risk of encountering him whenever she wanted food.

She'd refused suspended animation. After the interface, she didn't relish the thought of going back down into her brain, even if she wouldn't be conscious to experience it.

Still, after a while – without anything that served to delineate the time, either to a trade standard or a local schedule – she started wondering just how long she could manage. The accelerator's black walls were depressing and disorienting, like she was both adrift in starless space and confined in a space where the walls were too close. She could reach out and just barely not touch the walls of the room.

So eventually, she started wandering.

It was strange, how easily her body adapted to moving through the gravity of this place. As though her body was also accessing memories that weren't hers.

And eventually, she encountered Tarsul.

He was at rest, reclining on a little bench which may not have been a bench, in design. His hands were folded on his chest. He wasn't moving, but he was breathing deep and even; his eyes were open, so he wasn't sleeping. Kiu paused in the doorway to the little room.

"What are you doing?"

Tarsul tilted his head. "It's been a long time since I've been home," he said. "It's strange to realize I'm finally returning."

Kiu grunted. She let herself in, a few more handspans. Still kept a good distance between herself and Tarsul. "How long?"

Tarsul was silent.

Kiu narrowed her eyes at him, but she kept silent as well. Even so, Tarsul exhaled, sounding like he was disappointed in her. "I'm not sure, exactly."

"How many times have you made this trip?" Kiu asked.

At that, Tarsul actually looked surprised. He turned so that his whole body was facing her, head canted to one side.

"Me?" he asked. "The last time we sought resources from a star system was over a hundred twenty standard generations ago. How old do you think I *am*?"

"I remembered you," Kiu said. "You were there, in the accelerator's memory."

Tarsul's eyebrows knit together. "Two explanations," he said. "One: your own memories contaminated the accelerator's stored memory at the same time its contaminated yours. Pieces of your own experience became blended with what you remembered. None of the memories are faithful representations of anyone's experience. Two: coincidence. Someone on an historical resource-gathering expedition looked like me. Nothing more."

That would make more sense, she supposed.

Because what was the other explanation? He was over a hundred twenty standard generations old? – whatever that even *meant*, coming from his colony. Unlikely; the best genetic treatments couldn't extend life that far. He was cloned, or gengineered? Plausible, but why? She'd met plenty of heavily-gengineered humans, and they were without fail more impressive than Tarsul seemed to be. And if over a hundred generations had passed since that memory, they probably would have improved their gengineering, too. Why reuse the same models?

"You came out here. From your arcology."

Tarsul nodded, absently.

"How did you –" *Not go insane?* "Keep busy on the way out?"

"Meditation, mostly," Tarsul said.

"Really?"

Tarsul spread his hands. "I regarded it as a pilgrimage. I was chosen because I was... temperamentally suited to such a long journey. Unfortunately, that was a consideration I didn't have the luxury to make, for you."

Kiu made a disparaging noise.

"Maybe you'd prefer to sleep," Tarsul said. "We can still put you into suspension. I'm told that it's a dreamless sleep."

The same way that memory was supposed to be reassuring? Kiu thought. "No. Thank you. I'll figure something out."

"Of course," Tarsul said. "Let me know if I can offer any diversion."

"I'm not much into meditation," Kiu said.

Tarsul laughed, briefly. "I'd think not. Even so."

"Right."

Kiu lingered for a moment longer, then took herself away down the hall.

And occupied herself for some short span before folding, and admitting that stasis might be a more comfortable way of traveling by far.

* * *

Tarsul was right about this, at least – the sleep was dreamless.

She had no conception of the passage of time when consciousness infiltrated her mind again, arriving in a fog of sleepy confusion. She came to not quite knowing where she was; shivering very badly. Entirely psychosomatic, she'd been told, but she didn't believe it.

Tarsul was at the console beside her stasis bay, an inscrutable series of tones informing him of something. Kiu's arm ached, faintly, where an IV had gone in. "We're there?" she asked – but the apprehension of entering a new world, a strange station and culture, didn't have a chance to develop.

"We're off-course," Tarsul said. Maybe it was her imagination, but he sounded tired. "Something must have gone wrong with the calculations."

Kiu pushed herself out of the bay, and caught herself against the wall. It felt strangely warm against her palm. "I thought you said the accelerator handled all the actual calculations."

"With some form of input, some guidance, from the pilot," Tarsul said. "I don't pretend to understand the intricacies. But it has never failed, before."

And with that, a new apprehension rose in Kiu's chest. "What's that mean?" *Don't ask me to, don't ask me to –*

"It means we're traveling into nothingness," Tarsul said. "Unless you can correct the course. The accelerator *can* correct itself, I'm led to believe, even at these speeds."

The apprehension roiled into full-blown fear. "You want me to plug back into that thing."

"Unless the thought of drifting forever appeals to you." Tarsul turned his ear toward the hall. "Though 'forever', in our case, is bounded by the finite amount of supplies we have on board."

Slow deaths, then. Set against the immediate threat of all those voices, all those images, blooming up in Kiu's mind. Her heart sped.

As though he could hear that, Tarsul turned back toward her. "It can wait. A few hours will hardly make a difference."

Except that it would be a few hours more of sitting and dreading. Kiu grit her teeth. "No. I'll go now." Go under threat, but then this entire voyage had been under threat. That was nothing new.

She went back to the interface. Plugged herself in. Tensed her shoulders, tensed her hands, and all sensation of shoulders and hands and body dissolved.

Into –

A little planetoid was nothing. She stood at the helm of a planet, now – no atmosphere to shear off, but thrust turned it oblate. Their progress was slower. Not, however, slow. They could put together most of a system this way –

Or simply flee. Another time, another planetoid, another pilot, staring down at his gloved hands. Memories already coursing through his brain, which Kiu felt at one remove. The whole black body of the accelerator representing a theft as well as an escape. Looking up, to meet the eyes of an engineer who had no idea how to work any but its most basic functions, an entire body of knowledge left behind. Saying –

The tall man again, the one who looked like Tarsul, saying, No, it's futile. In the long run, the arcology will die. Of isolation. Of indolence. Of attrition. Saying, the prudent choice is to return to a star, and all the resources it offers. Not to continue out here, in the black.

Saying, I'll do my best for you, but I won't do anything beyond that.

Kiu didn't even remember the snap of the course correction; the driving need to go home. She snapped back into herself like a line under tension, shaking, with her hands in fists. And Tarsul, standing there, head cocked, as though he could *hear* the rage pouring off her. As though he'd neglected one of the traditional senses for some fleet of senses she had no knowledge of.

I won't do anything. So very like Tarsul, that.

She could have killed him, there.

Could have. That was a proven fact – and she'd thought, for the most part, that killers were people unlike her; people who didn't know what direction rationality lay in when it was pointed out to them, people whose brains were fried by some accident of genetics or chemical interest or brainwash mis-socialization. Not people like her, who got angry, yeah, but knew where the line was. And yet.

And *yet.*

There in no particular Erhat corridor, with no particular history of confrontation, in a bad half-second on a bad day in a bad string of days, some Erhat boy no older than her had looked at her and his face had twisted, the universal human expression of disgust, and he'd sent some social impulse off with an ostentatious tilt of his head. Something that had caused his networked friend down the hall to turn, and look at Kiu, and *laugh*, and Kiu, who'd been through too many homes already and knew, *knew* that she was still a piece of foreign debris in this one but would have liked to go a day without being *reminded* of the fact – had taught a lesson with a small stylus, just tapered enough to enter through human muscle and skin, given enough force.

Nothing said *I belong; I'm valuable, I'm worthwhile* than a staggering act of antisocial tantrum, huh. Even she knew that had been stupid.

It had stopped his friend from laughing, though. At the time, she hadn't seen past that – not one second, not one thought, not one millimeter.

Tarsul, now, had his eyes unfocused – they were *always* unfocused – but it seemed as though he was looking far afield. All the way out to his arcology, full of people whose skin was no thicker than that young man in the corridor. They could solve the problem of resource collection in the interstellar nothingness, but maybe they couldn't solve the problem of her.

"Kiu," Tarsul said. His tone made resentment march up her spine.

What are you going to do? she could have asked. *I'm the only one who can pilot this ship. I'm the only way your stupid arcology will have the material to keep breathing, keep eating, keep the lights on. You need me.*

To the exact extent that he needed this expedition to return successfully. And just what extent *was* that?

Was he the person in the accelerator's archived memory?

He let out a long breath, here and now. "Maybe you should sleep again."

"I don't want to sleep." She didn't want to stay awake, either. She wanted to crawl out of her skin. Get in a fight. Hurt someone.

Tarsul sighed again, and said, "I see."

"What are you going to do with me?" Kiu demanded. She realized, as she said it, how her breath sounded – ragged, rough, like she was looking for a fight. She *was* looking for a fight. She knew where she stood, when her fists hit flesh. "I'm bringing you home." *I'm doing my best.*

I won't do anything beyond that.

"I've yet to decide," Tarsul said. Like nothing, like this was easy.

Kiu jerked up from the interface chair.

Tarsul stepped back, and then turned, and walked away.

KIU RAN THE halls, as best she could. Tried to burn off the anger. It worked as badly as it ever had.

Between footfalls, between corners, she tried to think of options.

They were frustratingly few. She didn't know how to fix the accelerator so it would listen to her; she didn't know how to fix herself. So, maybe Tarsul would decide he was better off with her dead. She could strike first – she thought she'd be good at that – but if she killed Tarsul, what would she do? Show up at his arcology without him and expect them to let her in? They sounded like class-A xenophobes; Kiu didn't find the idea likely.

What else? Pilot the planetoid somewhere else? The accelerator alone would sell to just about any shipyard or research consortium for more than Kiu would need, but it seemed to have a mind of its own. Kiu had no idea how Tarsul had gotten it out to the Erhat system in the first place; maybe it was easier without a planetoid attached, but she couldn't even get it to go where *it wanted* to go. So that was out.

Which left... not much. Starve to death slowly as the provisions ran out.

She punched a wall. It didn't help.

In time, as though it had a gravity all its own, she went back to the interface.

She stood staring at it for a good, long time. The source of all her problems, this thing – or, at least, that was a tempting excuse. Much better than all her problems coming from her, or from genetics, or from ontogenic accident. If it caused her problems, maybe it could damn well fix them.

Of course, she couldn't just hit it until it agreed.

It and its memory, of people and things and places that all seemed to have so much more import than her haphazard little flight, her haphazard little life. All those people, coming into her brain and washing over her, more real to her than she was.

Then it struck her.

If this thing was meant to archive, then fine, it could archive *her*. Maybe she wasn't fit to live. But she'd still be remembered by someone. Something.

The thought appealed to her. Before she made a conscious choice, her body was already moving back to the seat.

Bad idea. Yes, well, probably, but she wasn't much use at having good ones. She growled to herself as she fit the connectors back against her scalp, but she'd decided; she was committed.

She activated the interface, and memory became the air around her.

Or – maybe not *memory*. Maybe just –

A sense of place, so strong as to be overwhelming. The corridors of the accelerator, but more present and real than they had been as she stood in them. These flooded her awareness, denying distraction, constructing themselves in her mind.

And in her mind, the man who looked like Tarsul materialized as though she'd simply forgotten that he'd been standing there.

But Kiu knew where she was. She didn't dissolve into it. Instead, she steeled herself, and spoke, with something that wasn't her voice:

"Who are you?"

Kiu Alee, the apparition said. It didn't sound like Tarsul; not entirely. Or maybe she just didn't know him well enough to catch this tone. *What an absolutely useless question.*

She had no sense of her body, here. She couldn't lash out. She couldn't feel her chest tighten, her breath draw in, her jaw and hands clench. It was freeing, in a way. It was also a little like death.

"Okay, then." She couldn't take a deep breath. Couldn't relax her muscles. And yet, she could still feel anger, like a sensation in a phantom limb. "Here's one: why can't I fly this thing right?"

Much more useful. Unfortunately, much more complicated. The not-Tarsul turned eyes on her: blank, flat, and still piercing. *You are not entirely similar to pilots in the past.*

No lip to curl. No teeth to grit, as she considered say saying, *No, I'm one of those accidents that happen from time to time.* What a waste of resources; what a waste of implants. If the Agisa medics could have pulled the filaments out of her brain and left them salvageable in any meaningful way, they probably would have.

Instead, she found herself here.

But it is an opportunity to learn, the apparition said. *I appreciate the chance to analyze your augments. And to analyze you. Of the two, you are more interesting.*

Slow realization crept through her. "You're not a memory," she said. "Are you?"

You aren't accessing the archived memories, not-Tarsul responded. *I understand the interface controls are erratic on your side, as well. Still, you chose how this interface was calibrated.*

"You're the engine," Kiu said. "You're the ship."

An acceptable explanation.

And that – all the questions she could ask, like *who made you* or *where did you come from*, vanished under the tide of annoyance. "You know where you're going," Kiu said. "Clearly, you have some kind of intelligence. Why can't you just fly yourself home?"

Calculations, it said, but Kiu thought there was a coyness to the answer. A slight tinge of lie. *Organic processors handle some calculations better.*

"If you needed organic processing, your builders could have grown a neural web on a substrate."

Before she could finish the thought, she was answered – *Well, just so. And once a human is connected, why not keep a piece for analysis?*

Kiu jerked.

And then she dove, back down toward her body, coming back to the surface of her consciousness with her hands on the connectors. But then the quick-trigger affront died back, just enough to let her close her eyes again, search for the connection.

"You're copying my neuron structure? Culling it? Replicating it?" Even in Agisa, that wouldn't have been possible. But moving a planetoid wouldn't be possible, either. Nor would moving anything but information at this ridiculous speed.

Not as you suspect it, the accelerator responded. *Your neuron structure, even with its augments, is not deterministic as to your experiential reality. I expand myself. But if you connected looking for immortality, pilot, all you'll receive is approximation. Still, this is valuable to me. Whether or not it is valuable to you hardly matters.*

She could have laughed. "Story of my life, isn't it?"

Well, it said. *Keep coming back. So far as the story of your life goes, it will matter here more than anywhere.*

That didn't sound like something Kiu was meant to understand. She moved past it. "If you study my augments, will you course correct? Is that what you need?"

No, the accelerator said. *That, I'd do for my own interest.*

"Wonderful. Great." This thing's intelligence was entirely unhelpful. "Can you just tell me why you won't *go home?*"

Kiu Alee, the accelerator said. *Why won't you* **let me?**

KIU WORKED HER body as hard as she could, after disconnecting. Made circuits of the halls, pushed and pulled against fixed points, did stretches and fast motions until she was gasping air. It bled off some of the boiling energy, if not all of it.

She came to Tarsul in the console room, a far-flung little space full of screens which he disregarded. She was almost too exhausted for rage, mostly just too cynical for anything. Tarsul tilted his head to acknowledge her entry.

"We are *still* not on course," he said. He sounded resigned. "I admit, I'm surprised. I don't know of any pilot who... experienced this much difficulty."

"I'm special," Kiu said, voice heavy. "My brain doesn't work right. Ace choice in pilots, though."

Tarsul turned to better regard her. His face, in that three-quarters turn, looked drawn and pensive. Kiu could almost hear the retort on his tongue: *I had no choice.*

Yeah, well. Seemed to be a common complaint, here.

Kiu glared at him for a while, and then softened, despite herself. Raw deal for him; surrounded by all this wonder, and he had a murderer with a broken brain on one side, a starving arcology so hidebound they needed a planet brought to *them* on the other. And hour after hour, he just kept doing what was in front of him to do.

Kiu felt a stabbing moment of powerlessness, of the attendant rage. She fought it back down.

"I can try again," she said. "One more course correction, right? No harm in trying."

"No harm," Tarsul agreed. Kiu wondered if, behind that easy agreement, he was already writing her off.

"Yeah," she said, and went back down the hall. After a moment, Tarsul followed her.

Maybe she'd go into the connection and not come out. Maybe she'd let Tarsul sedate her and let the accelerator mine her brain and learn her augments and maybe she would learn the command that would set their course correctly. Maybe that was the option left to her.

What had Tarsul said? *It's adaptive to fight when one's life is at risk.* Well, throwing a punch wouldn't save her, so maybe she should stop trying to throw the first punch. Maybe she should find something to pre-empt the violence that waited on the other side of every heartbeat. Maybe this was it.

"I think I can do this," she lied.

"I'm heartened," Tarsul said.

Maybe it was Kiu's imagination, but he sounded like he had as little faith in her as she did.

No matter.

She went back to the interface. Lowered herself into the chair.

Tarsul tilted his head at her. "You seem different," he said. His voice was curious. Maybe a shade wary.

I don't know if I've given up on life or had a breakthrough, Kiu didn't say. *Maybe a breakdown.* She grunted, vaguely, in reply.

"Are you well?" Tarsul asked.

"Fine. I'm always fine."

She reached for the interface wires, and pulled them down toward her head.

Tarsul was hesitating, as though he had something he wasn't sure he should say. Kiu paused with her hands on the wires, and raised an eyebrow she knew he couldn't see.

Whatever internal line of thought had occupied Tarsul wended its way to a close. "I wish you luck," he said.

"Huh," Kiu responded.

Then she attached the connectors, breathed out, and opened up, and surrendered herself to going home.

383

Thoraiya Dyer

INDUCTION

Thoraiya Dyer

INDUCTION

Induction n.

1. Provision of occupational health and safety training in a mining environment.
2. i. Inducting ii. Inducing iii. Production of an electric or magnetic state by proximity of an electrified or magnetic object iv. Drawing of a fuel mixture into the cylinder(s) of an engine. v. Reasoning (from observed examples) that a general law exists.

1.

DON'T LEAVE ME, Christian had begged his father.

I'm not leaving you, Dad had promised. *You're just going to stay with Granny for a while.*

Granny was tall. Her merry brown eyes and square, white-streaked haircut were high and far away, blocked by an oblong of flower-print dress and square-toed black shoes. Christian's father had lifted him to be close to the friendly face, but Granny had made a lowering motion and said,

He's old enough to walk, Godwin.

She took Christian's hand in her rough, dry palm. They walked down the palm-tree lined road until there was no more road, and then they took their shoes off and walked in the sand. That was when Granny first told him about the Freezers.

We found de Freezers when I was three. Took a fishing boat to Scrub Island and found dem, all de children running loose. We were completely free. De ocean was blood-warm. De town pool was blood-warm. De Freezers were limestone, cold water sea-caves. Dey went way down. We'd hold our breath, see how far we could go before we'd pop up in a pocket of air.

Granny's palm started to get sweaty. She swapped her shoes, stocking-stuffed, which she held by the heels, to her left hand, and Christian took her right. Now he was on the side of the sea. Pale topaz water lapped against the corpse of a broken umbrella.

Sandpipers ran from them, too light to leave footsteps in the sand.

I'm surprised nobody drowned, Granny went on. *Our parents didn't know about de caves. If a child didn't come home, dey wouldn't have known where to look. I was de smallest. My neighbour Viv looked after me. One time, dey all had to tie deir shirts together to get me out from a hole. Viv – his real name was Walter but he loved cricket and Viv Richards was Captain of de West Indies at dat time – always said dere was pirate gold, dat we'd find it if we went deep enough.*

And Christian, who never spoke if he could help it, whispered, *Can we go to de Freezers, Granny?*

'Fraid not, sweet boy, Granny answered, squeezing his hand. *Like many things around here, dat place has long ago been eaten by de sea.*

Granny's mind has now been eaten by old age, according to Christian's half-brother, Roy. Lung cancer, which she keeps forgetting she has, gnaws at the rest.

Christian stares out the window of the light aircraft, cowrie-brown knees wedged up against the seat in front. He listens to the whine of the engines; feels the roughness of the descent towards Anguilla's single airstrip in the much-reduced Valley; gets a glimpse of the now-separate island which his child-self called home.

There'll be no beach stroll to Granny's house this time, even if his brittle bones could hold together the whole way. It's different, seeing it in stark sunlight. Much worse than seeing it from space. The four ValleyPower rigs, once cornerstones of the long, leaf-shaped main island, still stand with their two hundred thousand ton concrete bases and hurricane-proof semi-circular shields, deriving over five hundred megawatts apiece from solar, wind and ocean thermal energy conversion.

Yet the towns supplied by the high voltage submarine cables are evacuated. Christian is here to convince Granny to leave. To force her if necessary.

The Irihana Wave arrives in three months.

A ROBOTROLLEY COLLECTS his luggage.

The airport exit is blocked by fluorescent orange panels diverting new arrivals to a kind of classroom. Individual desks form parallel rows. While some passengers stand, bewildered, by Christian's side, the Mexican and Barbadian labourers, their canvas bags hung with hearing protection and hard hats, settle into the seats with soft sighs.

Induction

A woman, six-foot seven with a shiny black beehive, drops heavy manuals, chunks of actual paper, on each desk.

"Dis an obligatory induction," she announces when the last booklet is dispersed, "as de entirety of Anguilla is classified a restricted work site. Even if you don't intend to approach de bore or de tailings, dere are heavy vehicles on de roads. Familiarise yourself with de risks. De Wave is not calculated to arrive before July, but dere is significant margin for error. In short, de island could explode at any time."

One of the workers whispers an explosion sound at his hunched-over neighbour, making his clenched fists fly apart with spread fingers. She rolls her eyes at him and continues replacing her plane-friendly plimsolls with thick socks and steel-capped boots. An indulgent smile plays around the lips of the woman with the beehive; she waves a manicured hand at three slim openings with simple keypads and screens inside.

"Pass de examination," she says, "and you may enter de site. Do not try to take de booklets out of dis room. De information is confidential."

Christian flips to a random page. There, a diagram of the bore is labelled with its dimensions.

Bore width: 5 metre (m) (diameter)
Bore depth: 30 000m
Volume of displaced basalt: 2 355 000m^3
Mass of displaced basalt: 7 088 550t
Volume to be vapourised, 50% = 1 177 500m^3 of SiO_2
(energy requirement 8 831 250 gigajoules (GJ))

On the opposite page, the font is large enough for preschoolers to read. Christian absorbs the information easily, impressionable as a preschooler, yet fails to react emotionally to its enormity; it's been difficult to feel, to care about much, since re-entry.

The remaining 3 544 275t of slag (consisting chiefly of Al_2O_3, CaO, FeO and MgO) will be raised 30km to the surface. There, it will be moved by haul truck to form solid channels and barriers. These peaks and valleys will guide the flow of magma.

Density of basaltic magma is 2.65 to 280gm/cm³; less than the density of solid basalt (3.011gm/cm³). The main process is simply that the magma is more buoyant. When the Irihana Wave arrives, molten rock will rise until it reaches the surface, restoring the main island of Anguilla to pre-climate change twentieth century dimensions of 26km long x 5km wide. New average elevation will be 200m.

In the event that cooling has been miscalculated and magma flow slows or stops, the slag-extracting pumps inserted into the bore can be reversed; seawater can be pumped into the magma. Injection of hot, new magma into the asthenosphere by the Wave will have already caused gases to come out of solution. This enhances artificial decompression caused by drilling the bore. Adding water will increase explosive force even further to blast away early-forming solid plugs.

IMAGE NOT TO SCALE.

* * *

Induction

WHEN CHRISTIAN ESCAPES the induction, night is falling.

Roy's driver waits for him on the other side, holding a smartpaper which reads MR. CHRISTIAN WATERS.

"Sorry," Christian says. "I need to use the bathroom before we go."

"Very good, sir," Roy's driver says.

In the airport restroom, Christian defecates into a ValleyFresh modular waterless composting toilet. It's the product that made his father's fortune, taken up en masse when metropolitan sewerage systems were switched into reverse by rising tides. The capital raised was then ploughed into ValleyPower.

Christian is the oldest son. He should have inherited ValleyFresh and ValleyPower when his father and Roy's mother, Lilah Spencer-Churchill, were killed in a light plane crash.

Christian didn't want them.

Roy manages both companies these days. Like an ugly, hand-crocheted hat your embarrassing poor relations gave you for Christmas, which you have to wear, sometimes, for politeness' sake.

2.i.

"WELL," ROY SAYS, staring. "I never expected to see you again. Weren't you supposed to plant the seeds of the human race beyond the solar system?"

The scotch in his glass is the colour of his skin. Impeccably dressed, even at this late hour, Roy wears light-bending fabrics which accentuate his shoulders, slim his waist and give the subtle impression of added height.

A straight fall of fringe brushes the noble brow where Christian can easily imagine Roy's coronet resting; he's a baronet or something; his mother's brother a duke. Yet he pretended to be pleased when they inducted him into the Anguilla Hall of Fame for his services to hygiene, handing over a plastic pageant crown.

"Here I am," Christian says, leaning back into a carved walnut armchair. It's at least two centuries old, one of the few antiques in the manor that hasn't yet been wrapped for transport to London. There, Roy has another house – or rather, four houses sutured into one giant Frankenhouse – where he'll wait out the rebirth of Anguilla in his image.

"You look terrible," Roy observes. Christian accepts a glass of water with a tremor in his wasted hand.

"Ten years in low gravity," he says. "They solved the cancer problem but not that one." He's no longer angry with Roy for failing to supply Granny with costly neoplasia preventatives. Anger slips away so easily; an ice cube melting in his hand.

"It's not catching?" A delicate pause before Roy's final word.

"No." Christian fishes the ice cube out with his left hand. Then, careful of the crystal against his chipped teeth, he downs the contents of the glass. "There's no space plague. The habitat leaked, that's all. We had to abandon it. The mission, too. So the engineers said."

"Engineers!" Roy attempts bracing brotherly camaraderie. "You'll want to watch that bothersome breed."

But Roy is a stranger.

"I didn't mean to force myself on you." Christian fights the urge to close his eyes. "I was going straight to Granny's but there was this thing at the airport. It took forever."

"My lawyers advised me on it," Roy says, and now his eyes are cold; he's the owner of all the power, the fresh water and the land. Not to mention the toilets.

"Lawyers. You'll want to watch them. They advised me to sign away all my inheritance."

"Because you were never coming back!" Roy's eyes bulge.

"Here I am," Christian says again, softly.

Roy scrabbles about at a polished rosewood writing desk. His computer, embedded, spits out permanent paper from a hidden cavity. He puts his palm to the paper, switching on an art deco lamp, but when Christian shows no sign of getting out of the armchair, he brings it to him.

"You want half of what father left behind? Here you are. I can't give you any part of the main island, it belongs to the corporation. So do the two rigs in Limestone and Auntie Dol. But the other two rigs, Sherricks and Windward Point, are still mine. You can have Windward Point and Scrub Island to go with it. Scrub Island is where your mother is buried, after all, isn't it?"

ii.

IN THE MORNING, Roy's driver offers to take Christian in a luxury private yacht from the island once called Anguilla, now called Valley Island, to the island now called White Hill Island, which overlooks the submerged township of Island Harbour.

Christian prefers to take the ferry.

He sits by an outside rail, the wind of their passage stinging his eyes. The engine screams defiance against the suck of the swell, sea birds hover over the white wake, but the briny dry makes him feel like he's crossing a Saharan saltpan; like the sea is a mirage all around.

Walls of slag sticking straight up out of the water and the rumble of monstrous, self-driving trucks recede. The ferry deftly avoids barges heaped with more slag and pale yellow sand. It detours around shallow reefs of hotel balconies crusted with cunjevoi.

Christian sees them clearly through the water.

When he disembarks at the church, ocean foam lapping at its arched white entryway, the robotrolley obediently brings his luggage, trundling at his heels like a dog. The shoreline is changed but the sheltered nook where Granny's house perches on tall wooden stilts is the same.

A narrow, uneven staircase rises to a small, shingled house. It has a peaked roof, balcony railings alternating turquoise and white. In contrast to Roy's glass-sealed, climate-controlled mansion, Granny's house is open to the trade winds with more shutters than solid walls.

The dirt beneath the house, once the shady refuge of piglets and hens, appears to be sporting rows of odd concrete mushrooms. Only, when Christian gets closer, he realises they are foot-long stakes, driven into the dirt, each one topped with a white or orange hard hat.

Each hat has a name and dates of birth and death scrawled on the plastic in black marker. Some of the hats are cracked or crushed. Some of them are stained. All of the death-dates fall within the past three months.

"Granny," he calls in a calm voice, once again strangely unengaged by the appearance of an apparent graveyard. But no, the hats are packed too close together for bodies to be buried there. A memorial, then.

The woman who wanders nonchalantly out onto the balcony, skin like copper-toned Tahitian pearl, is more stooped than he remembers, though her movement is less hindered than his; she always had good strong bones. A straw hat shades Granny's face. Long hoop-earrings with bits of shell and sea-glass rattle at her collarbones.

"Godwin, dat you?" she calls suspiciously, interrupted by coughing.

"It's Christian!"

"Christian!" She throws her arms wide. "For our light and momentary troubles are achieving for us an eternal glory dat far outweighs dem all! Our saviour's brought you home from de stars, sweet boy!" She hesitates. "I can't get down de steps easily. Come here to me."

Christian leaves the robotrolley measuring step size with its sensors and scales the balcony with frustrating slowness, hands on both railings. He wants to squeeze her but is wary of hurting himself.

"Your Granny not so frail," she scolds him when he pulls away, but she bites her lip to keep from coughing again. They beam at each other for so long that Christian's face hurts. Then she glances down the hillside and says something that makes his heart hurt. "Jeezum bread, but will you look at dat? De whole beach missing, Christian. You ever seen anything like dat?" She shakes her head in astonishment. "All de sand gone. Dat hurricane must have been a terrible one. What was it called?"

"Come inside, Granny," Christian says. The robot is half way up the staircase. "Show me my old room. I've never slept so peacefully as here." Not even in the cold and quiet of space.

In his old room, a stranger in beige overalls looks up from an expanse of glowing smartpaper unrolled across the bed. Her skin is the colour of kelp forests. A greenstone pendant hangs around her neck. Black hair is trapped in a neat bun at her nape. Her thighs spread like steak under a spatula over the sheets; she's almost as wide as she is tall, and big-breasted.

Her brown eyes measure him, top to toe.

"You're the grandson," she says, corner of her mouth twitching upwards. "The astronaut."

"I'm sorry but I'm not sure who you are, ma'am," Christian says, shocked back to schoolboy manners simply by being in the room. Granny has bustled away behind him to fetch clean towels.

"I'm Maata Irihana," she says, "Chief Geotechnical Engineer. Your grandmother seized hold of me in the fruit market and insisted I abandon my portable on-site office and stay with her. Also, I think she needed someone to carry the very large bag of rice she'd just finished haggling down."

Irihana, Christian thinks, blinking. *I know that name.*

"The oncology nurses come twice a week to check on her," Maata goes on, "but it's palliative care only. She can't remember that she has cancer. Thinks it's a cold. They told me she has weeks to live. I'm so sorry."

Christian steps back from her.

"I came to convince her," he says, "to come with me to London."

"Then you've come for nothing."

He realises what he's really come for even as he articulates it.

"I came to see her and the island one last time."

The corner of Maata's mouth twitches again.

"Better."

"I'll let you get back to it, then," Christian says, lingering in the room, wanting her to offer it to him even as it sinks in that every surface is covered in smartpaper. Wires connecting them to the single power socket twist in snarls around the bedposts.

"I work remotely from here," Maata says. "On the Anguilla

project and also one I'm due to start in Morocco when this one is done. Twice a week, when the nurses come to take care of your grandmother, I go to the bore site to supervise some. Pick up some shopping, but the main reason is to meet with the corporation chair. Your brother, Roy."

"Half-brother."

Maata laughs, a rich, smoky sound.

"Yes, he is objectionable, isn't he?" Her eyes return to the smartpaper. "I wouldn't have taken the job if I'd known."

Granny brings the towels and seems surprised to find Maata sitting on the bed.

"Jeezum bread, I'd forgotten. Christian, dis is my lodger, Maata. She's from New Zealand. You'll have to sleep in the guest bedroom, sweet boy."

New Zealand.

"You discovered the Irihana Wave." Christian is stirred to admiration and, at last, a little fear. She could have killed millions of people. She could have, but she hadn't. "You doubled the land size of New Zealand."

"Not that they're grateful," Maata mutters without looking up. Her hand touches her chin, seemingly without volition. "They needed it, though. All those Polynesians with their homes underwater and no place to go. A good doctor forces the medicine down whether the patient likes it or not." Her pudgy fingers tap the smartpaper and her lips purse. "Walter's complaining about pump fifteen parts being recycled instead of printed. Alignment isn't perfect. I could kill that brother of yours."

"Half-brother." Christian takes the towels from Granny, setting them down on top of the robotrolley, whose wheels grind a little; it needs recharging.

"Viv used to come with me to de Freezers," Granny says brightly. "We found dem on Scrub Island. So deep, and deliciously cold. Our parents never knew about dem. Much deeper dan dose sacred Arawak caves, Big Springs and The Fountain. Have you visited dem, Maata, young missy?"

"They're underwater, Granny," Christian tells her. "Just like the Freezers. Just like pretty much all of Scrub Island."

"Your mudda loved Scrub Island, sweet boy."

Christian smiles.

"That's why you buried her there."

"Dat's why," she stabs a gnarled finger at his chest, "we buried her dere."

"Roy gave it to me," Christian says. Maata looks up from the smartpaper.

"He gave Scrub Island to you? As in, complete title, sea bed and stones, underwater and over?"

Christian nods slowly.

"I've got the deed right here. On permanent paper. He gave me the north-eastern power rig, too, the one at Windward Point Bay. I suppose when you get your lava flowing up to form a new island, Scrub Island will re-form above water, too?"

"No," Maata says flatly. "Scrub Island is on the far side of the rig. It gets nothing."

"Wouldn't want my mother's grave smothered in ash anyway," Christian says too quickly, defensive of his naked naivety. The test to join the space mission hadn't been an intelligence test, or a physical fitness test. It had purely been based on people's ability to get along with others. Christian is forgiving. He doesn't hold grudges.

Perhaps he should.

"The Windward Point rig output is below ten percent of optimal," Maata follows up ruthlessly. "Roy hasn't maintained it at all, except as a storm break. The Wave comes from the north-east, from six thousand kilometres across the North Atlantic. It's coming slowly, but it's coming, because of the Greenland ice sheet melting. You don't redistribute 2.8 million cubic kilometres of ice without causing pressure changes in the mantle. I'm relying on Windward Point geothermal sensors to confirm the Wave's rate of travel. Which is beyond foolish. But your half-brother refused to pay for new sensors."

There's a knock at the door. Loud. The sound of footsteps running.

Christian and Granny share a confused glance.

Maata sighs deeply. She puts her palm to the smartpaper for a few seconds, waiting for it to switch off. Then she heaves her heavy body up off the bed, headed for the door.

Christian and Granny stand aside for her. They follow her to the front door. Something about her grim determination demands it.

On the top step, a scratched-up white hard hat balances on its crown. When Maata picks it up, Christian spots the black writing briefly before Maata tucks it under her arm.

"What is it, young missy?" Granny inquires, covering her mouth as she coughs. "You left your hat at work?"

"Yes, Granny." Maata forces a smile. "I'll pop it under the house with my dirty boots."

Christian carefully steers down the stairs. He searches the road for a retreating back but can't see anyone. When they're out of Granny's earshot, Maata murmurs,

"They think I can do something." She grips the hat's peak,

white-knuckled. It has a Spanish-sounding woman's name on it.

"Can't you?"

She shakes her head. Ducks under the house. Picks up the central rib of a palm frond and snaps it over her knee.

"Supply and demand," she says angrily, driving the new stake into the sand beside the others. "Too many human lives in this world. They signed theirs away when they came to the island. Somebody back home will get something, I suppose."

She brushes the hat off. Sets it gingerly on the stake. Kneels, holds it in both hands and kisses it like a mother tucking a frightened child to sleep.

"There are so many," Christian says, deeply saddened, though he knows it's nothing in the larger scheme of things. Maata's broad shoulders shake. She turns her head to tell him,

"Your half-brother!"

Her cheeks glisten with hot, furious tears.

Christian risks kneeling in the sandy soil with her. A memory flashes through him, of burying a pet budgerigar, a weightless bundle of blue. She allows him to lay an arm over her shoulders; through the short-sleeved overalls she feels fleshy and soft, so unlike the grim fellow skeletons in nanocloth he'd helped out of the landing module.

He likes the feel of her. Doesn't want to take his arm away even when she dries her eyes. There's a new awareness between them when her wet gaze lands on his. Sweat on her top lip, caught in the fine hairs there. Dirt on her hands.

BY LATE EVENING, the breeze has finally cooled.

The sunset, which should have been framed by silhouettes of

coconut palms and pleasure boat masts instead meets the naked gooseflesh of the sea. Two fluorescent amber dragons of cloud twine at the horizon. Granny leads the recharged robotrolley, with a tray of tea and reconstituted juice, onto the veranda.

"Jeezum bread," Granny gasps. She pauses to press one hand to her chest and cough her deep, ominous cough. "Christian, sweet boy, you ever seen such a high tide? De whole beach gone! Must have been a bad, bad hurricane just gone. What was its name, again?"

Christian, exhausted by the day, bends gingerly to pour the tea, porcelain stained orange by the light.

"I bet this view is always changing, Granny. How long have you lived here, again?"

"Practically born here," Granny says proudly. "My mudda was beside herself when we first came. A real city woman, you know. She thought dere would be more society. Why else were dere so many banks? And my fadda in charge of de biggest of all. But dose banks were for hiding rich men's money. Not for de local people."

Christian lets her soothing voice wash over him. Maata joins him at the railing. The sea and sky pull their gazes as easily as the receding blue jewel of the Earth had pulled Christian's gaze when he'd thought never to see it again.

"A real gentleman, my fadda," Granny continues. "Never raised his voice. Never laid a hand on us. When I was six months from starting school, my mudda was offered a job as a teacher's aide. She took it because if she turned it down, Lord knew when somebody else would move away, or die.

"My fadda told her: You don't need to work. But if you insist on taking dat job, just know I will not be helping you in de house. You are a mudda and a wife first.

"So my mudda went a bit crazy trying to prove she could do everything. Tried to hide it from us but she started drinking and smoking. Dese fifteen steps you see here? One time my fadda's car pulled in as we were carrying de shopping. She left two bags at de bottom of de steps for him. He did not even look at dem."

Granny hacks and hacks.

"My throat a bit dry," she says apologetically, taking a swallow of water. "Dis cold a nuisance. Anyway, my fadda won de best garden competition every year. He never touched dose roses. It was all my mudda's work. I thought she would murder the neighbour boy when he cut one and gave it to me!" She laughs, and chokes, and laughs. "Viv – his real name was Walter, but he loved de cricket with such passion, we called him Viv – he wanted to marry me. But he wasn't very handsome and his family was poor. My fadda would not allow it. Dey sold deir house so Viv could go to UTech in Jamaica. He bought it back for dem, ten years later, but I was married to your grandfather by den, sweet boy. With your mudda a babe in my arms, do you think I could still go with Viv to de Freezers?"

Christian leans deeper against the rail so that Granny won't see what's in his eyes; a vision of molten rock running over this place; over the rosebushes and the fifteen steps. Over the church with the ocean at its door and the grave that Granny hasn't filled, not yet.

"Granny," he says, "living here with you was the best time of my life."

"You'll keep it in your heart when you go," she says, "just like you did before, sweet boy. Be on your guard; stand firm in de faith; be men of courage; be strong. We will all see our brightest days again in de arms of our Lord."

Christian is distracted from the arms of the Lord by the

nearness of Maata Irihana. He wants to lean left so that his shoulder presses against her.

"You're sleeping in my bed," he says under his breath.

"It's my bed," Maata whispers, leaning against him. "There's room for two."

Christian doesn't go to her bed that night or the next night, or even the night after that.

But on the fourth night, he goes.

The bed is smaller than he remembers. Sex is more complicated and cautious than he remembers. Maata positions him like a doll and lowers herself with calculated care, keeping most of her weight off his dangerously porous skeleton. In the dark, his fingertips feel faint scars on her chin. She tells him they're from a tattoo removal and her insides tense deliciously when she hesitates on the brink of saying more.

The giggling, the attempts to stay quiet, are the same.

iii.

MAATA TAKES CHRISTIAN to the bore with her.

"I'll fake a name tag for you," she says. "There's too much ill-feeling. Towards Roy."

Christian accepts the advice. In the early morning, surrounded by mountains of slag and continuous noise, they stand at the brink of a shaft no wider than Granny's living room.

The engine housing of the drill, a six-storey square on four stumpy steel legs, hovers over them. They put on heat-proof suits with in-built radios for communication and oxygen tanks to avoid fumes from the hole. Standing on a gleaming silver safety net, Christian can't see down very far at all. The two-metre-diameter central pipe, sticking straight down from the housing like the inserted proboscis of a monster mosquito, is surrounded by a cog-shaped elevator whose scalloped edge permits the super-heated, vaporised rock to escape, uncaptured, into the atmosphere or to crystallise on the housing, forming stone daggers that a remote-controlled robot arm breaks off busily.

"Come into the elevator," Maata's voice says in his helmet. It feels strange being suited up and yet still so heavy; he associates suits with the absence of gravity. The tech is older and he doesn't trust it, but he goes along with Maata, as he's always gone along with everyone, except for his father on the one momentous occasion when he chose leaving the planet forever over completing a business degree at Cambridge.

Through the clear floor of the elevator, he glimpses the kilometres-long drop of the completed portion of the shaft. Oxygen being pumped into the cramped, space-module-like, ring-shaped space with opaque walls and transparent ceiling and floor makes a soft, reassuring hiss. Maata helps him peel off the uncomfortable suit.

"The drill head is the world's biggest plasma torch," she says simply with neither arrogance nor modesty. "I designed it. Half the rock is turned to gas. The rest is broken into rubble and sucked up the shaft. There are pump stations at one kilometre intervals. Quartz sand, shipped in from Florida, is pumped down to form the heat-resistant ceramic coating on the inside of the bore." She points. The coating gleams white in the artificial light; bulbs are set at ten metre intervals into hollows in the central pipe. "When the magma from the Wave rises up through the shaft, I can't have it losing heat through the walls. The drill head continuously forms the casing as it goes. Walter's the ceramic engineer in charge of overseeing that process. I've had a report from the electrician of some staining on the wall, close to the surface. We'll take a look."

They don't go far down into the bore before the elevator stops and Christian has to seal his suit. Maata opens a panel which is flush against the bore wall. Here, the white ceramic is rosy-streaked, or perhaps it's just Christian's filthy visor.

"You must have drilled this part of the bore three months ago," Christian says.

"Yes. But the lights have only now been repaired. To save money, your brother –"

"Half-brother."

"– stripped the initial lamps and cables from some local sportsground. Of course they eroded away almost instantly." She peers closely at the coating, torch in hand.

"Is it a different colour? More pink?"

"Yes. It shouldn't be." She opens another compartment, this one facing the central shaft, and unfolds a piece of smartpaper. It comes to life under her stylus. "What you said is true. This was done very early in the project. Yet there's no abnormality shown in the spectral analysis. Unless an abnormal result has been accidentally deleted. I'll ask Walter to run the checks again."

Christian licks his lips.

"What do you mean, an abnormal result deleted? Do you mean sabotage by someone?"

"I mean," Maata says hotly, "someone cares more about finishing the project quickly than investigating potential defects in the insulation!" She closes the panel and floods the elevator with breathable air again.

"Take off your suit," she commands, and Christian obeys.

She flicks some switches and the cramped, donut-shaped elevator begins another juddering descent. Before Christian can ask her if further evidence of his half-brother's disregard for human life was what she wanted him to see, her arms are around his neck and her lips searching for his.

"Careful," he rebukes her half-heartedly, words muffled against her mouth.

"Did you do it in space?" she breathes.

"No." The scallop-shape of the cog's edge conveniently supports his back. "Never met anyone I liked."

"Let's have the deepest fuck in the world."

"Yes. Okay."

Manoeuvring in the cramped space distracts him for a while. As the pleasure fades, though, he looks up through the clear elevator ceiling, sees on the display that he is eleven thousand metres underground and feels abruptly breathless.

"Get off me," he manages.

"I'm not on you," Maata says, eyes wide.

"Get off!"

She's as far from him as the elevator will allow. He still feels crushed. Like he'll never see the sky again. Ten thousand metres. He's as far from the surface, in the wrong direction, as passenger jets are when they cruise above the clouds. Like a bacterium in a human hair follicle, enclosed by poison gases and unclimbable walls, and heavy.

So unbearably heavy. Christian gasps for air.

Then the elevator stops. They are fifteen thousand metres down. Maata is putting his suit on, because someone is entering the elevator, and then she's taking it off again, gently, because the interior is flushed with air and the new arrival is guardedly answering her questions.

"De discoloration is due to de drill head hitting a ferrous pocket of de limestone." The man is black, desiccated and ancient. He's clean-shaven. Missing some teeth. Beneath his suit, he wears a grimy white singlet. A stained yellow do-rag covers his lumpy skull. "Some of de iron was incorporated into de insulation but it won't affect de integrity, I promise you."

It's Walter, Granny's once-sweetheart. Christian can't imagine him ever doing something as romantic as stealing roses. They're half way through the earth's crust and he's wearing sunglasses.

"I don't want promises," Maata says sharply. "I want test results."

Not sunglasses. They're bionic eyes. The lumps under the do-rag must be the receivers. Eyes come with clever processors these days; Viv won't have to do any measuring or testing with his hands; he'll only look.

Christian takes a deep breath. He feels calm again.

"I know who you are," Walter tells him, and Christian can't know if it's facial recognition software or just a resemblance to Granny that's given him away.

"You can't tell anyone, Walter," Maata says.

"We trusted Roy because of his fadda," Walter says accusingly. "De Lord took Godwin too soon, before he taught dat boy right from wrong. Sign dis, your brother says, and you'll be cosy in England til de island is stable and it's time to return. Only, dere's no return for de likes of us. Permanent climate change refugee visas, dat's what he's pissing on de crowd like punch at carnival. And our lands, underwater and out of water, transferred to de corporation."

"He didn't know," Maata says urgently.

"I've got nothing else to say." Walter shrugs. "Give my regards to your grandmudda, boy."

"You should visit her," Christian says. "She remembers you."

But Walter doesn't come out of the bore when his shift finishes that afternoon.

A heavy pounding and the sound of running feet signifies the delivery of his empty helmet to the front veranda of Granny's house.

There is a service for Viv at the church.

Most of his family have already packed and gone but his little brother, as puckered and dried out as Viv was, lays a battered cricket bat over a grave barely a metre above the high tide mark. A circle of workers sings a hymn and someone gives a bunch of flowers to Granny.

She touches Christian's arm.

"Dis a lovely party," she says brightly. "Is it your birthday, sweet boy?"

"No, Granny," Christian says unhappily. "Your friend Walter has died."

"Oh." She's utterly perplexed.

"You should go," Maata says at Christian's back in a low, hollow voice. "Take her home."

Christian glances back at the workers. Some of them have stopped singing and are staring daggers at him.

"They won't hurt me," he says. "I'm not Roy."

He takes Granny home anyway.

*   *   *

GRANNY DIES TWO weeks out from the arrival of the Wave.

This time, Maata, Christian and the pastor are the only ones at the graveside. The bore is completed, all thirty kilometres of it. The workers have gone and there are no inward-bound flights.

Roy is gone, his yellow convertible lifted easily by electromagnets, car and plantation house all loaded onto a barge beside the disassembled drill head and engine housing. Besides the three of them, there are only the terns and the wind in the sea-grape trees to bear witness. It's so quiet. Christian remembers women wailing and beating their heads at his mother's funeral. Granny had gripped his hand so tightly.

"De body dat is sown is perishable," the pastor intones. "It is raised imperishable. Sown in dishonour, it is raised in glory. Sown in weakness, it is raised in power."

Afterwards, he leaves Christian and Maata alone.

Maata touches her chin.

"They believe in the resurrection of the body," she says, seeing straight through the soil. "But my family disowned me for believing in the resurrection of the land. Stone can be brought back to life, I said, not by electricity applied to flesh, but by a magma transfusion, the planet's blood. They're the ones who told me as a child all about fire demons bringing volcanic heat to revive the dying guardian of the tribe. Now I summon fire demons. I am the guardian of the tribe."

They stand in silence while the wind soughs between them.

"You should go to London," Maata says, her tone instructing him that he is *not* to go to London.

"You should go to Morocco," Christian replies, smiling.

"I want to watch it. I don't want the last thing I see here to be death. Rebirth is better."

Christian nods tentatively.

"I'll stay with you. I'll watch it with you."

iv.

THE SANDY GROUND feels syrupy and softened beneath their feet.

In his old bedroom in Granny's house, Christian draws Maata away from pinned smartpapers showing columns with headings like *pumice wastage* and *limestone-basalt interface*. Electricity to the island is off but she has one small solar charger.

She's deep in thought.

"He lied," she says. "Your brother Roy. He lied about the initial survey. It wasn't a survey at all, it was a simulation. An extrapolation, and Walter knew all along. Walter knew!"

She's not in the kind of wild fury that Roy's lies usually provoke. In fact, the brightness in her eyes as she stuffs two stolen heatproof suits and a month's worth of rice and peas into a bag could be confused with excitement. Christian puts it down to the immanence of the island's transformation. He can't pull his father's lobster boat out from under the tall stilts of the house, so fragile-seeming yet proof against a hundred hurricanes, but he directs Maata. Most of her bulk is muscle. Sweat beads her curled upper lip as she avoids the memorial and drags it free.

Together they drain the deteriorated fuel from the outboard motor, inject it with butane and re-fill the tank. The robotrolley, whining, at the end of its battery life, carries the boat to the water's edge through a pressure release channel in the twenty-metre tall slag walls that enclose the nation's future borders.

There, the vintage engine starts on the second try.

"Let's go to Scrub Island," he says. "My kingdom."

"No," Maata says. "We'll need the safety of a hurricane shield. We'll go to the north-eastern power rig. The one at Windward Point."

Christian pats the folded permanent paper in his pocket.

"Also my kingdom," he says, grinning.

v.

THE NEXT MORNING, safely across the strait, they stand, half-suited, on the hurricane wall, gazing down on the empty cookie-cutter of an island to the south-west.

Waiting.

Drones perform last-minute fly-bys to check for human presence before snapping back to optimal, low-risk observation paths. Hot, blue, empty sky waits to be written on in ash and steam. The concrete battlements of the hurricane shield wait to be struck by ejected slugs of mud and stone.

Maata's bun is untidy. She tore a chunk out on the rusty, seventy-five metre exposed ladder they were forced to climb yesterday because Christian had the deeds to his kingdom but not the keys.

Looking fantastic to him in her unshowered majesty, she stifles a low laugh every once in a while and glances over her shoulder at Scrub Island on the other side of the rig.

"Coral sands," she wheezes at one point, barely restraining her hilarity, "substituted for the quartz. The records expunged and the lights sabotaged so nobody could see. He thought of everything, even before your brother sent for you. Planted the idea of Scrub Island as a sop in Roy's mind."

Christian would tell her she wasn't making any sense if memories of Roy's summons hadn't dragged his thoughts to Granny. He imagines her body where it lies under the sandy soil, waiting to wake and walk again with her saviour, or for a mountain to be born on her bones, or both.

What will he do, when he wakes from the fog of denial he's in and becomes fully part of the earth-world he abandoned? Dive on Scrub Island for pirate gold in the shadow of the corporation?

There's no warning of imminent activity other than the abrupt press of Maata's body. Bubbling laughter in her chest predicates bubbling lava in the sea. Her hands pull up and seal the filters of Christian's suit, and the hiss of the oxygen tanks makes him think of scuba diving through the Freezers.

"Duck," Maata commands, engulfing him in the double-safety layer of her cushiony limbs. Down they go.

Christian sees sun-warmed concrete on the other side of his visor. Raindrops strike it. The surface turns white with salt crystallising out as droplets evaporate immediately. He turns his head to better see the sky.

Billowing clouds fly upwards, not golden dragons this time but great grey banyan trees growing and being beaten down, fading branches falling towards the sea, swaying, to be swallowed by steam and new generations of trees, darker and more magnificent, rearing up behind them. Occasional ash arrows aim themselves at the outer atmosphere, trying to get back to the stars, discovering a new layer of constraint, trapped by gravity despite their best efforts.

The ash comes from the wrong direction.

The roar, like the sound of surf, rages from the wrong direction, too. It comes from Scrub Island. Waves smashing against the ten-metre thick shield send vibrations from the north-east and the sun is blocked by the cloud.

Yet the rig feels safe. Maata feels safe. Christian watches the cloud-patterns and wonders at what lies beneath the thin skim of semi-stability that humans call home.

Maata gently lifts him to his feet a few hours later, helping him along the increasingly pumice and ash-layered pathway to the section of wall overlooking his kingdom. There, they stand on a sheltered section of concrete that hasn't been covered. She checks a reading on his suit. Unlocks both their helmets. Christian expects a cool breeze and receives a blast of hot, dry air across his sweaty face instead.

It's not Granny's grave that's opened a burning hellmouth and stabbed a stone tongue towards heaven. It's his mother's. *Scrub Island is where your mother is buried, after all, isn't it?*

"It's the Freezers," Matta shouts joyously. "Viv – Walter – did it for you. The cave system formed a conduit and he weakened the bore insulation in exactly the right place. The corporation can't blame it on me because they're the ones who falsified the surveys. This is your new island, Christian!"

It's grey-skinned, showing luminous red through the cracks. An immolated bride. Or a dirty reptile egg with a bloodied hatchling pushing at the insides.

The long arms of it curl around a harbour that will be protected from hurricanes when it cools. The new kingdom's back is turned to the angry Atlantic. Its fingers don't quite touch the edges of Roy's cookie cutter. That expectant perimeter is destined to remain empty until continued rising sea levels fill it with salt water. Maybe also a mix of white quartz, rosy coral and black volcanic sands.

For the first time since his space mission was aborted, Christian feels his body fully inhabited. He's been sown in dishonour and raised in glory; he feels the surety of his future, not beneath his feet in the trembling earth's crust, but by his side.

"Stay here with me," he asks Maata, taking her heat-suited hand.

"I see things coming," Maata smirks. "That's why they took my name for the Wave. I already quit that Morocco job."

When he kisses her, she tastes of salt, fire and smoke.

415

Ken Liu

SEVEN BIRTHDAYS

Ken Liu
SEVEN BIRTHDAYS

7:

THE WIDE LAWN spreads out before me almost to the golden surf of the sea, separated by the narrow dark tan band of the beach. The setting sun is bright and warm, the breeze a gentle caress against my arms and face.

"I want to wait a little longer," I say.

"It's going to get dark soon," Dad says.

I chew my bottom lip. "Text her again."

He shakes his head. "We've left her enough messages."

I look around. Most people have already left the park. The first hint of the evening chill is in the air.

"All right." I try not to sound disappointed. You shouldn't be disappointed when something happens over and over again, right? "Let's fly," I say.

Dad holds up the kite, a diamond with a painted fairy and two long ribbon tails. I picked it out this morning from the store at the park gate because the fairy's face reminded me of Mom.

"Ready?" Dad asks.

I nod.

"Go!"

I run toward the sea, toward the burning sky and the melting, orange sun. Dad lets go of the kite, and I feel the *fwoomp* as it lifts into the air, pulling the string in my hand taut.

"Don't look back! Keep running and let the string out slowly like I taught you."

I run. Like Snow White through the forest. Like Cinderella as the clock strikes midnight. Like the Monkey King trying to escape the Buddha's hand. Like Aeneas pursued by Juno's stormy rage. I unspool the string as a sudden gust of wind makes me squint, my heart thumping in time with my pumping legs.

"It's up!"

I slow down, stop, and turn to look. The fairy is in the air, tugging at my hands to let go. I hold on to the handles of the spool, imagining the fairy lifting me into the air so that we can soar together over the Pacific, like Mom and Dad used to dangle me by my arms between them.

"Mia!"

I look over and see Mom striding across the lawn, her long black hair streaming in the breeze like the kite's tails. She stops before me, kneels on the grass, wraps me in a hug, squeezing my face against hers. She smells like her shampoo, like summer rain and wildflowers, a fragrance that I get to experience only once every few weeks.

"Sorry I'm late," she says, her voice muffled against my cheek. "Happy birthday!"

I want to give her a kiss, and I don't want to. The kite line slackens, and I give the line a hard jerk like Dad taught me. It's very important for me to keep the kite in the air. I don't know why. Maybe it has to do with the need to kiss her and not kiss her.

Dad jogs up. He doesn't say anything about the time. He doesn't mention that we missed our dinner reservation.

Mom gives me a kiss and pulls her face away, but keeps her arms around me. "Something came up," she says, her voice even, controlled. "Ambassador Chao-Walker's flight was delayed and she managed to squeeze me in for three hours at the airport. I had to walk her through the details of the solar management plan before the Shanghai Forum next week. It was important."

"It always is," Dad says.

Mom's arms tense against me. This has always been their pattern, even when they used to live together. Unasked for explanations. Accusations that don't sound like accusations.

Gently, I wriggle out of her embrace. "Look."

This has always been part of the pattern too: my trying to break their pattern. I can't help but think there's a simple solution, something I can do to make it all better.

I point up at the kite, hoping she'll see how I picked out a fairy whose face looks like hers. But the kite is too high up now for her to notice the resemblance. I've let out all the string. The long line droops gently like a ladder connecting the Earth to heaven, the highest segment glowing golden in the dying rays of the sun.

"It's lovely," she says. "Someday, when things quiet down a little, I'll take you to see the kite festival back where I grew up, on the other side of the Pacific. You'll love it."

"We'll have to fly then," I say.

"Yes," she says. "Don't be afraid to fly. I fly all the time."

I'm not afraid, but I nod anyway to show that I'm assured. I don't ask when 'someday' is going to be.

"I wish the kite could fly higher," I say, desperate to keep the words flowing, as though unspooling more conversation will keep something precious aloft. "If I cut the line, will it fly across the Pacific?"

After a moment, Mom says, "Not really... The kite stays up only because of the line. A kite is just like a plane, and the pulling force from your line acts like thrust. Did you know that the first airplanes the Wright Brothers made were actually kites? They learned how to make wings that way. Someday I'll show you how the kite generates lift –"

"Sure it will," Dad interrupts. "It will fly across the Pacific. It's your birthday. Anything is possible."

Neither of them says anything after that.

I don't tell Dad that I enjoy listening to Mom talk about machines and engineering and history and other things that I don't fully understand. I don't tell her that I already know that the kite wouldn't fly across the ocean – I was just trying to get her to talk to me instead of defending herself. I don't tell him that I'm too old to believe anything is possible on my birthday – I wished for them not to fight, and look how that has turned out. I don't tell her that I know she doesn't mean to break her promises to me, but it still hurts when she does. I don't tell them that I wish I could cut the line that ties me to their wings – the tugging on my heart from their competing winds is too much.

I know they love me even if they no longer love each other; but knowing doesn't make it any easier.

Slowly, the sun sinks into the ocean; slowly, the stars wink to life in the sky. The kite has disappeared among the stars. I imagine the fairy visiting each star to give it a playful kiss.

Mom pulls out her phone and types furiously.

"I'm guessing you haven't had dinner," Dad says.

"No. Not lunch either. Been running around all day," Mom

says, not looking up from the screen.

"There is a pretty good vegan place I just discovered a few blocks from the parking lot," Dad says. "Maybe we can pick up a cake from the sweet shop on the way and ask them to serve it after dinner."

"Um-hum."

"Would you put that away?" Dad says. "Please."

Mom takes a deep breath and puts the phone away. "I'm trying to change my flight to a later one so I can spend more time with Mia."

"You can't even stay with us one night?"

"I have to be in D.C. in the morning to meet with Professor Chakrabarti and Senator Frug."

Dad's face hardens. "For someone so concerned about the state of our planet, you certainly fly a lot. If you and your clients didn't always want to move faster and ship more –"

"You know perfectly well my clients aren't the reason I'm doing this –"

"I know it's really easy to deceive yourself. But you're working for the most colossal corporations and autocratic governments –"

"I'm working on a technical solution instead of empty promises! We have an ethical duty to all of humanity. I'm fighting for the eighty percent of the world's population living on under ten dollars –"

Unnoticed by the colossi in my life, I let the kite pull me away. Their arguing voices fade in the wind. Step by step, I walk closer to the pounding surf, the line tugging me toward the stars.

* * *

49:

THE WHEELCHAIR IS having trouble making Mom comfortable.

First the chair tries to raise the seat so that her eyes are level with the screen of the ancient computer I found for her. But even with her bent back and hunched-over shoulders, she's having trouble reaching the keyboard on the desk below. As she stretches her trembling fingers toward the keys, the chair descends. She pecks out a few letters and numbers, struggles to look up at the screen, now towering above her. The motors hum as the chair lifts her again. Ad infinitum.

Over three thousand robots work under the supervision of three nurses to take care of the needs of some three hundred residents in Sunset Homes. This is how we die now. Out of sight. Dependent on the wisdom of machines. The pinnacle of Western civilization.

I walk over and prop up the keyboard with a stack of old hardcover books taken from her home before I sold it. The motors stop humming. A simple hack for a complicated problem, the sort of thing she would appreciate.

She looks at me, her clouded eyes devoid of recognition.

"Mom, it's me," I say. Then, after a second, I add, "Your daughter, Mia."

She has some good days, I recall the words of the chief nurse. *Doing math seems to calm her down. Thank you for suggesting that.*

She examines my face. "No," she says. She hesitates for a second. "Mia is seven."

Then she turns back to her computer and continues pecking out numbers on the keyboard. "Need to plot the demographic and conflict curves again," she mutters. "Gotta show them this is the only way…"

I sit down on the small bed. I suppose it should sting – the fact that she remembers her outdated computations better than she remembers me. But she is already so far away, a kite barely tethered to this world by the thin strand of her obsession with dimming the Earth's sky, that I cannot summon up the outrage or heartache.

I'm familiar with the patterns of her mind, imprisoned in that swiss-cheesed brain. She doesn't remember what happened yesterday, or the week before, or much of the past few decades. She doesn't remember my face or the names of my two husbands. She doesn't remember Dad's funeral. I don't bother showing her pictures from Abby's graduation or the video of Thomas's wedding.

The only thing left to talk about is my work. There's no expectation that she'll remember the names I bring up or understand the problems I'm trying to solve. I tell her the difficulties of scanning the human mind, the complications of recreating carbon-based computation in silicon, the promise of a hardware upgrade for the fragile human brain that seems so close and yet so far away. It's mostly a monologue. She's comfortable with the flow of technical jargon. It's enough that she's listening, that she's not hurrying to fly somewhere else.

She stops her calculations. "What day is today?" she asks.

"It's my – Mia's birthday," I say.

"I should go see her," she says. "I just need to finish this –"

"Why don't we take a walk together outside?" I ask. "She likes being out in the sun."

"The sun... It's too bright..." she mutters. Then she pulls her hands away from the keyboard. "All right."

The wheelchair nimbly rolls next to me through the corridors until we're outside. Screaming children are running helter-skelter over the wide lawn like energized electrons while white-haired and wrinkled residents sit in distinct clusters like nuclei scattered in vacuum. Spending time with children is supposed to improve the mood of the aged, and so Sunset Homes tries to recreate the tribal bonfire and the village hearth with busloads of kindergarteners.

She squints against the bright glow of the sun. "Mia is here?"

"We'll look for her."

We walk through the hubbub together, looking for the ghost of her memory. Gradually, she opens up and begins to talk to me about her life.

"Anthropogenic global warming is real," she says. "But the mainstream consensus is far too optimistic. The reality is much worse. For our children's sake, we must solve it in our time."

Thomas and Abby have long stopped accompanying me on these visits to a grandmother who no longer knows who they are. I don't blame them. She's as much a stranger to them as they're to her. They have no memories of her baking cookies for them on lazy summer afternoons or allowing them to stay up way past their bedtime to browse cartoons on tablets. She has always been at best a distant presence in their lives, most felt when she paid for their college tuition with a single check. A fairy godmother as unreal as those tales of how the Earth had once been doomed.

She cares more about the idea of future generations than her actual children and grandchildren. I know I'm being unfair, but the truth is often unfair.

"Left unchecked, much of East Asia will become uninhabitable in a century," she says. "When you plot out a record of little ice ages and mini warm periods in our history, you get a record of mass migrations, wars, genocides. Do you understand?"

A giggling girl dashes in front of us; the wheelchair grinds to a halt. A gaggle of boys and girls run past us, chasing the little girl.

"The rich countries, who did the most polluting, want the poor countries to stop development and stop consuming so much energy," she says. "They think it's equitable to tell the poor to pay for the sins of the rich, to make those with darker skins stop trying to catch up to those with lighter skins."

We've walked all the way to the far edge of the lawn. No sign of Mia. We turn around and again swerve through the crowd of children, tumbling, dancing, laughing, running.

"It's foolish to think the diplomats will work it out. The conflicts are irreconcilable, and the ultimate outcome will not be fair. The poor countries can't and shouldn't stop development, and the rich countries won't pay. But there is a technical solution, a hack. It just takes a few fearless men and women with the resources to do what the rest of the world can't do."

There's a glow in her eyes. This is her favorite subject, pitching her mad scientist answer.

"We must purchase and modify a fleet of commercial jets. In international space, away from the jurisdiction of any state, they'll release sprays of sulfuric acid. Mixed with water vapor, the acid will turn into clouds of fine sulfate particles that block sunlight." She tries to snap her fingers but her fingers are shaking too much. "It will be like the global volcanic winters of the 1880s, after Krakatoa erupted. We made the Earth warm, and we can cool it again."

Her hands flutter in front of her, conjuring up a vision of the grandest engineering project in the history of the human race: the construction of a globe-spanning wall to dim the sky. She doesn't remember that she has already succeeded, that decades ago, she had managed to convince enough people as mad as she was to follow her plan. She doesn't remember the protests, the condemnations by environmental groups, the scrambling fighter jets and denunciations by the world's governments, the prison sentence, and then, gradual acceptance.

"... the poor deserve to consume as much of the Earth's resources as the rich..."

I try to imagine what life must be like for her: an eternal day of battle, a battle she has already won.

Her hack has bought us some time, but it has not solved the fundamental problem. The world is still struggling with problems both old and new: the bleaching of corals from the acid rain, the squabbling over whether to cool the Earth even more, the ever-present finger-pointing and blame-assigning. She does not know that borders have been sealed as the rich nations replace the dwindling supply of young workers with machines. She does not know that the gap between the wealthy and the poor has only grown wider, that a tiny portion of the global population still consumes the vast majority of its resources, that colonialism has been revived in the name of progress.

In the middle of her impassioned speech, she stops.

"Where's Mia?" she asks. The defiance has left her voice. She looks through the crowd, anxious that she won't find me on my birthday.

"We'll make another pass," I say.

"We have to find her," she says.

On impulse, I stop the wheelchair and kneel down in front of her.

"I'm working on a technical solution," I say. "There is a way for us to transcend this morass, to achieve a just existence."

I am, after all, my mother's daughter.

She looks at me, her expression uncomprehending.

"I don't know if I'll perfect my technique in time to save you," I blurt out. *Or maybe I can't bear the thought of having to patch together the remnants of your mind.* This is what I have come to tell her.

Is it a plea for forgiveness? Have I forgiven her? Is forgiveness what we want or need?

A group of children run by us, blowing soap bubbles. In the sunlight the bubbles float and drift with a rainbow sheen. A few land against my mother's silvery hair but do not burst immediately. She looks like a queen with a diadem of sunlit jewels, an unelected tribune who claims to speak for those without power, a mother whose love is difficult to understand and even more difficult to misunderstand.

"Please," she says, reaching up to touch my face with her shaking fingers, as dry as the sand in an hourglass. "I'm late. It's her birthday."

And so we wander through the crowd again, under an afternoon sun that glows dimmer than in my childhood.

343:

ABBY POPS INTO my process.

"Happy birthday, Mom," she says.

For my benefit she presents as she had looked before her upload, a young woman of forty or so. She looks around at my cluttered space and frowns: simulations of books, furniture, speckled walls, dappled ceiling, a window view of a cityscape that was a digital composite of twenty-first-century San Francisco, my hometown, and all the cities that I had wanted to visit when I still had a body but didn't get to.

"I don't keep that running all the time," I say.

The trendy aesthetic for home processes now is clean, minimalist, mathematically abstract: platonic polyhedra; classic solids of revolution based on conics; finite fields; symmetry groups. Using fewer than three dimensions is preferred, and some are advocating flat living. To make my home process such a close approximation of the analog world at such a high resolution is considered a wasteful use of computing resources, indulgent.

But I can't help it. Despite having lived digitally for far longer than I did in the flesh, I prefer the simulated world of atoms to the digital reality.

To placate my daughter, I switch the window to a real-time feed from one of the sky rovers. The scene is of a jungle near the mouth of a river, probably where Shanghai used to be. Luxuriant vegetation drape from the skeletal ruins of skyscrapers; flocks of wading birds fill the shore; from time to time, pods of porpoises leap from the water, tracing graceful arcs that land back in the water with gentle splashes.

More than three hundred billion human minds now inhabit this planet, residing in thousands of data centers that collectively take up less space than old Manhattan. The Earth has gone back to being wild, save for a few stubborn holdouts who still insist on living in the flesh in remote settlements.

"It really doesn't look good when you use so much computational resources by yourself," she says. "My application was rejected."

She means the application to have another child.

"I think two thousand six hundred twenty-five children is more than enough," I say. "I feel like I don't know any of them." I don't even know how to pronounce many of the mathematical names the digital natives prefer.

"Another vote is coming," she says. "We need all the help we can get."

"Not even all your current children vote the same way you do," I say.

"It's worth a try," she says. "This planet belongs to all the creatures living on it, not just us."

My daughter and many others think that the greatest achievement of humanity, the re-gifting of Earth back to Nature, is under threat. Other minds, especially those who had uploaded from countries where the universal availability of immortality had been achieved much later, think that it isn't fair that those who got to colonize the digital realm first should have more say in the direction of humanity. They would like to expand the human footprint again and build more data centers.

"Why do you love the wilderness so much if you don't even live in it?" I ask.

"It's our ethical duty to be stewards for the Earth," she says. "It's barely starting to heal from all the horrors we've inflicted on it. We must preserve it exactly as it should be."

I don't point out that this smacks to me of a false duality: Human vs. Nature. I don't bring up the sunken continents, the erupting volcanoes, the peaks and valleys in the Earth's climate over billions of years, the advancing and retreating icecaps, and the uncountable species that have come and gone. Why do we hold up this one moment as natural, to be prized above all others?

Some ethical differences are irreconcilable.

Meanwhile, everyone thinks that having more children is the solution, to overwhelm the other side with more votes. And so the hard-fought adjudication of applications to have children, to allocate precious computing resources among competing factions.

But what will the children think of our conflicts? Will they care about the same injustices we do? Being born *in silico*, will they turn away from the physical world, from embodiment, or embrace it even more? Every generation has its own blind spots and obsessions.

I had once thought the Singularity would solve all our problems. Turns out it's just a simple hack for a complicated problem. We do not share the same histories; we do not all want the same things.

I am not so different from my mother after all.

2,401:

THE ROCKY PLANET beneath me is desolate, lifeless. I'm relieved. That was a condition placed upon me before my departure.

It's impossible for everyone to agree upon a single vision for the future of humanity. Thankfully, we no longer have to share the same planet.

Tiny probes depart from *Matrioshka*, descending toward the spinning planet beneath them. As they enter the atmosphere, they glow like fireflies in the dusk. The dense atmosphere here is so good at trapping heat that at the surface the gas behaves more like a liquid.

I imagine the self-assembling robots landing at the surface. I imagine them replicating and multiplying with material extracted from the crust. I imagine them boring into the rock to place the mini-annihilation charges.

A window pops up next to me, a message from Abby, light-years away and centuries ago.

Happy birthday, Mother. We did it.

What follows are aerial shots of worlds both familiar and strange: the Earth, with its temperate climate carefully regulated to sustain the late Holocene; Venus, whose orbit has been adjusted by repeated gravitational slingshots with asteroids and terraformed to become a lush, warm replica of the Earth during the Jurassic; and Mars, whose surface has been pelted with redirected Oort cloud objects and warmed by solar reflectors from space until the climate was a good approximation of the dry, cold conditions of the last glaciation on the Earth.

Dinosaurs now roam the jungles of Aphrodite Terra, and mammoths forage over the tundra of Vastitas Borealis. Genetic reconstructions have been pushed back to the limit of the powerful data centers on Earth.

They have recreated what might have been. They have brought the extinct back to life.

Mother, you're right about one thing: we will be sending out exploration ships again.

We'll colonize the rest of the galaxy. When we find lifeless worlds, we'll endow them with every form of life, from Earth's distant past to the futures that might have been on Europa. We'll walk down every evolutionary path. We'll shepherd every flock and tend to every garden. We'll give those creatures who never made it onto Noah's Ark another chance, and bring forth the potential of every star in Raphael's conversation with Adam in Eden.

And when we find extraterrestrial life, we'll be just as careful with them as we have been with life on Earth.

It isn't right for one species in the latest stage of a planet's long history to monopolize all its resources. It isn't just for humanity to claim for itself the title of evolution's crowning achievement.

Isn't it the duty of every intelligent species to rescue all life, even from the dark abyss of time? There is always a technical solution.

I smile. I do not wonder whether Abby's message is a celebration or a silent rebuke. She is, after all, my daughter.

I have my own problem to solve. I turn my attention back to the robots, to breaking apart the planet beneath my ship.

16,807:

IT HAS TAKEN a long time to fracture the planets orbiting this star, and longer still to reshape the fragments into my vision.

Thin, circular plates a hundred kilometers in diameter are arranged in a lattice of longitudinal rings around the star until it is completely surrounded. The plates do not orbit the star; rather, they are statites, positioned so that the pressure from the sun's high-energy radiation counteracts the pull of gravity.

On the inner surface of this Dyson swarm, trillions of robots have etched channels and gates into the substrate, creating the most massive circuits in the history of the human race.

As the plates absorb the energy from the sun, it is transformed into electric pulses that emerge from cells, flow through canals, commingle in streams, until they gather into lakes and oceans that undulate through a quintillion variations that form the shape of thought.

The backs of the plates glow darkly, like embers after a fierce flame. The lower-energy photons leap outward into space, somewhat drained after powering a civilization. But before they could escape into the endless abyss of space, they strike another set of plates designed to absorb energy from radiation at this dimmer frequency. And once again, the process for thought-creation repeats itself.

The nesting shells, seven in all, form a world that is replete with dense topography. There are smooth areas centimeters across, designed to expand and contract to preserve the integrity of the plates as the computation generates more or less heat – I've dubbed them seas and plains. There are pitted areas where the peaks and craters are measured by microns, intended to facilitate the rapid dance of qubits and bits – I call them forests and coral reefs. There are small studded structures packed with dense circuitry intended to send and receive beams of communication knitting the plates together – I call them cities and towns. Perhaps these are fanciful names, like the Sea of Tranquility and Mare Erythraeum, but the consciousnesses they power are real.

And what will I do with this computing machine powered by the sun? What magic will I conjure with this matrioshka brain?

I have seeded the plains and seas and forests and coral reefs and cities and towns with a million billion minds, some of them modeled on my own, many more pulled from *Matrioshka*'s data banks, and they have multiplied and replicated, evolved in a world larger than any data center confined to a single planet could ever hope to be.

In the eyes of an outside observer, the star's glow dimmed as each shell was constructed. I have succeeded in darkening a sun just as my mother had, albeit at a much grander scale.

There is always a technical solution.

117,649:

HISTORY FLOWS LIKE a flash flood in the desert: the water pouring across the parched earth, eddying around rocks and cacti, pooling in depressions, seeking a channel while it's carving the landscape, each chance event shaping what comes after.

There are more ways to rescue lives and redeem what might have been than Abby and others believe.

In the grand matrix of my matrioshka brain, versions of our history are replayed. There isn't a single world in this grand computation, but billions, each of them populated by human consciousnesses, but nudged in small ways to be better.

Most paths lead to less slaughter. Here, Rome and Constantinople are not sacked; there, Cuzco and V nh Long do not fall. Along one timeline, the Mongols and Manchus do not sweep across East Asia; along another, the Westphalian model does not become an all-consuming blueprint for the world. One group of men consumed with murder do not come to power in Europe, and another group worshipping death do not seize the machinery of state in Japan. Instead of the colonial yoke, the inhabitants of Africa, Asia, the Americas, and Australia decide their own fates. Enslavement and genocide are not the handmaidens of discovery and exploration, and the errors of our history are averted.

Small populations do not rise to consume a disproportionate amount of the planet's resources or monopolize the path of its future. History is redeemed.

But not all paths are better. There is a darkness in human nature that makes certain conflicts irreconcilable. I grieve for the lives lost, but I can't intervene. These are not simulations. They cannot be if I respect the sanctity of human life.

The billions of consciousnesses who live in these worlds are every bit as real as me. They deserve as much free will as anyone who has ever lived and must be allowed to make their own choices. Even if we've always suspected that we also live in a grand simulation, we prefer the truth to be otherwise.

Think of these as parallel universes if you will; call them sentimental gestures of a woman looking into the past; dismiss it as a kind of symbolic atonement.

But isn't it the dream of every species to have the chance to do it over? To see if it's possible to prevent the fall from grace that darkens our gaze upon the stars?

823,543:

THERE IS A message.

Someone has plucked the strings that weave together the fabric of space, sending a sequence of pulses down every strand of Indra's web, connecting the farthest exploding nova to the nearest dancing quark.

The galaxy vibrates with a broadcast in languages known and yet to be invented. I parse out a single sentence.

Come to the galactic center. It's reunion time.

Carefully, I instruct the intelligences guiding the plates that make up the Dyson swarms to shift, like ailerons on the wings of ancient aircraft. The plates drift apart, as though the shells in the matrioshka brain are cracking, hatching a new form of life.

Gradually, the statites move into the configuration of a Shkadov thruster. A single eye opens in the universe, emitting a bright beam of light.

And slowly, the imbalance in the solar radiation begins to move the star, bringing the shell-mirrors with it. We're headed for the center of the galaxy, propelled upon a fiery column of light.

Not every human world will heed the call. There are plenty of worlds on which the inhabitants have decided that it is perfectly fine to explore the mathematical worlds of ever-deepening virtual reality, to live out lives of minimal energy consumption in universes hidden within nutshells.

Some, like my daughter Abby, will prefer to leave their lush, life-filled planets in place, like oases in the endless desert that was space. Others will seek the refuge of the galactic edge, where cooler climates will allow more efficient computation. Still others, having re-captured the ancient joy of living in the flesh, will tarry to play out space operas of conquest and glory.

But enough will come.

I imagine thousands, hundreds of thousands of stars moving toward the center of the galaxy. Some of them inhabited by people who still look like people, others by machines that have but a dim memory of their ancestral form. Some will drag with them planets populated by creatures from our distant past, others by creatures I have never seen. Some will bring guests, aliens who do not share our history but are curious about this self-replicating low-entropy phenomenon that calls itself humanity.

I imagine generations of children watching the night sky as the constellations shift and transform, as the stars move out of alignment, drawing contrails against the empyrean.

I close my eyes. The journey will take a long time. Might as well get some rest.

A VERY, VERY long time later:

The wide silvery lawn spreads out before me almost to the golden surf of the sea, separated by the narrow dark band that was the beach. The sun is bright and warm, and I can almost feel the breeze, a gentle caress against my arms and face.

"Mia!"

I look over and see Mom striding across the lawn, her long black hair streaming like a kite's tails. She wraps me in a fierce hug, squeezing my face against hers. She smells like the glow of new stars being born in the embers of a supernova, like new comets just emerging from the primeval nebula.

"Sorry I'm late," she says, her voice muffled against my cheek.

"It's okay," I say, and I mean it. I give her a kiss.

"It's a good day to fly a kite," she says.

We look up at the sun.

The perspective shifts vertiginously, and now we're standing upside down on an intricately carved plain, the sun far below us. Gravity tethers the surface above the bottoms of our feet to that fiery orb, stronger than any string. The bright photons we're bathed in strike against the ground, pushing it up. We're standing on the bottom of a kite that is flying higher and higher, tugging us toward the stars.

I want to tell her that I understand her impulse to make one life grand, her need to dim the sun with her love, her striving to solve intractable problems, her faith in a technical solution even though she knew it was imperfect. I want to tell her that I know we're flawed, but that doesn't mean we're not also wondrous.

Instead, I just squeeze her hand; she squeezes back.

"Happy birthday," she says. "Don't be afraid to fly."

I relax my grip, and smile at her. "I'm not. We're almost there."

The world brightens with the light of a million billion suns.

439

About the Authors

Charlie Jane Anders

Charlie is the author of L.A. Times Bestseller *All the Birds in the Sky*. Her stories have appeared in *Asimov's Science Fiction, The Magazine of Fantasy & Science Fiction*, Tor.com, *Lightspeed, Tin House, ZYZZYVA, McSweeney's Internet Tendency* and several anthologies. Her work has won a Hugo Award, a Lambda Literary Award, and the Emperor Norton Award for 'extraordinary invention and creativity unhindered by the constraints of paltry reason.'

allthebirdsinthesky.tumblr.com

Stephen Baxter

Stephen is one of the most important science fiction writers to emerge from Britain in the past thirty years. His 'Xeelee' sequence of novels and short stories is arguably the most significant work of future history in modern science fiction. He is the author of more than fifty books and over 100 short stories. His most recent books are *The Long Cosmos*, fifth in a series of novels co-written with Terry Pratchett, *The Medusa Chronicles* (co-written with Alastair Reynolds), and novella *Project Clio*.

www.stephen-baxter.com

Gregory Benford

Gregory is the author of more than twenty novels, including *Jupiter Project, Artifact, Against Infinity, Eater*, and *Timescape*. A two-time winner of the Nebula Award, Benford has also won the John W. Campbell Award, the Ditmar Award, the Lord Foundation Award for achievement in the sciences, and the United Nations Medal in Literature. Many of his best known novels are part of a six-novel Galactic Center sequence, *In the Ocean of Night, Across the Sea of Suns, Great Sky River, Tides of Light, Furious Gulf*, and *Sailing Bright Eternity*. His most recent novels are *Bowl of Heaven* and *Shipstar*, both co-written with Larry Niven. A retrospective of his short fiction, *The Best of Gregory Benford*, was published last year.

www.gregorybenford.com

Tobias S. Buckell

Called 'Violent, poetic and compulsively readable' by Maclean's, **Tobias** is a *New York Times* Bestselling writer born in the Caribbean. He grew up in Grenada and spent time in the British and US Virgin Islands, and the islands he lived on influence much of his work. His Xenowealth series begins with *Crystal Rain*. Along with other stand-alone novels and his over 50 stories, his works have been translated into 18 different languages. He has been nominated for awards like the Hugo, Nebula, Prometheus, and the John W. Campbell Award for Best New Science Fiction Author. His latest novel is *Hurricane Fever*, a follow up to the successful *Arctic Rising* that NPR says will 'give you the shivers.' He currently lives in Bluffton, Ohio with his wife, twin daughters, and a pair of dogs.

www.tobiasbuckell.com

Pat Cadigan

Pat is the author of about a hundred short stories and fourteen books, two of which, *Synners* and *Fools*, won the Arthur C. Clarke Award. Her story "The Girl-Thing Who Went Out for Sushi", originally published in *Edge of Infinity*, won the Hugo Award in 2013. She was born in New York, grew up in Massachusetts, and spent most of her adult life in the Kansas City area. She now lives in London with her husband, the Original Chris Fowler, her Polish translator Konrad Walewski and his partner, the Lovely Lena, and co-conspirator, writer and raconteuse Amanda Hemingway; also, two ghosts, one of which is the shade of Miss Kitty Calgary, Queen of the Cats (the other declines to give a name). She is pretty sure there isn't a more entertaining household. She is currently working on new novels *See You When You Get There* and *Reality Used to be a Friend of Mine*.

patcadigan.wordpress.com

Paul Doherty

Paul is a PhD physicist and a senior scientist at the Exploratorium, San Francisco's museum of science, art, and human perception. He has written many nonfiction science books, including the *Explorabook*, which sold over a million copies. With Pat Murphy, he writes a science column for the *Magazine of Fantasy and Science Fiction*. He has been the 'talent' in television programs from around the world including broadcasting from the rim of an active volcano in Antarctica, and is the winner of the Faraday Award for Excellence in Science Teaching from the National Science Teachers Association. Doherty was recently hired by the Dalai Lama to bring hands-on science education to Tibetans in exile in India. He is an adventurer who has worked as a scientist/writer at McMurdo station Antarctica where he joined in the culture of scientists doing research in an extreme environment. He has also done multi-day ski tours north of the Arctic Circle. Though he is a long-time science fiction reader, this is his first published science fiction story.

www.exo.net/~pauld

Thoraiya Dyer

Thoraiya is an Aurealis and Ditmar Award-winning, Sydney-based science fiction writer and lapsed veterinarian. Her work has appeared in *Clarkesworld*, *Apex*, *Cosmos*, *Analog* and a number of anthologies. Her most recent book is short story collection, *Asymmetry*. Her first novel, *Crossroads of Canopy*, a big fat fantasy set in a magical rainforest, is forthcoming from Tor in January 2017.

www.thoraiyadyer.com

Ken Liu

Ken is an author and translator of speculative fiction, as well as a lawyer and programmer. A winner of the Nebula, Hugo, and World Fantasy Awards, he has been published in *The Magazine of Fantasy & Science Fiction*, *Asimov's*, *Analog*, *Clarkesworld*, *Lightspeed*, and *Strange Horizons*, among other places. He also translated the Hugo-winning novel, *The Three-Body Problem*, by Liu Cixin. Ken's debut novel, *The Grace of Kings*, the first in a silkpunk epic fantasy, is a finalist for the Nebula Award and the winner of the Locus Award for Best First Novel. Sequel *The Wall of Storms* is due later this year. His debut short story collection in English, *The Paper Menagerie and Other Stories*, was published in March 2016. Coming up is the second 'Dandelion Dynasty' novel, *The Wall of Storms*. He lives with his family near Boston, Massachusetts.

http://kenliu.name

Karen Lord

Barbadian author, editor and research consultant **Karen** is known for her debut novel *Redemption in Indigo*, which won the Frank Collymore Literary Award, Carl Brandon Parallax Award, William L. Crawford Award, Mythopoeic Fantasy Award and the Kitschies Golden Tentacle, and was nominated for the World Fantasy Award. Her second novel *The Best of All Possible Worlds* won the 2009 Frank Collymore Literary Award, the 2013 RT Book Reviews Reviewers' Choice Awards for Best Science Fiction Novel, and was a finalist for the 2014 Locus Awards. Its sequel, *The Galaxy Game*, was published in January 2015. She is the editor of the 2016 anthology *New Worlds, Old Ways: Speculative Tales from the Caribbean*.

karenlord.wordpress.com

Karin Lowachee

Karin was born in South America, grew up in Canada, and worked in the Arctic. Her first novel *Warchild* won the 2001 Warner Aspect First Novel Contest. Both *Warchild* and her third novel *Cagebird* were finalists for the Philip K. Dick Award. *Cagebird* won the Prix Aurora Award and the Spectrum Award in 2006. Her books have been translated into French, Hebrew, and Japanese, and her short stories have appeared in anthologies edited by Julie Czerneda, Nalo Hopkinson, John Joseph Adams and Ann VanderMeer. Her fantasy novel, *The Gaslight Dogs*, was published through Orbit Books USA.

www.karinlowachee.com

Pat Murphy

Pat has won numerous awards for her thoughtful, literary science fiction and fantasy writing, including two Nebula Awards, the Philip K. Dick Award, the World Fantasy Award, the Seiun Award, and the Theodore Sturgeon Memorial Award. Her novels include *The Falling Woman, The City Not Long After, Nadya: The Wolf Chronicles, Wild Angel*, and *Adventures in Time and Space with Max Merriwell*. She has published many short stories, which are collected in *Points of Departure* and *Women Up To No Good*. In 1991, Pat co-founded the James Tiptree, Jr. Award, an annual literary prize for science fiction or fantasy that expands or explores our understanding of gender roles. This award harnesses the power of chocolate chip cookies in an on-going effort to change the world. In addition to writing science fiction, Pat writes about science for adults and children and makes strange devices from LEGO bricks and folded paper. Currently, she is employed as Activity Guru/Evil Genius at Mystery Science (mysteryscience.com), a web-based elementary-school curriculum designed to inspire kids (and their teachers) to love science.

www.brazenhussies.net/murphy

Larry Niven

Larry began freelance writing in 1964, the year of his first short fiction publication, "The Coldest Place", in *If*. He won his first Hugo in 1967 for "Neutron Star". His other Hugo winners are "Inconstant Moon", "The Hole Man", and "The Borderland of Sol". First novel *World of Ptavvs* began his Known Space future history. *Ringworld* won both the Hugo and Nebula and was followed by *The Ringworld Engineers, The Ringworld Throne*, and *Ringworld's Children*. His other solo novels include *A Gift from Earth, Protector, A World Out of Time, The Magic Goes Away, The Smoke Ring, The Integral Trees, Destiny's Road,* and *Rainbow Mars*. A frequent collaborator, Niven has written novels with Jerry Pournelle, Steven Barnes, Michael F. Flynn, Edward M. Lerner, David Gerrold, Brenda Cooper, and Gregory Benford. His short fiction is collected in more than 20 collections, including *Neutron Star, All the Myriads Ways, Inconstant Moon, A Hole in Space, N-Space, Playgrounds of the Mind, The Draco Tavern,* and *The Best of Larry Niven*. He is an SFWA Grand Master and has won a Heinlein Award and a Hubbard Award for Lifetime Achievement. He lives in Southern California with wife Marilyn.

www.larryniven.net

AN OWOMOYELA

An is a neutrois author with a background in web development, linguistics, and weaving chainmail out of stainless steel fencing wire, whose fiction has appeared in a number of venues including *Clarkesworld, Asimov's, Lightspeed,* and a handful of Year's Bests. An's interests range from pulsars and Cepheid variables to gender studies and nonstandard pronouns, with a plethora of stops in-between.

an.owomoyela.net

ROBERT REED

Robert was born in Omaha, Nebraska. He has a Bachelor of Science in Biology from the Nebraska Wesleyan University, and has worked as a lab technician. He became a full-time writer in 1987, the same year he won the L. Ron Hubbard Writers of the Future Contest, and has published twelve novels, including *The Leeshore, The Hormone Jungle,* and far future SF *Marrow* and *The Well of Stars*. A prolific writer, Reed has published over 200 short stories, mostly in *F&SF* and *Asimov's*, which have been nominated for the Hugo, James Tiptree, Jr., Locus, Nebula, Seiun, Theodore Sturgeon Memorial, and World Fantasy awards, and have been collected in *The Dragons of Springplace, The Cuckoo's Boys, Eater-of-Bone,* and *The Greatship*. His novella *A Billion Eves* won the Hugo Award. His latest book is major SF novel *The Memory of Sky*. Nebraska's only SF writer, Reed lives in Lincoln with his wife and daughter, and is an ardent long-distance runner.

www.robertreedwriter.com

ALASTAIR REYNOLDS

Alastair was born in Barry, South Wales, in 1966. He has lived in Cornwall, Scotland, the Netherlands, where he spent twelve years working as a scientist for the European Space Agency, before returning to Wales in 2008 where he lives with his wife Josette. Reynolds has been publishing short fiction since his first sale to *Interzone* in 1990. Since 2000 he has published thirteen novels: the Inhibitor trilogy, British Science Fiction Association Award winner *Chasm City*, *Century Rain*, *Pushing Ice*, *The Prefect*, *House of Suns*, *Terminal World*, and first in the Poseidon's Children series, *Blue Remembered Earth*. His most recent novels are the Poseidon's Children trilogy, *Doctor Who* novel *The Harvest of Time*, and *The Medusa Chronicles* (co-written with Stephen Baxter). His short fiction has been collected in *Zima Blue and Other Stories*, *Galactic North*, *Deep Navigation*, and *Beyond the Aquila Rift: The Best of Alastair Reynolds*. Coming up is a new novel, *Revenger*. In his spare time he rides horses.

www.alastairreynolds.com

KRISTINE KATHRYN RUSCH

Kristine started out the decade of the '90s as one of the fastest-rising and most prolific young authors on the scene, took a few years out in mid-decade for a very successful turn as editor of *The Magazine of Fantasy and Science Fiction*, and, since stepping down from that position, has returned to her old standards of production here in the 21st Century, publishing a slew of novels in four genres, writing fantasy, mystery, and romance novels under various pseudonyms as well as science fiction. She has published more than fifty novels under her own name, including *The White Mists of Power*, *Snipers*, and *The Enemy Within*, the seven-volume 'Fey' series, the Diving' series, and *Alien Influences*. Her most recent books are the popular, award-winning fifteen-volume SF 'Retrieval Artist' series, which includes *The Disappeared*, *Extremes*, *Consequences*, *Buried Deep*, *Paloma*, *Recovery Man*, and the story arc within the series, *The Anniversary Day Saga*. She will publish two Diving Universe novels in the next year, *The Falls* in October, and an as-yet-untitled novel in the spring. Her copious short fiction has been collected most recently in *Recovering Apollo Eight* and other stories. Her stories have appeared in, to date, over twenty best of the year collections. All of her short fiction is available as standalone titles online. She also reprints one story per week on her website for free, in a series she calls Free Fiction Monday. As of this writing, she has won the *Asimov's* Readers Choice award eight times, the AnLab award from *Analog* three times, as well as several other readers awards. She won the Hugo in 2000 for her short story

"Millennium Babies." She is also a multi-award nominee in the mystery genre (under both the names Rusch and her pen name Kris Nelscott), and in romance under her pen name Kristine Grayson. She also has a career as an editor, which she first retired from in 1997, after being honoured with the Hugo Award for her work on *The Magazine of Fantasy and Science Fiction*, and sharing the World Fantasy Award with Dean Wesley Smith for her work as editor of the original hardcover anthology version of *Pulphouse*. In 2012, she returned to editing with the anthology series, *Fiction River*. She also edits standalone projects like *The Year's Best Mystery and Crime Stories 2016* (with co-editor John Helfers) and *The Women of Futures Past*, a fiction anthology that honours the history of women in the science fiction field. For more information on her and her writing or to read a story for Free Fiction Monday, go to her website, kristinekathrynrusch.com.

www.kristinekathrynrusch.com

Pamela Sargent

Pamela has won the Nebula and Locus Awards, been a finalist for the Hugo Award, Theodore Sturgeon Award, and Sidewise Award, and was honored in 2012 with the Pilgrim Award, given for lifetime achievement in science fiction and fantasy scholarship, by the Science Fiction Research Association. She is the author of the science fiction novels *Cloned Lives, The Sudden Star, Watchstar, The Golden Space, The Alien Upstairs, Eye of the Comet, Homesmind, Alien Child, The Shore of Women, Venus of Dreams, Venus of Shadows*, and *Child of Venus*, as well as the alternative history *Climb the Wind*. *Ruler of the Sky*, her 1993 historical novel about Genghis Khan, was a bestseller in Germany and Spain. She also edited the *Women of Wonder* anthologies, the first collections of science fiction by women, published in the 1970s by Vintage/Random House and in updated editions during the 1990s by Harcourt Brace. Sargent sold her first published story as a senior in college at the State University of New York/Binghamton University, where she earned a B.A. and M.A. in philosophy and also studied ancient history and Greek. Her short fiction has appeared in magazines and anthologies including *The Magazine of Fantasy & Science Fiction, Asimov's SF Magazine, New Worlds, World Literature Today, Amazing Stories, Rod Serling's Twilight Zone Magazine, Universe, Nature,* and *Polyphony*, and in her collections *Starshadows, The Best of Pamela Sargent, The Mountain Cage and Other Stories, Behind the Eyes of Dreamers and Other Short Novels, Eye of Flame, Thumbprints, Dream of Venus and Other Science Fiction Stories,* and most recently *Puss in D.C. and Other Stories*. Her latest novel is *Season of the Cats*, a fantasy set in the present. Michael Moorcock has said about her writing: "If you have not read Pamela

Sargent, then you should make it your business to do so at once. She is in many ways a pioneer, both as a novelist and as a short story writer... She is one of the best." Pamela Sargent lives in Albany, New York.

www.pamelasargent.com

ALLEN STEELE

Allen became a full-time science fiction writer in 1988, following publication of his first short story, "Live From The Mars Hotel". Since then he has become a prolific author of novels, short stories, and essays, with his work translated into more than a dozen languages worldwide. His novels include *Orbital Decay, Clarke County, Space, Lunar Descent, Labyrinth of Night, The Jericho Iteration, The Tranquility Alternative, A King of Infinite Space, Oceanspace, Chronospace*, the Coyote Trilogy, the Coyote Chronicles, *Spindrift, Galaxy Blues, Hex, Apollo's Outcast, V-S Day*, and *Arkwright*. He has also published six collections of short fiction: *Rude Astronauts, All-American Alien Boy, Sex and Violence in Zero-G, American Beauty, The Last Science Fiction Writer*, and *Tales of Time and Space*. His work has appeared in most major US SF magazines, including *Asimov's Science Fiction, Analog*, and *Fantasy & Science Fiction*, as well as in dozens of anthologies. He won the Hugo Award for novellas *The Death Of Captain Future* and '*...Where Angels Fear to Tread*', and for *The Emperor of Mars* Steele was First Runner-Up for the 1990 John W. Campbell Award, received the Donald A. Wollheim Award in 1993, and the Phoenix Award in 2002. In 2013, he received the Robert A. Heinlein Award in recognition of his long career in writing space fiction. Steele is a former member of both the Board of Directors and the Board of Advisors for the Science Fiction and Fantasy Writers of America, and is also a former advisor for the Space Frontier Foundation. He lives in western Massachusetts with his wife Linda and their dogs.

www.allensteele.com